The Neon Madonna

THE NEON MADONNA

By Dan Binchy

St. Martin's Press
New York

Library of Congress Cataloging-in-Publication Data

Binchy, Dan.
    The neon Madonna / Dan Binchy.
      p.   cm.
    "A Thomas Dunne book."
    ISBN 0-312-07042-X
    I. Title.
PR6052.I7726N4   1992
823'.914—dc20   91-33292
                                                    CIP

First published in Great Britain by Random Century Group Limited.

First U.S. Edition: March 1992
10 9 8 7 6 5 4 3 2 1

This book is dedicated to my beloved Joy without whom it would never have been written. Also to our four children, Daniel, Gillian, Derek and Brian, without whom it would have been finished much earlier!

The Neon Madonna

1

'Eminenze, you wished to see me?'

When they were alone, Father Jerry addressed the Cardinal in English. If asked, neither of them would have been able to remember the reason for this. Perhaps it was simply because it offered a welcome change of pace from the frantic Italian that rattled along the marble corridors of the Vatican in short, staccato bursts.

'I believe the results of your tests have come back from the clinic?'

The Cardinal's face was unlined. It had the sallow, unblemished complexion that many well-fed Italians acquire at an early age and retain to the grave. Castelli looked younger, much younger, than his seventy-three years.

'Yes they did.'

Father Jerry had difficulty recognising his own voice. It sounded as though it came from a total stranger.

'And . . . ?'

There were no secrets within the walls of the Vatican. Castelli would have had the results on his desk within minutes of Professor Marti receiving them. None the less the pretence had to be maintained. The charade was interrupted as loudspeakers rasped a warning to the faithful jammed into St Peter's Square that the Pope would address them shortly. They paused for the announcement to end. Any day now the windows would be sealed against the summer heat and the air-conditioning switched on.

'Not good. It's ulcerative colitis. Professor Marti has put me on a course of steroids and some medication I can't even pronounce.'

'And the prognosis?' the Cardinal enquired.

'The treatment gives remission – anything up to ten years if I can avoid stress. Then probably cancer of the bowel.'

'What are his suggestions for the interim?'

Typical of the man. No time wasted on sympathy or idle speculation on whether the diarrhoea wasting his frame was the will of God. Which was just as well. It was better not to reveal his doubts about the existence of a God who could visit such suffering – and embarrassment – on his loyal servant.

'Complete rest and a change of climate.'

'That means going back to Ireland, does it not? Have you any relatives left there now?'

'I don't really know. My uncle died two years ago.'

Not quite accurate, but it would serve for the time being. There were certain members of the O'Sullivan tribe about whom he preferred not to think just at the moment.

'Left you an income *and* a legacy, I seem to remember?'

Like the Bourbons, the Castellis in learning nothing also forgot nothing. His uncle had indeed remembered him in his will. He had also paid his fees at the seminary and sent him money at irregular intervals ever since. Prone to drinking bouts, the cheques indicated that he had entered dry dock for essential repairs prior to his next immersion in a sea of bootleg liquor. The longer the binge, the larger the cheque. Father Jerry had long ago decided his uncle viewed these contributions as a form of fire insurance. A deeply religious man despite his unusual occupation, he had a lifelong dread of hell fire.

'Yes, the income goes into a bank account in Ireland. The legacy is on deposit here in the Vatican Bank.'

'What do you intend doing with it?'

'Well, I had hoped to buy a place in Ireland ... when I retire, that is.'

'From what your tests show, that will occur sooner rather than later.'

'So it would seem.'

Was he being deliberately unemotional? Castelli might as well have been discussing religious freedoms behind the Iron Curtain – or an errant priest sleeping with his housekeeper in Palermo – for all the feeling in his voice.

'Obviously there is no question of your staying on here. You know as well as I do what demands on mind and body this job makes. Has Professor Marti put you on some sort of diet – as well as avoiding stress?'

'No, as a matter of fact, he hasn't. Quite the opposite. He advised me to eat everything possible and try to put on some weight.'

'Lucky for some!'

A ghost of a smile flickered across the Cardinal's face as he spoke. It was the only flash of humour thus far. Castelli's ongoing war with his waistline caused much amusement among his staff. The merry-go-round of embassy dinners and his love of egg pasta ensured that that it was one battle he would never win. His expensively tailored cassock failed to hide the pear-shaped bulge. Whenever he mentioned

2

his ancestors, it was to refer wistfully to their baroque banquets that lasted for days rather than their contributions, spiritual or otherwise, to the one, true faith.

As a cardinal, Castelli had been shortlisted for Pope at the last conclave. 'Papabile' as Osservatore Romano had labelled him. It was rumoured that his was the last name to be eliminated before the Pole cantered home a surprise winner. Since then they had never been close. Luigi Marco Castelli could trace his lineage back to Charlemagne. His family still retained vast estates in Lombardy and Piedmont. Before his elevation to Prince of the Church, he had been Archbishop of Milan. His much criticised friendship with several leading communists paved the way for his appointment as head of the Vatican Diplomatic Corps.

It also scuppered his papal prospects. The Italian mafia in the *Curia* saw to that. A prelate who advised his priests to listen to the red orator, Palmiro Togliatti, so that they might improve their own sermons would never fill the shoes of the Fisherman. So they chose the Pole. Castelli had confided to Father Jerry more than once that in his view the frequent travels of Christ's current Vicar on earth were of greater benefit to Alitalia than the Roman Catholic Church.

Jeremiah O'Sullivan was his first secretary. He represented Cardinal Castelli on the cocktail circuit and ran discreet errands worldwide. In the byzantine workings of Vatican diplomacy, the true purpose of these was seldom clear. He had been assigned to the diplomatic service shortly after the death of Mussolini. He would have liked to imagine his tact and diplomacy had marked him out for this. Castelli frankly told him it was Ireland's neutrality that made him a suitable candidate for the job. Because the warring nations had yet to open proper channels of communication, they found the Vatican an ideal conduit. It had been an exciting era. Castelli's voice cut through his wool-gathering.

'. . . Nevertheless, the stress in this place is enough to kill a healthy man.'

If this were so, the Cardinal appeared to be thriving on it. But there was some truth in what he said. Even before Father Jerry began to feel unwell, it had been getting to him. The finer points of precedence in the seating plan for a modest lunch now annoyed rather than absorbed him. When minor diplomats squabbled over precedence, he became abrasive rather than attentive. The duties had changed too. No longer at the heart of intrigue, channelling information, threats or mere proposals from one embassy to another

3

in the cockpit of postwar Europe, the Vatican was now relegated to a quiet diplomatic backwater. The calibre of people assigned to the Holy See had deteriorated noticeably. Burnt-out cases from other, more demanding, outposts served out their time being saluted smartly by the Swiss Guards. Dammit, that was what could happen to him if Castelli's woebegone expression was any indication of what was to come!

'The Apostolic Nuncio in Dublin tells me there are several dioceses that would welcome your talents . . .'

For talents read private means! The number of parishes in Ireland unable to support even one priest were legion. Bishops had difficulty in finding volunteers to fill such vacancies. He hadn't spent years serving Castelli without being able to guess what was going on in his machiavellian mind. The pause lengthened. *You will have to spell it out, my crafty friend. Don't expect me to make it easier for you. Experience a little of the stress you were so concerned about a moment ago. You are going to have to come right out and say 'It's all over. No more diplomatic games. Time for you to go out to grass.' The Church is a caring employer but even she cannot carry passengers indefinitely – especially in the diplomatic corps. Wasn't that exactly what he had told poor Agostini? Now it was happening to himself.*

Of late, your hurried exits from meetings and receptions have aroused more than mere curiosity. It is not practical to explain them away by circularising the embassies and legations with notice of your illness and requesting that a vacant toilet be held in readiness for whenever you honour them with your presence. I have found you a nice parish in the sticks where you can live out the span allotted to you in peace and quiet on the generous income left by your rather mysterious uncle about whom you are so sensitive. Now run along like a good fellow, because I have a busy day ahead and lunch beckons . . . Of course it wasn't quite like that. When Castelli resumed after a pause for the response that never came, his tone was softer.

'He recommends one in particular. A small parish on the south coast. Brulagh, he called it. Its parish priest died recently. Sounds just the place to recover your health. When that happens, who knows? The Holy Father may well summon you back here. I shall certainly press him to do so.'

Castelli was living up to his nickname of the Red Fox. His words, though not a direct order, left no room for dissent. To gather all the relevant details he must have known the results from the clinic for some time. As for Brulagh, who had ever heard of the place? Must be some godforsaken dump at the back of beyond. Could he refuse to go? Don't be stupid. One of the first vows he took at his ordination was obedience. He had always experienced more difficulty with it than the others, celibacy included. If the Red Fox played true to form he would try to sugar the pill. As if reading his thoughts, the prelate resumed,

'We can make you a Monsignor, if you wish . . .'

Before he could decline the offer, Castelli was off on a different tack.

'. . . as for your deposit in the Vatican Bank, I am advised that there may be some difficulty in transferring cash or securities to Ireland. Heavy taxes at either end – that sort of thing. Since our brother Marcinkus . . .' his lip curled in distaste at the mention of the brash American, '. . . focused the attention of the world on our finances, the Bank of Italy have been creating difficulties for those wishing to transfer funds out of the Holy See. I don't suppose you wish to leave it behind you or to donate it to a worthy cause such as the Office for the Propagation of the Faith?'

Castelli, were he a civilian, would have been a millionaire several times over. It was whispered that his own personal fortune was safely tucked away in Switzerland, well out of reach of Marcinkus and his dangerous cronies. The lump sum Father Jerry had received from his uncle's ill-gotten gains had been more modest. Nevertheless, it would help ease his frustration at what might have been. Once he had believed that a new order would emerge from the smoking ruins of postwar Europe. An order, hopefully, based on Christian values, that would replace the old one based on pomp and privilege. It was something of a disappointment, therefore, to discover that this was not the prime concern of his superiors – unless the propping up of good Catholics like Franco, Salazar, Somoza and Peron could be regarded as such. Having seen their regimes at first hand, he did not think so.

No such doubts assailed the sleek diplomat who was waiting for a reply to his question. Castelli regarded the diplomatic game as a huge joke. If he took it seriously, as sometimes he had to, he viewed his role as that of a chess grandmaster destined to flourish his special skills before an admiring audience. If this troubled him, it did not show on his cherubic face. Father Jerry shook his head.

'In that case, you will have to turn it into something tangible. A valuable picture, perhaps? Diamonds maybe, or gold? Something portable that will hold its value in Ireland. Have you any ideas?'

He had. He knew exactly what he would do with this embarrassment of riches. If he was being condemned to an early retirement he would indulge himself. Were he an ordinary diplomat, a commercial attaché for instance, he would be presented with a silver tray or a gold Rolex. Since the clergy received no such bouquets, he would have to award one to himself. He most certainly did not want to become a Monsignor. It was a meaningless limbo between parish priest and bishop. Instead he would buy a car. Alfa-Romeo had introduced a new, powerful model. His eight-year-old Fiat was not worth bringing to Ireland. It was left-hand drive and would probably give up the ghost half-way across the Alps. As a sop to his parishioners he would order his Alfa-Romeo in clerical black. Then he would drive it across Europe to his native land.

The long journey would allow his mind and body to adapt to the change. He hadn't been back home in thirty-two years. It would take more than a two-week drive to readjust but it would be a start, at least. He would look up Agostini *en route*. The sly old devil had been put out to grass too, several years before. Perhaps he would have some advice on premature retirement.

'I was asking; have you any ideas?' Castelli prompted.

'Not at the moment,' Father Jerry lied effortlessly, 'I should have my desk straightened out within a month. Will that be all right?'

'Fine, fine . . . no great hurry. Well, do you want the pretty buttons?'

. Monsignors wore scarlet buttons as a badge of office.

'No thanks.'

He rose from the chair and let himself out through the oak door. There was no time to waste if he was to secure a right-hand drive car from Alfa-Romeo inside a month. Their machinery was beautiful but their administration left a lot to be desired. Just like the Vatican, he reflected.

6

2

The buzz of flying insects formed a choral backing to the drone of the voices. The stronger tone of Maggie Flannery began the mantra with 'Hail Mary, full of grace, the Lord is with thee'.

Before she could finish, the coarser voice of the older woman, Julia May, cut in with the response. 'Holy Mary, Mother of God, pray for us sinners now and at the . . .'

Before the end, Maggie picked up her refrain again, forming an unbroken chain of prayer. 'Hail Mary . . .'

Each started off on a high note, like a frisky racehorse at the tapes, only to falter at the half-way stage in the certainty of being caught and passed by the other. This produced a curious, surging resonance, not unlike the waves lapping against the nearby seashore.

To the west, behind the stark silhouette of the grotto, the sky was slashed with angry orange streaks. Grey clouds threatening rain swirled overhead, set ablaze at their fringes by the sun dying behind the dark purple mass of the mountain. Its last flickering light threw the stonework surrounding the grotto into sharp relief while cloaking its flaking paint and rusted railings in the warm dusk of the evening. A ring of dazzling white, a neon halo, hung suspended above the Virgin's head. Her statue stood in a rounded alcove set in the centre of a cut-stone grotto. Its smooth white surrounding wall further intensified the already piercing light blazing from the halo on to the faces of the two kneeling women. They wore loose-fitting cloaks of pale blue and white over their everyday clothes – the garb of the Legion of Mary. Each had a rosary clenched between finger and thumb which they advanced, one bead at a time, after each 'Amen'.

The Legion was a group of women who met regularly for prayer and discussion. They decorated the church with flowers, organised pilgrimages to holy shrines and kept vigil on special occasions in the church or – as now – at the grotto. The high point of their year was the trip to Lourdes, the most famous of the Marian shrines. It was there that the Virgin had appeared miraculously and the Brulagh grotto was meant to resemble its better known counterpart.

For as long as anyone could remember, Maggie had been the group leader of the Legion in Brulagh. It was a thankless task. Its only perk was a free ticket to Lourdes – contingent on her finding at least thirty others to accompany her. She saw to it that they paid for their tickets a month in advance of their departure. The parish priest and several invalids, hoping for a miraculous cure, also travelled free. This arrangement was not unusual. Many other branches of the Legion did likewise. It made the trip more expensive for the paying pilgrims but no one seemed to mind.

At least, not until their last meeting. It was then that Mary Mullarkey dropped a bombshell. She proposed that everyone, except the invalids of course, pay their own way. Claiming that her scheme would allow them to carry more invalids, she argued that now would be an ideal time to implement it. The new parish priest had yet to arrive. He could hardly take offence at the change as he had not been party to the original arrangement. Furthermore she had learned that Father Jeremiah O'Sullivan was not in the best of health. Having just motored across Europe from Rome it was unlikely that he would wish to set off again on a tiring pilgrimage so soon after his arrival. Uproar followed. Julia May, housekeeper to the previous parish priest and hot favourite to retain her post under the new regime, was furious. Before she could give vent to her fury, however, Maggie's voice had sliced through the uproar like a laser.

'It is appalling that the House of the Lord should be turned into bedlam like this. What's more, I am deeply offended that anyone should be so stupid as to suggest that I am taking advantage of my position to get a free trip to Lourdes. I declare this meeting adjourned here and now. At our next meeting I shall expect an apology for that insult and I pray to God and His Blessed Mother that cooler heads and wiser counsels will have prevailed by then!'

With everyone shouting at once, the meeting broke up in near disorder. There had been bad blood there ever since the Mullarkeys had stolen the post office from under Maggie's nose. She had assumed that when her aunt died, it would be hers. Mick Flannery, Maggie's husband, was the local TD, which should have made its transfer to the Flannery shop a foregone conclusion. Or so everyone thought – except for Mary Mullarkey. The moment the elderly postmistress had taken poorly, that lying bitch Mary Mullarkey had applied for it. In the application form for the job of postmistress there was a space reserved for 'any other relevant details'. In this the liar wrote that she had three years' experience of post office work before she married that string of misery, Pat. Then she claimed that she would be 'on call' twenty-four hours a day because she lived over the shop.

By the time Maggie discovered the treachery, 1.
appointment had already been ratified. When Mick .
with the Minister for Posts and Telegraphs he was to
gone to the better qualified applicant.

It had given the Mullarkeys a distinct advantage in the.
for the trade of the town which, until then, Maggie had had to
Farmers with fat milk cheques and fishermen exporting lobster   .1
salmon to France in giant lorries queued up to be served at Flannery's
long, wooden counter. There they would get credit and the promise
of political favour in return for their custom. Slowly but surely,
however, Mullarkey's supermarket caught on. At weekends when
there was still money circulating, people shopped at the supermarket
where everything was cheaper. When they were short of cash and
needed credit, they turned to Flannery's. With the squeeze on farming
and no more fish being shipped to France, few were able to pay
anything off their accounts in the big ledger beside the ancient cash
register. Those who were asked for payment switched their custom
to Mullarkey's.

The post office at the back of the supermarket lured even more
shoppers past the well-stocked shelves. It was very rarely that someone failed to buy something, even if they only dropped in to post a
letter. The harder times became, the more Mullarkey's prospered at
Maggie's expense. Now the rivalry between them had spilled over
into the affairs of the Legion. Maggie tried to concentrate on the
rosary which she had been reciting while her brain was set on auto-
pilot. The grotto where they were praying had been erected back in
the fifties. For no good reason that anyone could think of, the Pope
had decreed a Marian year, twelve months of special devotion to
Mary, the Mother of God. Ignored by the rest of the Roman Catholic
world, his edict was taken to heart by the Irish. In a burst of
enthusiasm for all things Marian, grottoes sprang up like mushrooms
at every crossroads. Parishes vied with each other to see who could
erect the biggest and most outlandish tribute to Mary, the Mother
of God.

When the Marian year ended, one by one the grottoes fell into a
state of benign neglect. The month of May rekindled a spark of
interest in them, it being regarded by the more devout as a time of
special devotion to Mary. The Legion organised a roster of members
to recite the rosary nightly at the Brulagh grotto while kneeling
outside the railings that protected it from the public. This evening it
was the turn of Maggie and Julia May. Earlier Julia May had

...ed to Maggie that her brief regarding the new parish priest was 'to put a bit of meat back on the craythur'. This had come from no less a source than the Bishop himself. As her previous charge had topped twenty stone when summoned to his eternal reward – a major factor in his unexpected demise – no one doubted her ability to put weight on her clergy.

They were half-way through a decade of the rosary which consisted of ten Aves and a Pater Noster. Suddenly Julia May let out a startled cry. 'Oh Holy Mother of God, did you see that?'

The panic in her voice was unmistakable.

'What, Julia May? Did I see what?'

'The statue of course, the statue! It's moving, surely you can see it move? Oh God between us and all harm, there it goes again!'

Maggie stared long and hard. Until then her head had been bowed in prayer, thus sparing her the discomfort of looking directly at the statue. Its neon halo hurt her eyes now that dusk was gathering fast. Yes, there *was* movement. The exact nature of it was impossible to define. The mass of the statue seemed to expand and contract. Peering harder into the oasis of light, Maggie imagined that she might have seen the tiniest flicker in the eyelids of the Virgin.

'I think I see something all right, Julia May, but what is it? I even thought her eyes opened for a second. Did you see that?'

Whatever happened, she was not going to upset her staunchest ally against the Mullarkeys by heaping scorn on her moving statue. Anyway, she did think she saw something. Furthermore she was not going to let it be said that she had been outdone in piety by anyone, not even the priest's housekeeper.

'Oh dear Holy God, Maggie, you're right! Is that a tear or what coming down her cheek?'

'It could be, Julia, it could be. I can't look any more with the light blinding me. I've a splitting headache as it is. Will we finish the rosary or would you prefer to go back to the house this minute?'

The avenue leading to the Flannerys' farmhouse was less than fifty yards away from where they were kneeling. They stayed where they were even though theirs was the last vigil of the night. As they prayed at a much quicker pace, they looked at the statue every so often to make sure it was still there. Occasionally they stole nervous glances at each other to gauge the reaction to the phenomenon they had just witnessed. Thankfully the statue appeared to have returned to immobility. Just as the rosary ended, Julia May gave another gasp of amazement. This time she was staring wide-eyed at the clouds.

There was just a fag-end of sunset lighting the sky and its fast-moving rainclouds.

'Oh dear God in Heaven, did you see him, Maggie? In the name of all that's holy, tell me that you saw him.'

She was pleading for reassurance, her voice breaking with excitement. Maggie decided the whole thing was rapidly getting out of hand. Whatever about the moving Madonna with her blinding neon halo, apparitions in the sky were stretching things a bit too far.

'Did I see what, Julia?'

'Padre Pio, of course. Looking down on us from that big cloud up there! Oh God between us and all harm, can't you see him for yourself? Up there, just above the grotto?'

She pointed to a dark, angry mass scudding across the sky.

'I can't, Julia. There's nothing there now.'

'Yerrah he's gone now. He was only there for a second or so, at the most. Smiling down on us he was, God love him, through that lovely beard of his.'

'I think we had better get back to the house. We can have a cup of tea and try to get our wits back.'

'I hope you're not insinuating, Maggie Flannery, that I'm losing my wits? Or imagining things, for that matter?' Julia May was seething with indignation.

'Didn't you see for yourself the Blessed Virgin move and her eyes blinking back the tears? I'm telling you 'tis a miracle we're after seeing and no mistake!'

Maggie nodded without conviction. Julia May's devotion to Padre Pio was legendary. The old Canon had tried vainly to discourage it but gave up in despair. The kitchen of the parochial house was festooned with portraits of the saintly friar, many of them displaying in gory detail the stigmata for which he was noted. Mother Church, in her wisdom, had so far declined to confer sainthood on him – a touchy subject with his many devotees. Julia May had already announced her intention of taking this up with the new arrival at the first opportunity. He was, after all, coming straight from Rome and should have the latest news on how the case for Padre Pio's canonisation was progressing. If that progress were not rapid enough for Julia May's liking, Father Jeremiah O'Sullivan was going to have some explaining to do.

'I'm not insinuating anything. It's just that I couldn't see Padre Pio, that's all. Oh God, I'm so confused I hardly know what I saw!'

Maggie hurried up the dark avenue leading to her house without

11

risking a backward glance at the grotto. Julia May, on the other hand, paused several times to look back. Maggie could hear her speculating aloud on the length of Padre Pio's trip back to Heaven and praying that nothing ill would befall him *en route*. The sooner she was sitting down in her own house and drinking a cup of strong tea, the happier Maggie would be. She introduced the next item on the agenda with all the delicacy of a bomb squad approaching a suspect device.

'I don't think we should mention this to anyone, not for the time being, anyway.'

'Dear Holy God, are you saying we should keep it a secret? As if we had something to be ashamed of? Is that what you're trying to tell me, Maggie Flannery?'

'No Julia May, that's not it at all. Of course we have nothing to be ashamed of. It isn't as if we were two young ones imagining things. It's just that they may not believe us. They might say we dreamed the whole thing up!'

'Let them – whoever they are – say what they like. You and I both know what we saw. Surely to God, they're hardly going to make liars out of the two of us . . .'

Maggie lifted the latch on the back door. At a big kitchen table, books scattered everywhere, her daughter Gillian was immersed in her homework. She barely raised her head as the two women came in. Julia May pursued her point relentlessly.

'Anyway, Maggie, so long as we're both of the one word about what we saw, where's the problem? It isn't as if we were a pair of flighty young ones who dreamt the whole thing up to get a bit of notice for ourselves. It's our bounden duty to tell the whole world, that's what it is. Why should we keep it under our hats? Isn't that the very last thing in the world Our Blessed Lady would be wanting us to do? If we kept quiet about it, we'd only be doing the Devil's work for him.'

'Maybe you're right but it's sure to make us the laughing-stock of the village and no mistake if we tell the whole world about it, that's why!'

Distracted by the argument and noting the hard edge creeping into her mother's voice, Gillian abandoned her studies to enquire. 'Why would you be the laughing-stock of the village, Ma?'

Before Maggie could reply, Julia May blurted out, 'The two of us were saying the rosary below at the grotto. Everything was fine until, I declare to God, didn't the statue of Our Lady start to move! The next thing we saw was the tears flowing out of her eyes by the bucketful. When I looked up at the sky who did I spot but Padre Pio smiling down on us from a heavenly cloud. He gave us his blessing and then he went away about his business. I declare to God it nearly put the heart crossways in me. I won't be in the better of it for many a long day to come.'

The story was improving with every telling, Maggie noted uneasily. Gillian's reaction was predictable. She giggled and smirked as she asked, 'Are you sure the two of you weren't at O'Shea's instead of the grotto? Speaking of O'Shea's Ma, he told me I could have a job in the bar during the summer holidays if I wanted it. Eight pounds a night. I told him I'd have to ask you first. What do you think? Please say yes. I'd love to do it, and think of the pocket money it would save you!'

'We'll discuss it later. Will you boil the kettle and bring us a pot of tea into the front room where we can get a bit of peace for ourselves. Come on, Julia, we'll get out of these robes, have a cup of tea and then I'll drive you back to the village.'

When Julia May had gone ahead, Maggie hissed to her daughter, 'I suppose you think you're very clever, saying what you did about us being in O'Shea's? You know perfectly well neither one of us would be seen dead in a place like that. I may well decide it's no place for you either, my girl. We'll see. In the meantime, don't breathe a work of this to anyone or you'll live to regret it, do you hear?'

Gillian nodded. She tried to look contrite now that her summer job – her only excuse to get out at night – was at risk.

'Not a word to a soul, Ma, I promise. Sure I was only joking. Wouldn't it be great gas, though, if Brulagh turned into another Lourdes or Fatima. The pair of you would be world famous!'

3

'Ah Jaysus Maggie, wouldn't you get a small bit of sense for yourself? If you go on like this we'll be the joke of the country. You no more saw the statue move than I did! As for Julia May, 'tis no secret that she's a crazy old bitch and a religious maniac into the bargain.'

Mick Flannery had just driven back from Dublin and was changing out of his suit into something less formal. Maggie replied through the open door of her bedroom.

'Fat chance of you seeing it move anyway. The last time you said a prayer was when you thought you'd lost the last election. As it was, you only just scraped in by a few votes. No doubt about it, Mick, the Devil looks after his own. As for Julia May, I'd leave her out of it, if I were you. Remember all the canvassing she did for you over the years when you couldn't be bothered to do it yourself.'

'You're talking nonsense and it's well you know it, woman. I go to Mass every Sunday and as for Jul . . .'

'Oh indeed you do. The poor Canon, God rest his soul, was afraid to start it without Mick Flannery in his best suit marching up the aisle to the front bench. I'd be prepared to bet big money 'tis the only front bench you'll ever sit on.'

'Very clever, Maggie, very clever. OK so I'll never be in the Cabinet or a front-bench spokesman. So what about it? Any time your relations want something, the bloodsuckers get what they want, don't they? As for my going to Sunday Mass, what's wrong with that?'

'I'll tell you what's wrong with it – as if you didn't know already. It's no secret that you don't say a prayer from one end of the week to the next. You only go every Sunday so that the voters will see what a good family man you are. And a good Catholic too, of course. Did you know that big lump of a prayer book of yours is out of date since Vatican Two? Still and all, how would you know? You never open the thing anyway?'

'Oh God give me patience. Are we talking about my religious practices or yours? You know as well as I do that if I missed Mass on Sunday I might as well advertise in the *Clarion* that I'm a homosexual atheist who beats his wife and abuses his children. As for the prayer book, it gives me something to do with my hands while I'm waiting for the Mass to end so that I can go outside for a cigarette. Anyway we're not talking about that, for God's sake. Why do you keep changing the bloody subject?'

His voice dropped several octaves and took on what he liked to think of as his persuasive tone.

'Why can't you just tell them that you only *thought* you saw something at the bloody grotto? Now that you've had time to think about it, explain to them it was only a . . . whatcha call it? . . . an optical dilution?'

'Illusion.'

'What?'

'Illusion, you fool. Dilution is putting water into something. Like whiskey – a subject you should know all about!'

'Oh yes, how do you make that out?'

'The dogs in the street know that you're drinking your skull off these days. They say it's because you're afraid Pat Mullarkey will take the seat off you in the next election.'

'Well isn't that lovely, fucking lovely? You can tell whoever *they* are that if that long string of misery is daft enough to run against me, I'll have him for breakfast. I suppose "they" are that crowd of eejits dressed up like yourself. God Almighty, the whole lot of you look like Brulagh's answer to the Ku-Klux-Klan!'

'I wish you wouldn't use that filthy language in this house. Now if you're referring to the Legion of Mary . . .'

'I am, I am!'

'I thought as much. Well, it's no more than I would expect from a third-rate politician. Trying to drag everyone else down into the gutter along with yourself! Now I must go. We're meeting in the church in a few minutes.'

She had gone out the door before he could think of a suitable reply. It was unfair of her, she admitted as she hurried towards the church, to bring up the matter of Sunday Mass. She knew perfectly well how important it was to his political survival.

Mick used religion as just another means of retaining his seat in the dail. Every Sunday he marched to the top of the Church, the family trailing uncomfortably in his wake. Dressed in his best suit and clutching an enormous Sunday missal, he genuflected reverently before the altar and took his place at the head of the congregation, as befitted a public figure. Without so much as a sideways glance at the Mullarkey family across the aisle, he would bury his face in his hands as though lost in prayer. When the Canon emerged from the sacristy to celebrate Mass, flanked by two altar boys trying hard not to smirk at their friends, Mick rose slowly from his knees. With a flourish he made the sign of the cross, employing dramatic gestures that seemed to embrace the entire congregation. It was his way of telling the Canon that he had assembled his people in this place at considerable inconvenience and now it was high time to get on with the show.

At the communion bell, he was out of his seat quicker than a greyhound out of traps. His hands were clasped across his groin as though guarding against an unexpected blow from Pat Mullarkey, whom he had beaten yet again to the altar rails by the shortest of heads. Communicants were expected to be in a state of grace. That meant, even for the most pious, regular attendance at the Sacrament of Penance where sins were confessed to the priest and duly forgiven. Mick hadn't been inside a confessional for thirty years – though not for the want of something to confess, Maggie suspected.

The key to the door of the church was massive – like something presented to Saint Peter by a bearded deity in a medieval painting. Lest it be lost, it was attached to a timber block by a chain. Julia May was wrestling with it in the lock when she was joined by Maggie Flannery.

'Are we the first?' Maggie asked.

The question was unnecessary. There were still five minutes to go before the meeting. While charity and chastity were highly thought of among its members, the Legion of Mary attached less importance to the virtue of punctuality. Eight o'clock on the evening of the first Tuesday of every month was when they gathered in the church for prayer, contemplation and discussion. The first two of these elements were conspicuous by their absence at the last meeting, which broke up in disorder over the pilgrimage to Lourdes. There was no reason to believe tonight's meeting was going to be any better. The fact that the new parish priest had not yet arrived only added to the problem.

'Yes, we are, by the looks of it. Just as well too. I wanted to ask you something before the meeting started. Did you put it on the agenda?'

Maggie looked mystified.

'Did I put what on the agenda?'

'God give me patience! What the two of us saw at the grotto, of course. The whole village knows about it by now. Didn't you see the crowds there for the last few nights?'

Julia May's exasperated tone gave due warning of a major eruption at any moment.

'Well they didn't hear it from me, that's for sure,' Maggie replied. Already on the defensive, Maggie just could not summon up the courage to suggest again that the incident would best be forgotten. To do so would have upset Julia May who, even at the best of times, was prone to frenzied outbursts at those who crossed her. Were she to unleash one now, Maggie would lose the support of her strongest ally just when she needed it most. It was a pity that Julia May was forever trying to draw attention to herself by acts of excessive piety but perhaps it was only to be expected of a priest's housekeeper. The old Canon had abandoned all attempts at curbing her religious zeal long before he died. It would be interesting to see whether his successor would fare any better. That, however, was his problem. Maggie's was that Mary Mullarkey was undermining her position as group leader by demanding that she pay her own way to Lourdes.

So it was more essential than ever to keep Julia May on her side, even if it meant supporting her increasingly bizarre tales of what happened at the grotto. Anyway it was probably too late to withdraw gracefully from the whole thing. By now it had taken on a momentum of its own.

As Julia May had observed, every night there were more and more people milling around the grotto, waiting for something to happen. Already some of the younger Flannerys were planning to turn their mobile home into a chip van and use the front field as a car park.

'I can promise you, Maggie, it didn't come from me either. I didn't breathe a word about it to a soul. Maybe it was Gillian. She was the only one who knew apart from ourselves. Probably told the girls in her class. Anyway it doesn't matter any more. The whole village knows by now.'

It was all Maggie could do to choke back her indignation. Julia May had told everyone she met. The sceptical she referred to Maggie for confirmation. It was yet another of Julia May's ploys to demonstrate her religious fervour. It was the same at the rosary. Her voice was always loudest, as though sheer volume could be equated with sanctity. At Mass, she chimed in with the responses a split second before the rest of the congregation. Before Maggie could defend her daughter, Julia May had taken up the running again.

'Thanks be to God Father O'Sullivan is arriving tomorrow. Trying to keep the church tidy with strange priests arriving at every hour of the day and night to say Mass and hear confessions, not to mention them expecting to be fed and found, was getting on my nerves. That's why I have the door locked. 'Tis even worse than nursing the poor old Canon though, God Himself knows, that wasn't easy either . . .'

The lock gave a loud click and the heavy door swung open. She interrupted her litany of sorrows to place the key and its accoutrements back in her handbag. She continued, but on a different tack.

'I declare to God if the Bishop's secretary hadn't the cheek to phone the parochial house yesterday. Wanted to make sure I had everything ready for the new arrival, if you please. You can be sure I wasn't long in telling him 'twas easily known he had never set foot inside the parish of Brulagh or he'd have realised that there was no need to tell Julia May to have everything in readiness.'

Maggie did not reply. The opportunity to deny that her daughter was the source of the leak would be lost for ever in another torrent of words of she didn't act now.

'I'm sure Gillian never breathed a word to anyone. You heard me warning her that evening in the kitchen, didn't you?'

Julia May nodded distantly. She had now lost interest in that topic, preferring to dwell on her triumphs over the Bishop's secretary.

'For all his cheek, he didn't seem to know much about our new man except that he was arriving tomorrow. Said he was driving from Rome, for God's sake. Did you ever hear of anything so silly? In the name and honour of God why couldn't he fly like everyone else, especially when he's not well in himself?'

'That's what Mary Mullarkey said at the last meeting. How did she know, I wonder? About his health, I mean?'

'Is it joking me you are, Maggie Flannery? You know the answer as well as I do myself. That one listens in to every telephone conversation. With the exchange at the back of her shop, why wouldn't she? Do you mean to tell me you didn't see the look I gave her at the last meeting when she was going on about Father O'Sullivan not being in good health? Of course she was only trying to make out that he wouldn't be interested in going on the pilgrimage to Lourdes so soon after arriving here from Rome. If she brings it up again tonight, I won't be long in telling her to mind her own business and not to be listening in to other people's telephone calls, especially when it concerns Our Holy Mother, the Church.'

'She's probably right, all the same. About him not wanting to go, I mean. And it will be hard to justify my travelling for nothing if she has an invalid to go instead.'

'Yerrah that's all nonsense. We'll have our work cut out for us to make up the usual four as things stand, not to mind finding any extra invalids. The only one we can be sure of at the moment is the Widow Slattery.'

Before Maggie could reply, they were joined inside by the rest of the members, including Mary Mullarkey. Julia May turned on the lights in the darkened church as Maggie called the little group to order. She wondered nervously how this meeting would go.

'We all remember how our last meeting ended. I think we should say a decade of the Most Holy Rosary so that Our Blessed Lady will guide us. Let us pray that she will show us a way to resolve our differences!'

Without delay, she intoned, 'The fourth glorious mystery, the Assumption of Our Blessed Lady into Heaven. Our Father who art in Heaven, hallowed be thy Name, thy Kingdom come . . .'

Maggie's voice changed when reciting the rosary. It had a hollow, robot-like timbre not noticeable in her everyday speech. She recognised this but was powerless to correct it. The old Canon was the same. When he implored Almighty God to look with pity on his flock and to steer them back to the paths of righteousness, he could have been a tub-thumping evangelist of the old school. Yet his ordinary voice was a reedy semi-quaver to which careful heed had to be paid lest his words be lost in thin air.

Her closing prayer was 'Glory be to the Father, the Son and the Holy Ghost.'

The response surged back, Julia May in first, as usual. 'As it was in the beginning, is now and ever shall be. World without end. Amen.'

Maggie cleared her throat. It was now time to open the discussion.

'As you may have noticed, I picked the fourth glorious mystery of the Holy Rosary to open our meeting tonight. It seemed to be particularly suitable for the month of May . . .'

She saw Julia May waving frantically from the back of the group.

'Did you want to say something?' Maggie enquired.

'Indeed I did. Before you go any further, can I make an announcement?'

It would have been easier to stop a herd of wild elephants. Maggie shrugged her shoulders and prepared for the worst. 'Of course. Go ahead.'

Everyone turned to look at Julia May as she spoke.

'You all must have heard by now what Maggie and I saw at the grotto last week.'

19

She paused for effect. Some exchanged nervous glances while others stared fixedly at the stained-glass window above the altar, which the evening sun had transformed into a blinding kaleidoscope of colour.

'Well there's no point in trying to keep it quiet. Myself and Maggie saw the statue of Our Blessed Lady moving and weeping. I saw Padre Pio and he looking down on the pair of us. He gave us his blessing and promised that Our Lady would have a message for the world on her special day. That's August the fifteenth, the feast of the Assumption of Our Blessed Lady into Heaven. Indeed 'twas only right and fitting for Maggie to pick it as the mystery for the decade of the rosary we just said.'

To say that her interruption made an impact would have been a gross understatement. They were struck dumb. Maggie tried feverishly to find her voice, but to no avail. This was an entirely new development. Until now, there had been nothing about a message. The ante had been upped yet again. Julia May, obviously pleased at the effect of her revelations, still held the floor.

'While it's not for me to tell you all your business, I think we shouldn't go to Lourdes at all this year. We'd be far better off looking after our own grotto and getting ourselves ready for the fifteenth of August.'

'But that's the day of the festival opening!'

Mary Mullarkey had spoken for the first time. She could not conceal the dismay in her voice. Having got the floor from Julia May, she was not about to relinquish it.

'Did Maggie see Padre Pio or did she hear him talk about Our Lady's message?'

Though the question was addressed to no one in particular, all eyes turned on Maggie. She fully realised the critical decision she had to make. To confirm Julia May's latest fantasy would lock her into a position she might not be able to sustain. At the very least it would label her a religious eccentric on the same level as Julia May. The alternative was to deny that she saw anything. This would hold her only ally up to ridicule and, no doubt, greatly please that lying Mullarkey bitch. She chose her words with care.

'I saw what Julia May saw and heard what she heard.'

Amid the gasps of astonishment, she saw Julia May nodding complacently. Victory was hers. Suddenly everyone was chattering excitedly to each other.

Before any further questions could come from the floor, Maggie announced in as steady a voice as she could muster, 'I declare this meeting adjourned until further notice. The pilgrimage to Lourdes will be postponed until we can come to a decision under the guidance of our new parish priest, who arrives tomorrow.'

With that she gathered up her blue and white cloak and swept out of the church. An excited group surrounded Julia May, pressing her for more details. She was only too happy to oblige them.

4

The lair of his old friend was not easy to find, hidden as it was in the heart of the mountains. Though swift motorways cut through the plains of Tuscany, the road that led to Boggola was breathtaking. Not alone for its beauty but also for the sheer drops that loomed around each bend on the tortuous climb to where Giuseppe Agostini lived out his days in paradise. His tiny church was surrounded by a neat vineyard, a pool full of carp, several peacocks, a harem of cats and three dogs of indeterminate ancestry. One of these seemed permanently attached to the hem of Agostini's threadbare cassock. As they sipped the rich Chianti and gazed out across the mist-laden valley with its patchwork of vineyards carved from the mountainside, Agostini enquired how Father Jerry felt about returning to his native land.

'I really don't know. I haven't been back in over thirty years. Obviously a lot must have changed in the meantime. Yet from what I read in the papers, many things remain the same – particularly the less attractive elements. They continue to kill each other in the name of God. The young still leave in droves in search of a brighter future. The changes brought by the Vatican Councils have scarcely touched them. Nor have I been able to find Brulagh, the place I am going to, on any map. Would you believe that I had to ask someone how to pronounce it? I was told it was Broo-lah, so now you are as wise as I am about the place.'

'Now that is a good thing, my friend. Here in Boggola, that's Boggo-lah, we too are a little off the beaten track. It makes for a peaceful life, I can assure you. I have a flock of four hundred or so yet my Sunday Mass attracts fewer than twenty. Perhaps I should regret this. The truth is that I don't. The state pays me a modest salary. With my garden and vines, I have all that I require. Should I feel in need of excitement, I can visit il palio in Sienna. The Irish also love horses, no?'

'Oh yes. Still do, from what I hear,' Father Jerry assured him.

'That is as it should be. I always enjoy the palio. I have a friend whose parish enters the race each year. He invites me to his balcony overlooking il campo where the race is run. His entry never wins because his parish is a poor one and it cannot afford a good horse or rider. Nevertheless we enjoy ourselves. If I need to stimulate the mind, I take a bus to Florence. There I look at the pictures in the Uffizi and pay my respects to Michelangelo and his *Pietà*. It is a relief, I can tell you, to get back here, far away from the crowds of tourists.'

'Hope I feel the same way about Brulagh. I suppose I'll manage to get in a bit of golf. The truth is I know nothing of where I am going. I could have found out more about the place if I wanted to but I prefer to see for myself. By the way, Castelli sends you his regards.'

Agostini spat delicately on the dust. 'Aaah, the Red Fox . . . ! Do you know, Jerry, I used to hate that man? Since he banished me here, the bad feeling has evaporated. That is true healing. Now I just feel sorry for him.'

'Sorry for him?'

'Yes, sorry, and a little sad. The man was a true Prince of the Church. In Milan he did a terrific job working with the communists for the good of the region. He should have stayed there instead of propping up tinpot dictators and trying to ignore the financial scandals that surround him. Pity . . . he would have made a good Pope. Did he offer you anything?'

'Not really. Asked if I wanted to become a Monsignor.'

'And?'

'I declined, of course.'

'Very sensible of you. Those buttons are the very devil to replace. Expensive too. I lost mine years ago and never bothered to get any more. Your uncle might have liked to see you sporting them, though.'

'He died a few years ago.'

'I'm sorry. I didn't know. Was it easy? His death, I mean?'

'Not from what I hear. Cirrhosis of the liver, as might have been expected. I was in Lima when it happened. He was buried by the time I heard about it.'

Agostini chuckled drily as he murmured half to himself, 'Those who live by the sword . . .'

Then, more loudly, 'and yet did he not deserve better after all those Masses you said for him? He sent you enough money to say them down through the years.'

Father Jerry shrugged but did not rise to the bait. He stayed another day, most of it spent in desultory talk about the past. His

23

uncle was not mentioned again. Then there was nothing left to say except a brief farewell.

As he made his way down the corkscrew road to the *autostrada* leading to Sienna he thought long and hard about his friend. Agostini had been troubleshooter for the Vatican diplomatic corps. Anyone stepping out of line had to answer to him first. The prospect had caused more than one senior prelate to resign rather than submit to such an ordeal. When his uncle back in Ireland had got into trouble, Agostini got wind of it somehow. It took an hour's interrogation before he was satisfied that Father Jerry was sufficiently isolated from the scandal to avoid any embarrassment to the Church. The experience had made him realise that the Inquisition was not just confined to the Middle Ages.

Now the Grand Inquisitor had become a simple country priest, the Don Camillo of Boggola. His transformation from globe-trotting man of the world to contented, threadbare shepherd of a tiny flock was complete. As Father Jerry gingerly edged his way out on to the fast lane of the *autostrada*, he wondered if he, too, would grow old as gracefully as Agostini. Or, more to the point, whether he would live long enough even to begin the experiment. The rest of the journey was pleasant and free of incident. He joined the sightseers in Florence, Paris and London. He negotiated the Saint Bernard Pass and fed the ducks on Lake Geneva. He celebrated Mass in the ancient cathedral of Chartres and marvelled at the mountainous slag heaps of Wales. He spent time with friends in Geneva and a night in the presbytery adjoining the abbey in Bath. As he cruised slowly into Brulagh, he reflected that the Alfa had been a joy to drive.

As a village it was unremarkable. It doggedly preserved its ordinariness behind the plastic facias of shops, a pub and a bank that lined its main street. Though signs everywhere pleaded to keep the place free of litter, the habits of past generations died hard. Cigarette packets, crisp bags and sweet wrappers scarred the pavements while hungry yellow litter baskets remained unfed.

True its setting between the mountains and the sea was spectacular, especially when the sky was full of sunlight and fleeting clouds, as it was today. The equal of anything he had seen on his travels. Yet despite its natural surroundings the place was a monument to drabness, a lacklustre gemstone set in an exquisite mounting. The grey buildings crowned with dark slates brooding over a black tarmacadam street were worlds apart from the cheerful red-tiled roofs and sunlit piazzas of his beloved Italy. An important fishing port at the turn of the century, the sudden departure of its staple catch, the pilchard, for warmer waters had started a steady decline in Brulagh's fortunes that continued to the present day.

It looked best from a distance. When he had braked hard to avoid an old blue Ford driven at lunatic speed in the middle of the narrow, pot-holed road, he had climbed out of the driver's seat to stretch his legs and recover his composure. Below him, the soaring spire of the church was the hub of a village clustered round it like a devout congregation. A small, stubby pier jutted into the blue crescent of sea to form a tiny harbour. To the left of the spire, just outside the village, a huge mound rose out of a field that was part of a patchwork quilt of green squares stitched together by grey stone walls. The darker patches of green on the mound were thorny brambles that soon would yield a harvest of blackberries. Only a stranger, however, would pluck them for here lay the remains of a fairy fort.

The fort of Brulagh after which the village was named predated Christianity. Its origins were lost in an age when tribes, possessed of magical powers, lived in such places. To walk through them, much less touch anything there, was to disturb the spirits. All silly superstition, of course, but a surprisingly large number of people gave these places a wide berth. Some even claimed to have heard fairy music coming from them on May Eve. The Church officially condemned such nonsense but privately did not concern itself unduly about it. As the Bishop had confided late last evening, the superstitions of today were of more immediate concern.

These focused on the grotto. It, too, was visible from the mountain road. Its garish blue-and-white colours were in stark contrast to the ring fort with its subtle shades of green. A bright light, the neon halo above the Virgin's head, burned defiantly as if to cow the ancient spirits of the fort. Suddenly he remembered the consternation in the Vatican when the Marian year had been declared. The Irish descended on the Holy City in their hordes, each demanding a personal audience with the Pope. It was part of his duties to explain that this was not possible. The best he could do was to ensure that his fellow countrymen would receive a Papal Blessing delivered from the balcony of St Peter's. He traced the start of his illness to those trying times.

Last evening his new Bishop had warned him that the twin problems of his parish were two women claiming to have seen 'something' at the grotto and the vexed question of what to christen the new GAA stand. The Bishop suggested with a rather forced laugh that such trivia should present little difficulty to a skilled Vatican diplomat. Shrugging off the clumsy compliment, Father Jerry was, nevertheless, secretly relieved. From the gravity of the expression on his host's face as he introduced the topic over an atrocious dinner of boiled chicken and mashed potatoes, he feared much worse. A schism, perhaps, or even a minor heresy. Gentle probing over the jelly and custard evidently satisfied the Bishop that his latest recruit had sufficient funds to support himself and was unlikely to be making any demands on the coffers of the diocese.

Father Jerry remained unforthcoming when quizzed about his health. For one thing, he regarded it as a personal matter for as long as it did not affect the performance of his priestly duties. More importantly, he had little of interest to impart. Ulcerative colitis conveyed nothing to most people. It was the length of the remission that mattered. In that also, Professor Marti was not of much help. It all depended, he insisted, on lifestyle. Plenty to eat and a stress-free routine was the correct regime. Father Jerry's first priority should be to put on some more weight. If this meal was a fair sample of clerical fare, that should be the least of his problems.

A steep, cobbled road led from the main street down to where green and blue nets lay drying on the smooth wall that ran the length of the pier. Lobster pots were piled high waiting for their bait of rotten fish before returning to the deep. He supposed he should have inspected his church and parochial house first but the sea was more inviting. There was no one about. He sat on the wall and looked upwards at his new parish. Even from here, the spire was the dominant feature. How was he going to cope with his new surroundings? Despite it being the very core of the Church, the Holy See had remarkably little truck with religion. His duties had been almost entirely of a diplomatic nature. Apart from saying morning Mass and reading his daily office, he might just as well have been a lay person. Now here he was in a community where the Church played a dominant role – cast as the leading actor.

A warm breeze blew in from the sea. It was good to clear his lungs and relax after the last lap of his journey over such terrible roads. Already he was doubting the wisdom of bringing back such a powerful car. The Bishop had examined it without comment. To hell with it. It had been worth it even if the drive down the mountain into Brulagh had left him a nervous wreck. The hairpin bends on the road to Boggola were child's play by comparison. Then there was that idiot who had almost forced him off the road. Before he could so much as raise his fist, the offender had disappeared at speed round the next corner.

As he turned the car by the pier, he decided that the houses and farms looked more prosperous than when he had last seen them three decades before. The people were better dressed too. Parks filled with flowers graced many towns and villages. But the roads were bad as ever: pot-holed tracks with the grass growing wild at the verges for the most part. Motorways were few and far between. Even then the fast lane was often blocked by a car travelling slowly as less patient drivers passed it on the *inside*. As he inched the large car back up the cobbles to the main street, he reflected that some things never change.

From the road, his new home was impressive. A square house with large windows, it was built from the same grey stone as the church beside it. He tried to look inside the church but found the door to be locked. As he drove up the avenue, the front door of the parochial house opened and a plumpish woman in her sixties was framed in the doorway. She wore a long black dress of some heavy material. Over it was a white, frilled apron and the whole ensemble was topped off with what could only be described as a maid's bonnet. The last time he had seen a similar outfit was at a performance of *Charley's Aunt* staged for expats in the British Embassy.

''Tis yourself that's as welcome to Brulagh, Father, as the flowers in May.'

'You must be Mrs O'Hara.'

'I am. Father I am. But no one calls me that around here any more since my poor husband passed away fourteen years ago. Now I'm plain Julia May.'

With that she attempted what might have been a curtsy.

'Here, let me help you with your bags,' she said. 'We don't want you to be tiring yourself out after the long drive, do we?'

He decided the question was rhetorical and let it pass.

'I see the church is locked. Is there any particular reason for that, Mrs O'Hara . . . sorry, Julia May?'

'I thought it better to. Just in case.'

'In case of what?'

'Well . . . in case anything was taken out of it while there was no priest here. I have the key inside. I'll get it for you now if you like.'

'Yes, please. I very much want to see the church first – on my own, if you don't mind. After that, I'll come back here and you can show me over the house. Is that all right?'

She nodded without enthusiasm and turned on her heel. While she

27

was gone he took in the view from what now was his front door. A green expanse of lawn swept down in a graceful curve to a low stone wall that bordered the main street. In the middle distance he saw once more the harsh neon light at the grotto. It seemed out of place in the bright sunshine. When Julia May returned with the massive key, he asked, 'Is the light always on at the grotto?'

'Only in May, Father, Our Lady's month. It's her halo. Is there something wrong, Father?'

He resisted the temptation to inform her that he was already quite well versed in Marian devotion.

'No, not all. I just thought it strange that the church should be locked during the day, yet a light still burns at the grotto. Putting the cart before the horse, I would have thought.'

'Well, Father, I suppose I'm to blame for that too. I declare to God but didn't myself and another woman see the statue of Our Blessed Lady move. There were tears pouring out of her eyes and I even saw Padro Pio himself, the lovely man, smiling down on us from the clouds! Of course I suppose 'tis yourself knew him well?'

Taken aback by the unexpected outburst his simple question had provoked, he could barely stammer out, 'Who? Did I know who well?'

'Padre Pio, of course. I was only saying to myself a while ago that I'm sure Father O'Sullivan is one of those holy men trying night and day to get the poor man made into a saint.'

'If you're asking me did I know Padre Pio, I have to say no. I met him twice, that was all. As for his canonisation, I assure you it has nothing whatsoever to do with me. That is a matter for the Holy Father himself.'

'And did you know him too? The Holy Father, I mean?'

'Yes, as a matter of a fact I did. I had to report to him twice a week. Julia May, tell me, do many others claim to have seen what you and this other lady saw?'

'Maggie, Father, Maggie Flannery. That was the other lady, Father. Oh yes, lots and lots of people. Mind you, to tell nothing but God's own truth, they've all seen different things. You can take a look yourself tonight. There will be hundreds there after it gets dark. In the dark it's just like being at Lourdes what with the lighted candles and the whole crowd saying the Holy Rosary. Oh it's grand altogether, Father, absolutely grand so it is. You'll love it!'

'I wonder, Julia May. I wonder if I would really love it. His Lordship the Bishop did mention that two ladies thought they saw something at the grotto. I was not aware, however, that my house-keeper was one of them. We must have a good, long talk about the whole thing very soon. In the meantime, I would like to take a look at the church.'

Taking the key from her outstretched hand he strode briskly along the gravel path that led to the locked door. He needed to be alone to gather his wits. He had thought the inspection of his first parish church would be a moving occasion for him. In fact he barely took in his surroundings, his mind in a turmoil from the unwelcome news that his housekeeper was one of the visionaries. So much for the stress-free retirement Castelli had stage-managed for him.

5

Before Mick Flannery left home to walk to the parochial house, a sheet of paper with an official stamp at the top caught his eye. It was peeping out from the bottom of an untidy pile of correspondence by the phone. Oh sweet Christ, he had completely forgotten about it. It was the most recent VAT assessment. For one reason or another he hadn't filed a return in years. God be with the days when all he had to do was to lift the phone to old Johnson in the tax office and the matter would be sorted out over a few drinks. Now Johnson was dead and the tax office was swarming with beardless youths whose sole ambition appeared to be to screw every last penny out of him. A while ago a little shagger, still wet behind the ears, called to the shop about the missing VAT returns. When they couldn't be found, he asked permission to examine the books. Maggie, her mind on other things like bloody moving statues and the like, told him to go ahead. After five hours of inspecting them, he left with the promise that Maggie would be hearing from him. He was unimpressed when she mentioned that her husband was a member of the Dail.

Probably another of those smart-arsed socialists that were taking over the civil service lock, stock and barrel, he decided. The sort of pencil-pusher that would look down his nose at the likes of Mick Flannery trying to get one of his supporters off a drink-driving charge – or pooh-poohing an £11,000 VAT assessment on himself. He didn't know how the young brat arrived at such a crazy figure. What he did know was that if Maggie ever found out about it, she would take leave of her last few remaining senses. He hoped the VAT people would agree that a lot of those accounts in the big ledger would never be paid. Even without this extra worry, the shop was going through a difficult patch. When Mullarkey's joined that bloody buying group, he pleaded with Maggie to do likewise. There were at least four other groups to choose from and any of them would have welcomed an old-established business like Flannery's.

She wouldn't hear of it, insisting that while independence was important to her, it was even more so to her customers. She would be damned if she was going to replace the elegant script above the door that proclaimed Flannery's to be Grocers since 1913 with a plastic monstrosity bearing the giant logo of some group and their own name in tiny lettering at the bottom, almost as an afterthought. Fine for upstarts like the Mullarkeys with no tradition behind them but quite unsuitable for a long-established concern like theirs.

To preserve the shop as an island of good taste in a sea of vulgarity, she refused to have any truck with 'special offers'. She dismissed them as a cheap trick that the people of Brulagh would wake up to, given time. Well not so far, Mick reflected sadly. Maggie's prediction that their customers would flock back in greater numbers than ever when they discovered that they were getting the shadow rather than the substance had yet to be realised. As a politician he knew that the shadow was often worth more votes than the substance. It was also much easier to deliver.

His suggesting minor concessions to the twentieth century such as getting a modern cash register and pricing the items individually met with a like response. Everything in the shop bore a tiny label written in a code understood only by his wife. She had explained it to him many times but he forgot it almost immediately. Anyway he could never understand why prices should be shrouded in secrecy. He suspected that she charged what she felt the market would bear and that those she liked might pay less than those she did not. Having chosen an item, a pair of wellington boots for example, the customer would hand them across the counter to her and ask the price. She would peer at the coded label, start wrapping the purchase and then announce that they cost six pounds. It required unusual strength of character to abort the proceedings at that stage. The inevitable result was that cash customers preferred Mullarkey's, where they could see the prices before buying. It was only those obliged to buy on credit who endured the byzantine procedure at Flannery's.

As he tied a large Windsor knot in his tie, the spectre of a tax inspector leafing through the big, leather-bound ledger came back to haunt him. Maggie always kept it in the same place, at the end of the wooden counter that ran the length of the shop. It lay beside the enormous cash register that emitted a sharp ring when its handle was jerked downwards, causing the cash drawer to slide open. Until decimalisation, purchases had been keyed in and the total appeared in a window at the top of the ornate dinosaur like symbols in a gaming machine. When converting it to the new currency proved impossible, she disconnected the display mechanism. Another link with the past broken, she complained to Mick, as though he were solely responsible for the fiscal policy of the government. For a time, he feared she was going to insist on doing business in the old currency – but that would have been going too far, even for Maggie.

That had been her sole concession to modernity. Everything else carried on as though marooned in a time warp. Tea was a case in point. Though the rest of the free world had taken to tea-bags like ducks to water, Maggie continued to buy tea by the chest. A family friend was a tea merchant. He sent on a chest whenever he deemed a shipment suitable for her customers. Such an arrangement made for an irregular supply. Sometimes the shop was awash with tea. Then again it could be out of stock for weeks on end. The merchant had a genuine concern to send her only the best and so live up to the legend embossed on the side of the packet: 'FLANNERY'S FINEST TEA – *A blend of the very best teas from all over the world brought together to please even the most discriminating palate.*'

The tea scales were another treasured relic. Kept under the counter they were produced only when a fresh consignment had to be weighed into the distinctive paper bags. Weighing the tea acted as a balm to Maggie's increasingly frayed nerves. Perhaps it was the soothing aroma of the dark, dry leaves as she scooped them from the plywood chest into the open bag on the silver platform of her precious scales that caused her to sing happily to herself. Or maybe it was the tingle of excitement she got from prising open the top of the chest and cutting through the taut silver paper that acted as an airtight seal. Could it be that she still half believed her father's warning about the snakes? He had told her as a little girl that while he was opening a tea-chest a black snake had slithered out on to the floor. He had rushed to the back of the shop for a spade to kill it. When he got back, it was gone. For long afterwards she had nightmares of a colony of wriggling, writhing black serpents under the floorboards. Too often she reminded Mick of what her father said when she finally plucked up the courage to ask him if it was true.

'Yerra not at all, girl. You should know better than to believe a single word out of the mouth of a politician – even if he is your father. But I'll tell you one thing. Always and ever take a good look before you put your hand inside a new chest. You can never tell what those foreign shaggers might be leaving in there after them!'

She took care to cut the silver paper evenly off the top and sides of the chest. She would hand it up to the schoolteacher, who sent it off to Africa where, in some unspecified way, it was used to 'help the black babies'. Those missionaries with the tired faces and prematurely white hair were most insistent that silver paper and an 'offering' from her parents were the only way to help the black babies. Mick kept his views on the subject to himself. Religion was a bone of contention between them. To her, it was the central point in her life. Early in their marriage she had placed the family under the special protection of Mary, the Mother of God. Mick felt that as a form of insurance, it did little to reduce the stress in her life. She continued to worry incessantly, especially about their son, Sean.

In this case, it seemed as though the Blessed Virgin's protection was working quite well at first. Maggie's proudest moment was when they brought Sean to the ivy-covered building that housed the Seminary of St Joseph. Looking at the enormous steeple towering over the manicured lawns, he said 'It reminds me of a prison – a *holy* prison, of course!'

That made Maggie weep with happiness. Mick told himself he should have known there was something amiss when his son, who had never been away from home before, appeared so relaxed about spending the next six years in such gloomy surroundings. The place gave Mick the creeps. He wanted to put as much distance between himself and St Joseph's as possible.

He had always been ambivalent about religion. He recognised the Church as an institution to be wary of, together with the Gaelic Athletic Association and the farmers' associations. The GAA was no problem, and he could talk rings round the farmers. But organised religion, in the person of God's representatives on earth, was something else. He hoped the new man would be different from his Bishop. That bloody man could not be satisfied. No sooner had Mick got planning permission for a new school than the prelate wanted the damn thing built. Didn't he know that these things take time, for Jaysus' sake? When the Bishop didn't get immediate action, he complained in a pastoral letter read out at every Mass that the local representatives were 'dragging their heels on this important matter'.

As the only politician for miles around, he might as well have named Mick and be done with it. Such public censure from the pulpit upset Maggie. No sooner was the bloody school built than the Bishop tried to take all the credit for it. When he discovered the way to reach Mick was through Maggie, he exploited this weakness mercilessly. Maggie was elevated to group leader of the diocesan pilgrimage to Lourdes. But for some brazen lying Mick would have been roped in as a helper. A weekend ministering to the sick and reciting the rosary was not exactly his idea of a junket to France.

'His Reverence is at his lunch, Mister Flannery. I'll show you into the parlour. You can wait for him there.'

Julia May ushered him through the hall into a large room. He did not enquire after the well-being of Padre Pio or make any reference to the grotto. Instead he nodded and followed her across the polished floor, bare save for a few expensive-looking rugs that hadn't been there before. The place smelt of wax polish and sizzling bacon. The walls of the parlour were panelled in oak half-way to the ceiling, creating a gloomy effect lightened somewhat by the huge windows. The wall between the ceiling and the panelling was a soothing beige that highlighted the swirling brown grain in the oak to good effect. The furniture overwhelmed the room. A large sideboard, elaborately carved, filled most of one wall. Its four thick columns supported an elegant canopy under which a mirror duplicated Julia May's flower arrangement. Mick believed he could have made a better attempt at it himself. Yet the heavy vase that held the scrawny blooms was worth a small ransom – as was the old Canon's collection of silverware surrounding it. The sideboard had delicately carved rope-edge borders, a feature repeated on the big dining table and chairs that occupied the centre of the room. When it came to furnishings, the clergy did not stint themselves.

Except for two pictures propped against the sideboard, everything else in the room belonged to the old Canon. The new man must have bought the contents unseen before moving in. Mick examined the pictures. Saint Sebastian looked unhappy, as ever, to collect yet another arrow in his bosom, while the *Adoration of the Magi* was a beautifully hand-painted copy. Both were encased in heavy, ornate gilt frames.

'Father O'Sullivan will see you now.'

He had not heard the door open. For such a large woman, Julia May padded silently as a cat. His shoes squeaked shrilly on the parquet flooring as he followed her back through the hall to a study. It was very different from the room he had just left. The walls were lined with bookshelves, holding matching leather volumes in neat rows. Stacked high on the floor were hundreds of paperbacks, still waiting to be sorted and put on the shelves. The big desk was strewn with newspapers, correspondence and pamphlets. A battered typewriter basked in the warm glow of a reading lamp. The Very Revd Jeremiah O'Sullivan, Parish Priest of Brulagh, was composing his Sunday sermon. A thin, frail man with a dangerous pallor, he rose with a smile and extended his hand.

'Hallo, Mr Flannery. I'm glad to meet you. Both my housekeeper and the Bishop speak well of you. They tell me that you have represented the people of this area for over three decades. That's quite an achievement, especially in Irish politics, is it not?'

'When you put it that way, I suppose it is, Father. Still there are a few round here who think it is thirty years too long.'

'If that is so, I have yet to meet them. May I ask if this is a purely social call? Because if it is, I would offer you a drink. On the other hand, if you have something of importance to discuss, perhaps we had better dispose of that first and have the refreshments later.'

'Well it's a bit of both, really. Naturally I wanted to welcome you to the parish, both on my own behalf and that of the village.'

'Thank you, Mr Flannery. I assure you that I am pleased to be assigned to Brulagh and look forward to working among you all. Perhaps the first small step towards that goal would be if you were to call me Jerry. Or Father Jerry, if you prefer.'

'And I'm Mick. They only call me Mister around here when the news is bad or they want something done for them. Did you have a good trip? That's some car you have outside the door.'

'It has always been my ambition to own an Alfa. Like good race-horses, they have a long pedigree. In the Vatican I could never afford one. Anyway there was nowhere to park it. Alas, stealing cars is now a national industry there. I was advised that to save on tax the best way to get money out of Italy was by buying something with it – hence the car. All perfectly legal, I assure you!'

Mick heaved a sigh that seemed to come from the soles of his shoes.

'You can't tell me anything about taxes that I don't know already. . . . What speed will she do?'

'Well over the hundred. I gave her a bit of a gallop on the motor-ways. Very fast, I must say. Not really suitable for the roads around here though.'

'You could be right there, Father. I'm damned from people pestering me morning, noon and night about them. The trouble is the County Council hasn't any money to spend on places like Brulagh. What small bit they have goes on the major roads. I suppose it's the same in Italy?'

'Not really. Of course they mainly have toll roads which work out quite expensive. But they don't have any pot-holes. What was it you wanted to ask me, Mick?'

'Well, it has been the tradition here all along that the parish priest is the chairman of Saint Fintan's GAA Club. I wanted to check that you would have no objection to taking on the job.'

'None at all. I hear you are a famous hurler yourself. Four All-Ireland medals in a row, wasn't it?'

'That's right. But things were easier then. If you had a good team in those days you were in with a great chance. Nowadays, all the teams are good. That's why the record still stands.'

'I'm sure you're being far too modest. It would be a pleasure to take on the job. While we are on the subject, are there any other similar jobs that I am likely to be given?'

'Oh buckets of them. The Development Board, the Festival Committee, the Dramatic Society. Then, as you know, there is the Pioneer Total Abstinence Society, the Society of Saint Vincent de Paul, the Legion of Mary and I know for a fact that the Golf Club will want you as their president.'

'Good! Golf was one of the things I really wanted to take up again when I came back here. It's far too expensive in Italy. Do you play yourself?'

'Whenever I can. I usually play with the Doc Buckley and the Sergeant, Gus Moriarty. You would be more than welcome to make a fourth any time you wish.'

'Thanks, I'd like that. As soon as I get settled in, of course. As you can see, I haven't half my things unpacked yet.'

Which was perfectly true. Quite simply, he hadn't the nerve. Julia May had been fussing over him like an old hen ever since he set foot inside the house. He had collected few possessions worthy of being carted across Europe in the Alfa. Of those he had only dared to bring in his collection of paperbacks and two of the three oil paintings under the disapproving nose of Julia May. From her demeanour, he gathered that she regarded books as objects to be admired rather than read. A vast array of leather volumes filled one wall of the study. He wondered idly if any of them had ever been opened, much less read. They did not inspire him to take them down and browse. Many were now relegated to mere fiction by the edicts of recent Vatican Councils.

An example of this was the beautifully bound omnibus edition of *The lives of the Saints*, most of whom had been demoted by Castelli and his brethren. What happened to saints whose status had been so reduced? Were they put on a lower perch in the celestial pecking order or did they just ignore the lunacies of mere earthlings and continue the same as before? Whatever their fate, the whole lot of them would soon be banished to the basement to be replaced by his own less elegant but well-thumbed favourites. That is, when he plucked up enough courage to do so.

After barely twenty-four hours, a titanic struggle was already looming. Julia May evidently considered it her duty to preserve the house as a shrine to his predecessor. The two pictures waiting to be hung in the parlour were merely pawns in the game. They were skilful copies done by a vagrant artist who had called at his apartment in the Vatican on the same day that an extremely generous cheque had arrived unexpectedly from his uncle. It was accompanied, as always, by a request to be remembered in his daily Mass. Since the size of the cheque always reflected the duration of the drinking bout, Father Jerry was only mildly surprised when it was followed some days later by word of his uncle's death. He had spent the rest of the money on his portrait by the same artist.

It remained in the car along with four cases of malt whisky, an unexpected but none the less welcome present from Castelli. The discreet 'D' decal on the car assured an untroubled passage through two sets of customs. Would that it could perform the same feat with Julia May. He toyed with the idea of enlisting Mick in an attempt to smuggle them into the house. A complexion of such purplish hue as Mick's must virtually guarantee his support in any activity even remotely connected with whisky. It was the portrait that made him dismiss the notion for the time being. He did not yet know Mick well enough to let him see it, and as it was so skimpily wrapped in newspaper, he could scarcely avoid doing so.

Like the pictures in the parlour, he would just have to bide his time. When he had told Julia May that he intended removing a woodcut of the Blessed Virgin emerging from what at first appeared to be a nuclear holocaust but on closer inspection proved to be the engraver's impression of a well-lit paradise, she pretended not to hear. An inner voice warned him to get on top of the situation before it took control of him. Julia May would have to be faced down sooner or later, be it on the issue of rearranging the furnishings in his new home or the even more delicate matter of the grotto. All very well, he admonished the inner voice, but what's the point in going out looking for trouble? All his life he had worked on the principle of letting trouble find him. This was no time to abandon a principle that had served him so well in the past.

'. . . What's this about a festival?' Father Jerry enquired.

'Saint Fintan's GAA Club. It's a hundred years old. We're holding a festival to celebrate its centenary. Nothing special, just the usual thing. Fancy-dress competitions, a flower show, a cake stall, a donkey derby and that sort of thing. Should be a bit of a laugh. I'll probably be opening it but you're welcome to say a few words off the platform if you want. It isn't until the middle of August anyway so there's no rush about making up your mind.'

Father Jerry examined the bearer of this lukewarm invitation more closely. He was a big man in an expensive suit. His tailor had managed to conceal a thickening waist by clever venting of the jacket, but even he could do little when his client chose to relieve the pressure. It was then that the result of endless fund-raising dinners could no longer be camouflaged by even the most skilful stitching. Its sudden release from the corset of his jacket allowed his stomach to surge forward in all its majesty, filling the spotless white shirt to overflowing. Every button strained furiously to hold in the wobbling mass. A tie of psychedelic colours with a knot the size of his fist loyally traced its contour to end somewhere just above his navel.

Even his gestures were larger than life. As he emphasised the lack of urgency in deciding whether to bask in his reflected glory, his hands sliced the air, chubby pink palms outstretched and shoulders hunched, as if to say, '*Make a speech if you really want to, but I'll act you off the boards!*' He might have been conducting a symphony or merely adjusting the volume of his booming voice, which decades of speech-ifying had moulded into a throaty roar. He looked familiar, as if he had played a different role much earlier in the play. Father Jerry couldn't put his finger on it just then but it continued to scratch around the edges of his subconscious. He replied as was expected of him.

'I think not. The people will have had enough of my sermons by then.'

His gaze strayed back to the typewriter where he had been trying to find something to say to his flock. Preaching was new to him. Apart from one retreat a year he gave to a convent in Rome, he hadn't spoken from a pulpit since he went to the Vatican.

'. . . that is if I can think of anything original to say to them.'

This was addressed as much to himself as to Mick, who quite agreed.

'I know what you mean. In my job if I said anything original they'd run a mile. I feed them the same old rigmarole every time. I tell them how wonderful they are and that their future is secure as long as they keep on re-electing me. Then I predict a bright, new dawn for everyone and wrap it up inside five minutes. My father-in-law warned me that if you don't strike oil in the first few minutes, stop boring. He knew a thing or two about politics, I can tell you, Father. I took over his seat when he died, God rest his soul.'

Father Jerry replied, 'I may well follow your precept – certainly where the five-minute rule is concerned. However, as my position does not depend on a fickle electorate perhaps I can afford to be more daring in my choice of subject matter. Do you find the electorate fickle, Mr Flannery . . . sorry, Mick?'

'Indeed I do. Just between you, me and the wall I expect a lot of trouble in getting re-elected. Which brings me to the new stand.'

Well here it comes. Will he try flattery, cajolery or veiled threats? Perhaps a cocktail of all three? Well, let's play this fish a little and test his fighting qualities.

'Oh yes. I seem to remember His Lordship the Bishop referring to that. Is there not some discussion as to what it should be called?'

'You can be sure of it. There will be a meeting soon about it in Doc Buckley's house . . .'

'I haven't met him yet.'

'You will, you will. A decent skin if ever there was one. As you will be chairing that meeting, I wanted to sound you out first. Some people think the stand should be called after me, others think it should be named Saint Fintan's Stand after the club. Then there's some who think it should be calling nothing at all.'

So that was it! Now he remembered who Mick reminded him of. The Mayor of Palermo had led a delegation to the Vatican on some long-forgotten mission. One of his henchman did most of the talking. Father Jerry found out later that he was a *capo* in the Mafia with several executions to his credit. The Mayor was his puppet. That *capo* was freshly reincarnated before him as Michael Flannery. The resemblance was striking. The upraised palms and protruding lower lip to emphasise the utter reasonableness of their outlandish demands were almost identical. He hoped Mick's corpses were only political and wondered if he would be added to the hit list if he did not acquiesce.

'What do you think yourself?' Father Jerry asked tentatively.

'Obviously I'm biased. It would help me a lot if they named it after me. Mullarkey, he's the trainer of the team and the treasurer of the club, knows that damn well so he will fight me all the way. There's no love lost between us, I can tell you.'

Frankness, that was to be his chosen weapon! The most difficult to counter, Castelli had often warned him. Not at all what he would have expected, in fact. There was much more to Mick Flannery than met the eye. He was becoming more likeable by the minute.

'Does the chairman have the casting vote?'

'Yes he does.'

'Oh dear. Do you have any idea of how the voting may go?'

'Well, not really. I'll have to abstain since I'm involved. I expect the Doc and the Sergeant will vote for me. Maybe Bernie the secretary too. Mullarkey will vote against me and so will his boss.'

'Who is that?'

'Mossy O'Connor. He runs the Department of Agriculture around here. Or he's supposed to. Mullarkey does what little work there is. Mossy spends most of his time in O'Shea's bar.'

'So there's a possibility that I may have to cast my vote after all?'

'A possibility, yes.'

'And you would like to know which way I am going to cast it?'

'Something like that, yes.'

Father Jerry had no intention of making life any easier for this large, friendly giant of a man. Why should he? Yet Mick's candour was refreshing. He made no effort to disguise his hatred of Mullarkey. Father Jerry's inherent caution triumphed over his desire to make an instant friend of this *capo*.

'Well Mick, you must appreciate that you are putting me in a difficult position. I haven't been here twenty-four hours and already I'm embroiled in controversy. If I support you, I antagonise Mr Mullarkey and vice versa. No doubt he will be along shortly to put across his point of view. The best that I can promise you right now is that I will do nothing for the moment. It really seems to be a matter between the two of you. It would be impertinent of me to come down in favour of one side or another. I would, however, be prepared to act as an intermediary, if that would help. By the way, I don't believe I'm familiar with Saint Fintan. Who was he?'

Mick hid his disappointment well. He was obviously another graduate from the academy of hard knocks. Another point in his favour.

'I haven't the faintest idea. I remember being told in school that he was a monk who lived in a stone hut like a hermit. Is that any help?'

'It might be. I'll look him up in the Canon's reference book and see if he is worthy of having a stand called after him. If he's not, you're the odds-on favourite. Will that satisfy you?'

Mick nodded glumly. 'I suppose it will have to. Now, I have something else to ask you.'

'Go ahead, this seems to be a day for it.'

'My wife, Maggie, thinks she has seen the statue at the grotto move. She has the whole family driven mad over it. Not only that, but a lot of strangers are hanging round the grotto every night. It's getting so I can hardly get my car in my own driveway. Would you try to talk some sense into her, Father?'

The priest took a deep breath before replying.

'Julie May imagines the same thing – only more so. I have tried to persuade her that it was a trick of the light but without much success thus far. Still, it's early days yet and I am more optimistic in the longer term. If you think I am now going to incur the wrath of your good wife by casting doubts on what she saw, then you are not the sound judge of character I took you to be. I haven't even met her yet, Mick. If she wants to discuss it with me privately, then that's a different matter.'

'Can I tell her that you'll talk to her if she calls on you?'

'Of course, Mick, that's part of my job, after all. Just don't expect any miracles. On second thoughts it might be better if I dropped into the shop casually. Julie May tells me that's where she buys the groceries. That way there would be less formality about the whole thing.'

On an impulse he added, 'Now perhaps you might do something for me?'

'Of course, anything at all.'

'I have four cases of whisky in the boot of my car. I want to get them inside without Julia May seeing them. Regrettably they are too heavy for me to lift. Would you bring them in for me?'

'Of course. Anything for the sake of a good cause!'

'Then we might open a bottle, just to check that it hasn't deteriorated in transit, of course.'

Mick nodded happily as they approached the car. Father Jerry had forgotten that he had opened one of the cases to give a bottle to Agostini. To save time he had torn a hole in the bottom. As Mick was carrying the last carton across the hall, a bottle slipped out through the opening. It exploded into tiny shards on the parquet floor. Golden pools of precious Glenmorangie disappeared for ever down between the parquet tiles. The aroma of the Highlands replaced that of beeswax floor polish. Both men stared in awe at the destruction they had wrought. Then they started to laugh. At first it was an almost silent heaving. Then from somewhere deep inside, a rumbling belly laugh erupted from Mick. Father Jerry let loose a higher, more delicate guffaw as counterpoint. Mick scythed the air with his hands, helpless in a paroxysm of mirth. The priest stooped over the disaster, hands clasped to his knees and bent double, laughing uncontrollably. Mick was first to recover the priceless gift of speech.

'Oh dear Jesus, I'd prefer if it was blood!'

This sparked an even louder outburst of merriment. It was cut short by a rasping voice from the top of the stairs.

'Stop thief! Remember you are in a priest's house!'

As they turned to face Julia May, she recoiled in a dramatic gesture of shock and horror. Making a hurried sign of the cross, she clutched the banister rail for support. They heard her not so silent prayer.

'May the Divine Jesus and His Blessed Mother protect us all. If the poor Canon could only see the sort of carry on that's happening in his house, he'd turn in his grave!'

With that she fled upstairs. As Mick walked down the avenue, the clatter of the typewriter shattered the stillness. Jeremiah O'Sullivan, PP, had returned to his sermon. Before leaving, Mick had jokingly suggested it might deal with the virtue of temperance. It was only then he remembered that the promised drink had never materialised.

6

'That's a nice straight line you have there, Sergeant.'

Gus had been concentrating so hard on the job of marking the pitch that he hadn't noticed Father Jerry's arrival. The surprise made him flustered. He stammered, 'Oh hello, Father. Nice to meet you. I'll be with you in a moment – as soon as I get to the end of this line. If I stop now the whole thing will be banjaxed.'

Waiting for the Sergeant to finish, Father Jerry took stock of his surroundings. The pitch was a good one, level and grassy. Overlooking it and facing seawards was the new stand, its steel girders resplendent in dazzling orange paint. An undercoat more for rust protection than decoration, he hoped as it clashed badly with the dark purple of the brooding mountain that served as a backdrop. The concrete walls and corrugated iron roof remained in their pristine grey and galvanised silver.

So this was the structure whose christening threatened such discord. It hardly seemed worth it. After Mick Flannery had departed, Father Jerry had traced the troublesome Fintan in the reference books of his predecessor. A brisk walk was needed to clear the cobwebs from his mind after a second sleepless night. At 4 a.m. he had decided that high on his shopping list would be a new bed. The Canon's had a cavity which may have cocooned his enormous frame but caused its new occupier to thrash around nervously at the prospect of being smothered in its airless womb. Getting out of it required the agility of a mountain goat.

A small girl with red hair directed him to the pitch. She admitted to being called Deirdre but dissolved in giggles when pressed for further information of a personal nature, such as her age and surname. Julia May said that the Sergeant could be found there if he wasn't in the dilapidated guards' barracks that nestled between the supermarket and the office of the Department of Agriculture.

'Sorry I couldn't shake hands with you just then . . .'

The Sergeant carefully wiped his hand with a grimy handkerchief before extending it in greeting.

'Father O'Sullivan isn't it? I'm Gus Moriarty. I saw your car outside the parochial house but I didn't want to disturb you before

43

you got settled in properly. Now I'm embarrassed that you have to come looking for me. Nothing wrong, is there?'

'No, not at all. I just wanted to stroll around and see the sights. That's a fine pitch you have there. As for the stand, it's a credit to you. Julia May tells me you built it almost single-handedly.'

'Ah no, Father, that's not so. Pat Mullarkey did most of the fund-raising.'

Which was quite true. When Pat and himself approached Donnelly, the bank manager, for a loan, the bastard almost wet himself laughing.

'What in the name of God do you want with a stand? The club hasn't drawn a decent crowd in years. It's more spectators you want first. Then go and build your stand!'

While he hadn't come right out and said it, the implication was clear. To get a crowd you needed to win matches occasionally. This they had failed to do. Typical of the bloody man, of course. A true rugger bugger who could barely conceal his contempt for the Gaelic Athletic Association. That was two years ago. The tireless efforts of Mullarkey and himself to raise the money through raffles, bingo sessions, monthly draws, sponsored walks and anything else they could think of had finally paid off. With the matching grant Mick Flannery prised from the GAA they now had a fine stand built and paid for without turning to Mister bloody Donnelly for a brass farthing.

For Gus, the GAA had always been the focal point of his life. He made no apology for it even when its blatant nationalism attracted well-deserved criticism. He never defended its ban on members play-ing 'foreign' games like rugby and soccer. Instead he simply ignored it. Nor did its sectarian songs trouble him unduly. 'Faith of our fathers' sung at Croke Park was no more or less offensive than 'Bread of Heaven' at Cardiff Arms Park. To him, the GAA was the soul of Ireland and it was as natural for a bishop to throw in the ball to start an All-Ireland final as it was for a duck to take to water. It was no secret that Gus had got his chance to play in Croke Park at the insistence of his club-mate, Mick Flannery. During the trial, Mick had taken him under his wing by feeding him a succession of easy passes and half-murdering his opposite number. All to no avail. The best Gus could achieve was a place on the substitutes' bench. Even that, he suspected, was due to Mick's influence.

'I just helped out where I could,' he continued.

'That's not what I'm told, Sergeant. Look at you even now. Surely there must be some young fellow that you could get to mark out the pitch for you.'

'Oh there are for sure but I prefer to do it myself. If you spill this stuff, not alone does it look awful but whatever chemical is in it burns the grass yellow for months afterwards. I want everything looking its best for the big day.'

'Of course,' Father Jerry replied. 'Mick Flannery called on me yesterday. He mentioned that the opening would be part of the Festival. Around the middle of August, I think he said.'

'That's right. The Feast of the Assumption used to be a Pattern Day round here long ago. While we don't want to bring back the faction fights or the drunkenness, we would like to restore some of the excitement that surrounded the same weekend long ago.'

'Indeed. It sounds like a good idea as long as it brings the whole community together. It would be a pity, though, if it became a source of division.'

'How do you mean, Father?'

'Well, Mick was saying that there is some disagreement over what to call the stand. What do you think it should be called?'

'Oh the Flannery Stand, of course. No doubt about it . . .'

And why not? Didn't he owe more to Mick than any other man alive. Were it not for him putting a word into the right ear, Gus might have been stationed hundreds of miles away from his beloved Brulah. Instead he served a mere six years in barracks around the country before being transferred back here as sergeant. Even during his brief exile he had never lost touch with the place. He returned each summer for his annual leave – long after his parents died and the rest of the family had scattered around the globe. The gaunt face of the priest swam back into focus, jerking him out of his reverie.

'. . . except, of course that Pat Mullarkey won't hear of it.'

'So where does that leave us? I say "us" because Mick tells me that I am to be the chairman of Saint Fintan's. Normally I would view the job as an honour but the more I hear about this stand business the less sanguine I become. Do you think there is any way you could resolve the question before the next meeting, whenever that might be?'

'Perhaps you should have a word with Pat. He's reasonable enough most of the time but he's got the bit between his teeth over the stand. I suppose if he threatens to kick up too much of a row you could always call it after Saint Fintan.'

This nut was not to be cracked easily. Perhaps not at all. The

Sergeant, for all his deference, appeared to have his own way of doing things. It was obvious that he had not the slightest intention of tackling Mullarkey on such a delicate issue. That he would leave to the fabled diplomacy of the Reverend Chairman of St Fintan's GAA club, Father Jeremiah O'Sullivan. Castelli could hardly have managed it better. He explored another avenue.

'Or call it nothing at all.'

'The stand with no name? Not such a bad idea, Father, even if it would be a bit of a setback for Mick. By the way, did Mick say who is to perform the opening ceremony?'

'As I recall, he said he expected to be doing it himself. In fact he asked me if I would like to say a few words from the platform.'

'I see. Well I suppose Mick is the obvious choice for that, too. Still it will get up Mullarkey's nose if it looks like Mick is trying to take over the show at the last minute. You see, apart from getting the grant out of the GAA, he hasn't done a damn thing compared to Mullarkey. It puts me in a difficult spot, I can tell you. No one thinks more of Mick than myself but having worked with Mullarkey I've developed a respect for the man. Sure he's hard to get on with but he gets results. If he were to get offended and resign from the club, we might as well close it down.'

So you want me to play God too. I think you are being too devious by half, dear guardian of the law. Do you really expect me to sail into the meeting, say a few well-chosen words that will oil the troubled waters, decide on a name for your stupid stand, choose the speaker to perform the opening ceremony, impart my blessing to one and all and then slip away quietly into the night? Let's confine the miracles to the grotto at the other end of the village, if you don't mind, Sergeant. That way we can keep the state whose laws you enforce separate from those of our Holy Mother, the Church. It might even give me the opportunity to preach the gospel and save a few sinners, myself included, rather than act as unpaid ombudsman to a lot of squabbling idiots.

'Well, we don't want that to happen, do we? I'll be visiting the Doctor shortly. He may have something to say on the subject. I'll try to see Pat Mullarkey too before the meeting. Maybe we can work something out in advance. Do you happen to know when the meeting is?'

'To tell the truth, Father. I don't. There's no fixed time for it but there's one due about now. We were waiting for you to arrive before we held it.'

Wasn't that very civil of you all?

'I see. Well let's not be in any great hurry to hold it until we get closer to agreeing on a name. Now there's something else I must ask you.'

The Sergeant eyed him warily. 'What would that be, Father?'

'This grotto business, Sergeant. I have heard Julia May's version so I know what she thinks she saw. What I want to find out from you is the type of person Mrs Flannery is. I mean, is she excitable and likely to imagine things?'

'I wouldn't think so, Father. In the normal way, she is a calm, sensible sort of woman who divides her time between the shop and her family. I would have thought her the last person to get involved in that sort of thing.'

Father Jerry continued. 'Is it causing you any trouble, I mean from a policing point of view?'

The Sergeant pondered the question for a moment before replying.

'Not yet, but it could any day now. The traffic is beginning to build up around the grotto for sure. It's only a matter of time before there's a major traffic jam. Did you have a look at it yourself, Father?'

'Only on my way into the village the day I arrived. If I went there now it would look like I was giving the whole thing my blessing.'

'So it would, to be sure. Still there's nothing stopping you taking a quiet look when they're all hard at it about nine o'clock. Hardly anyone knows you round here yet. It might be harder for you to see what's going on next week when they've all had a good look at you at the altar. I suppose you have to report to your boss like myself?'

'I'm afraid I don't quite follow you, Sergeant.'

'I mean, my Superintendent was on to me about it. Wanted to know if there was anyone breaking the law or anything like that. I told him that unless you count Julia May giving out the rosary as disturbing the peace, he had nothing to be worried about. Anyway I told him that yourself was coming and that you'd have the whole thing sorted out in no time.'

'Thank you, Sergeant. Your confidence in me is touching, if a trifle misplaced. My Bishop, as you guessed, would be more than happy to see an end to such carry-on. Like yourself, he is leaving precisely how that should be achieved entirely up to me. I think I'll take your advice and take a look for myself. Is it true that Mrs Flannery is turning her front field into a car park?'

It was more a statement than a question. Gus decided that for a man who had been in the village barely two days, Father Jerry seemed to have heard a lot.

'Pat Mullarkey won't like that, with him being on the Planning

Committee and all. He's already hassling Mick over a bit of a shed at the back of the shop. He claims it spoils the view from the pier. Mick says he had to put it up because the insurance people insist he keeps the gas cylinders outside. Now the car park will cause more bad blood between the two of them. You're supposed to have planning permission before you break a new entrance on to a main road.'

'I gather that there is a political element to some of it?'

'Of course. The dogs in the street know that Mullarkey is after Mick's seat. He might get it too if Mick isn't careful.'

'Is that a fact?' Father Jerry asked.

Oh dear God, I'm even beginning to talk like them already. In another world, nuggets of information such as he was seeking could be mined more easily. Here it involved prolonged haggling more suited to Arabian *souks*. To ask the whereabouts of the post office would be met by another query such as 'Is it a stamp you're looking for?' The intricacies of diplomacy were child's play by comparison.

'I thought Mr Flannery had it all sewn up,' he went on. 'The votes, I mean. Is it that he doesn't meet the people often enough?'

'Could be. He runs a clinic in O'Shea's pub now and again but that's about as far as it goes. The people that go there will vote for him anyway. Most of the time they talk hurling and greyhounds. If they're trying to get something done, they'll turn to Mullarkey. He's only on the County Council but he's a real live wire. It's getting to the stage that if you want a favour nowadays, you go to him rather than Mick.'

'I see. Well that's not going to make our task any easier. Where naming the stand is concerned, I mean.'

'*Our* task, Father? I don't quite follow what you mean. Thanks be to God it won't be my vote that will decide the issue. I will have voted for Mick long before it gets around to the chairman's casting vote.'

This innocent-looking man was not going to become embroiled in the controversy if he could help it. His veneer of respect for Holy Orders was wafer thin. The priest suspected that deep within this soft-spoken giant lay a dormant dread of the power of the Church. To prod it back to wakefulness by seeking his support over the stand would be foolhardy. He might never come right out and say so but Father Jerry sensed that the Sergeant believed in the strict separation of Church and State. The message was to leave the laws of the land to the likes of Gus Moriarty, Sergeant of the Garda Siochana. He, in return, would not interfere with the priest's enforcing the command-

48

ments of the Church. As a concept, it seemed reasonable. Unfortunately it did not work that way in this forlorn lump of rock, the most westerly outpost of Europe. The two forces were inextricably entwined.

'I take your point Sergeant. By the way, Mick invited me to make a fourth in your game of golf. Is that all right with you?'

'Of course it is, Father. Just remember to bring money!'

As a jest, it was only moderately successful. A gushing invitation it most definitely was not. It ranked even lower than Mick's one to join him on the platform. Nevertheless the priest acknowledged it with a thin smile.

'I will, Sergeant, I will. Well I had better let you finish marking the pitch. Goodbye for the moment.'

With that he turned on his heel and left. The Sergeant stroked his chin thoughtfully as he watched the thin figure in black striding briskly down to the village. Then he lifted up the marker carefully and set it up for the difficult run along the touchline.

After a dinner that would have left Castelli's ancestors begging for mercy, Julia May cleared away the plates and announced that she was going out for a few hours. Father Jerry went into his den and looked at his notes for the opening sermon to his new parishioners. Whatever muse it was that inspired preachers, it had evidently followed his housekeeper's example in taking the night off. He pushed the typewriter away from him and pondered whether to unwrap the portrait. He decided that he wasn't in the humour to look at that almost unrecognisably youthful face, so full of hope and confidence that it could put the world to rights in next to no time.

Now, he reflected, almost a generation later, nothing much had changed. His Church was still in conflict, threatened by schism from within and by torture and scepticism from without. His own faith had not been strengthened in the meantime. The sudden changes in direction wrought by the Vatican Councils had troubled the older clerics without revitalising the younger. He was trapped in a vacuum somewhere between the two. On the one hand he regretted the passing of the Latin Mass with its resonant phrases. They were the same all over the globe, differing only in accent or pronunciation. Now each country used its own dialects and the Church had lost its common voice yet he appreciated the fact that it had probably become more meaningful to its people. Or those that still attended its services. He stretched himself lazily and glanced at his watch. Time to slip upstairs and don a sweater and slacks. He slipped out of the parochial

49

house in the gathering dusk. It was barely five minutes' brisk walk to the grotto.

As he drew near the crossroads he noticed cars abandoned, rather than parked, along the side of the road. Near the grotto, it would have been impossible for any vehicle to pass through the throng kneeling on the tarmac road or the knots of curious people standing around the crossroads, undecided whether to join in the prayers or just gape. The air was heavy with barely suppressed excitement. Though he couldn't see her from the back of the crowd, he could hear the unmistakable voice of Julia May and another woman giving out the rosary in a loud voice.

He felt safe in the gathering darkness. The loose sweater and faded slacks should be enough to preserve his anonymity from the few that had met him since his arrival. The late Pope John strolled around Rome in similar garb until his security advisers objected. The Pole tried to do the same. Castelli claimed that he slipped out of the Vatican dressed as a beggar. He chuckled that if Archbishop Marcinkus, persisted in his fiscal policies, the Pole's disguise would soon become his everyday garb.

From the back of the crowd the drone of the rosary being mumbled by upwards of four hundred people rose and fell like an angry swarm of bees. '*Hail Mary, full of grace. The Lord is with thee . . . Holy Mary, Mother of God, pray for us now and at the hour of our death, Amen . . . Hail Mary, full of grace . . .* '. The mantra went on and on. The women knelt on the hard road, a handkerchief or scarf protecting their knees from the tar. The men dropped on one knee to the ground, one elbow resting on the other. One hand supported their bowed head, the other fingered their rosary beds. The priest was both impressed and appalled by such spontaneous devotion.

The grotto curved like a half-moon. It was about twelve feet at its highest post, directly below which was an alcove of pale blue. Inside this, standing on a plinth, was the object of their devotion. It was a plaster statue of Mary, the Mother of God. She was gazing Heavenwards, in the same pose as the woodcut hanging in the parlour. A red rose had been placed in her clasped hands, and bouquets of wild flowers strewn at her feet. Suspended a few inches above her head was a circle of neon, which emitted such a dazzling light that Father Jerry's eyes blinked defensively. This gave a sense of movement to the whole scene. The outline of the grotto against the night sky became blurred at first, then wavy. Turning his gaze to the statue, he could quite easily have persuaded himself that it moved.

Set well back from the road, the grotto was guarded by a low wall, on top of which was set an iron railing. A gate of wrought iron with a matching design opened on to a short path which led to the base of the statue. Worked cleverly into the ironwork design of the gate were the words AVE MARIA. On either side of the path was a tiny lawn on which two plaster figures knelt in prayer. The boy was dressed in shepherd's clothing, the girl in white veil and blue dress identical to what Julia May was wearing when she left the house earlier that evening. It was the uniform of the Legion of Mary.

His eyes were dragged back to the statue as though by a magnet. Raised to the elevated statue, they also took in the backdrop of a blazing sunset with fast-moving clouds overhead, further increasing the illusion of movement. Then, of course, staring at the halo for any length of time caused the pupils to dilate. The effect was similar to gazing at a naked bulb in a dark room. It required just one small step further to persuade oneself that the eyes wept or the lips moved. With the drowsy hum of the rosary fuelling the barely suppressed hysteria, anything was possible.

Satisfied with his night's work, he walked back to the house. He paused outside a bar with a garish plastic sign that proclaimed it to be 'O'Shea's Motel and Singing Lounge'. The script was entwined with shamrocks of a green hue he had not seen before. With his housekeeper safely occupied at the grotto for some time to come, and while he was still unknown to his parishioners, it seemed an ideal time to investigate what Brulah had to offer in the way of entertainment. He opened the door and went inside.

7

Father Jerry's first sight of the inside of O'Shea's made him want to turn on his heel and make good his escape. The appalling plastic sign should have warned him of what to expect. O'Shea evidently viewed life through a green haze of which the décor was but one example. The clash of so many emerald hues pushed the boundaries of bad taste well beyond acceptable limits. The carpet was green with an intricate shamrock pattern woven into it. The wallpaper sported a similar motif, though the shade was a touch more bilious. The wrought-iron work that framed the bar counter incorporated metallic green shamrocks of varying sizes into its delicate filigree. It may well have been the same hand that wrought the AVE MARIA into the gates of the grotto.

The pictures on the walls were the usual collection of long-dead patriots. Only two from the present generation were represented. Predictably they were John Fitzgerald Kennedy and the priest's late employer, Pope John. It was not a flattering portrayal of the portly figure. He was imparting the two-fingered papal blessing in a manner that was open to serious misinterpretation. In contrast, Kennedy looked positively saintly. As he eyed the lone figure engrossed in a newspaper at the far end of the counter, Father Jerry reflected that of all the leaders of failed rebellions who adorned O'Shea's wall, only the late Pope had met a peaceful death. He gave an involuntary shudder as he remembered the Kennedy entourage engulfing the Vatican. Marcinkus had had the time of his life agreeing security procedures with the presidential bodyguards. Even the cynical Castelli had been won over by the young couple despite JFK's formidable reputation as a womaniser. Or maybe because of it. One never knew the workings of Castelli's mind. Then came the appalling film clips of the killing. Would the keeper of Camelot have been amused at his position between a dead Pope and a collection of failed revolutionaries?

As he waited for someone to serve him, he recalled that even the last Irish uprising had flopped. Its final hours were featured in the huge reproduction behind the bar. It was an impressive scene, awash with blood and dying rebels firing from a blazing building. High above the flames and smoke flew the tricolour, the flag of the newly declared Republic. As a rebellion it won little support and its leaders were shot out of hand. It was this outrage rather than the uprising that sparked a countrywide rebellion. O'Shea would no doubt have described it as casting off the yoke of the British Empire by a blood sacrifice. Success through failure was a concept Father Jerry found strangely comforting. He saw a wiry man in his seventies appear behind the bar, polishing a glass and holding it up to the light as if hoping to find a pearl left there by a grateful customer.

The man at the far end of the counter was first to speak. He did so without lowering his newspaper.

'A nice slow pint, Tom, from the middle of the barrel. You can take the price of it out of the ninety-five pounds you owe me!'

The Cork accent had a singsong quality that the priest thought was part of an elaborate joke. It was, he discovered, quite genuine.

'I suppose you're talking about the ad in the *Clarion*?'

O'Shea's Boston twang cut through the air like a knife. He was small with steel-grey hair cropped short in a military crew cut. He wore a white Aran sweater over baggy tweed pants. The raised floor behind the counter made him look taller. References to his height – or lack of it – were to be avoided. He had a quick temper and did not hesitate to use his fists on men twice his size and half his age. Charley Halpin, well aware of this, chose his words with care.

'Indeed I am. Would you believe I'm tired from people stopping me on the street saying *"Wasn't that a grand advertisement for O'Shea's?"* They loved the shamrocks around the border. They made it jump right out of the page at you.'

That they certainly did. The editor asked him if he had gone barking mad. It took time to persuade him that it was what O'Shea wanted. Had he seen the sign over the door he would have been more easily convinced. To a man capable of such an assault on the senses, shamrocks around an advertisement were a mere trifle.

'It would have jumped all the better if you had put it where you promised you would.'

There was a sharp edge to O'Shea's tone. Selling advertising around a feature was tricky at the best of times. Everyone wanted to be at the top of the page. O'Shea's advertisement in the Easter Shopping feature, plugging the overwhelming welcome he would extend to his patrons over the Easter Weekend, was at the bottom.

'I only said I would *try* to get it put at the top. That's not quite the same thing as promising, now is it, Tom?' Charley answered.

O'Shea refused to be mollified. Ignoring the reply, he turned to the priest at the far end of the counter with a curt, 'Yes?'

'A glass of stout, please.'

Father Jerry was glad that O'Shea's unusual décor did not extend to bright lights. Where he was seated was in semi-darkness, for which he was immensely grateful. He was already regretting his sudden whim and had decided that the sooner he beat a hasty retreat the better. To do so without ordering a drink would have been to attract, rather than dispel, further attention. He was relieved that O'Shea had neither greeted him nor made any attempt at drawing him into the conversation.

'You reporters are all the same. Every damn one of you is trying to pull some kind of stroke. I had a guy on the phone about an hour ago. Wanted to know about the grotto. I told him it was nothing, just a couple of crazy old bats imagining things. Then I hung up on him.'

When Charley was startled his accent became more pronounced. This news item drove it to new heights.

'How did you know he was a reporter?'

'Because he told me, stupid! The guy gave his name as Colum something or other. Said he was from the *Journal*, or some rag like that.'

'Oh sweet Jesus! Would his name have been Jones . . . Colum Jones?'

'Yeah, that's the guy. Know him?'

'Do I *know* him . . . ?'

The fat little man's voice became shrill with excitement. 'Of course I bloody know him. He's their top man. Collects awards like a dog picks up fleas.'

His voice dropped to a lower pitch as he peered at his persecutor through half-closed eyes. He now sounded more suspicious than startled.

'Are you sure you're not making it all up just to get a rise out of me?'

'No siree, I'm not making it up. It's the gospel truth.'

It was obvious to the priest as he sipped the dark beer that O'Shea was enjoying himself immensely. His weatherbeaten face was creased in a smile. Torturing the reporter on the rack was his reward for burying the advertisement in the cemetery at the end of the page. He made no effort to disguise the mockery in his voice. Charley eyed his persecutor bleakly. The priest could read his thoughts. '*An orphan's curse on every Yank that ever returned to his native soil. They're all miserable bastards to a man. The whole damn lot of them should be shipped back to Boston and their daft societies like the Hostile Sons of Saint Malachy or the Ancient Order of Bogtrotters!'* Naturally Charley's prayer was a silent one. He tried cajolery as a last resort.

'Ah come on, Tom. Give over! This is important. It's as much as my job's worth to walk out of here without being sure about Jones. Give me a break, will you? Is it really true or are you just having me on?'

'Will you give me something off the ninety-five quid for sticking my ad so far down?'

'For Christ's sake, Tom, I can't. You know that yourself. I only work for the paper. The editor decides what goes where and how much it costs. I'm only the messenger boy!'

Had poor Charley realised it, no further concessions were necessary. Once he had purged his guilt by demeaning himself, O'Shea was satisfied. Unaware of this, the harassed reporter tried another approach.

'I'll tell you what I *can* do. I'll guarantee you the best position on the Festival edition, you have my word on it. What's more, I'll give you a free plug in the feature itself, something like . . .'

He paused, trying frantically to think of something positive to say about O'Shea and his dreadful bar. 'How about this: "When you are exhausted from the Festival celebrations, take the weight off your legs and visit O'Shea's Motel and Singing Lounge where you are always assured of good drink and a warm welcome!" How about that for a free plug?'

'It'll have to do, I suppose. Change "a warm welcome" to "Céad Míle Fáilte" and you've got yourself a deal.'

Mockery gave way to triumph. O'Shea was beaming like a lighthouse. He was one of those who loved to win . . . and showed it.

'Good, I'm glad you're satisfied. A hundred thousand welcomes it will be. Now if you could give me the cheque and tell me if the new parish priest has arrived yet, I could be on my way.'

'Oh he's here all right. No one has seen him yet except Mick and the Sergeant. He has a big black car with foreign plates parked outside the parochial house. That must have cost him a few quid. According to Julia May he's been ill and needs building up.'

'Well, she's the one to do it. The old Canon must have been well over twenty stone by the time he died. I interviewed her last week about what she saw at the grotto.'

'Well, did she say anything you could print?'

'Not much. You can read all about it tomorrow. I won't spoil it for you by telling you now. Can I use your phone? I have to talk to Mick.'

'OK, you know where it is. While you're phoning I'll get you that cheque.'

O'Shea threw a questioning look at the priest and his half-empty glass. 'Do you want another of those?'

Father Jerry shook his head. When O'Shea disappeared out the back, the reporter slid off his stool and made for the phone in the corner of the bar. Lifting the receiver he cranked the handle three times.

'Hello, Mary. Charley here. Put me on to Mick Flannery, if you please.'

Mick's deep voice came through almost immediately.

'Mick Flannery speaking.'

'Mick, Charley Halpin here. Can you fill me in about the stand?'

'How do you mean, Charley?' There was a distinct note of caution in his voice.

'Well, like when it is being named. Are they going to call it after you, for instance?'

'Jaysus Charley, have a heart! How do I know? And even if I did, you don't think I'm going to tell you, certainly not over the phone, now do you?' This was directed at Mary, if she were still listening.

'No, I suppose not . . .'

Charley noted, not for the first time, Mick's habit of finishing his replies with a question. He found it disconcerting. He decided it was time to change direction.

'There's a reporter from Dublin enquiring about the grotto. Did you hear anything about that?'

'Not a word, Charley. He wasn't in touch with me, if that's what you're asking.'

'What about Maggie?'

'What about her?'

'Was anyone looking for her?'

'Not as far as I know. Why should they be?'

'Well, there's the business of the grotto and all . . .'

'Listen Charley, get this into your skull. Maggie is not giving interviews to anyone about anything. Least of all the grotto business. Just remember that. Any interviews that are to be given by my family will be handled by me. Understand?'

'Sure, Mick, of course I do. One last question. Will you be here for the Festival?'

'Of course I'll be here for the bloody Festival. Whoever says I won't be is a liar!'

'Calm down Mick, for God's sake. No one is saying you won't be. There was a rumour that you were off to Blackpool for a conference of some sort around the same time, that's all.'

'Well I'm not and you can quote me on that. I'll be here for that weekend, giving out the prizes, making a few speeches and helping out in any way I can. Anyway it's not for bloody months yet so what's all the fuss about? As regards the stand, there's a meeting about it on Saturday night. Nobody, and I mean nobody including Mister bloody Pat Mullarkey, has a clue what it will be called until then. As for the grotto, I would be obliged if you kept Maggie's name out of whatever you write about it.'

'OK, Mick. I'll do the best I can. But if that Dublin shagger starts sniffing around you'll understand. I have an editor to keep happy too.'

'Sure I understand. Just remember that when he's gone back home, you'll still be here, trying to earn a living like the rest of us.'

The click indicated that Mick had hung up. The threat was unmistakable yet Charley was not unduly worried about it. Mick appreciated better than most that publicity was the oxygen by which politicians survived. The Festival would be an ideal platform for Mick, especially if they ever got around to calling the stand after him.

As Father Jerry walked back in the warm night air, the drone of the rosary from the grotto was just audible above the lapping of the waves against the pier. As he turned the key in the lock of the heavy front door and let himself in, he wondered what his housekeeper had told Charley Halpin. It would appear that far from fizzling out through lack of interest, as the Bishop had predicted, this drama was in for quite a long run.

8

'Julia May, come in here, will you? I want to read out something that may interest you.'

The priest's voice called from his den. Abandoning the dishes in the sink, Julia May dried her hands on her apron. Then dipping her finger in the holy water font hanging from the wall, she made an elaborate sign of the cross with her right hand. As she did so, she looked at her friend and mentor and begged, *Padre Pio, guide and protect me in my hour of need!* She whispered it so quietly that it emerged as a sibilant hiss.

From the moment the *Clarion* dropped through the letterbox, she had a premonition that this would be the day of reckoning. Though she would never dare to wrinkle its velvet-smooth pages by opening it before the old Canon had time to digest its contents, she had been sorely tempted to intercept it before her new charge got his hands on it. If it contained something she would prefer him not to see, she could have dumped it in the kitchen range without his ever being aware of its arrival. He might not have known of its existence and what he didn't know wouldn't trouble him. A hurried consultation with her conscience and a nervous glance at what she believed was a disapproving Padre Pio gazing down on her from his place of honour above the kitchen door decided the issue. She would not stoop so low. Instead she would place herself under the dual protection of Our Lady and the saintly, if not yet sainted, friar.

Despite her apprehension, she couldn't help registering disapproval at the scene that met her eyes. Books and papers scattered everywhere bore testimony to the fact that it was the only room in the house she was not allowed to tidy. Everywhere else she had a free hand to do as she pleased. The chaos reminded her that Father Jerry's den, as he had christened it, was sacrosanct. It was an oasis of disorder in a desert of polished floors and gleaming mahogany. It was aptly named, she reflected sourly. Its occupant became more fox-like by the hour. Their initial confrontation over the grotto had not been repeated. The long talk that he had promised to have with her very soon had yet to materialise. She wondered if it was going to happen now. Or could it be that he was going to read out something completely different? Maybe he wanted to discuss the unresolved matter of the pilgrimage to Lourdes. Could it be a new recipe that had taken his fancy in the cookery section of the *Clarion*? When Charley Halpin called last week to ask those stupid questions, she had raised that very topic with him.

'Charley,' she told him, 'the *Clarion* is a fine paper. No pictures of half-naked women plastered all over it, thanks be to God and His Blessed Mother. But let me tell you something. I don't like the cookery section. Too many of those fancy dishes with foreign names. Tell whoever writes it that they would be better employed giving us something useful like new ways to use up leftovers or a good recipe for a Christmas pudding.'

Charley promised to make her views known to the editor and resumed his probing on what Padre Pio had said to her about the message. As for the catering end of things, in the absence of instructions to the contrary she continued with the food she had dished up to the Canon. Her meals did not vary. They had two fixed points in the week – fish on Fridays and a Sunday joint of well-done roast beef. Mondays offered hairy bacon with a thick layer of fat dividing the salted meat from the crusted rind through which the pig's hairs bristled defiantly. Accompanied by mounds of potatoes and boiled cabbage, the food was camouflaged in a thick veil of white parsley sauce. It was preceded by an enormous bowl of soup and followed by any one of Julia May's three desserts. These were steamed bread pudding with custard, thick-crusted apple tart and whipped cream, and what she coyly described as roly-poly pudding. Chicken, Irish stew, boiled mutton and shepherd's pie completed her main course repertoire. Half-way through the programme, Father Jerry was already missing the feather-light salads and delicate veal *piccatas* from the Vatican kitchens.

He had to admit reluctantly that in the brief period under her care he had put on two pounds – if the scales in the bathroom were to be believed, that is. Now if only she could be persuaded that her visions were mere tricks of the light, the two of them might yet learn to survive together under the same roof. Midway through her first dinner he made a deal with his Maker. He would eat everything she put before him. He did so for several reasons: out of a sense of duty to his medical advisers, in reparation for the sins of his past life, to avoid arguing with Julia May. The irony of it did not escape him. Whereas the hermits of old fasted in the wilderness, he gorged himself to the verge of gluttony in a large, cold house that could have

59

comfortably provided shelter for at least three large families. Presumably both he and the hermits believed what they were doing to be the will of God.

In exchange for his compliance, he asked God for ten more years of useful life. Since confirmation of this arrangement was hard to come by, he would just have to assume that it had been agreed. At the very least, it would have the spin-off effect of making life with his housekeeper that much easier. Already her tours of inspection while he was eating were becoming less frequent. He supposed that she was checking that the wagonloads of food were going into him rather than his pockets.

'I wish to God you'd let me give this place one proper going-over. If anyone laid eyes on it, they'd say I was neglecting my duties,' Julia May said reprovingly.

He chose to ignore the remark. Instead he held up the *Clarion* between thumb and forefinger as though it were a fish that had gone off. Adjusting his glasses until they were perched almost on the top of his nose, he sighed deeply and began to read aloud in a disapproving voice.

'Brulagh Notes by Charley Halpin. The village is buzzing with excitement at the strange happenings at the grotto just outside the village. Some members of the Legion of Mary who keep vigil at the grotto during the month of May report that they have seen the statue move. Rumours, as yet unconfirmed, suggest that it was seen to weep. It is also claimed that a vision of Padre Pio appeared in the sky above the grotto during which he promised that a message from Our Lady will be sent via the statue at some future date. Readers will recall with great sadness the passing of our beloved and respected parish priest, the Very Reverend Canon Denis Sheahan two months ago. The *Clarion* is pleased to announce that the Very Rev. Jeremiah O'Sullivan, late of the Vatican Diplomatic Service, has been appointed in his place. He has taken up residence in the parochial house within the past few days. The *Clarion* and its many readers take this opportunity of extending to him a hearty welcome. We wish him a long and happy stay in the parish of Brulagh.'

He coughed to clear his throat and resumed in his normal voice, 'Well, Julia May, what do you think of that?'

'It was nice of him to welcome you, I suppose.'

'Quite so, most generous of him but that was not what I meant. I suspect that you know that as well as I do. What I wanted was to hear from you, in your own words, exactly what is going on.'

'How do you mean, Father?'

'I mean, Julia May, what was it you thought you saw at the grotto? I have refrained from questioning you further about it since you introduced the topic within moments of my arrival. I assure you that this was not because I was not deeply concerned about the matter. It was rather that I wanted to give you time to reflect. Indeed I prayed that you would have had second thoughts about the whole affair.'

As he spoke, he shot a quick glance in her direction to see how she was taking it. Her lips were pursed and her eyes were fixed at some point about two feet above his head. So far so good. At least she hadn't marched out of the study in high dudgeon, as he had feared. Definitely a case for 'softly, softly, catchee monkee!' he decided. Before she could respond, he pressed on.

'You must consider the possibility that your eyes may have deceived you. I went down there a few nights ago to have a look for myself. I stood at the back of the crowd and after a few minutes staring at the statue my eyes became so strained that I could quite easily have imagined that it moved. After I closed my eyes to rest them from the glare of the halo and opened them again, everything, including the statue, danced around for a moment or two before my eyes got used to the light in the dark once more. Did you find that yourself, by any chance?'

'What are you trying to tell me, Father? That I'm imagining things or what?'

'Nothing of the sort, Julia May, nothing of the sort. From what I've seen of you since I came here, I can't imagine anyone less likely to make up something like this. No, that was the very reason I went to have a look for myself. I said to myself, if an intelligent woman like my housekeeper has seen something out of the ordinary, then there must be some rational explanation for it. Tell me, had you been kneeling at the railings for long before you thought you saw something move?'

'We were saying the rosary, Father, Maggie and myself. Oh I suppose we were there over an hour when it happened.'

'But that's it then, Julia May . . .'

He tried to seem reassuring rather than triumphant. 'If I thought I saw something move after only a few minutes, God alone knows what you two must have seen after an hour and a half. Wouldn't you agree with me?'

She nodded her head doubtfully and said nothing.

61

'You see, I have to find out for His Lordship the Bishop exactly what happened. He's very worried that this thing may balloon out of all proportion. You know yourself how the Bishops don't like anything out of the ordinary going on in their dioceses.'

He shot another covert look at her to gauge her reaction to the lies he was so blithely concocting. The Bishop had made it abundantly clear that he didn't care what happened about either the statue or the stand as long as he was kept out of it.

'If you really believe that you saw the statue of Our Lady move and weep, then you would have to go and tell him all about it yourself. It wouldn't be enough for you to tell me and for me to pass it on to him. That way there would be a danger of some vital element of the story getting left out. His Lordship did, however, suggest that I have a good talk with you, like we're having now. Mind you, that was before the *Clarion* got hold of your story. Still the good thing about this otherwise dreadful situation is that neither you nor Mrs Flannery are actually mentioned by name, although I'm sure everyone knows by now that it's the two of you who are involved. It's only a matter of time before they print that you are my housekeeper and then you can imagine what the headlines will be. I believe the Dublin papers have already got wind of it. After that, the radio and TV crews will be looking to interview you. What will you say to them?'

'I hadn't thought of that, Father.'

She sounded taken aback but not in the least contrite. If they wanted to talk to her, well and good! She would have a thing or two to tell them about their filthy TV programmes that were turning young and old alike into sex maniacs. And the radio wasn't much better, with its non-stop talk of sex and contraception. Her thoughts were interrupted by Father Jerry's soft, persuasive tones. She was relieved that he had been so nice about it up to now. It would be a pity if they were to finish up shouting at one another.

'Well, maybe it's time you started thinking about it. I doubt if His Lordship would let me keep you on as housekeeper if you were to persist with your story of moving statues, you know . . .'

He waited a moment for the veiled threat to sink in. Then he continued, 'Now why don't you begin by telling me exactly what happened.'

'It's hard to know where to begin, Father.'

'Then tell me when you first thought you saw something.'

She started off uncertainly, her voice becoming more confident as she got into her stride. She insisted that the statue not only moved but wept. Maggie Flannery would confirm this if he had any doubts about it. The hesitancy returned when she described Padre Pio and the promised message.

'The fifteenth of August, you say?'

'That's right, Father. The Feast of the Assumption of our Blessed Lady into Heaven.'

'I am as aware as you are of the significance of the date, I assure you. And you say that Padre Pio gave you the news of this impending message? Why not the statue?'

This time he made his voice harder and less sympathetic. It was the old ploy of the interrogator. Start off gently, then suddenly switch. The mood change often threw the victim into confusion.

'I don't know, Father.'

'You realise that a lot of people are going to say that you are imagining all this, don't you?'

'I suppose so. But they said the same thing about Lourdes and Fatima.'

'Quite so. But this is totally different. What we are talking about here is a weeping, moving statue at a shrine already dedicated to Our Lady, not an apparition on some lonely hillside. And you and Mrs Flannery aren't exactly innocent peasant children either!'

'Indeed we're not . . .'

He had at last pierced her defences. Her voice seethed with indignation.

'We're nothing of the sort! But we're not complete eejits either like some are making us out to be. We know what we saw. The statue of Our Lady moved first, then the tears flowed down her cheeks. A moment later I looked up in the sky and there was himself smiling down on the two of us. He gave us his blessing and said that Our Lady would have an important message for the world on her Feast day.'

'What exactly did he say?'

Whatever her answer was to be was lost in the jangling of the phone on his desk. Impatiently he picked up the receiver.

'Father O'Sullivan? This is the Sergeant here. I've just had a call from Pat Mullarkey. There's an emergency up the mountain. Pat couldn't say much but apparently someone's tried to hang himself. I know where the place is but I haven't got a car at the moment. Could I get a lift from you? You'll probably have to anoint the misfortune anyway.'

'Right, Sergeant. I'll pick you up outside the barracks in two minutes.'

He rummaged in a drawer for the box that held the holy oils. As he made for the door he called over his shoulder, 'An emergency, Julia. We must continue this talk we were having very soon. Think hard about what I said in the meantime. I'll be back as soon as I can. If there's anyone else looking for me, tell them I'm out on a sick call.'

No need to tell them it's the first of my life, he added to himself. Seconds later the throaty roar of the twin exhausts signalled his departure in a spray of gravel.

9

A child's bright red wheelbarrow was abandoned outside the door of the farmhouse. Across the yard a rusty tractor of uncertain age ticked over noisily. The whitewashed buildings surrounded a clamp of silage neatly wrapped in black polythene and weighted down against the mountain winds by old car tyres. In the neat paddocks cows, a few calves and an evil-looking bull grazed contentedly. Inside the house, the mother sat at the kitchen table surrounded by her five children. The eldest, a girl, looked barely eight years old. She was standing behind her mother, her arms encircling her heaving shoulders. The woman was rocking to and fro on the kitchen chair, her fists knuckling her eyes as though trying to gouge them from her head.

The child was pleading with her mother.

'Mummy, please stop crying, will you? Everything is going to be all right.'

This was repeated in a dull monotone, over and over again. Father Jerry tried to think what it reminded him of, then he remembered. It was the same singsong voice Julia May used to give out the rosary at the grotto. The mother did not respond. She just continued to rock in silent grief, not wanting to remove the fists from her eyes and face up to the disaster that had just befallen her. He was appalled by his own helplessness. Was there nothing he could do or say to ease this tortured creature's burden of sorrow? What could he dredge up from his store of honeyed words and silver-tongued diplomacy that would suit the occasion? Nothing, absolutely nothing. His cupboard was bare. The apprenticeship he had served in the Vatican, scurrying from embassy to legation and back again, finally to report all to Castelli, was no preparation for this. Hollow words of consolation would have ricocheted around the walls of the kitchen, re-echoing ghoulishly their complete inadequacy to meet the situation. One of the younger children piped up, 'Are you the new priest, the one they told us about in school?'

'I am child, I am.'

'What do they call you?'

His sisters were mortified by such impertinence. They nudged each other and glared wide-eyed at their brother as if he had committed a much graver offence than their poor father.

'Jerry, Father Jerry. What's your name?'

'Andrew, Father. That's a great car you have. Will it go fast?'

Though a welcome relief in one respect, it hardly seemed a suitable topic for discussion in the circumstances.

'It will. It's not locked. Would you like to go out and have proper look at it?'

The child looked at his mother enquiringly. Oblivious to what was going on around her, she was lost in a cocoon of misery and grief. Taking her silence for assent, the boy rushed outside with a whoop of excitement to examine the sleek Alfa. The Sergeant whispered quietly, 'Perhaps now would be a good time to say the rosary?'

He left the suggestion hanging in the air for a moment before he continued, 'That would give me the chance to slip out quietly and look after things outside.'

Father Jerry nodded numbly. 'Things outside', as Gus had so delicately put it, were the body of a man in his thirties hanging from a steel girder by a length of blue nylon cord. He had noticed that it was the same as that used to bind the rectangular bales of straw that were so neatly stacked in the barn. When he and Gus arrived, Pat Mullarkey was already going through the poor wretch's pockets. Father Jerry whispered an act of contrition into the dead man's ear. *Oh my God, I am heartily sorry for having offended thee and I detest my sins above every other evil. . . .* Then, with an overpowering sense of futility, he administered the Last Rites. These were designed to comfort the dying and send the soul on its way to the final judgement. They seemed inappropriate, to say the least, in this instance. Nevertheless, it was what was expected of him and so it had to be done.

The body would have to remain as it was until Doctor James Buckley arrived. He was out on his rounds and Mary, Pat Mullarkey's wife, was trying to contact him at one of the few houses that had a phone. The Doc had to sign the death certificate. As he was also the coroner, Gus had said it would be better to leave 'things' as they were until he arrived. It would save a lot of embarrassment for the family at the inquest if the gruesome details did not have to be read out in evidence. This would be unnecessary if the coroner had seen for himself what had happened.

'The first sorrowful mystery, the Agony in the Garden. Our Father who art in heaven, hallowed be thy name . . .'

Half-way through the rosary the woman started to mutter the

responses, at first incoherently, then in an increasingly strong voice. It was as if she were coming back to life. To the priest, this was a greater miracle than all the moving, weeping statues in the universe. If only the soothing mantra had the power to bring back her husband, he thought as he started to put away his beads.

'Hail Holy Queen, Mother of Mercy, Hail our Life, our Sweetness and our Hope . . .'

The sound of a car driving into the yard shattered the protective shell that he had built around his prayer group. Unwelcome reality in the person of Doctor James Buckley walked into the kitchen.

'Nora, sorry to hear about Paddy. . . . Oh hallo Father, not interrupting anything important, am I?'

'Well, we were just finishing the rosary and . . .'

'That's fine so. Nora – the district nurse is on her way with groceries from Maggie Flannery. Father O'Sullivan here will make the arrangements for the funeral, the Mass and that sort of thing. Don't worry about the inquest, the Sergeant and myself will look after that end of things. I had a word with the bank before I came and they'll see that you're all right for money so that's another worry off your shoulders. Johnny Slattery has promised to do the milking for you and keep an eye on the cattle until you get better organised.'

This breezy man in the rumpled tweed suit was behaving as though it were the most normal thing in the world to find the head of the family dangling, bug-eyed and purple, from the end of a cord. Yet the formula was working. The mother dried her eyes and was nodding gratefully as the Doctor reeled off the list of things that need not worry her. To hear him tell it, she had never had it so good. As a performance in attitude adjusting, it was a *tour de force*. It also confirmed Mick Flannery's assurance that the Doctor was 'a decent skin if ever there was one'. A supreme diplomat too, it would seem, if this performance was anything to go by.

'Now Nora, I want you to do something for me. I want you to take three of these tablets right away, then one every four hours after that. Imelda, won't you see to it that your mother does as I say. You can be the doctor when I'm not here.'

The eldest, who until then had been trying vainly to console her mother, now swelled with pride. This was something concrete that she could do to help. It also clearly marked her out as the most important helper among her brothers and sisters. She smirked at them now in a superior fashion as she lisped, 'Of courth I will, Doctor Buckley. You can rely on me.'

'I knew I could, Imelda. Now children, the rest of you are to help your mother in every way you can. Don't worry about the farm or the animals, they will be looked after by Johnny. You can have the rest of the week off school, can't they, Father?'

'Of course, Doctor.'

He was grateful that his role in this damage limitation exercise was so minor. Nothing so far in his life had prepared him for this. The Doctor was still in full spate.

'Now when the nurse arrives in the ambulance I want you all to stay in the kitchen. She'll have sweets from Flannery's and something stronger for your mother, I hope. Then she, and the driver and Sergeant Moriarty will take Daddy away so that he can get ready for his long journey to Heaven, aren't I right, Father?'

This time the priest was so moved that he could barely trust himself to nod in agreement. However slender his belief in a merciful God, he had to admire the Doc's selling of the concept on this occasion. The children looked solemn, in complete agreement that this was the proper way to deal with their father who had behaved so strangely. James Buckley was now doing the priest's job as well as his own. He was doing it far better than Father Jerry could have managed even in his wildest dreams. The children were wide-eyed in anticipation of the sweets. They would remember this dreadful day as much for them as for the tragedy that provided the unexpected treat. Nora had swallowed the tablets and was already sitting up straighter in the chair.

'That's settled then. Father O'Sullivan must go back to the village now. The rest of us will wait here for the ambulance. It should be along any minute now.'

Taking his cue, he gave the family his blessing, nodded his gratitude to the Doctor and left.

10

Father Jerry parked the car on the empty pier and strolled along the seashore for an hour or so before facing Julia May. With screaming gulls wheeling overhead and the surf sighing as it broke in small, rolling ripples on the beach, he tried to regain his composure by taking stock of his situation. His retirement from the hurly-burly of the Vatican to this sleepy backwater was turning out nothing like he expected. The trauma of the widow and her children was only worsened for him by his own utter helplessness. Apart from saying the rosary in the kitchen and administering the last rites to a corpse, his contribution had been minimal. Where was the shrewd manipulator of old? Where was the supreme diplomat capable of defusing the most explosive situations Mother Church got herself into with the civil power in any of a dozen strife-torn countries? *You are going to have to shape up, Jerry my boy. You must not let Marti's diagnosis be an excuse for opting out.*

Like it or not there are several problems requiring your immediate attention. Your housekeeper first, then Maggie Flannery, must be persuaded that all this nonsense about moving statues is merely a trick of the light. That surely won't tax your powers of persuasion overmuch! Then there is the question of what to call the blasted stand. Look on it as a chance to perform your celebrated tight-rope act and do not be unbalanced by that likeable rogue, Flannery. From what you saw of his rival, Mullarkey, he seems an efficient if somewhat officious individual. Perhaps the circumstances in which you met were less than ideal for forming a balanced judgement of the man. As chairman of the GAA, you must steer a middle course and leave the two of them to fight it out between themselves.

Then, of course, there is the little matter of asserting yourself in your own house. Though you are reluctant to admit it, you are afraid of Julia May. Should diplomacy fail, you are going to have to confront her. You could start by hanging the three pictures you brought with you, even if they will have to displace some of the old Canon's more dreadful woodcuts. And don't forget the four cases of whisky in the boot of the car. You can hardly ask her to lift them in yet they are too heavy for you to carry. Last but not least, you have yet to compose a sermon for your flock.

By the time he got back from his walk, Julia May knew all the grim details of the tragedy. 'The poor craythur!' was her sole comment before relaying the message that Doctor Buckley wished to see him when convenient.

He was now complying with this wish. The lion was familiar. Cast in bronze, it served as Doctor James Buckley's door-knocker, and Father Jerry tried to remember where they had met before. The elderly computer of his mind sorted and crunched its way through the probabilities. With gratifying speed it spewed out the answer. Yes of course. It was a Florentine lion. He had stumbled across the original, carved in marble in the fourteenth century, while searching for his car parked in a crowded piazza. He remembered the look of utter disgust on the *carabiniere*'s face when he realised that a priest was driving such a *bella macchina*. Since the days of the Medicis, Florentines didn't have much time for the clergy. Now the same lion's head, miraculously transported to Brulagh, was glaring balefully at him. Such memorabilia had been all the rage with souvenir sellers for as long as he could remember. He banged it twice and gave the doorbell with 'Surgery' taped beneath it a push for good measure.

Under his arm was the large manila envelope containing his medical report from Professor Marti. Might as well kill two birds with the one stone, he thought, before deciding that the phrase was inappropriate for the occasion. As the envelope was unsealed he had looked inside. It held his medical file and a brief letter setting out the recommended procedures. Both were in English, their flawless translation providing further proof that his departure from the Vatican was no sudden whim of Castelli's. The information in them was sparse and revealed nothing new. As a death warrant, it was unimpressive.

'That was quick. I didn't mean you to rush.'

The lanky figure ushered him into a small room off the hall. Its door bore the legend su GERY in stick-on letters that curled up at the edges. The R looked as if it had been missing for some time.

'Didn't get a chance to introduce myself properly this morning. You might as well call me Doc, everyone else does. Terrible business, wasn't it?'

His handshake was dry and firm. The priest introduced himself.

'I'm called Jerry O'Sullivan. In Italy I was "Jerry" but anyone I've met here so far calls me "Father". Jerry would be much easier. Yes, indeed it was a bad business. About the worst I've seen, in fact.'

'Oh really? Happens quite a lot round here, I'm afraid . . .'

As he spoke, the Doctor looked at the frail priest and thought to himself:

70

Will I tell him the truth? Which is that farmers have been doing themselves in since Adam was a boy? It's the isolation that gets to them in the end. If someone in the village has a row with the wife or gets a stiff letter from Donnelly about his bank account he can drop into O'Shea's. There he will have a drink and a chat and forget about it, for the time being at least. On the side of that bloody mountain there's nowhere to go and no one to turn to. You're not going to talk to the animals unless you are already half mad. Long before this, farmers were hanging themselves, walking off cliffs, drinking weedkiller or blowing their heads off with shotguns on a regular basis. The only difference nowadays is that everyone hears about it. Of course no coroner would ever dream of bringing in a verdict of suicide. And rightly so. This is a Catholic country! Suicide is both illegal and a mortal sin on this island where Christians bomb, maim and execute each other every hour of the day. No one, not even a hill farmer, could bear the stigma of having a relation in hell. That's why we have the lowest suicide rate in the world. No, I won't tell you. You can work it out for yourself!

'. . . still,' the Doctor continued, 'it's always worse when a young family is involved. The reason I wanted to see you is that Gus and I agreed that an inquest would cause too much trouble for the family. We decided that it was an accident. As a witness we need you to sign a statement to that effect. Gus typed it out before lunch. Just sign it and I'll post it off with the rest of the paperwork. That way there will be no need to hold an inquest, not even in camera. Saves a lot of bother in the long run.'

Taking the proffered biro Father Jerry held it poised in mid-air over the typewritten sheet and enquired, 'What exactly am I signing?'

'I thought you might ask that. Well, actually it says that it was "death by misadventure". He fell off the bales and cracked his skull on the concrete floor. Actually it happens quite often with those bloody bales of straw. Rarely results in death, though, I'm glad to say. Better to die of an unstable bale than an unstable mind, I always say. Wouldn't you agree?'

'Better for whom, may I ask?'

He was reluctant to sign such a blatant lie, especially on such flimsy acquaintance with his accomplices. Then the truth hit him like a thunderbolt. That was precisely what he had been doing all his life. Except, of course, that in the diplomatic service the lies were called communiqués.

'Oh for everyone, I think. For his family in particular. There was an insurance policy. Nothing enormous but big enough to pay off the bank loan and tide them over for a few months. Suicide renders it

71

null and void. If you don't sign that bit of paper, I'll have to hold an inquest. That means a full report in the *Clarion*, the kids being jeered at in school and the widow afraid to raise her head in public with the shame of it. Of course I would have to instruct the jury to bring in a verdict of *felo de se*. That probably means the family will end up on the side of the road with the farm sold over their heads. Suit yourself but you'll have to decide one way or another immediately. That report must be sent off right away or else I'll have to convene an inquest.'

'What about the insurance company?'

'What about them?'

'Sounds dangerously like fraud to me.'

The Doc made no attempt to hide his impatience.

'Not to me, it doesn't. Any city I've ever been in has been desecrated by glass boxes, ten storeys high. Most of them house insurance companies or banks. They make their money by taking in more than they pay out. You can call it commerce or usury, whichever you prefer. That poor wretch was in hock to the bank for more than he was worth. Where there is bad borrowing there also has to be bad lending. He took the only way out he could think of. The fact of the matter is that he did his family a favour in the long run. Now they have a fresh start once they get over their grief. The insurance company is none the wiser, and pays up. Donnelly gets his money and the bank are happy. Are you going to bugger up the poor devil's heroics by refusing to put your name to a harmless piece of paper?'

Your conscience, Jerry, what happened to your conscience? You have been signing your name to bigger lies than this harmless canard in the name of God. Yes, literally in the name of God. Now it's your turn to play God and you have no sleek Castelli to turn to for advice. Odd that you should have had to come so far to meet yourself face to face. Still there it is, Jerry. This is 'make your mind up' time.

'I take your point. I just hope this sort of thing doesn't happen too often. I doubt if my Bishop would approve of his new recruit doing time behind bars.'

He signed the document with a flourish. The tension between them evaporated. The Doc's face split open in an infectious grin.

'Well, you'd be in good company there with the Sergeant and myself. Pat Mullarkey signed it too, I might add. As would Mick Flannery if he hadn't gone to Dublin at cockcrow this morning. I see you've brought something along with you. Is it for me?'

'Yes, my medical records. The specialist in Rome asked me to pass them on to you.'

Pushing them across a desk even less tidy than his own, he tried to reconcile this disorganised medic with the cheerful saviour of a devastated family. Try as he might, he could not get the pieces to fit. He abandoned the exercise in favour of asking, 'Anything there to be worried about, Doc?'

He kept his voice casual. He was curious to see how the Doc would handle yet another delicate situation. Telling new patients that they had a life-threatening disease could not be easy.

'Not much. As your Professor Marti may have told you already, your condition is incurable. The length of remission varies. You could live out your normal span and never be troubled by it again if we get the treatment right. Then again, it could strike quite unexpectedly. There is no set pattern. Your man recommends steroid treatment so I'll give you a prescription for those. Tricky things, steroids, though. The sooner you can get off them the better. They're great for weight-lifters and cattle but they can have weird side-effects on mere mortals like you and me. We'll just have to see how it goes. Do you have some to keep you going? Good, because I doubt if the chemist has any. He'll probably have to order them and that could take a week. As you can see, we are pretty isolated here.'

'Yes, so I've noticed. That road down the mountain is really something.'

The Doc chuckled without showing a trace of remorse for his reckless driving.

'Yes, we nearly ran into each other already, so to speak. That was a mean-looking machine you were driving. Mick Flannery tells me you drove it back from Rome. Nice city, that. I went there with the old Canon back in the fifties – during the Marian year. By the time we got back home, some lunatics had erected that monstrosity of a grotto. The poor man nearly had a fit. To his dying day he regarded it as a blot on the landscape but he didn't dare say a word. That would have seemed ungrateful and given offence to the more pious members of his flock. Anyway the thing was built. Nothing short of gelignite could remove it by then. Now there's a crazy mob running round it like headless chickens, waiting to see if the statue will move. What do you think of it all?'

Father Jerry warmed to this man. Doc Buckley said what he thought. There had been no beating about the bush when it came to his illness. Now he was echoing his own sentiments on the grotto. Nevertheless his instinct urged him to be cautious.

'Hard to say. The Bishop is less than enthusiastic, as you can imagine. He's all for religion, of course. The more of it the better in this day and age, he believes. I agree with him – up to a point. But I think he would prefer such piety to be a bit more structured. So would I. This spontaneous combustion makes us both nervous.'

'I wish to God the whole thing would go away this minute. My phone has been hopping off the wall since Maggie and your house-keeper started the ball rolling. Half the village think they have seen something moving. The other half are suffering from anxiety-related depression because they can't see anything! With the amount of tranquillisers I'm prescribing, the chemist must think Christmas has arrived early this year. I'll be taking them myself soon, if the pressure doesn't ease up. Normally the whole thing would fizzle out after a while but with this message nonsense it could drag on till the middle of August, if not longer. That's nearly three bloody months away, for Heaven's sake! Now, speaking of pressure, I was on my way to call on the Widow Slattery when you came in. She's Johnny's mother . . .'

'The lad that's looking after Nora's farm?'

'One and the same. Though lad hardly describes him. He must be sixty if he's a day. Anyway she has an infection and I didn't have the right antibiotic with me this morning so I have to go back again. You should see her too, by the way. She's not got long more. The problem is, you'll never find her place by yourself. Would you like to travel with me?'

'You mean now, this minute?'

'Yes, right away. If you come with me you won't wreck that grand car of yours on what passes for a road up to her place.'

Father Jerry barely hesitated. He had nothing urgent to do for the rest of the day. He had thought of looking up Pat Mullarkey with a view to doing some ice-breaking but that could wait. Far better to make a start on the parish visits right away. Particularly when he now had the services of a guide to the remoter regions.

'Yes, I'd like that. You don't think the widow will die of fright when she sees the priest and the doctor arriving at the same time?'

'Yerra not at all, she's well used to it by now. The Canon and myself used to share the driving quite a bit. Cuts down on petrol expenses and makes the journeys less boring.'

'Will I need to anoint her?'

'Wouldn't bother if I were you. Now *that* would frighten the life out of her. Despite what they are told off the pulpit, round here they still believe the Last Rites are just that. They haven't yet grasped what preventive medicine means, not to mind preventive religion!'

The Doc flung whatever flotsam had gathered on the front seat of the old blue Ford into the back and held the door open for his passenger. The engine fired at the fourth attempt. For the second time that day, the priest was heading towards the barren purple mountain that loomed menacingly over the village.

11

'Not too bad, Doctor. It catches me in the chest sometimes. The trouble is that I can't go outside to feed the hens any more. Johnny tries to look after them but his hands are full with watching the few sheep, not to mind having to keep an eye on that poor Nora's place after the accident this morning. Would yourself or the priest drink a cup of tea or maybe something stronger out of the bottle?'

'No thanks. You don't want a drop of the hard stuff, do you, Father? No, I thought not. As I didn't have time this morning when I came over for Johnny, I had better take a proper look at that chest of yours now. Could you open the top few buttons and I'll give a listen to what's going on inside.'

Father Jerry excused himself and went outside. He was glad he had heeded the advice about the Last Rites. He would come back another day to prepare her for the long journey to eternity. With any luck the wind might be blowing from a different direction. Then what served as kitchen, parlour and bedroom might not be so choked with the acrid turf smoke that belched from the open fire and made his eyes water. Outside he inhaled deeply to clear his lungs. He hadn't seen poverty like it since the *barrios* of Buenos Aires. The hovel had a thatched roof. It was visibly rotting, and sagged dangerously in the middle like the Canon's bed. The walls must have been two feet thick and made of mud and whitewashed plaster.

From where he stood high up on the mountainside he could see other white-walled dwellings dotted here and there, their roofs golden in the sun. He wondered if they too might not bear closer inspection. Well he would find out soon enough. He would have to visit them at least twice a year. If they housed the old or the sick, every month would be nearer the mark. The farm where this morning's tragedy unfolded must be nearby even though it was on a different road to the one they had roared up with a screaming engine and a fine disregard for the craters masquerading as potholes. It was beginning to dawn on him why the Doc did not drive something more in keeping with his profession. More to the point, he was having twinges of anxiety about how long his own sleek thoroughbred would survive roads that were more like dry riverbeds.

A figure approached, striding through the yellow gorse. At the same instant the door opened and the Doc signalled him to come back in. When he spied the new arrival he shouted, 'Johnny, meet our new parish priest, Father O'Sullivan. Father this is Mrs Slattery's son, Johnny. He's the biggest bootlegger in Brulagh . . .'

When his remark passed without retort, he continued, 'How are things over beyond?'

'Not that bad. She's coming round a bit. As I was leaving the kids were making her a cup of tea. There's a heifer due to calve any minute so I'll keep an eye on things for the time being.'

'Good man yourself. Come on, we'd better go back inside. I see you told your mother 'twas an accident.'

Johnny nodded as they stooped low to get back in through the doorway. Opening the door launched another belch of smoke. The ash from the fire danced in the sunlight streaming in through the tiny windows before it swirled up the chimney. The widow took a fit of coughng that ended in a throat-rattling wheeze. Johnny, too, cleared his throat noisily before enquiring, 'How do you think she is, Doctor?'

For all the concern in his voice, he might as well be asking after the well-being of one of those scrawny sheep eking out a meagre existence on the mountainside. It reminded Father Jerry of Sicily, where life was hard and death often a merciful release. He was still reeling inwardly from the discovery that Johnny was a bootlegger. On the rare occasions when he had given 'the business' any thought while he was in Rome, he had assumed that it had gone the way of other skills like basket-weaving and turf-cutting. When his uncle died, he had thought it to be not only the end of an era but also the final curtain for poteen-making. If Johnny were the biggest, did this imply that there others busily distilling moonshine around Brulagh? It would be ironic if he, the nephew of a man who was once the biggest and most notorious bootlegger in the country, had ended up in the midst of those he had sought so long to avoid. For a fleeting moment he considered the possibility that Castelli had planned the whole thing before common sense told him not to be so ridiculous. The Doc's voice scattered his fears.

'I was just telling your mother that she'll have to go to the hospital for a bit of a check-up. There's no great hurry about it but it would want to be done before the autumn. I'll keep an eye on her in the meantime. Now that Father Jerry knows the way, I'm sure he will drop in on her every now and then.'

Father Jerry bowed his head in agreement.

'Johnny, make it your business to see that she takes two of these tablets at night to ease that cough a bit.'

'I will, Doctor. 'Tis as well that she's going into hospital. There are times when she can hardly get her breath at all. Will she be gone long, I wonder?'

Still not a hint of emotion in the voice. He had a long, angular frame which appeared to be permanently bent somewhere around his navel, giving him a stooped appearance. A long, pointed nose ran continuously. He relieved this condition by sniffing a lot, sometimes wiping the problem way with the sleeve of his pullover.

'Probably not. Just a week or two to find out the cause of the trouble. The way things are right now I mightn't be able to get her in for ages. They're only taking emergency cases at the moment. They would regard your mother as a routine admission so she will have to go on a waiting list. It's a long one, I can tell you, but I'll see what I can do.'

Was this conversation going to last for ever, Father Jerry asked himself? He longed to escape from the kitchen to breathe again the mountain air perfumed with gorse and purple heather. Bootlegging, it would appear, was no longer a money-spinner if Johnny's surroundings were anything to go by. Or perhaps he was just a mediocre practitioner. Johnny seemed to be a great man for the questions.

'I suppose a trip to Lourdes wouldn't do her any good, Doctor?'

'It might. T'would be no harm to book a place on the pilgrimage with Mrs Flannery anyway. I'm sure Father Jerry will put in a good word for her. That way she might even get to travel free as an invalid. Then again there's talk that they mightn't be going at all this year. Did you hear anything about that, Father?'

He shook his head. Julia May had muttered something about his chairing a meeting of the Legion of Mary. Did she say it was to discuss a trip to Lourdes? He couldn't remember. He was developing a technique of switching off while she was in full flow. If appearances were anything to go by, Johnny Slattery would have been as likely to book a flight to Mars with NASA. Once blue dungarees, now rigid with dirt, only partly covered a grimy woollen pullover and a pair of manure-encrusted wellington boots. Unless the widow could travel free as an invalid, of course. Otherwise the bootlegger would have to sell a hell of a lot of poteen. Christmas, his busy period, was still a long way off.

'How's the business, anyway?'

It was out of Father Jerry's mouth before he could stop it. He felt it was time he joined in the conversation, even though the fresh air outside beckoned invitingly.

Already the Doctor had clicked his bag shut and was heading for the door. He froze in his tracks at the question. No one ever referred to Johnny's sideline as anything but 'the business'. How did this exile know the jargon? A coincidence? Maybe. Perhaps the priest wasn't quite so much up in the clouds as he pretended.

Father Jerry was aghast at this slip of the tongue. Part of his mind raced madly as it tried to see whether anyone in the smoke-filled kitchen would notice it.

Another part of it sped back in time to the morning his father was carried into the yard on a horse-drawn cart that the family used to collect seaweed from the strand for fertiliser. On this occasion its cargo was a corpse, its legs dangling grotesquely over the rough timber sides. His father had been found dead in a ditch, into which he must have fallen while in a drunken stupor. During the night heavy rains had swollen the mountain streams and filled the ditch as he lay unconscious from the poteen which he and his brother had run through the still the previous day. It was traditional to sample the first run of 'the business' but his father must have overindulged while his brother managed somehow to find his way back to his own house. From that day on, Father Jerry was reared by a doting mother and a remorse-filled uncle. It was not something he ever spoke about again nor did he wish it to be known that his modest nest egg came from his family's involvement in 'the business'. Poteen, a lethal spirit distilled from potatoes, could damage the brain, cause blindness or even death. As a punch, with plenty of hot water, lemon and cloves to mask the taste, it was barely drinkable. The more prudent used it only as an embrocation.

The portable gas cylinder gave a new lease of life to 'the business'. The police could no longer find stills by the telltale smoke from the fires used to heat the mash. As Christmas drew near the *Clarion* would run pictures of grinning policemen with axes poised to smash barrels seized in a raid. The reports varied little from year to year. '*A large still for the manufacture of poteen has been discovered on a lonely mountainside. Though no one was found at the site, an early arrest is expected. In the meantime, the vigilance of Sergeant Gus Moriarty of Brulagh has prevented forty gallons of this dangerous spirit from playing any further part in the Christmas celebrations!*' Charley Halpin would pen a long article on the perils of drinking poteen. It was a subject on which he was quite an expert since he supplemented his income from the *Clarion* by distributing Johnny's output to trusted customers for a commission of two pounds per bottle.

'Oh it's tough enough, Father,' Johnny replied. 'With all that cheap whiskey being smuggled across the border, 'tis only the old and the feeble are drinking the stuff nowadays.'

Suddenly remembering that the Doc was a good customer, he tried hard to retrieve his gaffe.

'And, of course, those with sense enough to know where to get the real mountain dew!'

'Perhaps if you gave a drop of it to your mother now and again, it might ease the pain in her chest a bit,' Father Jerry suggested.

The barb bounced harmlessly off Johnny's hide.

'Aren't I blue in the face from telling her the same thing, Father? Take a sup of what's good for you, Mother, says I to her but she pays no heed. "Leave it to them that have the taste for it", she tells me. Isn't it true for me, Ma?'

'Oh indeed it is, Father. He has my heart broke from pestering me to try it. Me, who never let a drop of liquor past my lips. I told him and his father before him that it was the Devil's brew, but they wouldn't listen.'

'Well, we must go . . .' He had caught the signal in the Doc's eye.

'I'll just give you my blessing and I'll call again next week. *Benedicat vos omnipotens Deus . . .*'

He shut the door gently behind him so as not to cause another eruption. He found his driver standing by his battered blue Ford. The Doc had seen the rosary beads clenched in the Widow Slattery's gnarled hands and was gazing out to the distant sea, lost in thought. *She knows that her time is up. The look on her face as she waited for you to place the cold stethoscope on her bony chest should have told you that she, too, was just playing the game. What game would that be now James Buckley, Doctor of Medicine and purveyor of homespun philosophy? The game of life, you fool! The one you've been playing since you left college a million years ago. The same one you debate with Mick Flannery when the two of you get drunk and find the answers at the bottom of a glass only to lose them again the next morning. The old Canon, God rest him, didn't know a damn thing either. You could see it in his eyes. He anointed, absolved, christened and buried but he didn't really understand the game either. His successor isn't any wiser, if his performances so far are anything to go by. Still he is only doing his best, I suppose.*

The bit of Latin could well be just as effective a drug as those little blue

80

capsules you gave her. Both have a pretty coating to hide their contents. Interesting how he used the Latin blessing. The old Canon was the same. Any time he sounded as if he really meant it, he invoked God's blessing in the Roman tongue. It really did sound more impressive than plain English. Wealthier colleagues in his own profession had long ago discovered that using it allowed them to charge much more. Had Shakespeare written 'You too, Brutus, my lad?' no one would have given the line a second thought. It's the same with Father Jerry. Despite his Vatican service it seems that the decrees of its Councils discouraging the use of Latin sit lightly on his hunched shoulders. Does it really matter a damn what language we use when we are all merely actors in a bad play? We can't even make up our minds if it is comedy or tragedy, though the plot never seems to change. Philosophers, I would remind you, dear Doctor, make lousy medicine men.

Rattling down towards the village the Doctor recalled the last time the road had been repaired. Just before the last election. It was another of Mick Flannery's vote-catching ploys. Mick promised the six families who lived along the road that he would personally see to it that it was made good as new. When the job was being done he visited each of them to announce, lest they had been struck both deaf and blind, that the work was in progress. When it was completed a week before the election, he called on them again to confirm that everything was now in order. That way he got three bites of the cherry. Well Mick, he reflected, I hope you can get the widow moved up in the waiting list or she will die where she is.

Banishing dark thoughts of political chicanery, he shared the magnificent view with his passenger as they slewed around dangerous curves in their corkscrew descent. Father Jerry purred happily as each new vista unfolded. Even the Doc could not fail to admire the scenery despite its familiarity. As craggy grey rock gave way to lush pasture on its downward sweep to the sea, the priest announced that they must be close to paradise. Eden, he speculated aloud, must have been something like this.

Squares of green, each a different shade, blended in perfect harmony. It may well have been the effect O'Shea's décor had strived for with such spectacular lack of success. The tiny fields stretched right and left as far as the eye could see, stitched together in a giant patchwork quilt by grey stone walls. Many of the patches imprisoned tiny black-and-white ants. They were Friesian cows. Father Jerry was first to break the silence.

'Some things never change, do they?'

The Doc was concentrating on keeping the car between the ditches.

Nevertheless he stole the occasional glance at his passenger's face. He hoped it was the splendour of the scenery and not his squealing brakes that accounted for the awed expression.

'What do you mean?'

'Oh just life and death, the scenery, those cows in the fields. The whole shooting match in fact. Despite our puny efforts to change it, life seems to go on just the same.'

'Pat Mullarkey wouldn't agree with you there, Father. Not about the cows anyway.'

They were the unwitting cause of all those files piled high on Mullarkey's desk. Under those heaps were booklets produced by the Department of Agriculture, designed to wean dairy farmers away from these black-and-white ants. Some expert had christened it 'alternative farming'. What he meant was 'anything but milk'. The benefits of deer production, rearing ducks, geese or pheasants, breeding rabbits or snails were all discussed at length. You name it and some genius driving a desk in the Department of Agriculture was working on it. He may have missed out on Johnny Slattery's sideline but no doubt he would stumble across it, sooner or later. The legal problem could surely be overcome, given goodwill on all sides!

The poor genius. He would have been better employed crawling under his desk with a bottle of Johnny's month-old paint-stripper. The men and women working those patchwork squares were an independent breed. Every expert from here to Timbuktu could tell them that there was no future for them in milk. They would just go back home and farm the same way as before. If the pressure from banks became too great they would retreat behind their farm gates and live off the land. It would be no picnic but they would survive. Mullarkey had often said that if milking cows were made a hanging offence, most of his farmers would happily march to the gallows. Now it would be the task of both himself and this very ill priest to attempt to change Pat Mullarkey – or rather his attitude to the naming the blasted stand.

The Doc's attention had strayed. He realised with a start that Father Jerry was speaking to him.

'Oh you surprise me. I thought he would have been all for the cows. Surely his job depends on them!'

'Not the way he says it. He spent the last six years trying to change the farmers from hay to silage-making. Having succeeded, he now finds that the effluent from silage kills all the fish in the rivers.'

'So what is he going to do about it?'

'Not much he can do. He tells them to build effluent tanks but they don't want to know. They can't make money out of holes in the ground. No wonder he's tearing his hair out. He is in no mood to listen to reason about the stand, that's for sure.'

'I'm sorry to hear it. I had thought of calling on him and sounding him out on the subject. In fact I promised the Sergeant that I would do so before the next meeting. Mick Flannery tells me that the job of chairman automatically goes to the parish priest.'

The Doc gave a hollow laugh. They had come to a fork in the road.

'Mick's right. Here, let's go back by a different road. This links with the main road into the village. It's only a mile or two longer but it will help you get used to the lie of the land. The scenery's not bad and we'll be passing the Golf Club. Mick tells me you play. We could use a fourth. I'm fed up with parting money to Gus and himself.'

'I haven't played in a long time. Vatican staff used to have playing rights on a course outside Rome. Then Archbishop Marcinkus got into trouble with the Italian authorities and couldn't leave the Vatican or he would have been arrested. He was also our best golfer so the club cancelled our playing rights. I haven't played since then.'

'Sounds an interesting type, Marcinkus.'

He was not going to rise to the bait. The secrecy of the confessional was as nothing compared to the silence of his colleagues on that subject.

'His methods were unusual, if that's what you mean, but he was a good golfer . . .' To change the subject he pointed to a rose-covered cottage with a 'For Sale' sign.

'That's pretty. Surprising it's not sold.'

'Rose Cottage? It belonged to an uncle of Maggie Flannery. He died a few months ago without making a will. There's about a dozen beneficiaries involved. The place is for rent until they can agree on a price and how it should be divided. Mick Flannery is executor. He says it would be easier to mind mice at the crossroads than to get them to agree on anything. One crowd wants to go this way, another wants to go that way and the rest want to stay where they are. 'As you say, it *is* pretty even if it is a bit isolated.'

'Mick Flannery seems to be at the heart of most things round here, doesn't he?'

'That's a fact. Mick's a survivor. He scraped in by barely fifty votes last time. He'll tell anyone who'll listen that he is in danger of losing his seat next time. Which, even though he is my closest friend, is hardly surprising.'

'Oh, why? I thought he embodied political life round here.'

'Yes and no. He made a lot of promises.'

'That's usually what is expected of politicians, isn't it?'

'Yes of course. Except that Mick hasn't delivered on any of them. Not yet, anyway.'

'Do you mean that there are some still in the pipeline?'

'Well I suppose so . . .' The Doc sounded dubious. '. . . I expect Mick would claim that Fort Electronics was still in the pipeline.'

'And what was Fort Electronics supposed to make?'

'Microchips. Mick was going to turn Brulagh into the Silicon Valley of Europe. No longer would the people have to rely on the whim of Mother Nature to scratch a living from the soil or the sea. Instead they would rise up and take their rightful place at the leading edge of high technology. I'm quoting him almost verbatim, you understand?'

Father Jerry nodded. It only confirmed his view that things had not changed much. Politicians had been saying much the same thing when he was a student in the Seminary.

'Mick promised secure jobs at top wages in modern surroundings. The young would no longer have to emigrate to find work – it would be right on their doorstep. As for their parents, they could rest from their labours and live out their days in the warm glow of prosperity from the rising sun of Japan. The microchip, he promised, was going to change everyone's lives. Even the likes of Johnny above in the mountain would benefit from it. All they needed to do was to vote for Mick.'

'What happened?'

'Well Mick got elected and nothing more was heard of Fort Electronics. Anyone who asked was told that development problems had cropped up unexpectedly. Apparently the Japanese were working like beavers day and night to get it right. Once the bugs in the chip were sorted out, they would go ahead with building the factory. That was four years ago.'

'Some would say that's a longish pipeline,' Father Jerry observed.

'Indeed. Then there's the pier . . .'

'The pier? You mean the one in the village?'

'Yes. If you've seen it, you will have noticed that it's slowly falling into the sea.'

Indeed it was. He rather liked it though. It was wide enough to park his car when he walked by the shore. He didn't say any of this. He did not want to break the flow.

'Yes, well it's the winter storms that do the damage. Before another election Mick promised to have it repaired. Not just repaired, mind you, but improved to the extent that it would rival the best on the coast. And not just a pier but all the extras that go with a thriving fishing industry. Mick painted a picture of factories lining the seafront to process the catch of a huge fishing fleet being unloaded by giant cranes. An auction hall would dispose of that part of the sea's harvest surplus to their needs. Another plant would make ice to keep the catches fresh on board ship. A later stage in the plan included a marina and luxury hotel on the far side of the bay. There was even the possibility of a lobster-breeding station and an oyster hatchery. The best news of all was that not a penny of this was to come from the taxpayers' pockets.'

'Did anyone really believe this?'

'Hard to say. It made sense at the time. Charley Halpin wrote that Brussels had selected Brulagh as a Regional Fund pilot scheme to exploit European fish stocks. He quoted a well-informed but anonymous source to the effect that this was a direct result of intensive lobbying by Mick. It was implied that little else was discussed at EC headquarters except the exciting new developments in store for Brulagh. All that was needed was the continued presence in power of our Mick. Only in that way could the project be safeguarded against the backsliding for which the EC bureaucrats are notorious.'

'And what happened then?'

The question was asked out of politeness. When he had seen the pier it was unchanged since the famine times in which it was built. That was over a century ago. The only new structure that he remembered seeing was a ramshackle shed at the back of what he now knew to be Flannery's shop. It housed bright yellow gas cylinders.

'Oh, the usual. Nothing. Mick told everyone that the plans were sabotaged at the last moment by the Brussels bureaucracy. It may even have been true. Didn't matter anyway. He was re-elected by then.'

As they drove through the gate that led to the Golf Club, Father Jerry realised the truth of Mick's claim that naming the stand after him was vital to his re-election. Whether Mick deserved it was another question altogether.

'I suppose we had better hold that meeting sooner rather than later.'

85

'Yes, I think so, Father. Though there was never a hard and fast rule, we usually met in my place on the first Saturday night of the month. That was to accommodate Mick, who is away during the week when the Dáil is in session.'

'Your place it is then, next Saturday night. Let us hope the Divine Providence will direct our actions!'

The unspoken thought in the Doc's mind was that whatever deity looked after Brulagh was far too preoccupied with events at the grotto to bother with trivialities like naming a GAA stand. Instead he pulled up in the empty car park and got out.

'I will now show you Brulagh's answer to St Andrews. It has certain features not usually found on a golf course, that flock of sheep over there being but one of them . . .'

12

Anywhere else but in Brulagh, the view from the office would have been worth a fortune. One big window looked out to sea, the other framed the mountain. It had dawned another cloudless day. The sun blazed down the valley throwing the yellow gorse and square, green fields into sharp relief against the brooding, purple mountain. Turf smoke from the whitewashed cottages nestling in huddled groups on the mountainside spiralled upwards in the still air. A heat haze fudged the line where the sea met the sky. Explosions of light erupted here and there as the sunlight flashed messages from wavecrests to the screaming gulls. Most of them pursued a half-decker that was ploughing a creamy furrow through the shimmering swell.

It was Joe Gallagher's boat. Good man Joe, Pat thought as he grimaced at the telephone six inches from his ear. What with the lobster fishing, growing early carrots, running a guesthouse and drawing the farmers' dole, Joe must be worth a fortune. Then, of course, there was his pension from the Water Utility in Chicago. If anyone knew how to work the system, it was Joe. Yet for as long as anyone could remember, he had been a pillar of the Church. Not content with acting as usher at the two Sunday masses, he steered the wooden box with the long handle through the congregation to take up collections for worthy causes such as The Propagation of the Faith and the Foreign Missions. If an altar boy failed to appear, Joe would serve the mass. It was suggestd only half in jest that he could have celebrated the mass in the period between the canon's death and the arrival of the new priest. A daily communicant, Joe led the church choir in a reedy baritone.

Pat's eyes focused vacantly on the middle distance as the voice at the other end burbled on. When it stopped, Pat raised his eyes despairingly to the ceiling and spat out the words like orange pips.

'Are you trying to tell me that our proposals are unacceptable to the bank?'

Another sentence crackled through, only to be cut short by, 'You know damn well that we couldn't meet those repayments. Why the hell can't you be realistic for once?'

Now a pause, followed by a more subdued chattering.

'Well that's the best we can do. Absolutely our bottom line. Think about it again and come back to me on it.'

With a snort, he slammed the receiver back in the cradle. Christ Almighty, he had tried his best to reassure that misfortunate swinging from the blue cord. He had promised him the bloody bank would never sell the farm out from under him no matter what. No one in their right mind would buy a farm sold out by a bank, not in the land that spawned Captain Boycott. And who had ever seen a banker in pinstripe suit and wellies trying to milk a cow? No, he told the poor wretch, what was needed was a calm appraisal of the situation.

'Go back home and carry on just as before. Draw up a list of what you own. Write down what it costs you to run the farm and feed your family. Then put in how much you earned last year. When we have those figures down on paper we can work out a plan to repay the bank. Not in their time but in yours. When that's done the two of us will go and talk to Donnelly about a rescue package. Go home now like a good man and start writing down the information we need. That way you won't forget about it or leave out something important.'

He had his lines off by heart. Sometimes he recited them in his sleep, to the consternation of his wife. Some, like yesterday's victim, made for the pub after their first interview with Donnelly. Then they would call on Pat at the office, so helplessly drunk that he had to drive them home. They were the worst. Getting them into the car was difficult enough but bringing a drunken father home to his wife and family was shattering. Often they had never seen him in that condition before. Naturally the explanations were left to Pat.

'Well Ma'am he went to see the bank manager and he got a bit upset. After that he went to O'Shea's, had a few drinks too many and then called in to see me at the office. I thought it better to bring him home before he got any worse. No, there's nothing really to worry about, just a few details Mr Donnelly is looking for. Yes, he's handling it himself now. No, it's not necessarily a bad sign. It just shows he's taking more interest in the account now that it's gone so high. Oh, didn't he tell you about it? I see. Well, yes, it is rather high, actually. It would be as well if you had a proper talk with himself about it when he's feeling better. No, don't worry, the farm will be all right. You'll just have to tighten the belt a bit more, I suppose. Look I must get back to the office or Mossy O'Connor will have my life. No, not at all. It was no trouble at all. When he comes round tell him to get to work right away on those figures I asked him for. Oh he'll remember all right, never fear! I must go now. Goodbye!'

Then back to the office, to Mossy and to a growing mountain of files. Well, he would have one less to contend with after yesterday. Mossy was his boss and had been a lifetime with the Department. He viewed Pat with a benevolence that lasted for as long as Pat did the work and left Mossy to discuss the state of the nation, perched on a bar stool in O'Shea's. Anyone with a problem he sent to Pat, assuring them with a wave of his hand, 'Pat's the man you want for that! Knows more about money than anyone else I know. Doesn't have a shilling to call his own, mind you, but you don't have to be a chicken to make an omlette! He's got a great head on his shoulders. If you have any problems, he's the man for you.'

There was a time when Pat had been flattered by such praise. No longer. Now he regarded Mossy as a lazy, bitter old drunk. Someone was tapping sharply on the door. A dark shape was outlined against the frosted glass on which 'Department of Agriculture' was painted in gold script. Putting his hand over the mouthpiece he shouted, 'Come in, it's open.' The pale but delicately chiselled face of Jeremiah O'Sullivan peered around the door – Mullarkey snapped out of his reverie, dredged up a thin smile and said, 'Welcome to Brulagh, Father. Sorry if I've kept you but that was the bank manager. The Doc asked me to work something out with him – about yesterday. Well, wasn't that one hell of an introduction to your new parish? I'm sorry we couldn't have met in pleasanter circumstances.'

'Thank you, Mister Mullarkey. No need to apologise, I quite understand. As for bank managers, I expect they are much the same all over the world. When they whistle the rest of us must jump. As for our meeting, you can hardly blame yourself for the tragic circumstances . . .'

Oh sweet Jesus, I hope you are right! I was the one who advised him to expand. 'Buy more cows and put up a decent milking parlour', I told the poor bastard. Probably he believed he'd never see another hungry day. Then those damned bureaucrats in Brussels changed the goalposts!

'. . . Have there been any further developments?'

'Not really. The Doc was back from Slattery's with Johnny before the ambulance arrived. We cut him down and sent him off to the mortuary. Then the Doc wrote his report. Gus and I signed it and that was that.'

'I know. I signed it too. Eventually.'

Pat's laugh was harsh and without humour. 'Death by misadventure, of course. We haven't had a proper verdict round here in years. That was the third suicide in my area so far this year.'

'That many? You surprise me. We were always told that Ireland had the lowest suicide rate in the world.'

'Now you know why. The Doc will bring in a verdict to suit everyone. A great man for consensus is our Doc. That way the system is safe for the next hundred years or so. A nod here, a wink there and "sure aren't we all only passing through this life and we might as well leave well enough alone". Which is what has us the way we are. Nothing is going to change until someone gets up off his arse and shouts STOP! Pardon the language, Father, but you caught me at a bad time.'

'I can easily call some other time, if that would help.'

The Doc was right. This man was in no mood for compromise.

'Not at all, Father. Just give me a moment to make a note of what Donnelly said while it's still fresh in my mind. Then I'm at your service for as long as you wish.'

With a sigh he reached for a buff folder. Selecting a sheet from the file he wrote slowly and methodically, his tongue curling out of the side of his mouth in concentration. Dropping the folder back in the filing cabinet he turned to the priest.

'Did you have much paperwork in your last job?'

'Yes indeed. It is one of the things I'll be happy to leave behind.'

'Will you miss Rome, do you think?'

'Too soon to say. Anyway this is my home for now. I was born and reared in a place like this. Though I admit thirty years is a long time to be away from anything.'

The phone rang. Pat shrugged helplessly and answered it.

'Yes, I got him home all right . . . Not really drunk, it was more that he wasn't used to it . . . Yes, that was it, he'd never been inside a bank before . . . No, well the news wasn't great for him . . . I left him at home with his wife and told her I'd phone Donnelly. He must have woken up, gone outside and done it there and then. Yeah, I was just speaking to him a moment ago. Sure what would you expect from a pig but a grunt? That's it, then?'

During the call, Father Jerry examined the unlined face before him. It had the boyish looks of a Kennedy and, perhaps, a matching ambition. Even the hairstyle with the fringe brushed across the forehead added to the likeness. Mullarkey replaced the receiver.

'That was my boss. Enquiring about yesterday.'

'Are there many more like him? The dead man, I mean.'

'Too many. They thought the good times would never end. Now the banks want their money back. I know it's stupid to blame them for everything but there's a right and a wrong way of going about it.'

'And you think they are doing it the wrong way?'

'I most certainly do.'

He saw again the ghastly look on the face of the man they had cut down. The blue twine had cut deep into his neck. There had been no note. His wife knew of no reason why he should take his life. Pat did. This was confirmed when he went through his pockets.

'It has come to the notice of the Directors that your account had not been active for some time. It is the policy of the bank, in such cases, to try to come to an arrangement regarding repayment of outstanding monies. However since you continue to ignore such efforts on our part, you leave us with no option but to pass on your file to our Legal Department for immediate action.'

It conjured up a picture of worried directors sitting round a boardroom table, wringing their hands in anguish as they cast about in every direction seeking vainly for some way out of the impasse. Reality, Pat knew, was that some bloody computer hiccupped out a list of delinquent accounts. Then lackeys like Donnelly were dispatched to call in the loans before farming went down the tubes. Even his own department had seen the writing on the wall. It offered early retirement to older staff. Because he was still young the package did not apply to him. Anyway, he could hardly desert those whom his advice got into trouble. His boss, Mossy O'Connor, was different. He would have left the job without a backward glance. Though he was the type any organisation would have been glad to see the back of, Mossy was too old to benefit from early retirement. To get his full pension he had to stay in harness for two more years.

'I wanted to talk to you about the meeting on Saturday night,' Father Jerry said.

'Is that so?' Pat's voice had suddenly acquired a hard edge to it. 'I thought it was going to be a routine meeting. Just preparing for the festival, that sort of thing.'

Still the bright, innocent expression. Father Jerry groaned inwardly. He was beginning to dislike Pat for no particular reason. Perhaps he envied the younger man's boyish looks and overbearing self-confidence. The priest decided that Pat knew exactly what was coming next but wanted to make him jump through the hoops like a performing seal.

'I hear that you have a motion down for debate on naming the stand. Is that correct? I ask because I understand that I am to be chairman of the GAA committee, *ex officio* as it were.'

'Yes, I have.'

'And what are your views on the matter?'

'Well, for what they're worth I think it should either be called after Saint Fintan or not called anything at all.'

He gave a toothy smile that others might have found engaging. Father Jerry did not. He stuck with his task.

'Why not call it after Mick. The Flannery stand or something like that? After all, what's in a name?'

An original thought if ever there was one. Nevertheless it was the best he could come up with on the spur of the moment. Anyway the ball was now in Pat's court.

'Why not indeed . . . ?'

The smile had been wiped off Pat's face. It was replaced by a frown that threatened to darken into a full-grown scowl at any moment.

'I'll tell you precisely why not, Father. Some of us have worked hard for that stand. When the bank turned us down flat, most people said that was the end of it. Mick himself is on record as saying it would be more in our interest to turn out a winning team before going into debt by putting up a stand that no one would use. He as good as told me I couldn't train ivy up a wall, not to mind a hurling team. OK, maybe we haven't won anything but the team tries hard and it gives the kids something to do in the evenings.'

'I appreciate that but . . .'

Pat used the politician's trick of pressing on as though he hadn't heard the interruption.

'Anyway the fact remains that we now have our stand. Underneath it, I hope we will build a clubhouse which can double as a community hall and a function room. It will be somewhere that all the village can meet and play bingo, have a drink or a game of cards and anything else they damn well like. They won't have to pay subscriptions or put their names forward for election like the Golf Club. It will be open to everyone, rich and poor alike. When that's built and paid for, we'll put in a squash court, possibly a tennis court and maybe even a running track. We'll do it from within the community by our own sweat. It will happen, I promise you, but I don't know when. Maybe not even in our lifetime. But happen it will! Not like the microchip factory we're still waiting for, nor the new pier, nor the processing factory, nor the ice plant, nor the marina and God knows what else. Unlike all of Mick Flannery's promises, this stand happened. It is there as a monument to what the people can do if they buckle down to it. And it's only the beginning. Now after all that, you're asking me to name the only thing we have ever achieved in Brulagh after a conman like Flannery. You must be joking!'

Not once during the tirade had he raised his voice but there was little doubt that he meant every word. Castelli's technique was that when all else failed, try cajolery.

'Come on now, Pat! I know yourself and Mick aren't exactly close friends but you've got to admit that he's the best hurler the village ever produced. Would it not be fitting to call the stand after such a man?'

'Of course he was a great hurler long ago. No one can deny him that. But I believe the Mick Flannery that you want to call the stand after is the politician, not the hurler. If so, you are calling it after the worst sort of political animal in the whole zoo. To call anything, even the public toilet we so badly need, after him would only honour his total neglect of the village. Tell me of one job he has created round here in the last thirty years. Tell me just one promise he has kept in the time he has been a TD. Come to think of it, tell me one thing he has done for the club that is now proposing to call the stand after him. If you're going to say that he got the grant from the GAA, I would remind you that we were fully entitled to it anyway. The very most he did was to get it a bit sooner, that's all. He saw his chance to act the big man and pretended to use his influence with the Council. If he's so bloody influential, why can't he get on the Council in the first place? Then he would have real power. Well I can tell you that from what I hear they wouldn't touch him with a forty-foot barge pole. I hope you don't take offence but the question was asked. I hope I've answered it for you.'

'No doubt about that, I would say.'

He tried to match Pat's smile but abandoned the effort half-way through. This nut was not going to be cracked today – or any time in the foreseeable future. Mick would do well to look to his laurels. This man would make a better friend than an enemy. That being so, there was little point in alienating him further. Might as well wrap it up with one last question.

'Do you intend to say all this again at the meeting?'

'If I have to, yes.'

'Do you mean that someone is going to have to write all that into the minutes?'

'If you like I'll give Bernie a copy of my press release. She could paste it into the minute book. It would save her a lot of writing.'

'Who is this Bernie?'

'Sorry, I forgot you were new here! Bernie runs the Golf Club. Stewardess, I think they call her. Anyway she doubles as unpaid secretary of our committee. Between ourselves, I think she has a crush on the Doc but don't quote me on that.'

Refusing to be distracted by such an obvious red herring, Father Jerry pursued his quarry relentlessly. It was difficult to divine from his fixed smile if Pat were serious about the press release. Assuming for a moment that he was, it was a new development that could be very well done without.

'But that's blackmail, Pat. You can't go around forcing people's hands like that.'

'Hold it right there, Father! Are you trying to tell me that Mick didn't drop the word to someone that it would be a nice idea to have the stand called after him? Am I to believe that the Holy Ghost descended on the heads of the committee and inspired them to do it? It's one thing to have a walkie-talkie statue but to believe that the GAA committee is inspired by God is taking religion too far.'

'It's still blackmail Pat, no matter where the idea came from.'

'Call it what you like, but that's how things are at the moment.'

Father Jerry rose wearily to his feet. Pat remained seated. This did nothing to endear him further to the priest.

'Well, if that's your last word on the matter I won't take up any more of your time.'

'I'm afraid that's the way it is, Father. Nothing personal, I assure you.'

'Glad to hear it, Pat. See you on Saturday night then.'

13

Father Jerry looked around the table. The only two unfamiliar faces were those of Mossy O'Connor and Bernie, the secretary. She had read the minutes of the last meeting quickly before the first three items on the agenda were quickly dealt with. After a brief introduction by Pat Mullarkey, Mossy had taken no further interest in the meeting – or its new chairman. He sat slumped in his seat, apparently oblivious to what was going on around him.

Pat stopped examining his fingernails long enough to stare long and hard at Father Jerry. He wasn't quite sure how much of their earlier talk had filtered through to the others. He hoped they realised that the question was far from being resolved. He, too, examined the faces around the mahogany table. What did the Doc need with such a huge piece of furniture? It wasn't as if he did any home entertaining. A wedding present, he supposed, that he couldn't bring himself to part with when his wife died. It must be worth a fortune. Not that you'd think it, the way glasses, ashtrays and notepads were scattered all over it. Certainly not to keep up appearances. The Doc had never been one for that. His clothes might have been rejects from a sale of work. His car was an ancient rust-bucket in need of a wash. It was no secret that most nights he took a drink or two or three in the Golf Club, untroubled by the gossip it caused.

The same could not be said of Pat's boss. Mossy O'Connor wore a well-cut suit and drove a car in keeping with his status as Chief Agricultural Officer for the region. Seated at the far end of the table he was having difficulty in keeping his eyes open. His chin would drop down on his chest, eyelids flickering shut, until something disturbed him. With a start he would shake himself awake, look around furtively to see if anyone had noticed his lapse and then nod off again. Not that it interfered with the business of the meeting. Mossy had been co-opted to make up the required number on the understanding that he wasn't expected to contribute very much. The old Canon had quietly advised him to say nothing at all and just accept the perks that came with the job. These were tickets, rare as diamonds, to the All-Ireland finals. Mossy sold them to the highest bidder. When asked why he didn't go to the matches, he insisted that he saw more of the game on TV. Next to him sat Bernie busily taking notes in longhand, teeth clenched with the strain of keeping pace with the discussion.

'. . . and now we come to Mister Mullarkey's motion, number four on the agenda, concerning what, if anything, to call the new stand. I'm sure he would like to say a few words on the subject.'

'Thank you, Chairman, I would indeed.'

Pat was unsure whether to address Father Jerry as 'Reverend' or 'Mister' chairman. Everyone called his predecessor 'Canon' and that was that. He noticed that tonight the new man was addressed as 'Father'. Because Pat was a stickler for proper procedures he preferred to speak, as protocol demanded, through the Chair.

'Good. Just before you begin, Pat, perhaps we should try to agree on a format for the opening ceremony. You will understand that I know little or nothing of the arrangements for the festival. For instance, do you intend holding two separate ceremonies? One to inaugurate the festival and the other to open the new stand. Perhaps someone might enlighten me?'

Father Jerry's question hung in the air for a moment. Eventually the Doc cleared his throat and replied.

'That's something we never really settled. Originally it looked like there might be two separate events. But that seems to make less sense now. Especially since it looks as if this grotto business might be coming to a head at the same time. If that happens, we'll have enough trouble attracting a good crowd to one opening ceremony, not to mind expecting them to turn up for two!'

Ignoring the reference to the grotto, the chairman pressed on in a level voice. 'That sounds very sensible. If there are no amendments, could I have a seconder for the Doctor's proposal?'

After a brief silence, the Sergeant raised his hand and murmured, 'I'll second that.'

For a brief moment Pat considered objecting on the grounds that what the Doc said was a suggestion rather than a formal proposal but abandoned the idea when he caught the steely glint in the chairman's eye. Better to keep his powder dry in case he needed it. Anyway the bloody priest should be in no doubt as to how he felt about the stand after the discussion earlier in the day. In the pause that followed Mick Flannery went to the sideboard to refill his glass from the whiskey decanter.

'Good, that's settled then. The opening of the festival and the stand will take place at one and the same time. Now would someone fill me in on the details?'

Again the Doc obliged. It had not escaped him that Father Jerry had invited Pat to speak and the effectively shut him up before he could oblige. He wondered whether what he was witnessing was an accident or an old Vatican ploy to disconcert the opposition. Whichever it was, it had the effect of making Pat look distinctly ill at ease.

'We were thinking of putting up a platform outside the church gates. Then we could have the opening immediately after last Mass on the Feast of the Assumption. If you have no objection, that is?'

'None that I can think of at the moment. Do the rest of you agree with the idea?'

His gaze swept round the table. It was met with a series of nods and grunts.

'So far, so good. Now who is going to make the speech or did you intend having one speaker open the festival and another declare the stand open? Has anything been agreed about that?'

To judge by the pall of silence that descended on his listeners, it seemed not. For an occasion that was generating so much fuss and bother, very little seemed to have been accomplished up to now. Father Jerry decided to concentrate on the minutiae, thereby putting those expecting to sink their teeth into larger issues off their stride.

'Well then perhaps we had better settle that next. We'll go round the table. You're first, Sergeant. Will you be addressing us from the platform?'

The reply was predictable.

'Not on your life, Father! I'd sooner hang myself than make a speech . . .'

When he realised the unfortunate phrase he had used, the words tumbled out in a barely coherent torrent.

'. . . what I mean is, I couldn't even if I wanted to. I'll have to be moving around all the time and keeping an eye on things. My assistant is away on sick leave and may not be back by then. Not that I'm expecting trouble or anything but it's no harm to be on the look-out all the same. No, Father, I won't even be on the platform, not to mind speaking off it. What about yourself?'

That was the longest contribution he had made to any meeting in living memory. He slumped in his seat, mortified by the embarrassment that his untimely reference to hanging himself had caused.

'God forbid, Sergeant. They will have had enough of me from the pulpit by then. If they saw me standing up to speak again they'd run for their lives!'

'With respect, Chairman, I think we should take the items the other way round. That is, we should settle the question of what to call the stand first. After that, we can then decide who will make the speeches.'

At last he had the chance to break in. For a while there Pat had felt like a nervous actor waiting in the wings to make his début as the rest of the cast hogged the limelight. The chairman had no sooner invited him to say his piece than another topic had been introduced. Perhaps it was the priest's way of paying him back for threatening to use the press release. An empty threat, as it happened. When he phoned Charley Halpin afterwards he had missed the *Clarion*'s deadline by several hours. He wondered if the priest was aware of this. It wouldn't surprise him. He was a smooth operator, a very different kettle of fish from the old Canon. Pat hoped the matter of the press release would be forgotten by the chairman. Even if Charley's editor was prepared to print it in a week's time, by then it would be far too late to have any effect.

Anyway the implication of what he had just said was clear. If Mossy had been awake, even he would have grasped it. *Shaft me on the issue of the name and you can damn well find someone else to share the platform with Mick.* If the priest sensed this, he didn't show it. His face was a picture of contentment. Not a single line creased his brow. He had lit a large, yellow pipe and was sucking on it happily as though he hadn't a care in the world.

'Fine, Pat . . . I'll call you that, if I may . . . as I say, that will be fine. If the rest of you have no objection, we'll take the items in the order Pat has suggested.'

Another pause as he looked round the table to see if any there were any dissenters. Mick shuffled uneasily in his chair as if he was about to speak. Then he thought better of it and remained silent. The Doc found something of interest on his ceiling and stared fixedly at it until the priest concluded his remarks.

'As chairman, I'll stay out of it for the time being . . .' –

Unless, of course, I have to use my casting vote to bring some semblance of order to this circus. From what you said in the safe haven of your office, Mister Mullarkey, I thought you would already have launched into an impassioned diatribe against the country in general and one Michael John Flannery in particular. Instead of which you are letting me make all the running. Well, that may be the rock on which you perish. If you had been playing this game for as long as I, you would realise that you have to make your point at the beginning. Having the last word can be futile when everyone else has settled on a course of action within the first five minutes. Then the rest of the time will be frittered away on trivialities. If you are going to make your move, this could well be your last chance.

'. . . so we'll hear from each of you. Pat, as you tabled the motion, you speak first.'

Pat would have much preferred to speak last. Then he could see which way the cat was going to jump. Being first off the mark, he decided to test the water before diving in. In the mildest of tones he said, 'If we *have* to call it something, it should be after Saint Fintan. If that's not acceptable to some of you, I propose we don't call it *anything at all.*'

He pushed back from the table and folded his arms to show that he had finished. *That was a far cry from your outburst this morning. Have you lost your taste for battle or are you just biding your time?*

'What about you, Sergeant?'

'The Flannery Stand. No doubt about it. It's high time Mick got a bit of recognition from his home crowd. Like it or not, the man is a legend.'

This was addressed to no one in particular though he looked towards Mick, who was busily engaged trying to persuade his lighter to work. Nor did he make eye contact with Pat on his right. When Gus stopped speaking he too discovered something of interest in the ceiling. He was still looking at it when Father Jerry intervened.

'Perhaps at this stage it might be better if Mister Flannery were to leave the meeting until this matter is resolved. It might prove embarrassing for him and for us should he remain.'

Mick shrugged his shoulders to indicate it didn't matter to him either way. Gathering up his cigarettes and glass, he left the room. Mossy was next to give the meeting the benefit of his thoughts. Draining his tumbler of whiskey, he placed it noisily back on the table. It was obvious that he was thirsting for a refill. He sighed, suppressed a huge yawn and declared firmly, 'I'll abstain on this one, if you don't mind.'

Like a dog expecting a bone, he glanced expectantly at the Doc. He had hoped that such evenhandedness would be rewarded with a fresh drink. It wasn't. The Doc had other things on his mind. He was next to speak.

'I have to go along with Gus on this one. If we called it anything else, it would be a slap in the face for Mick. Leaving aside for the moment the fact that he is the best hurler ever to come out of Brulagh, he is also the president of our club. Anyway I think that the Flannery Stand has a nice ring to it. I must say this, however. In my view unless the meeting is unanimous about it, we shouldn't call it anything at all. We'd look right eejits to fall out at this stage over a small thing like a name.'

He had run out of steam. At least he could look Mick straight in the eye and say that he had supported him. No need to tell him how much he had hedged his support in the hope of avoiding a blazing row. Had he but known, Mick had the empty glass pressed against the door, listening in to every syllable that was uttered inside the room. He smirked with satisfaction at the Doc's contribution. It was no more than he would expect from him.

'Now, last but not least, our honorary secretary.'

They watched anxiously as Bernie put away her notepad. Much depended on what she had to say. Mick was a regular at the Golf Club bar – something that incensed O'Shea, who complained that the Golf Club could remain open half the night while he had to shut up shop on the stroke of closing time. The fact that Gus and Mick played together merely aggravated matters. If the truth were known, his real complaint against the Sergeant had to do with the banning of the Easter lilies. Since he came back to Brulagh O'Shea had appointed himself keeper of the Republican conscience. He sold paper lilies outside the church on Easter Sunday. They were to commemorate the Easter Rising so graphically portrayed behind his bar. On the suspicion that the proceeds went to swell subversive coffers, Gus had received a directive from his Superintendent to stop such activities. When he passed on the word to O'Shea, there had been an ugly scene. Eventually they worked out a compromise whereby the lilies were given out free from behind O'Shea's bar and Gus turned a blind eye to whatever contributions O'Shea received in exchange. What the takings were and how they were kept separate from his bar sales was anyone's guess.

Whether Mick's custom was enough to win her support in naming the stand after him remained to be seen. What was beyond dispute was the fact that Bernie was an excellent secretary. No one had ever questioned the accuracy of her minutes. Pat wondered how she would report this meeting. It was going fine so far. No rows, no thumping the table and, even more important, no vote. The Doc had handled that expertly. Everybody was being studiously polite. Pat wondered was it in deference to the new chairman. Mossy, his boss, hadn't been of much help either. He watched Bernie's expression as she started to speak.

'I propose that we defer the naming of the stand to some future date.'

She thought her voice sounded like it was coming from the bottom of a well. It was as if a stranger had taken charge of her vocal chords. It might seem to the others that she was evading the issue, but that couldn't be helped. It had to be done if this stupid game was to end without anyone getting hurt. She liked Mick but she admired Pat. He was a complex individual. His disapproval of the Golf Club and its trappings irked her more than she cared to admit. He made no secret of the fact that he regarded the place as an exclusive drinking club for the over-privileged. Everybody knew he was going to contest Mick's seat at the next election but that was a matter between the two of them. It should not be allowed to spill over into this meeting. But of course it would, unless the silly game was stopped dead in its tracks. Men were so stupid where their pride was concerned. It was obvious that the priest was trying everything in his power to avoid a row. The Doc and Gus were perched uncomfortably on the fence. Nobody took any notice of Mossy, and Mick was skulking out in the hall.

If the stand were called after Mick, that would be a famous victory for him and one in the eye for Pat. The downside would be that Pat would probably resign and the Club would be all the poorer for that. Calling it after St Fintan would be seen as a successful guerrilla attack by Pat. The idol that was Mick Flannery would prove to have feet of clay. Her proposal would result in an honourable draw for both parties.

'I'll second that!' The Doc was in almost before the words were out of her mouth.

'Do we have any amendments to the proposal, gentlemen?'

The chairman looked around the table. This could be the anti-climax of the century. To think he had actually lain awake at night in the giant maw of that dreadful bed, worrying what would happen at this non-event. The very last thing he wanted at this stage was a damned amendment. None the less, it was his duty to seek one. If he didn't, Mullarkey might feel aggrieved. Worse still he might challenge the correctness of the procedure. The Doc was first to weaken.

'Before you look for an amendment and maybe a divisive vote, may I say something?'

'Of course, Doctor. Go ahead.'

101

Father Jerry was relieved that the spotlight had shifted. He didn't care what they called the blasted stand as long as he didn't have to cast the deciding vote. Why was he in the hot seat? What had building stands and running festivals got to do with eternal salvation? Or what had they to do with a dignified retirement in a quiet backwater that would end, sooner or later, in easeful death? Not much, he decided, as he waited for the Doc to speak. Those who accused the clergy of having a finger in every pie were the first to nominate them for a job that no one else would touch. Yet he knew that communities had been split for ever over lesser issues than the one before them tonight. He prayed the Doc's healing powers would extend to what he was about to say. Of those he had met so far, the Doc was the most impressive in every respect. The fact that he appeared not to give a damn about anything made what he had to say worth hearing. The journey down the mountain in the old Ford had been a revelation: he had learned more about the geography and the people of his new parish in that short twenty minutes than he had in all the time since he'd arrived. His informant was talking in a relaxed, almost bored fashion.

'This is getting too complicated for me. As far as I can see, two of us want the stand called after Mick and two more would rather we didn't call it anything. The chairman and Mossy are abstaining for the moment. Am I right?'

Everyone signalled their agreement. He continued.

'It seems to me that Saint Fintan is not a serious contender. If we take a vote on it, whichever side is beaten is going to feel wronged. So, instead of a vote, why don't we try to sort the thing out with a bit of sensible talk? Mind you, we don't want to take all night over it. There are plenty more items left on the agenda. Well, what do you think?'

Again everyone agreed – this time with varying degrees of enthusiasm.

'All right then. As Gus and Pat are the two who put most effort into getting the stand built, the rest of us should stay quiet for a while and let them sort it out between themselves. What do you say to that, Gus?'

'That sounds reasonable to me,' the Sergeant replied. 'Like I said before, I think it should be called after Mick. I soldiered with him through the All-Irelands and a finer hurler I never laid eyes on. I said it once and I'll say it again – the man is a legend in his own lifetime. However, I have also campaigned with Pat here and I can honestly say that the stand would still be a pipe dream only for him. So if he wants to open it without a name, I'm prepared to go along with that. I agree with the Doc that it would be daft to call it after Saint Fintan. I hope you'll pardon my saying so, Father?'

'Oh most certainly, Sergeant. I couldn't agree more, in fact!'

He could not hide the relief in his voice. It would be a brave man – or a lunatic – who would break up this mutual admiration society. The debate was over. The rest would only be window dressing. He added his own trivia to the winding-down procedure.

'To be honest, I have my doubts about him. Saint Fintan, I mean. From what I can discover in Church history, he didn't set a shining example to our youth. Very fond of the ladies, it seems. They had some pretty peculiar monks back in those days, I can tell you. Are you happy with Bernie's proposal, Sergeant?'

'Put it this way, Father. I can live with it,' Gus replied.

'Thank you, Sergeant. And what about you, Doctor? Will you go along with Sergeant Moriarty?'

'Yes, of course. As it's unanimous now, do we need a vote?'

'No, I don't believe we do. I mean it is unanimous, isn't it? Mister Mullarkey did say that if the name Saint Fintan did not suit, he would be happy to leave the stand nameless. Did you not, Mister Mullarkey?'

Pat agreed. He was trapped by his own words. He noticed that the chairman had reverted to 'Mister'. The sound of a glass breaking in the hall reminded them that Mick could now be recalled. As he resumed his seat Father Jerry addressed him.

'Mister Flannery, it has been decided that the stand remain without a name for the moment. We would like you and Pat to do the honours for the opening ceremony. Perhaps you might be good enough to address a few words to the people on the festival opening. Mister Mullarkey might then declare the stand open. Does that seem like a good idea?'

It didn't, but neither of them could think of a valid objection to the proposal. They nodded without enthusiasm, studiously avoiding looking at each other.

'Good, that's settled then. Now the next item on the agenda is . . .'

After the meeting, Mick Flannery approached him in the hall as the others were heading for O'Shea's.

'Would you care to join us?'

'I think I had better not, thanks all the same. Could I persuade you to join me back in the house for that drink we never had?'

As he waited for a reply he saw no reason to tell Mick that he had already been in O'Shea's and was in no hurry to repeat the experience. Anyway he felt like a drink of decent whisky after the anticlimax that was the meeting. Mindful of Graham Greene and his whisky priests, he preferred not to drink alone.

'Sure, that would be great. I hope it tastes as good as it smelt on Julia May's floor!'

They followed the straggling procession down the dark street and made a discreet turn up the short driveway to the parochial house. Not discreet enough to avoid the bleary eyes of Mossy O'Connor. Turning to Pat he remarked, 'I see Mick slipping into the priest's house. I wonder would it be his blessing or his whiskey he's after?'

14

'Do you know what I'm going to tell you?'

Mick leaned towards the priest as if he were in the confession box. Though clearly rhetorical, Father Jerry thought it only polite to acknowledge Mick's question by shaking his head.

'I've found that the things you expect to be the worst are never half as bad, and vice versa, of course.'

A silence followed while this nugget of wisdom sank in. Father Jerry sucked thoughtfully on his pipe while Mick lit a cigarette from the stub of its predecessor. Mick took a gulp of scotch that lowered the level in his glass by at least fifty per cent before further developing his theory.

'Take tonight, for example. The whole place thought there were going to be fireworks between Mullarkey and myself over what to call the bloody stand. Instead of which, the whole thing was as dull as ditchwater.'

'Perhaps they were just being nice to their new chairman.'

'You must be joking! When Mullarkey wants to get something off his sunken chest, he couldn't give two knobs of goat's . . .'

He corrected himself, remembering that he was in the presence of a man of God and hastily rephrased Mullarkey's lack of concern for the norms of debate.

'He wouldn't care if 'twas the Pope himself was chairing the meeting. When that shagger gets the bit between his teeth, there's no stopping him.'

'Well, to be frank, I had expected more from him. His timing seemed a bit off, if you ask me. He left his contribution a little late. If he had got his spoke in earlier, the outcome might have been different. Still one never knows . . .'

'You're dead right there, Father. Early bulling means early calving, I always say. If you've got something up your nose, better to spit it out there and then and be done with it rather than hanging around, waiting for the right time.'

Father Jerry did not neglect his duties as host while he tried to unravel this very mixed metaphor.

'Here, let me get you a drink, your glass is empty. . . .'

He got to his feet slowly. As he did, the effort caused a rictus of pain to flicker like lightning across his face. He poured a generous measure for Mick and a lesser amount for himself. He considered quoting *There is a tide in the affairs of men*, but thought better of it. He continued, 'Were you pleased with the result? Of the meeting, I mean.'

'Yes and no . . .'

'I hope you didn't mind my asking you to leave before we started to discuss the stand?'

'Yerrah not at all. I'd have done the same myself had things been the other way round.'

Mick was grateful of the reminder that he had left the room. Having listened in to every word that was said from outside the door it was quite on the cards that, because of the Glenmorangie and the lateness of the hour, he would refer to something that he wasn't supposed to have heard.

'But to be honest, like I told you before the meeting, t'would have been a help in getting re-elected to have the bloody thing called after me.'

'I remember you saying that but are you really serious about not getting re-elected? After thirty years they can hardly throw you out.'

He nearly added 'at the end of your days', but bit it off just in time. Anyway Mick looked far from a spent force, politically or any other way for that matter. Indeed Julia May had hinted darkly that he was still something of a Lothario though, like the rest of her gossip, it was more suggestion than straightforward assertion. Normally he allowed her to ramble on as much as she wished. The more communication between them, the easier he hoped it would be to talk her out of her visions. But he had cut her short when she began to elaborate on Mick's bedroom escapades. He now regretted doing so.

'Why not? They do it all the time. Especially if some young upstart like Mullarkey is promising them the sun, moon and stars and whispering that I'm past it . . .'

He did not explain precisely what his rival claimed he was past. In a moment he had brightened up again as he continued, 'Anyway, Saint Fintan didn't get the nod either.'

'No, he didn't. He was quite a ladies' man, I believe. I said as much at the meeting.'

Inwardly he smiled at the similarities between Mick and the unlisted saint.

'Look Father, I know you did the best you could for me and no man can do more than that.'

Mick raised his glass in salute to his benefactor and turned his gaze on the picture, still wrapped in newspaper, propped up against the wall.

'What's the picture of, Father? I hope to God it's not another saint. Between Julia May and the poor old Canon this house looked like a match programme for Heaven. All that was missing was the bit of writing below the pictures giving their weight, age and what position they played in!'

'I take your point, though I doubt if my housekeeper would agree. No, in fact it is a portrait of myself, painted a long time ago in Rome. I have been trying to pluck up enough courage to hang it here in my study.'

'And what's stopping you?'

'Julia May for one thing. The comparison, for another.'

'I can understand about her but what do you mean by "comparison"?'

'Oh I suppose the difference between how I was then and now. Not just my appearance, I might add. The face in the picture has a fire in the eye that is no longer there, I fear.'

Mick said nothing. He sensed that the priest was thinking aloud. His head was cocked to one side, his eyes focused on the middle distance.

'It was painted just before my uncle died. He put me through boarding school and the Seminary. He sent me money regularly when I was in Rome. Said it was for Masses, the poor man, but I think he really meant it as an allowance.'

'What did he do, for a living I mean?'

After a long pause Father Jerry's answer came slowly and uncertainly.

'Oh, he was in business. He came from Donegal.'

The tone of the reply did not invite further questions on the subject. They were well into the second bottle, sitting in the study and eyeing the young cleric they had just hung on the wall, when Mick divulged that he had a son a priest. Well, not exactly. 'A spoiled priest', was how he described Sean. 'That a fact? What made him leave?'

He noticed the thickening in his own speech. It irritated him that Mick seemed unaffected by alcohol.

'God knows. I don't anyway. It nearly broke his mother's heart, I can promise you. She was dead set on making a priest out of him.

When the letter arrived from St Joseph's saying he was on his way home, she nearly lost her mind. To tell the truth, she hasn't been the same ever since.'

He did not add that it had also changed their sleeping arrangements. Maggie had moved into a separate bedroom. The Doc had warned her that another pregnancy might be fatal. Mick brought back a packet of contraceptives from Dublin. Producing them at what he believed to be an opportune moment resulted in one of their more spectacular rows. It ended in Maggie moving to another bedroom and the condoms being flung into the kitchen stove.

'I'm sorry to hear that. By a strange coincidence I, too, was a product of St Joseph's. I served the full sentence of six years, but only just! Sean's not the first and certainly won't be the last to decide that the priesthood was not for him. Far worse that he should stay on against his will.'

He said this with such sadness that even Mick, not the most sensitive of men even when completely sober, got most of its import. The Church was swarming with clergy who had been railroaded into Holy Orders. Many families, particularly in the remoter parts, regarded it as a high honour to give a son to the Church. The fact that he might not have been consulted about it was neither here nor there.

'Maybe you're right there, Father. Then again, maybe not. He didn't improve his lot much by coming home, that's for sure.'

'Oh! What happened?'

'Yerrah I sent him to university. He went off on a debating team to Oxford and was caught trying to steal a bloody statue.'

Statues seemed to loom large in the Flannery family.

'A statue? That was rather ambitious. In my day we usually settled for beer mugs or ashtrays. What sort of statue was it?'

'A bust of some bloody writer or other. Sean decided its proper place was back in Ireland. When he was drunk he tried to smuggle it out of the museum under his coat. Someone spotted him and called the police.'

'And then?'

'Oh can't you guess? I pulled a few strings and the charges were dropped. Got it passed off as a silly, student prank. The Embassy weren't a bit pleased, I can tell you. They'd enough on their plates as it was with the shagging IRA blowing up half London at the time without having to bail out the likes of Sean on account of his father. And do you know the thanks I got after it was all fixed up?'

It was hardly necessary to shake his head. Mick was going to tell him anyway.

'Sweet shag all, in pardon to you, Father. That was the thanks I got. Maggie blamed me for making him join the bloody debating society in the first place. Said I wanted him to follow in my footsteps. She was right there, by the way. Sean could make a speech better than myself. He didn't thank me either. Wanted it to go to court, if you don't mind. To attract publicity for the bloody statue or something like that. Didn't bother his arse worrying about what sort of an eejit I'd look with a son barely out of the priesthood when he ends up in jail!'

Mick was beside himself with indignation. He took a drag from his cigarette so deep that it must have sent the smoke down to his toenails.

'What was the end of it?'

'I gave him a one-way ticket to England. Told him not to come back till he got himself straightened out. That was six years ago. Not a squeak out of him since. Could be dead, for all I know. Or in jail, more likely.'

'Does his mother miss him a lot?'

'I'd say so. She never mentions him, though. Keeps it all bottled up inside her, so she does. Between you, me and the wall I'm going to make an appointment for her with the Doc one of these days. She's gone stone mad over this grotto business. Can't talk of anything else. I'll get him to give her something to calm her down before she has the rest of us as bad as herself.'

Another long silence ensued while they digested what had passed between them. Clouds of tobacco smoke swirled around the light overhead. The light blue wisps from Mick's cigarettes played tag with the denser, greyer thunderclouds that issued from the yellow bowl of the pipe.

'That was a bad business up the mountain.'

'The suicide you mean?'

Father Jerry instantly wished he had not said that. Mick was quick to correct him.

'Accidental death was the verdict, they tell me.'

'Death by misadventure, actually. Probably much the same thing. I should know. I signed the papers, didn't I? Have you any idea why he did it?'

'Same as the rest of them, I expect. Thought the good times would never end and farm prices would keep rising for ever. With the banks falling over themselves to dish out money to farmers who could barely sign their names, 'tis hardly surprising that some of them overdid it. Then there was Mullarkey and his likes egging them on to spend big money like there was no tomorrow while I was telling them off the platform that the good times were going to get even better. Yerrah, if we had any sense we'd have known that nothing lasts for ever. Now the prices are dropping, bank interest is going through the roof and Donnelly is looking for his money back. Some poor buggers are caught between the Devil and the deep blue sea. No wonder some of them take what they think is the only way out. If the poor eejits only had the sense to stand their ground and tell the likes of Donnelly to shag off there's not a lot he could do about it!'

'Couldn't the bank sell the farms out from under them?'

'Anywhere else but in Ireland, they could. Not in the land that spawned Captain Boycott. If they only knew it, they could get a good deal from the banks. It's a pity that clown Mullarkey hasn't the brains to see it. No bank that wants to stay in business would dream of evicting anyone, no matter how much money is owed to them. It's all to do with our history, Father. Eviction is a dirty word round here. Reminds people of the Redcoats and rack-rent landlords, so it does. Not the image the banks want, I can tell you. Even if they were daft enough to try a forced sale, no one would buy. At the end of the day, the farmer could buy it back for half nothing. Anyone else buying it would have no neighbours to talk to. His stock would get sick or go missing, that kind of thing. The shops wouldn't serve him either.'

Father Jerry understood. The Mafia did exactly the same thing where they held sway. He refilled their glasses as Mick enquired innocently, 'You'll be burying him in the graveyard, of course?'

Unsure whether it was a question or a command, he nodded to confirm that such was the case. Church law excluded suicides from burial in consecrated ground but now that a sensible verdict had been brought in, the cruel edict did not apply. As for the all-seeing God, he would surely understand. Why he allowed such things to occur if he were truly omnipotent was a question for another day – or night. It was getting late. They would have to finish up after this one. Tomorrow would be challenging enough without the added burden of a hangover.

'I expect you have to go to a lot of funerals – in your official capacity?'

110

'Three a day sometimes, Father. That's more than you'd manage yourself!'

Was there the merest hint of mockery in his voice? Funerals were a major source of income for the clergy. Yet another reason for the Bishop's difficulty in finding a pastor for Brulagh. With its tiny population and their obvious good health, funerals were a rarity.

'I hope so. I would be just as happy to miss tomorrow's, I promise you!'

'Can't say I blame you. More often than not we're burying some poor divil that everyone thought was dead years ago. No matter who it is, any politician worth his salt has to be there. Both the night before for the removal of the remains from the house to the church and then the next day for the funeral Mass and the burial in the graveyard. Not that it does any good being there. It's missing one that counts. Then the relatives will spread it about that Mick Flannery is getting too big for his boots. Make an excuse and try telling them that you are out of the country on "government business" and all they'll say is "government business my backside! More likely the shagger is stuck in some pub, drinking his skull off!" Oh sometimes I think you can't win!'

Sins of omission, Father Jerry ruefully decided, were often the worst. 'Goodnight Mick, we both have a long day tomorrow.'

As he watched Mick's broad back disappearing down the short avenue, he noticed that the only other light visible from the front door was the white neon glare from the Madonna. Dropping the two empty bottles in the rubbish bin, he reflected that to judge by the amount of Glenmorangie Mick had demolished, it might have been a perfectly reasonable assumption on the part of the electorate.

15

'In nomine Patris et Filii et Spiritus sancti. Amen. Introibo ad altare Dei. Ad Deum qui laetificat juventutem meam.'

The Latin rattled around the peeling walls, soaring into the oak rafters supporting the sharply angled roof and re-echoing downwards, finally to settle like an invisible cloak over the bowed heads of the congregation in the half-full church. Well, Father Jerry thought as the familiar words rolled off his tongue while his mind flew on verbal auto-pilot, it makes a change from the cathedrals on the journey from Rome. His swan-song in the Sistine Chapel was performed before a busload of twittering Japanese. They exploded flashbulbs with a fine disregard for the warning notices. A fireworks display on his *grande finale* seemed appropriate. Then *il Duomo*. The Florentines had given him a time slot of 5.30 a.m. in their enormous Medici warehouse of black-and-white marble. It reminded him of those square liquorice allsorts of his youth. Again hordes of tourists chattering among themselves and oblivious to his transforming bread and wine into the Body and Blood of Christ.

To be fair, Chartres had been different. In a dark corner he celebrated the sacrament unobserved. The elderly verger was surprised that he chose Latin. After some hesitation he chimed in with the responses as though Latin were still the dynamo that had powered his church before it became just another flabby multinational. Now that each country prayed in its own dialect, he might just as well have been a salesman for Exxon or IBM. Thankfully Brulagh had not yet adopted guitars and earnest folk-singers. Only a matter of time, he decided glumly as he intoned, 'Lord hear my prayer.'

'And let my cry come unto Thee.'

The cry was discordant. The scattered response gave him a chance to scan forward to his next line. This was in English so the auto-pilot had to be switched off. He hoped his hesitancy with the unfamiliar prayers would be mistaken for extreme piety. Were it not for Joe Gallagher and Julia May he might as well have been conducting a monologue. They shared the front bench with the Flannery family and were first in with responses every time. The altar boy, the youngest Flannery, was so overawed by the occasion as to be rendered speechless. Father Jerry shot a glance at his partner in the revels of last night. Other than looking a trifle pale, Mick seemed unaffected by the second hanging within a week. He wished he could claim the same for himself. His head throbbed unmercifully. Those large whiskies were lethal. Parts of last night were coming back to him in great, indigestible chunks impatiently waiting to be processed into his memory. That blasted portrait had been the cause of it all.

'A reading from the Holy Gospel according to Saint . . .'

Julia May was several lengths ahead, rasping out the response in a voice like a corncrake's that set a raw nerve between his eyes throbbing violently.

'Glory to Thee, O Lord.'

Joe Gallagher cantered in a poor second but was still well clear of the rest of the field.

'In the name of the Father, the Son and the Holy Spirit. My brothers and sisters in Christ, let me begin by saying how happy I am to be among you. In case there are some of you who do not know my name despite the best efforts of the *Clarion* . . .' – an awkward pause here for a communal chuckle that never came – '. . . it is Jerry O'Sullivan. I have served Our Holy Mother the Church in Rome for almost thirty years. Now for health reasons Our Holy Father the Pope has sent me back to my own people to pursue my ministry. It is sad that my first Mass among you should be one for the dead. I would ask you all to bow your heads in prayer for the soul of Patrick for whom this Mass is offered. May the Lord welcome him into his Heavenly Kingdom to find peace among the angels and the saints. May He console Nora and her young family and lessen their grief at his departure from this life . . .'

He caught a glimpse of the bereaved three rows back from the altar. The widow wore black, a veil of fine lace shrouding her face. Her head was bowed and her shoulders heaved in silent grief. A red-eyed Imelda, obeying the Doc's instructions to the letter, was keeping her brothers and sisters in check. Johnny the bootlegger, who was looking after the farm for them, was sitting directly behind the widow.

'. . . The funeral will take place immediately after this Mass. Now some announcements . . .'

He read out details of bingo sessions, collections for the foreign missions, the names of the dead whose anniversaries occurred around that time and the news that the local Praesidum of the Legion of Mary would meet on the following Friday. *Would that be when the grotto business was to be settled once and for all? He still hadn't resumed his interrupted discussion with Julia May on the topic. What about the pilgrimage to Lourdes? Apparently the two visionaries now wished to cancel it. Well that plan should be knocked on the head as soon as possible. Calling off the pilgrimage would only lend respectability to the grotto nonsense. How he was going to get that across without causing offence was a different matter altogether.*

'Go in peace, the Mass is ended.'

Dear God in Heaven, how am I going to live among these people? I know they are my own flesh and blood but they seem so different. Maybe it's just the passage of years that has made them seem so. Yet looking down at the gloomy faces staring back at him with just a hint of curiosity, he had his doubts. Even Mick Flannery in his best suit and shining shoes looked the essence of the respectable burgher. Is there no light left in their lives – no joy, no gaiety – just a suffocating drabness covering their smug indifference?

No, that's not quite fair. Pat Mullarkey seems to have the good of the people at heart. A pity that he has to be so serious about it – and abrasive. And what of Mick, your newfound drinking partner? He wears his world-weariness like a winding sheet. In time it must surely strangle him. Oh to be sure he is a witty and amusing companion! His anecdotes of a lifetime in politics could make the very stones laugh. But he's no longer a serious player. More of a clown prince, really. If he ever had ambitions to change the world, they must have drowned long ago in a sea of drink and cynicism.

As he struggled out of his heavy vestments and asked the junior Flannery to get the incense burning for the blessing of the coffin he pondered what lay ahead. The rubric for the funeral service had seemed quite straightforward when he studied it last evening. Dressed in his black clerical suit, he would march out of the sacristy, past the marble altar, genuflect before the tabernacle and lead the mourners down the aisle and out through the heavy doors to the graveyard behind the church. As he walked slowly ahead of the coffin, he would recite the prayers for the dead:

Requiem aeternam dona ei, Domine. Eternal rest grant unto him,
    O Lord.
Et lux perpetua luceat ei. And may perpetual light shine upon him
Requiescat in peace, Amen. May he rest in peace, Amen.

A mound of fresh earth heaped by a dark gash in the green sward marked the grave. A few muttered prayers, a hurried decade of the rosary – the sorrowful mysteries, of course – then back to Julia May for lunch. He moved towards the bereaved as the first spadefuls of soil crashed down on the coffin. *Why can't they leave that till later? Must they squeeze every last drop of misery out of the terrible tragedy? Why must the mindless idiots start filling in the grave now in front of the grieving family – as though their cup of sorrow were not already full?*

As he placed a comforting hand on the widow's shoulder and braced himself to whisper a few meaningless platitudes in her ear, he saw a familiar face contorted with rage. Almost immediately it started shouting across the open grave. It was hurtling abuse at a well-dressed couple he hadn't noticed till then. Perhaps they had arrived late. The face belonged to Johnny Slattery. His nose still running freely, he was shouting louder now and his words were all too easy to understand as Joe Gallagher grasped him by the shoulder and tried to restrain him.

'It was you, you fucking bastard, that put him in the grave! You and the rest of the bloodsuckers in that fucking bank of yours. If I could get my hands on you I'd . . .'

Before he could finish, Gus Moriarty grabbed him by the scruff of the neck and clamped a hand over his mouth. With the help of Joe Gallagher, the collar of his coat was pulled down to pinion his arms as they frog-marched him away. At first he struggled mightily but by the time they reached the gate he had gone limp between the two men. An uneasy silence descended on those who remained by the graveside – frozen in a tableau of shock and embarrassment. Father Jerry took his hand away from the widow's heaving shoulder and busied himself by putting his breviary in its leather case with great deliberation and then placing his rosary beads back in their pouch. This done, he put it, with studied care, back into his coat pocket. All of this was accomplished in slow motion as though an elaborate mime had to be played out before they could all leave the graveside and go their separate ways. The end could not come too soon, as far as he was concerned.

Julia May was comforting the widow, wrapping her beefy arms around Nora as though to shield her from the raw savagery of the burial ceremony and the eruption that followed it. Donnelly, the bank manager, against whom the tirade had been directed, was preparing to leave with his wife as soon as it was decently possible to do so. He was standing next to the Doc though they had not exchanged a glance, must less a word. Donnelly and his bank, it would seem, had suddenly become the pariahs of Brulagh. Bernie, who had saved the day at that damp squib of a GAA meeting last night, was dabbing at the corners of her eyes with a tissue. Pat Mullarkey, a clearly hungover Mossy and Charley Halpin formed a compact, whispering group. Every so often they cast an anxious glance at the priest to see if he had any notion of bringing the proceedings to a close.

Though his wife was still nowhere to be seen, Mick was slowly but surely taking control of the situation. His children were whispering with Imelda and her brothers and sisters as he signalled the grave-diggers to stop their horrific shovelling. In a suit of shiny blue mohair, gleaming patent leather shoes and a back tie, Mick could have been mistaken for a chief mourner. Which, presumably, was his intention. Father Jerry had started to move away from the graveside when the widow, her eyes swollen and red-rimmed from crying, broke free from her comforters and wordlessly pressed a crumpled brown envelope into his hand. As a mixture of anger and embarrassment welled up inside him, he was distracted by snatches of singing coming from the far side of the stone wall that surrounded the cemetery. Moments later, he recognised it as a hymn from his childhood.

'I'll sing a hymn to Mary, the Mother of God.
When wicked men blaspheme Thee, I'll love and bless Thy Name.'

Maggie, dressed in the flowing robes of the Legion of Mary, was leading a large group in similar garb along the road that led from the grotto. They swarmed through the gates and positioned themselves around the grave, still chanting. Everyone froze in amazement as Maggie addressed the grieving widow.

'I'm sorry we're late, Nora. We would have been in time for the Mass but for what happened at the grotto.'

She said this just loud enough to be heard by those around the grave. What came next was addressed in a much louder voice to everyone present.

'Padre Pio appeared again in a cloud above the grotto. Lots more people saw him this time. He repeated that Our Lady would have a special message to deliver from the grotto on her Feast day. Now I beg all of you to follow me back there to say the holy rosary in preparation for this great honour.'

She approached the bereaved family and invited them to go with her. After a moment's hesitation, they did, leaving Julia May seething in their wake. The dumbstruck priest heard her mutter aloud, 'God knows t'would be more in that one's line to look after her shop and make sure her flour isn't crawling with weevils.'

As Maggie passed her husband, she addressed him sourly, 'I don't

116

suppose we'll be expecting the likes of you to join us. Or that murderer of a bank manager either!'

Without further ado, she swept out through the open gates, shepherding the widow and her family before her. They were followed by her own group and many more who had been attending the funeral. Among them was Charley Halpin, who could be seen fumbling for his notebook.

Mick recovered his composure with admirable speed and made for where Donnelly and his wife were rooted to the spot, not knowing which way to look.

'Sorry for what she said. It's obvious that she's gone clean out of her mind.' In a lower tone he added, 'I know it won't make up for it but I'd like to buy you a drink in O'Shea's. I think we need one after this.'

Without waiting for a reply he took Donnelly's wife by the elbow and steered her towards the gate. Looking back over his shoulder, Mick raised his eyebrows quizzically at the priest as if to say, 'Do you want to join us?'

Father Jerry shook his head and walked along the tarmac footpath that led around the front of the church to the parochial house. In the sanctuary of his study, he flopped down in the padded armchair and let out a deep sigh. He snatched the meerschaum from the pipe-rack and feverishly packed the dark tobacco into its bowl as though his very life depended on it. Scrabbling in his pocket for matches his fingers found the envelope instead. He cringed inwardly as he tore it open. It contained two tired-looking ten-pound notes – a small fortune to the bereaved family. Dear God in Heaven, this was really the last straw! How could he return the money without giving offence? The question preoccupied him for the next hour. Just as he finished lunch, the doorbell rang. Julia May answered it.

'Well I declare to God if it isn't Charley Halpin himself, no less!'

Her glare would have made a less determined caller take to his heels. Instead he dredged up a weak smile and enquired, 'Well, Julia May. Did you enjoy my piece about the grotto? I never mentioned your name, like I promised. Is himself at home?'

'Even if you didn't itself, the whole world and his wife knew well that it was me all the same. Anyway, that's all in the past. I'm not so sure about the whole thing any more. And I, turning it over in my mind, I began to think that Our Blessed Lady jumping around the place might just have been a trick of the light or something.'

117

'Maggie Flannery doesn't think so. Did you see her performance at the funeral?'

'Oh glory be to God, indeed I did. I'm afraid the poor craythur is after losing the run of herself entirely, if you ask me. As for that whelp, Johnny Slattery, I hope the Sergeant lets him rot in jail for the rest of his born days. He deserves no less for fighting on consecrated ground. Not that Donnelly and that brazen wife of his didn't have it coming to them sooner or later. Did you see the skirt she had on her? It hardly covered her backside. There wasn't enough cloth in it to make a coat for a gooseberry.'

Charley was learning fast that when Julia May was in full flow, it was better to cling to the wreckage until her frenzy subsided.

'Can I quote you on that?'

'Indeed you cannot! God knows I'm in enough hot water as it is without you making things worse for me. Did you tell that editor of yours about giving a few sensible recipes in the cookery section?'

'Indeed I did . . .', the lie tripped off his tongue easily and without a moment's hesitation, '. . . the very moment I got back to the office. He said he would attend to it right away.'

She beamed with satisfaction.

'Good, I hope he heeds what I said. Now, you were asking about himself?'

'Yes, I was. Do you think I might have a word with him?'

'Do you have an appointment by any chance?'

'No, I'm afraid not.'

'Then I'll have to ask him first. He usually takes a rest for himself after his lunch. Something he got used to in Italy, if you please. Fine for some, that's what I always say. Wait here till I find him.'

She was gone for a minute or two; then, 'His Reverence will see you now. He's in the study.'

As he crossed the hall in her wake, he could see his reflection in the parquet floor. An elegant grandfather clock with an ornate brass dial ticked like a metronome against the far wall. A carved hall stand with an inlaid mirror stood like a sentinel by the hall door. In its well, intended for walking sticks and umbrellas, stood a few elderly golf clubs. The leather straps that formed their grips flapped loose and their iron heads were pitted with rust. In their midst stood a new fishing rod with a complicated-looking spinning reel attached to its butt. On the white marble top lay a breviary in a black leather case, several unopened envelopes that looked like bills and three rubber eels with vicious-looking hooks protruding from their innards.

A few nondescript woodcuts of faces with sad expressions decorated the walls; the haloes above their heads showed them to be saints. Charley would have expected them to look happier now that their eternal salvation was assured. He avoided stepping on the rugs scattered across the slippery floor as he neared his quarry, a frail-looking cleric in late middle age.

'Hello! My housekeeper tells me you are from the press. The *Clarion*, I believe. I have not had time to read it yet but Julia May speaks highly of it. I understand that she has been interviewed by you. Thank God you didn't quote her direct. What was the name again?'

'Halpin, Father. Charley Halpin.'

'Well now, Mr Halpin, what can I do for you?'

The tone was free of accent as he steepled his fingers and looked the reporter straight in the eye. His voice bore no trace whatsoever of his long stay in Italy. Nor did it reveal that he had observed Charley in his difficult confrontation with O'Shea.

'I'd like to get your own views on the grotto business for a start. I need the official line the Church takes on the matter, as well. Then there is the business of what happened in the graveyard. What do you have to say about Johnny Slattery's attack on the bank manager? I understand that you were at the scene of the – ah, how shall I put it? – accident, I suppose is the best word for it. And what about Maggie Flannery and her followers dragging off the poor widow and her family to the grotto and the corpse hardly cold in the ground?'

Father Jerry emitted a dry chuckle. The sides of his mouth crinkled in a smile that was not reflected in his eyes. They had a steely glint that would have warned off less sensitive reporters than the one seated across the desk from him.

'Certainly, Mister Halpin. That's easily done. As parish priest of Brulagh I have no views whatsoever on any of the matters you have just mentioned. As far as the grotto is concerned, you could best describe my attitude as one of "wait and see". As for Our Holy Mother the Church, I suspect that you may find her views to be much the same. Extreme caution could best express them. Should you require further elaboration, I suggest that you contact the Bishop's secretary. You will find his number in the telephone directory. His views may well carry more weight with your editor than those of a newly appointed parish priest like myself. Likewise the incident in the graveyard. That is a matter for the civil authority. I'm sure

Sergeant Moriarty is well able to handle it. Now, before you go, is there anything else you wish to know, Mister Halpin?'

The silky voice might just as well have been enquiring if he would care for a cup of tea, except for the fact that the speaker had risen from his chair. The interview appeared to be at an end.

'I don't think so, Father. Not for the time being, anyway. I was just hoping to get your angle on the stories before reporters from the big dailies descend on you.'

'I'm afraid I don't quite understand you, Mister Halpin. Why would they do a thing like that?'

Charley had taken enough needling from this urbane cleric. Now it was his turn.

'Because, Father O'Sullivan, when I get back to the office, I'll be filing the story not only with the *Clarion* but with every daily paper in the country. If I get lucky the English tabloids may pick up the story. Moving statues are big news all over the world, Father, and it isn't every day that a story like this ends up in my lap. Out of respect for the widow and Mick Flannery, I'll overlook both the fracas in the graveyard and Maggie leading her troops into battle. But if anyone else gets hold of story, I'll have to write about that too. What's more, I think I may have an interesting angle to it!'

The priest's eyebrows arched questioningly.

'Oh yes . . . ? And what might that be, Mister Halpin?'

'I'll keep my powder dry on that one for the moment, if you don't mind, Father.'

'As you wish, Mister Halpin. I am already only too familiar with your profession's never-ending quest for what you term "interesting angles". I find that it sometimes gets in the way of the truth, however. Do you find that, Mister Halpin?'

The barb struck home.

'No, I don't, Father. What I do find, though, is that people in the same profession, be it mine or yours, tend to cover up for each other.'

'Indeed I suppose they do. But I fail to see the relevance of it in this instance . . .'

He wished he could stop talking like a damn robot and find some way of reaching out to this potentially dangerous enemy. He had a gnawing fear of what was coming next.

'Oh it's relevant all right, Father. I can promise you that. It's just that I don't see where it fits in at the moment. All I'll say for now is that those of us in "the business" usually look after each other and I hope that you're no exception.'

120

Like the grin on the face of the Cheshire cat, the threat hung in the air long after Charley had departed.

16

The snug in O'Shea's was an oasis of solitude. Outside those who had resisted Maggie's invitation to the grotto pressed around the counter trying to catch O'Shea's eye and get a drink. Mick had taken over the snug and slid the bolt home from the inside, thereby ensuring that they would be safe from unwelcome visitors. Through the tiny serving hatch he called for large brandies all round.

'Jaysus, that was awful. I'm in two minds about which was worse!'

'I don't quite follow you, I'm afraid.'

As he spoke, Donnelly harrumphed several times, then swiftly lowered the level of his brandy by half while staring sourly at its provider. His disapproval at the turn the conversation was taking enveloped them like an invisible cloud. Mick decided he had better keep this feast of reason and flow of the soul going for as long as possible. There were fences to be mended and now was the time to do it. Courvoisier, like time, was a great healer.

'I mean it's a toss-up as to which of the pair of them, Maggie or Johnny, made the bigger eejit out of themselves.'

Though it appeared on the surface to be an explanation of sorts, Mick uttered it in the form of a question. He was desperately trying to assess just how offended they were by Maggie's accusation. Because of his large overdraft in Donnelly's bank and the increasingly strident tone of his letters requesting a meeting 'at your earliest convenience', Mick was determined not to worsen his already delicate situation. Maggie's calling Donnelly a murderer was not calculated to lessen his zeal for recouping his bank's money from the Flannery tribe.

'To be honest, she's not been well in herself this past while. The damn grotto has her driven half mad.'

Josephine Donnelly decided to rescue this large, awkward man from the hole he was digging for himself. She had met him many times before but never at such close quarters. He had invariably been surrounded by a phalanx of stocky men wearing tweed caps and shiny suits with waistcoats. To a man they affected a gold chain and a pocket watch, drooping just below the naval, which they examined uneasily when their man dallied over-long on the voters' doorsteps. They wore the chain as a badge of integrity and respectability in an otherwise decadent world where a vote wrongly cast could plunge the world into turmoil – if not outright war. They would descend from their mountain fastnesses before every election to answer the call to get out the vote for Michael John Flannery – hurler *extraordinaire* and defender of the people's rights for longer than anyone cared to remember. They knew the names and voting habits of everyone, even those who lived at the end of the long, twisting roads that wormed their way through the Flannery bailiwick.

Without his henchmen, Mick seemed isolated and vulnerable. Not bad looking either, despite his years. Understandable, she supposed, when he was once reputed to have been the fittest man to take the field at Croke Park. Not that she would have known anything about those dreadful Gaelic games. Her family regarded them as the sport of the masses. As for Tom, he was a rugger bugger to the core. He regarded the GAA as somewhere between the Mafia and the Provisional IRA. Josephine attempted to console Mick Flannery by saying, 'She's not the only one. That old cow Julia May thought she saw Padre Pio smiling down on her from the clouds, for crying out loud! Wonder how he got there? Alitalia I suppose. Or maybe by Aer Lingus, our friendly airline. They call their planes after saints. "We regret that Saint Patrick will be late landing in Lourdes due to problems with his undercarriage!" '

Josephine's mimicry of a harassed air hostess was perfect. Mick laughed aloud, a mixture of relief and amusement. She was off again.

'Did you see the look on the priest's face? He must have thought he was at a pantomime or something. When Johnny started effing and blinding I thought he was going to fall into the grave with embarrassment. That really would have cast a gloom over the whole proceedings!'

'You may be closer to the truth than you think! I had a few drinks with him last night. I can tell you this. The man is not well in himself at all, that's for sure. He has a painting of himself done a few years ago and you'd think it was his son rather than himself that was in it.'

'Ah good old Dorian Gray again, I suppose.'

'I don't know who painter was, it might have been for all I know. But however bad he's looking, I can tell you he's a good judge of whiskey. That and Julia May's cooking will have him back in shape in no time.'

Ignoring the gaffe, she burned away the smirk starting to form around her husband's mouth with a ferocious glare. So fierce, in fact, that he muttered something about having to get back to the office, and left almost immediately.

'Or out of shape more likely, a bit like yourself . . .' She mocked his waistline with a mixture of disapproval and awe.

'By any chance did he tell you why they sent him back to a dump like this after Rome?'

'No he didn't. But, like I say, the man's not well.'

'So they sent him home to die, you mean? Well they sure as hell sent him to the right place. Everyone's half-dead already round here, if you ask me.'

'You don't find life in Brulagh too exciting then?'

She didn't nibble at the bait. She swallowed it hook, line and sinker. She was much younger than her husband. Her wanton pose was slowly but surely driving Mick to distraction. Seated well back from the table, a double brandy in one hand, a cigarette in the other, she was both a balm and a temptation to his troubled mind. Languidly she crossed one leg over the other to display an expanse of thigh that would have aroused a dead monk. Did she realise the effect she was having on him, he wondered? Of course she did! The sheer muzzle velocity of her reply staggered him momentarily.

'Jesus Christ Almighty the place is like a bloody morgue. There isn't a decent pub or restaurant within miles of here . . .'

While Mick agreed with her, he wished she would keep her voice down. O'Shea was notoriously sensitive, especially regarding the décor of his premises, and had barred people for less. Though Mick disliked O'Shea intensely, he did use his place for the occasional clinic and the next pub was seven miles away. But there was no stopping her. She was in full flight.

'. . . For God's sake, the biggest thing on the calendar is the Harvest Festival, would you believe! Oops, sorry, I forgot about the centenary thingummy. My husband tells me the whole show is really to honour you.'

Not quite what he had said. Nothing remotely like it in fact. '*A booze-up to celebrate the miracle that the biggest bloody conman since Barnum has avoided cirrhosis up till now, despite all the odds*', was how the dreary bastard had described it. When he heard that Mick had failed to get the new stand named after him, Donnelly had perked up and become almost cheerful. Only the fact that it had been a clear victory for Pat Mullarkey had dampened his jubilation. Even so, he had indulged himself in an unprecedented second glass of sherry while his wife downed her fourth vodka martini before dinner. She was bored out of her mind and fighting with her husband. She wished she could tell this great bear of a man that she was looking for a new focus to her life, as recommended in the current issue of *Cosmopolitan*.

'Yerrah not at all, girl,' Mick said dismissively. 'It's all in aid of the GAA. If I'm lucky, I get to make the opening speech, that's all.'

'Talking of speeches, I hope you'll take care of that side of it at the wine-making competition.'

'Sure, no problem at all. That's my job, after all. I tell everyone how great they are and how good things are going to be in the future for them!'

'And do they believe you?'

'Some do, some don't . . .'

The latter were a growing majority, he reflected ruefully. He perked up again as the full significance of her remark sank in. He suddenly remembered that the pair of them were to give out the prizes for the wine-making competition.

'I hear they're going to make a judge out of you. For the wine competition, I mean,' he said.

'Yeah, someone talked me into it. Wasn't you, by any chance, Mick? If it was, I'll have your guts for garters.'

'Oh I swear to God it wasn't me, Josephine. I hope you don't mind if I call you that?'

She shook her head so vehemently that her long blonde hair temporarily dropped like a curtain over her face. She delicately drew aside the veil of hair with fingers tipped with a blood-red nail varnish and peered out at him in a way that aroused him to an almost unbearable extent. So much so, in fact, that he shouted the order for two more brandies to O'Shea rather than risk the embarrassment of standing up and whispering it discreetly through the serving hatch.

'Oh most certainly not,' he went on. 'I'd never walk a fine-looking woman like yourself into something like that. I'd be more inclined to think it was Pat Mullarkey. Or his wife. If either of them had any brains they'd be dangerous. Nothing they'd like better than to drop you in it, I can tell you. Or rather your husband. But if they can't nail him, then you'll do nicely!'

'Well thanks a lot, Mick. You really have the knack of making a girl feel wanted!'

Her sarcasm was softened by a wide smile that showed off her perfect teeth to good effect. Before he could correct himself she had the floor again.

'Anyway, that's no way to talk about the treasurer and trainer of the famous Saint Fintan's hurling team?'

Her voice had a lilt to it that he found quite entrancing. How, he asked himself, had he failed to notice what a beauty she was until now. Well Mick, he consoled himself, better late than never. Mention of the hurling team momentarily changed his lust to exasperation.

'Jaysus, you don't call that lot a hurling team, do you? They wouldn't win an argument for God's sake. As for Mullarkey, that little bollix couldn't train ivy up a wall!'

'Such language! I'm surprised at you, Mick Flannery. I thought all politicians were silver-tongued charmers.'

'Sorry, I got carried away there for a minute . . .' He tried to look suitably contrite as she interrupted him.

'Tell me, Mick, do you often let yourself get carried away?'

He paused and drew a deep breath. It was always the same. There came a time in some encounters, sporting or amorous, when you had to throw caution to the four winds and go for it bald-headed, regardless of the consequences. Much of his success on – and off – the playing field lay in recognising when such a moment had arrived. It was heralded by a tingling sensation running up and down his spinal vertebrae, which caused the hairs on the back of his neck to stand out like so many antennae. Now, for the first time in ages, the tingle was back.

'Only when I'm alone with a really beautiful woman like yourself,' he replied.

They stared at each other for a what seemed a lifetime, until she broke the spell by lighting another cigarette. He took a sip from his glass and luxuriated in the warmth of the brandy sliding down his throat like a torchlight procession. Her skirt, whether by accident or design, had ridden up even higher. Perhaps it was just the awkward shape of the chair that caused it. Like every other item of furnishing in O'Shea's establishment, it seemed to have been designed with the customer's utmost discomfort in mind. Hungrily shifting his gaze from thigh to bosom he slowly raised his eyes till they locked on to hers. He was fascinated by her sensuous lips as she inhaled deeply from her cigarette and drained her glass.

'Do you think we could meet again? Somewhere more private than this, of course, like my apartment in Dublin or Rose Cottage?' he asked.

For Mick, the world stood still. The sounds from outside the snug suddenly became magnified and crystal clear like voices drifting across calm water. It seemed that Johnny's name was on everyone's lips. No snatch of conversation that drifted into the silent vacuum of the snug failed to include him in some shape or form. Josephine took a deep drag on her cigarette, exhaled a cloud of smoke and watched it spiral slowly towards the ceiling. Then, as if Mick had never made what might have been considered an improper suggestion, she asked about Johnny's future.

'What's going to happen to him? Do you think Gus will press charges?'

'Not unless you or your husband presses charges, I'd say. Mind you, I don't think Johnny's your husband's biggest fan.'

'I know that. Neither are you, for that matter. I gather you are high up on his mailing list!'

'Oh indeed I am. Nearly number one, I'd say . . .'

The only number one he was likely to get from the smarmy bastard, he thought, before pressing his suit further.

'I need another one of these just to even think about it. Will you join me?'

She nodded. He relished the gloss on her lips. He had never seen anything like it before, certainly not in Brulagh. It made her look like a film star. When she smiled those teeth semaphored all kinds of erotic messages to his confused brain. He tried to remember what it was they reminded him of . . . Ah yes, that was it, of course! They were just like the tombstones he had seen on a junket to the war graves at Arnhem. Rows and rows of even, rounded marble slabs. The memory of that enormous cemetery jerked him back to his original purpose for being here.

'Jesus, that was an awful carry-on in the graveyard wasn't it?'

'Would Johnny have taken a sup of his own brew?'

'He's no genius but he's not that big an eejit either. Sure that bloody stuff is only for greyhounds and sick animals.'

'What do you mean, greyhounds?'

'The woman who was in the bank before you could have told you all about it. She used to race them. Or try to, only she was too mean to feed them properly. Then someone told her that if you spat a mouthful of poteen into the dog just before he went into the traps, it would make him run like the Devil himself was after him. She was arguing for a week with Johnny over the price of a naggin of poteen – she was too mean to buy a full bottle. Anyway they struck some sort of a deal in the end. She had the fill of the naggin in her mouth, with the jaws of the dog held open like a crocodile so that she could spit the poteen down his throat and close the jaws again to make sure he swallowed all of it . . .' He paused to gulp down the Courvoisier.

'Well go on, for God's sake, don't stop now! What happened after that?'

She was beside herself with excitement. She simply had to know the fate of the daft old bat who lived above the bank before she arrived on the scene.

'Well just as she had her mouth full of Johnny's cheapest, didn't someone clap her on the back and say "Hello Missus, I haven't seen you in ages!" '

He took another gulp, which drained the balloon glass.

'Two more Tom, like a good man, and don't be all day about it. I've a thirst on me that would drown a whale.'

'Are you going to tell me what happened, Mick, or do I have to drag it out of you?'

He concluded the story before her impatience turned to truculence, 'Yerrah the slap on the back made her swallow the whole lot herself. It took the best part of a week in the intensive care with a stomach pump working day and night to get Johnny's poison out of her.'

He had to pause to allow her to get her breath back. Tears of laughter were streaming down her face as she groped for a cigarette.

'. . . That's how bad it is. So don't say you haven't been warned!'

'Oh Mick, that's the funniest thing I've heard in ages. You really are a scream. Are you always like this? Did that really happen or were you only having me on?'

The thought of having her, on or off, filled his mind to the exclusion of all else. Then, discarding the glorious dream, he dragged himself back reluctantly to the here and now.

'That I may be struck dead by a bolt of lightning if every word of it wasn't the gospel truth itself. Mind you, he might have given her a bad drop on purpose. Johnny never liked banks.'

'You don't have to tell me that! Your wife seems to hold similar views.'

'Sorry, I didn't mean it like that.'

'I know. Forget it – especially the last crack. My husband always tells me that I get tetchy as I get tiddly. Look, as we're here, hadn't we better get something organised about the bloody wine thing. Remember you promised to do all the speechifying. Do you want to help me judge the wine too?'

'Not on your life, I'll leave that to you. I've enough enemies as it is without making more by not picking their bloody bottle.'

'Yeah, maybe you're right at that. Right then, I'll do the judging and you do the rest. OK?'

'Fine. How will you decide which one is the winner?'

'Oh it won't be so difficult. Most of them will have mysterious rope-like things swirling around inside the bottle. Others will be bubbling – fine for champagne but not what you want in a still wine. More of them will taste like vinegar. That should only leave one or two in with a chance. Simple, really!'

'Well I hope so. A few years back Johnny Slattery won the first prize for vegetables with a cauliflower he bought from Maggie. I wonder if he'll have an entry in the wine competition. If he does, be sure not to swallow it or you'll finish up in intensive care like that other one.'

'Does he really make a lot of poteen?'

'No one knows for sure. Gus Moriarty says he has the trade of the whole county. Though to look at Johnny, you'd give him a penny if you didn't know he was in the business. His mother looks after him. They live in a cottage at the top of the mountain that you'd be ashamed to give to a pig.'

'Does he keep pigs?'

'Funny you should say that. Mullarkey went up to him one time to try to get him to go in for pigs. He was going on about the great money there was in them, the grants that Johnny could get which would mean he'd have the whole piggery for half nothing, how much money he'd make out of them, all the usual nonsense that an agricultural instructor goes on with. Anyway Johnny kept on saying it wouldn't be fair. Eventually Mullarkey got mad and asked him what the hell he meant by "it wouldn't be fair".'

'I'll tell you, you four-eyed bastard, if you'll only let me get a word in edgeways! My mother already cooks my meals, washes my clothes, looks after the house, the sheep, the few cows and the hens. It wouldn't be fair to ask her to look after a whole lot of pigs as well, now would it?'

'That's a great story, Mick. Sorry but I don't believe one word of it. Now, while you were rambling on about Johnny and his pigs, I was considering what you suggested earlier. About us, I mean.'

He tried to divine his fate from her expression. He cursed himself for blowing it. His clumsy attempt at seduction had offended her but she was too vain to let it show. She's going to walk out on me with a withering look of disdain. The brandy she had drunk might even spark a scene, which would please O'Shea no end. It would be yet another incident in an already hectic day. The whole bloody village would hear about it before nightfall. What she *did* whisper, as she leaned across the table to peck his cheek, was much more encouraging than he could have expected.

'Sounds like a great idea, Mick. It not every day a girl gets invited to bed with a legend in his own lifetime. Nevertheless, I need time to think about it. The bank will appraise you of its decision on your application in due course, as my dear husband might put it.'

Her laugh tinkled like crystal bells as she gathered up her cigarettes and lighter and put them back in her handbag. Wordlessly she closed it with a click, rose to her feet and swept out of the snug. Only the cupid's bow of her lipstick on the glass was proof that it had not been just an erotic daydream. Mick finished his drink and settled up with O'Shea. His next call would be to Father Jerry. He would have to apologise for Maggie and see how the poor man had survived his first funeral.

17

'Hallo, hallo! Is that Father O'Sullivan? It is? Good. Can you hold
on and I'll put you through to the barracks, the Sergeant wants to
talk to you.'

After a good deal of static and two loud clicks as Mary Mullarkey
made the connection, the voice of Gus Moriarty crackled across the
line. It might have been easier for him to stand outside the door and
bawl his message up the street to the parochial house. Father Jerry
decided that if the bright new future heralded by Mick Flannery was
about to dawn in Brulagh, it might well begin with the telephone
system. With one ear glued to the handset, he sealed off the other
with the palm of his hand the better to determine what it was that
was troubling Gus.

'Hello Father. I hope I'm not disturbing you but I have a man
here who you might want a word with . . . Johnny Slattery, that's
who . . . No, can't call up to your house because I'm holding him
here under lock and key . . . Well not until he promises to behave
himself . . . I know, sure I've been trying to talk some sense into his
thick skull but he doesn't take a blind bit of notice . . . I was hoping
you might succeed where I failed . . . T'would save a lot of trouble
for everyone if you could try to talk a bit of sense into him . . . Right
then Father, I'll be expecting you shortly.'

*What does he want me to do? Threaten Johnny that by the Divine Power
vested in me by Almighty God I'll stick him to the floor of his cell or transform
him into a mountain sheep? Better not, on second thoughts. Turn him into a
sheep, I mean. Johnny might regard that as more of a blessing than an affliction
if the rumours concerning his vices of mountain men are to be believed.*

It was his first time inside the barracks. Its dilapidated exterior
was not reflected inside. Though the floorboards were bare, they were
well scrubbed. The walls were painted a dull cream and draped with
notices warning of the dire penalties in store for those who encouraged
the spread of rabies, noxious weeds, the warble fly or the non-
payment of dog licences. A sturdy table, piled high with official-
looking papers, was the centrepiece of the room. On it lay a few
biros, two pencils and a large pair of scissors neatly arranged round
a wooden mushroom with hooks from which hung an assortment of

important-looking rubber stamps. The Sergeant's blue cap with its shiny black plastic peak lay on the table next to the telephone. Beside it a 'sit-up-and-beg' typewriter, even older than the Smith-Corona in his own study, took pride of place in the middle of the table. A sheet of typing paper protruded from its top. When Father Jerry walked in, Gus abandoned whatever he was writing, his index fingers poised in mid-air like a concert pianist about to pound the closing bars of a concerto. He rose from his chair and extended a hand in welcome.

'Thanks for coming, Father. I have himself locked in the cell. 'Twill give the rogue a chance to cool down a bit while I make up my mind what to do with him. I phoned the bank and Donnelly won't press charges, thank God, though I haven't told our jailbird that yet. I can't let him out if he's going to create ructions again the minute he's free. He won't listen to me so I was hoping you might be able to get through to him.'

Father Jerry nodded without enthusiasm. If Gus had failed, he wasn't optimistic of his own chances of success. However, it would seem churlish to refuse. He was beginning to like the Sergeant. Their first meeting had not gone all that well. He felt that Gus had been less than helpful about naming the stand in front of which they were talking while Gus took a breather from marking the pitch. He seemed quite unconcerned about the grotto business as long as it did not create a traffic problem. He had been less than forthcoming when questioned about Maggie. That and other straws in the wind left Father Jerry with the impression that one didn't have to scratch Gus too deeply to find a devout anti-cleric. Later, at the meeting, he had shown his true colours. What looked like a case of running with the hare while chasing with the hounds, in the struggle between Mullarkey and Mick Flannery, proved to be a result of the Sergeant's genuine respect for both parties coupled with an understandable wish not to offend either. It was this that made him seem ambivalent. Now the man was almost effusive in his welcome and the priest decided to respond in like manner.

'I can but try, Sergeant. Where is he?'

They went through a narrow door with panes of frosted glass to light the dark, narrow corridor. At the very end was a stouter door with a small iron grill bolted into it. Behind this languished an unrepentant Johnny. Father Jerry went inside while Gus returned to his desk.

'Well Johnny, this is a fine mess you've got yourself into and no mistake. If your mother heard about your performance in the grave-yard she'd have your life. How is she keeping anyway?'

'Only poorly, Father. Her chest is at her day and night. Doctor Buckley is still trying to get her into the hospital. For all the good 'twill do her!'

This last was said more to himself and in so quiet and dejected a voice as to make it almost inaudible.

'I'm sorry to hear that, Johnny. But I'm sure you'll agree that news of all this won't make her any better. The Sergeant says he'll let you out of here this minute without a charge or anything if you'll sign a bit of paper promising that you will be of good behaviour for the future.'

'Does that mean I have to stand aside and leave Donnelly get away with it?'

'Get away with what, Johnny?'

'With selling the farm out from under Nora and her children, that's what I mean . . .'

His tone had suddenly become aggressive, so much so that the priest felt vaguely uneasy at sharing the small confines of the cell with him. He let him continue.

'I know you're only new to the job but I thought you would have known that much, at least.'

'Nobody told me anything like that was going to happen. I'm sure neither Mr Donnelly nor his bank would dream of doing such a thing.'

'They won't if I can help it, that's for sure and certain, because I'll strangle the bloodsucker with my own bare hands the moment I get out of here. What charge is Moriarty holding me on, anyway?'

'He didn't tell me. I hardly spoke to him on my way in. But I expect it's for something like causing an affray or disturbing the peace. If he thought you were drunk, he could charge you with being drunk and disorderly as well as everything else. It could work out expensive for you, in the long run.'

'Hang the expense! I'll see Donnelly in hell first. After that I'll worry about the money.'

'Johnny, Johnny . . . Can't you go easy?'

He tried to make his voice as soothing as possible.

'Who's going to look after your mother when you go to jail? Because that's where you'll go, if you don't leave Donnelly alone. Who will mind the farm? Not to mention your promise to Doctor Buckley that you would help that poor widow, Nora, with her farm too? How can

133

you manage to do all that if you are locked up inside a jail for the next couple of years?'

Johnny lapsed into a sullen silence. It was obvious that some of the steam had gone out of him as he sought an answer to the questions posed by the priest.

'I won't apologise to that bastard, if that's what you're asking me to do. Nor will I sign anything for that shagger out there . . .' – he cocked a thumb towards the corridor lest the priest was in any doubt to whom he was referring – '. . . He's been out to get me since Adam was a boy. Just because he never managed to catch me with the still, he thinks he can get his own back on me this way instead.'

'Oh I don't know so much about that, Johnny. I'd be surprised if the Sergeant was as small-minded as that. He's only doing his job, after all. I mean, you did kick up quite a rumpus in the graveyard. You may have meant well but you know as well as I do that you can't carry on like that and expect to get away with it for long. You gave me such a fright I nearly fell into the grave. As for Nora, I don't think she approved of it either.'

'Well I'm sorry, Father, if I gave you a bit of a start. That's the very last thing in the world I intended. God knows, my mother talks about you all the time. As for Nora, I wouldn't want to harm a hair on her head. It was only for her sake I had a go at Donnelly. The man means nothing to me.'

'If that's the case, how can you blame him for what happened?'

'The lousy bastard was writing letters to poor Paddy this while past. That was what drove him to it in the end. Donnelly and that other lunatic Mullarkey with his grand schemes. Paddy should have run him out of the farmyard with a pitchfork like I did instead of paying heed to his daft ideas. Paddy, the poor eejit, spent a fortune on milking-machines and fertiliser when he would have been better off putting what money he had under the mattress. Anyway, neither you nor I can do much to bring him back now.'

'Indeed no, Johnny, you're right there. Look, what do you think of this for an idea? If I tell the Sergeant that I'll be responsible for your good behaviour, then you won't have to sign anything or apologise to Donnelly either.'

'Would you really do that for me, Father? You hardly know me.'

'Of course I would, Johnny. That's what I'm here for, isn't it? But, of course, you would have to give me your word that you won't go gunning for Donnelly, or his wife for that matter, the minute you're out of here.'

Johnny spat on the floor in disgust.

'Whatever about him, I wouldn't touch that hoor of a wife of his with a forty-foot barge pole. Did you see her at the funeral? You'd think 'twas a dance she was going to with the get-up of her! No, you have my solemn word Father, I'll leave the two of them alone if you'll just get me out of here.'

'I'll do better than that, Johnny. I'll just have a quick word with the Sergeant to make sure everything is in order for your release, then I'll drive you back to your own place myself. I'd been meaning to call on your mother again, anyway. Not that we'll breathe a word of all this to her.'

'Begod Father, you're one decent man and no mistake. When I saw you first with that big car under your backside, I thought you'd have your nose stuck up in the air like the rest of them. Now I'll be the first to admit that I was wrong about you. I'll be gathering up my few things here while you square it with Moriarty.'

The moment he got in the car, Johnny slumped in the front seat and lapsed into a deep silence. It was another perfect summer day. Bird song mingled with the throaty burble of the Alfa as it accelerated out of one corner before braking for the next one on the torturous route to Johnny's lofty retreat. Father Jerry had the sun roof open to its fullest extent, as well as all four windows. The reasons for this were twofold. One was weather. The other was the unmistakable fact that his passenger had not washed for some time. In the silence, he tried to convince himself that Johnny was immature, rather than raving mad. What happened in the cemetery when linked to his sudden mood changes did little to support the case for his sanity. Suppose he were to become unhinged again and attack him in the car? He told himself to stop over-reacting. The wretch was just one of those people who were easily upset, that was all. Whether this was fuelled by his own brew or by hatred of Donnelly and his ilk remained shrouded in mystery. The silence was unnerving. Father Jerry was trying to think of something to say when the sight of an old man on a steep hillside with two donkeys hitched to a plough caused him to stop. He watched in amazement as the ploughman stopped to lever a large rock from the path of the furrow with a heavy crowbar.

'What's he doing that for, Johnny? Wouldn't you think he would have a bit of sense, whoever he is, and let the grass grow into hay instead of making all that work for himself? What else would grow on that bit of ground anyway?'

What sounded like the side of the car scraping against the low stone wall proved to be Johnny laughing uproariously.

'Oh faith then there's no fear of him, Father. He's a second cousin of my mother's. I told him that if he grew a certain class of spuds for me I'd pay him well for it. He's ploughing the ground for them, that's what he's doing now . . .'

A short pause for another cackle before he resumed, 'The auld shagger is too mean to hire a tractor so he tackled up the donkeys to do it on the cheap.'

'Won't he be half the year at it?'

'More than likely, Father . . .' – Johnny was untroubled by the prospect of his distant relative working himself to death – '. . . but I won't need the spuds for a long time yet. When the Lord made time, he had plenty of it.'

'Do you grow any spuds yourself?'

'No Father, 'twould make it too obvious. Are you from farming stock yourself?'

'Indeed I am. Everyone belonging to me came from the land. From the same sort of terrain as this, but in Sligo. All my family were farmers.'

'Were they now? Begod you wouldn't think it from the look of you . . .'

He wondered whether that was meant as compliment or not as Johnny persisted in his cross-examination.

'You'd be well used to making hay then, I suppose.'

It was somewhere between a statement and a question.

'Indeed I would, Johnny, though it's nearly forty years since I held a hayfork in my hand.'

Suddenly Johnny, the car, even the scenery drifted away to be replaced by a big hayfield. In the twinkling of an eye he was trapped in the past. It was a golden day with all the family and three sets of neighbours as well in the meadow. Haymaking brought out the best in them because it needed co-operation. When the hay was ready for harvesting on several farms at the same time there was nothing for it but to organise themselves into groups who moved from one field to the next transforming the swathes of hay into wynds. These were golden cones, six feet high, sculpted with two-pronged forks by men who had learned the skill from their forefathers. To build a wynd that would withstand storm and rain until it was brought into the barn was no easy task. To make two hundred of them on a hot summer day was sheer slavery.

136

The work could only be done in fine weather. As a boy, Jerry would welcome the sudden showers that poured out of a clear sky. They offered a respite from piking the hay up to the man on the wynd, a back-breaking job whose only reward would be a mug of strong tea from a big milk churn and a thick wedge of home-made bread smeared with butter. And, of course, the talk. That was the best part of all. It only happened at teatime. He would sit in the shade and listen to the men talk of summers long ago and the oddities of neighbours alive and dead. He remembered the drowsiness that descended on them along with the swarms of midges that plagued them as they sweated through the long hours.

Then there were the horse-flies. Those horrible, long-winged vampires that landed so gently on exposed flesh and bit deep until they found a vein. The bravest would let them drink their fill, painful though it was, until they gorged themselves. Then, like a pricked balloon, they would burst, leaving flecks of dried blood on the arm as a badge of valour. He tried to do it a few times but always slapped the bloodsucker dead before it exploded. Even now he remembered the agony of an aching back as he got to his feet for another four hours of piking before the evening dew made the hay too damp. What drove him to such superhuman efforts was the age-old dream of youth – to prove himself as good as his elders.

When a field was finished they moved on to the next one. It seemed never-ending. Even when the last wynd had been fashioned and secured with ropes to prevent it being blown off the mountainside, the harvesting was far from over. Wynds were left to 'cure' in the field for a month and then winched up on to a horse-drawn hayfloat. The winch was worked by levers with long wooden handles at the front of the float. As the ratchet bit into the cog of the winch, it made a grating sound like a corncrake. Sometimes the ratchet slipped and the load slid back down the float on to the grass amid a flurry of curses and wildly spinning cogs. It was then that accidents happened.

And when all went well and the weight of the wynd forced the float back to the horizontal with a loud crash, even the quietest horse might take fright. It was Jerry's job to hold the horse's head while the safety bolt was banged home. He would perch precariously on the end of the float with the wynd blocking him from the driver's view. A bumpy field or stony gap would work the locking bolt loose and the float would suddenly tip backwards into the loading position. When this happened anyone sitting behind had to jump off quickly or their legs would be crushed between the back of the float and the

137

hard ground. Though it was forbidden to ride on the back, the driver could not see and it was more fun than a long walk from the hayfield to the barn after every load.

Of course it had to happen. His mother caught him at the dangerous game of hitching a ride. The shock of it made her lose her temper. As she slapped him across the face, her words stung even more than the blows.

'Do you want to end up dead in a ditch like your poor father? Is that it? 'Tis bad enough to have to drag you up without a man in the house except that drunken fool of an uncle of yours without you trying to kill yourself like that!'

It was the only occasion on which she referred to the circumstances of his father's death. It wasn't until years afterwards that he prevailed on his uncle to reveal the gruesome details. The two brothers had been celebrating a particularly good sale of poteen by drinking the brew straight from the still. One brother staggered home from the mountain where they had hidden the equipment. The other fell asleep in a ditch. It rained heavily that night and a mountain stream overflowed into the ditch, drowning the senseless bootlegger.

The family concocted some story to satisfy the coroner but it wasn't believed. At the inquest, the police claimed the circumstances were still unclear and applied to have the inquest adjourned. Though everyone in the locality knew the true story, no one assisted the law in their enquiries. When the coroner resumed the hearing, he found the police no nearer the truth. He made some remarks about their being met with a wall of silence and brought in a verdict of accidental death.

His uncle remained unmarried but looked after his brother's wife and her only son. In time he became the most prosperous bootlegger in the west of Ireland. When Jerry was twelve, he was sent to a boarding school run by the Jesuits. It was, in reality, a nursery for the priesthood. His fees were paid every term but when he went on for the priesthood, they were refunded to his uncle. This money was put in trust for him. His progress through the Seminary was smooth but unspectacular. There had been no Road to Damascus, rather it seemed as if by common consent his future would lie in the Church. He never remembered discussing his vocation, if he ever actually had one, with anyone. His mother did not live long enough to hear him say his first Mass but the uncle threw a lavish reception in a local hotel to celebrate his nephew's ordination.

He was studying for a doctorate in theology in Rome when Castelli headhunted him for the diplomatic service. As he wafted out of the time warp, Castelli's cherubic features gave way to the gaunt face of Brulagh's leading bootlegger. He hoped Johnny's silence was caused by trying to come to grips with enormity of his behaviour at the graveside. Then again, perhaps he was contemplating his recent good fortune. The intervention of one Jeremiah O'Sullivan to effect his release from the clutches of the law must surely be preoccupying him.

If the truth were known, such speculations were well wide of the mark. Johnny was trying to decide if he should take this kindly cleric into his confidence. He had an innate distrust of uniforms of any sort. That included black suits and dog collars. When he eventually recovered the priceless gift of speech it was to drop the biggest bombshell yet in a day that had not been lacking in incident for the new shepherd of the Burlagh flock. Digging deep inside his coat pocket, Johnny fished out a grimy envelope.

'I got this last week. I wasn't going to show it to you at all. I didn't know how you would take it, for one thing. Anyway I didn't want to admit it straight out to you that I'm in the business. But now that you've treated me fair and square, 'tis only proper order that I do the right thing by you.'

He took the letter out of the envelope and passed it across. It read

Dear Johnny Slattery,

You don't know me from Adam but we're both in the same line of business. I hear your merchandise is as good as my own. I have a big sale for it around the border. The trouble is that between the police and the military, there's no chance of making enough of it to keep up with the demand. I'll be calling on you in the near future to talk business. In the meantime I hope you have plenty of stock laid in somewhere safe.

All the best for now,
Freddie O'Sullivan

p.s. I see by the newspaper that your new parish priest is a cousin of mine. Perhaps he'll give us both his blessing! We might even cut him in on the deal if he's able to keep the law off us!

As the Alfa surged ever upwards, the two men were lost in thought. So this was to be the last judgment. Each man must confront his destiny at some stage of his life. Father Jerry had been close to it on several occasions. There was a time in the *barrios* of São Paulo when he thought to throw in his lot with those fighting desperately for justice. In the end he packed his bags and went back to Rome. He thought for a moment that the bleak family skeleton might fall out of the cupboard when his friend and colleague, Gianni Manolo Agostini ran the ruler over him before appointing him secretary to Castelli. But if he found anything, he kept it to himself. Agostini certainly knew about the uncle. When he enquired about him in Boggola, he seemed amused that he should have succumbed to cirrhosis of the liver and muttered something about 'Those who live by the sword . . .' Never in his wildest fantasies did he dream that his chickens would come home to roost on the side of a barren mountain, part of an inhospitable offshore rock called Ireland. Johnny was talking again.

'I knew you were in the business the moment you asked me "How's the business?" the first time you called up to see my mother. Is your man really a cousin of yours or is he only having me on?'

'I expect he must be if he says so.'

'Jaysus, I hope you don't mind if I do business with him. I've a lot of stuff left over from last Christmas. I could do with a few bob to send the Ma to Lourdes. It might cure her. What do you think yourself, Father?'

They were at the gate to Johnny's farmyard. Father Jerry turned the car with difficulty, not concentrating properly on what he was doing. His mind was racing madly, a maelstrom of emotions from fear through panic to a cold anger. Trying hard to keep the exasperation out of his voice, he replied.

'It might cure your mother indeed. Won't do her any harm anyway. Now Johnny, about this letter. I don't want to know anything about your business. Or Freddie's either, for that matter. The business has caused me enough heartache already. Now will you promise me that you'll behave yourself and keep away from the Donnellys?'

Johnny nodded and climbed out of the car.

'In case you're worried Father, I won't breathe a word to anyone about that auld letter. 'Twill be the same as if I never got it at all.'

It was the priest's turn to nod as he let out the clutch and roared off down the mountain.

18

Donnelly was arranging the papers strewn about his desk into some semblance of order when the intercom buzzed like an angry wasp. Who the hell could want him at this hour? Those three clowns at the front desk knew damn well that he was taking his wife out to dinner. It was such a rare event that he was surprised it had not made headlines in the *Clarion*, his firm favourite for the worst newspaper in Christendom. The restaurant was almost forty bloody miles away across the mountains. With a table booked for seven o'clock sharp, he needed to be out of his office on the stroke of five. That is, if he were to wash, shave yet again and change his clothes. Otherwise he would have to race like a demented rally driver whose contract was under review if they were to make it on time.

With his luck they would strike rush hour. By some edict lost in the mists of time, cows were milked at six o'clock. The narrow, twisting road would be jammed with shambling black-and-white monsters, their udders bulging with milk, who effortlessly thwarted his most reckless efforts to pass them. In retaliation, they were quite capable off spurting a stream of the brown and smelly over his pride and joy, the almost new Volvo that he had bought last month. Even meeting the stupid things head-on was frightening. He waited in the car as they lumbered towards it, parting at the very last moment like the Red Sea but brushing against the gleaming paintwork with their dirty carcasses and sending the wing mirrors dancing on their self-correcting ball joints. Those humans supposedly in charge of this lethal caravanserai were even more stupid than the beasts themselves. They loped along behind their charges, a cigarette glued to their lower lip, tipped their cap and smiled oafishly at those motorists whose progress they were impeding.

To make matters worse, today was late closing for the bank. The rest of the week they put up the shutters at three o'clock. It was understood that no customer got near him an hour before closing time. All the more surprising therefore that someone should have slipped through the protective screen he had erected. The intercom was used only when someone other than the staff wanted to see him.

He tried without success to keep the testiness out of his voice as he pressed the speaker button and asked, 'Yes Marie, what is it now?'

'Father O'Sullivan wants to have a word with you.'

'What . . . now? Oh all right, send him in.'

Surely to God the bloody man could have called earlier in the day. Even God's representative in Brulagh must have realised by now that Wednesday was the late opening day. Anyone with a modicum of good sense – not to mention courtesy or consideration – would have known better than to try to see him at the one time of the day when all the staff shared the same goal, that of getting to hell out of the place as fast as possible. Add in the dinner date with his wife and the bloody priest must have had Divine inspiration to select the worst possible time to call. As he looked up from his desk a slim, slightly stooped figure in a well-cut clerical suit was framed in the doorway.

'Come right in, Father, and take a seat.'

It was noticeable that he did not rise from his own as he issued the lukewarm invitation. Father Jerry ignored the discourtesy and sat down opposite this very agitated man in a rumpled suit. Donnelly was going bald on top. His hair was artfully arranged to conceal the fact; it gave an odd shape to his head that the priest found disconcerting.

'Well Father, what is it I can do for you?'

He made no effort to disguise his glance at the clock on the wall. In fact he checked its accuracy by glancing impatiently at his watch. Had he been even remotely civil, the priest would have made his excuses and left. He would have said, quite truthfully, that the matter he wished to discuss was not urgent and would keep for a later date. As things were, he decided to take his time, however uncomfortable it might make Donnelly.

'I have been looking through the parish accounts. There seem to be seven different accounts that I can find. Six are overdrawn and one is in credit, is that correct?'

'Well Father, without looking up the file, I can't confirm that that is so. For the time being, I'll have to take your word for it.'

'Well Mr Donnelly, when you do find the time to look them up, you might do something for me.'

Donnelly arched his eyebrows as he stared at the priest with a new respect. He was not often addressed so coldly. He tried, with scant success, to inject a little warmth into his next question.

'Yes Father and what might that be?'

'My arithmetic is somewhat rusty but the rough calculation I have done seems to indicate that the deposit account more than covers the liabilities in the six other accounts.'

'I see. And . . . ?'

The question hung in the air for some time before Father Jerry answered him patiently.

'Well, for one thing it seems unnecessarily complicated to have all these different accounts for such relatively trifling sums. More importantly, the interest being paid on the overdrafts is considerably greater than that which the deposit account attracts.'

'Nothing strange about that, Father . . .'

The hearty laugh died in his throat as he saw the bleak expression across the desk. He put on his most patronising voice to explain, as if to a child, '. . . it's the way all banks operate. If the two rates were the same, where would we make our money?'

'I take your point, Mr Donnelly and indeed it had not escaped me. However in the case of the parish accounts, if they were all compounded into one, the slight surplus would attract deposit interest, would it not?'

'Indeed it would, Father, indeed it would. I see now what you're getting at. But the old Canon preferred to have a lot of separate accounts. Said it made his own accounting procedures simpler. He also liked the idea of having a substantial sum on deposit. Provision against the rainy day, as it were.'

'I see. Well I, too, am all for providing against the rainy day. Not at any cost, however. For example . . .'

It was now the priest's turn to become patronising. To make matters worse, he seemed to be enjoying himself.

'I do not believe that paying interest on borrowed money when we already have more than we need on deposit makes good commercial sense. From the point of view of the parish I mean. I can more easily see the attraction of such an arrangement from your side of the desk.'

The rebuke was administered so gently that Donnelly looked sharply at him to confirm that he was hearing the words correctly. The bloody fellow was hardly installed a wet week before he started to chop and change. The poor old Canon, God rest him, had left such minor details to him. The change would be all the more hurtful because the parish accounts were by far the most profitable on his books.

'So what exactly do you want me to do?'

The tone had again become impatient almost to the point of rudeness. There was nothing to be gained by humouring this troublemaker any further. The sound of the front door of the bank closing forced Donnelly to look again at both the clock and his watch as he waited for an answer.

'Simply this, Mr Donnelly. As and from now, I want just two accounts. A checking account and a deposit account. When the checking account is in credit for more than one hundred pounds, I will expect you to transfer the excess to a deposit account.'

'And when it is overdrawn?'

'Should that situation arise, I would expect you to provide over-draft facilities as in the past.'

'Do you expect to incur any exceptional expenses in the near future? Either on behalf of the parish or of a personal nature?'

Father Jerry was taken aback. His plans for the future did not need explaining to this surly individual. Yet he had better remain civil. After all, they had to live in the same small fishbowl.

'As regards the parish, it's too early to say. I can see that you are in something of a hurry, so we had better leave my own personal arrangements for another day.'

'Right, Father, I'll attend to that matter first thing tomorrow.'

The priest stood up and extended his hand. It felt like a dead mackerel. Donnelly showed him out through the hall, now that the bank itself had been locked up for the night. The assortment of locks, chains and bolts on the door were impressive. To his left was a well-carpeted staircase leading, presumably, to the bank manager's living quarters. From somewhere overhead there came a loud bang, immediately followed by an exasperated outburst.

'Oh sweet Jesus, wouldn't you know the bloody thing would break just when I needed . . .'

To whom the speech was directed was unclear; it may well have been a soliloquy. Donnelly squeezed out another smile as he almost pushed the priest out of the door.

'My wife seems to be having trouble with the hairdrier . . .'

Just before the door clicked shut another muffled oath floated down the stairs.

Upstairs in the bedroom Josephine Donnelly jumped with fright as her hairdrier exploded. An acrid stench of burning rubber oozed from somewhere inside its plastic casing. Cursing fluently, she unplugged it hurriedly and wondered aloud to herself what she was going to do with her hair. Josephine Donnelly wasn't speaking to her husband

144

and anyway he was downstairs, probably preening himself in his blasted office. As her daughter, who always took her father's side in any argument, was at a friend's house, she addressed her remarks to her reflection in the mirror. Nothing much wrong with the body anyway, she consoled herself as she let the bathrobe fall to the ground. Nothing that a bit of jogging wouldn't fix, she decided as she examined her breasts, firm and rounded. Thank God they showed no unsightly veins from suckling that bad-tempered little bitch, Moira. It was really amazing how that child believed the sun, moon and stars shone out of her father's anus.

Well, maybe her waist might have done with an inch or two less but the shapely hips and thighs more than compensated for that. It was a pity that Tom didn't appreciate her. Or if he did, he kept it a dark secret. The cause of the current coolness was the same as usual. It was bad enough to have to listen to him talking shop all through dinner but when he announced that he had a briefcase full of work to get through before bedtime she really blew her top.

'Ah for Chrissakes, Tom, that's the flaming limit! Where do you think you are? Bloody Wall Street? When are you going to accept that we're stuck here in the arsehole of nowhere with you managing the smallest bank in the whole damn group? So tell me again why you must bring your bloody briefcase all the way upstairs every night! Does the economy of the free world depend on your finishing what's in it before you go to sleep? I can see the headlines in *The Financial Times* – MARKET COLLAPSES AS DONNELLY DUCKS HOMEWORK! You know perfectly well it doesn't matter a tinker's curse whether you finish those reports tonight or tomorrow morning. From what you've been telling me those cowboys are already washed up no matter how many reports you write. Who reads the damn things anyway?'

He remained silent and continued writing as though he hadn't heard a word she said. Storming over to his desk, she screamed, 'I asked you "who reads them?" Have you lost your tongue as well?'

'As well as what, Jo?'

'Oh . . .', she stamped her foot furiously, wishing she hadn't gone so far, '. . . as well as bloody everything else, for Heaven's sake. As well as your interest in me, in Moira, in our life together, the whole bloody shooting match in fact!'

'Don't be ridiculous, Jo. You know perfectly well I haven't lost "interest", as you call it. And I have no illusions about my importance in the scheme of things as far as Allied Banks of Ireland is concerned. With a staff of four I'm hardly their star performer.

145

Maybe that's why the work mounts up. Nearly every account on the books is in trouble and I have to find something to say, something helpful and optimistic mind you, about each and every one of them.'

'So when do you think you'll be finished with that lot?'

'About midnight, with any luck.'

He was already immersed in a folder, sucking the end of a pencil as if hoping to draw inspiration from it.

'I see . . .' Her tone of voice was icy enough to stick a dog to a lamp-post. 'Well if that's how it is, I'll take myself off to bed. Don't even think of waking me when you come up.'

'Goodnight, Jo.'

Looking around frantically for a towel to substitute for the hair-drier, she drew some consolation from his attempts at placating her over breakfast this morning.

'It's ages since we had a meal in a restaurant. Would you like to go back to that Indian place again?'

'Better than staying in, anyway. When will we go?'

'Why not tonight?'

'Why not indeed, lover boy. I'll book a table before you change your mind. Would seven o'clock be all right?'

'Fine, it's late closing today but we should make it by then.'

Now the bloody hairdrier had packed up and Tom still hadn't appeared. Probably nattering with that stupid Sergeant. Since the IRA had turned their attention to robbing banks, security pre-cautions, even in a dump like this, were beyond belief. A land where subversives could knock over banks at will was not the image the government wished to project to the world at large. What made it even more galling was that the proceeds of such robberies went towards boosting the war chests of an organisation dedicated to getting rid of them as a matter of some urgency. Private enterprise in the persona of ordinary criminals masquerading as Provos got in on the act. They emptied bank safes to cries of 'Up the Republic'. The Provos showed their disapproval of such tactics by leaving the mutilated bodies of those involved wrapped in black plastic refuse sacks by the roadside. They justified these executions by claiming the amateurs were giving their organisation a bad name.

Nowadays the Sergeant made phone calls at any hour of the day or night to satisfy himself that all was well. Sometimes, if the exchange were busy, he bestirred himself sufficiently to walk the fifty yards to the bank. As if that were not enough hassle, their own front door was fitted with three heavy mortice locks which took ages to open or close and a push-button speaker through which callers were expected to identify themselves. Up till now it had been used only by young brats to test their choicer expletives and flee before she made it down two flights of stairs to wring their scrawny necks. Everyone else used the doorbell as before.

There was a remote-control device for opening the door when the mortice locks were off but the damn thing either jammed or the idiots outside didn't push hard enough at the right time. Either way she seemed to spend half the day flying up and down the stairs – which might have been good for her waistline but did absolutely nothing for her temper. From now on she was going to leave the entire system switched off, which, she felt, would leave it in perfect harmony with the rest of Brulagh.

Anyway, half the joy of eating out was in getting away from the village – if only for an evening. She still hadn't made up her mind about Mick. Though it wasn't the only improper suggestion she had fielded in the course of her marriage, it was the first to which she had given serious consideration in the cold and sober light of dawn. Her fidelity, she told herself, was due more to a lack of temptation than to a surfeit of virtue.

As she tried to do something with her hair, she ran the pros and cons of an affair with Mick across the spreadsheet of her conscience. In her present frame of mind, the only negative element to the equation was the possibility of being found out. Whatever doubts she harboured about the suitability of Rose Cottage as a love-nest, his Dublin apartment sounded perfect. Should she decide to go through with it, distance would certainly lend enchantment as far as her husband was concerned. It would be easy to concoct an excuse for a trip to the capital city. She went there as a matter of course to stock up on things they had never heard of in Brulagh. Victualling the beleaguered garrison, as she referred to it, though Tom didn't consider this especially amusing or witty. There was a time when her witticisms had him falling about in paroxysms of laughter; now he seemed to regard her attempts at levity as a form of mental derangement that should be nipped in the bud before they developed into full-blown dementia. Further thoughts about Mick had to be shelved due to the arrival of her spluttering husband.

'I thought he was never going to leave. If I didn't know better, I'd have said the bloody fellow knew I was in a hurry to get away and deliberately took his time.'

'Ah Gus is not so bad. What did he want? Your signature on our shore leave pass or what? Did you tell him we were going out and to keep an eye out for someone trying to steal the bank?'

She laughed happily as she spoke. As usual she found her joke much funnier than he did. If this was growing old together, he could have her share of it. The expression on his face was one of unrelieved misery. At least Mick made her laugh. That would be a change. What's more, he seemed to find her amusing. Tom was saying something.

'. . . wasn't Gus at all, more's the pity. It was our new parish priest. He marches in on the stroke of five and demands that I change the whole system of parish funding. I honestly think he meant me to do it there and then.'

'Did you tell him to go and jump off the pier?'

'I told him I'd attend to it tomorrow.'

'That was really telling him! I'll bet he went back to that old cow, Julia May, trembling with fright at the flea you put in his ear!'

Instead of reacting to the barb, he switched on the electric razor and steered it around the smooth curve of his face. As he did so he took stock of his appearance much as he might have assessed the merits of a loan application. Not bad for forty-one, he supposed. Admittedly the pate was getting a little bare but the strong growth of hair around the sides was sufficient to make up the deficit. Like a prudent merchant he simply reorganised his assets by careful brushing of the sides upwards so that they could meet at the dome. It was true, as Josephine said, he was going grey. But only at the temples, he insisted. More of a fleck really, like a light dusting of snow. He thought it gave him a more dignified appearance – more mature than the ruddy-faced rugger bugger of yore. The sort of face that Personnel would select for high office, thereby rescuing him from the dangerous quagmire that was Brulagh.

It was a relief to be getting out of the place for a few hours. Josephine loved Indian cooking and regarded the marathon trek across the mountains as well worth the effort. He would charge everything, including the petrol, to expenses. His last entry on the 'cheat sheet' had been the round of drinks in O'Shea's after that dreadful business in the graveyard. Entertaining clients was not a feature of banking in Brulagh. A more justifiable expense, in his view, would have been the hiring of a hit-man to improve the repayment situation. Because the trip was meant as a peace offering after the row, he supposed it would be only proper that he should offer to drive. That would allow her to indulge herself, though he would have to be more careful. The dried-up riverbed that passed for a road was a right bastard, especially with a lot of drink on board. It wouldn't do his promotion prospects much good to have the albatross of a drunken-driving conviction about his neck.

They made the restaurant with minutes to spare. He had a small dry sherry as Josephine sank two large vodkas and tonic while they scrutinised the menu. They settled for a carafe of chilled house white when he suggested that even the generosity of Allied Banks of Ireland might not rise to her original choice, a magnum of vintage champagne.

After just one glass of wine Tom switched to mineral water. Out of bravado mingled with frustration at the direction their night out was taking, she demolished the carafe and chased it down with three large brandies. She was determined to enjoy herself despite her husband's unwelcome bout of temperance. They had another blazing row on the way home. She was feeling romantic: she wanted him to stop the car and make love like they did in those far-off days when Brulagh was just an unknown flyspeck on a map. When he politely but firmly rejected her advances in favour of getting home first she felt deprived and scorned. Choosing her words with care, she told him he was a boring, middle-aged, impotent shit and then lapsed into a tearful sulk.

The next morning she was hit by two thunderbolts. One was the worst hangover she ever had experienced. It started somewhere in the region of her toenails and worked its way slowly and painfully up to the roots of her long, blonde hair. The other was that she really lusted for Mick Flannery. Not being one to dither, she sent a postcard to his Dublin address. It took him some time to decipher it two days later. It was brief and to the point. In a leisurely scrawl it stated, *'The white flag has been raised. We are now under starter's orders!'* It was signed with a flowery yet unmistakable 'J' that when linked with the Brulagh postmark caused him to spill his black coffee as he threw the postcard in the air and whooped with joy as the full import of its message dawned on him.

19

The meeting had just begun. At the back of the church there was a large, empty space between the door and the first row of seats. A rack held pamphlets, many of them dogeared with age, with titles like *Company Keeping* and *Family Planning within the Church*. Posters advertising a Perpetual Novena in Honour of Our Lady in a neighbouring parish and the telephone number of an advice centre for intending emigrants drooped wearily from the notice-board. Its green baize had ensnared balls of multicoloured fluff and several dead flies. On Sundays the back of the church acted as a foyer for Mass-goers who arrived late, wished to leave early or simply preferred to chat in hushed tones while the celebrant got on with saying the Mass. Joe Gallagher fought a never-ending battle with these people. He assured them that there was plenty of room in the seats further up. While the less hardened gave in and reluctantly took their place nearer the altar, the majority nodded civilly at their persecutor as if to suggest they would comply with his wishes in a moment. They would then resume their conversation, happy in the knowledge that Joe's other duties during Mass would prevent him from bothering them further.

A trellis table and chairs had been placed there for the meeting. Those who could not find a chair sat on the benches and turned to face the door. Someone had lit votive candles at the feet of the statue of the Blessed Virgin at the top of the church. Their scent wafted down the aisle to where about twenty women were listening intently as one of their number addressed them. Father Jerry sat at the head of the table, a look of concern etched on his face.

It was gloomy. The only light came from the big stained-glass window high above the white marble altar. The rays of the sun were just starting to catch the coloured shards of glass that made up the crucifixion scene on Calvary. The garb of blue and white worn by Mary, the Mother of God, was almost identical to that of the Praesidium of the Brulagh section of the Legion of Mary that was now in session. To the casual observer, were it not for their dress they might have been a group of middle-aged housewives meeting for a cup of tea and a chat rather than a prayer group hell-bent on tearing itself apart.

'. . . so in view of what has happened and is still happening at the grotto, I propose that the pilgrimage be cancelled here and now. It would be far better for us all to concentrate our efforts on the miracle that is happening on our doorstep rather than rushing off to Lourdes.'

Maggie sounded like a robot. Though strong and confident her tone was devoid of emotion. It was as if she was reading from a prepared text. Julia May was on her feet before Maggie had finished. Eyes blazing, her voice shook with fury.

'As I stand before God, Maggie Flannery, that's the greatest load of nonsense I've heard in a long, long time. To tell nothing but the truth, when you and I *thought* we saw something that evening, little did I think it was going to come to this. Half the village think they have seen the statue moving and the other half are convinced that we have taken leave of our senses. To make matters even worse, we have a mob flocking in from God knows where to see for themselves. I declare to God and His Blessed Mother, if we don't call a halt to the farce here and now, we'll be the laughing-stock of the whole country. Now before anyone reminds me that I was the first to claim I saw the statue do strange things, I want to tell you all something very important . . .' Her voice took on a lower, more confidential, tone as she pressed on, '. . . I'm not telling one word of a lie when I say that ever since that first night I've been going over and over in my mind to try to remember what actually happened. At the time I was very upset by the poor Canon's death and the arrival of Father O'Sullivan here . . .'

She nodded briefly in his direction. He tried to look suitably grave yet supportive of what she was saying. This was too good to be true. Had he written her script, he could hardly have bettered it. It was exactly what was needed to defuse the crisis. Or so he thought. A lot would depend on what she would say next.

'. . . and now that I have had the time to think about it properly, I realise that I must have imagined the whole thing . . .'

An explosion of excited whispering filled the church. Her recanting was as surprising to him as it was to Maggie. Of course he had been working hard at undermining her faith in the moving statue, not to mention the unscheduled appearance of Padre Pio. Scarcely a day passed but he mentioned how tricks of the light could play havoc with tired eyes, especially in the twilight time between dusk and darkness. The neon halo over the Virgin's head, he gently suggested, could have the same effect as staring at a torch in a dark room. Causing the pupils to expand so quickly, he explained, could easily give the impression of movement where there was none. He chose to ignore the face of the saintly friar in the clouds. Some things defied explanation. It was as gratifying as it was surprising that his efforts had been so well rewarded.

'. . . because of the sunset and the clouds moving in the sky,' Julia May went on. 'It's as plain as the nose on my face that the whole thing is getting out of hand – especially after the carry-on at the funeral. That was disgrace entirely, especially as some people I won't name were wearing the Legion robes at the time. We could all be expelled for that sort of thing, you know! Anyway I completely disagree with Maggie about the pilgrimage. We would all be better off going to Lourdes as usual and forgetting about the grotto. We have a duty to our invalids if nothing else. I know I was the one who talked to Charley Halpin of the *Clarion*, and I wish I hadn't. If we don't stop this nonsense soon, the village will be crawling with reporters before we know where we are and the rest of the world will think we are nothing but a pack of religious maniacs. The month of May is over and done with, thanks be to God, so why don't we go back to normal? My advice is to forget about the prayer vigils at the grotto from now on. Time is a great healer and in a week or two the papers will have found something else to write about. The crowds will stop coming and we can get back to living our normal lives again.'

With that she sat down abruptly, folded her arms and glared defiantly at Maggie. When the staccato burst of chatter died down, Maggie again rose to her feet. This could be her last chance to repair the damage Julia May had done before any more of the fainthearted took the easy way out.

'Julia May is entitled to her opinion, just like each and every one of the rest of us here tonight. The first evening we saw the statue move it was she who convinced me that something out of the ordinary was happening. Then I saw it for myself. If she now wants to change her mind and say it was just a trick of the light, then that's her own business. Whatever or *whoever* caused such a change of heart . . .' – here she paused to stare hard at Father Jerry before continuing – '. . . is no concern of mine. What is of deep concern to me, however, is an attempt by some people to imply that I am going mad. Worse still, it is being whispered that people like myself hope to make money out of the whole affair. Those who know me well . . .' – the venomous look she directed at him this time indicated that he was not one of these – '. . . would realise that I have been in charge of this Praesidium for a long time. In all those years I have never gained a single penny from my position. At the last meeting it was suggested that the fact that I am entitled to travel free as organiser was unfair – even dishonest. Mary Mullarkey suggested that I was taking up the place of some poor, deserving invalid. Well, to set her mind at ease, I am resigning as group leader here and now. The accusation that I am profiting from my position is more than I can take. I will, of course, remain on as an ordinary member. Even she can't take that away from me.'

She sat down abruptly. Father Jerry looked around for a reaction. There was only a stunned silence. Eventually he spoke in a low, measured tone.

'I have listened with interest to the two speakers. In the case of Julia May, because she is my housekeeper I can hardly be expected to have a completely unbiased view. Nevertheless I am glad she has had the courage to come out and say what she did. As for Mrs Flannery, I respect her views but would urge her to reconsider her position. It would greatly surprise me if anyone seriously thought that her beliefs were in any way connected with personal gain. In that regard however, I think this might be a good time to read to you a press statement prepared by the Bishop's secretary. It will be issued if and when the Bishop sees fit.'

He was reluctant to play his trump card. The Bishop had asked him to draft something in case Charley Halpin might ask for a statement. The Bishop confessed that neither he nor his secretary, a newly ordained priest, had any experience in dealing with reporters thirsting for headlines. He implied that an old Vatican hand should be able to take such things in his stride. So what he was about to read out was all his own work, though his listeners believed it to have come from the Bishop himself. The opening paragraphs were run-of-the-mill stuff, welcoming such devotion to Our Lady at any time and praising the parish for its strong faith. It then issued a stern warning about the Church's lack of enthusiasm for 'individuals or groups claiming to have seen statues move, receiving messages from Padre Pio or, worse still, seeking to impose these notions on other people'. The real sting was in the tail. 'The faithful should well know that God does not display his power in such ways. To portray Our Lady or Padre Pio as giving endless streams of messages – some of which border on the absurd – is but a further indication of unreliability.'

After they had digested that broadside an uneasy calm descended on the meeting. All eyes were fixed on Maggie to see how would she react to the suggestion of 'unreliability' – which, after all, was just a polite way of suggesting that she was taking leave of her senses. She rose to her feet, gathering up her veil to prevent it touching the ground, tucked her handbag under her arm and left the meeting without a word. After that, the rest sidled out through the big arched door in ones and twos leaving a bewildered priest to wonder whether he had just won a famous victory or scored an own goal.

In the weeks that followed events took on a momentum of their own. At first he viewed them in a rather detached fashion, as though he were floating far above, high up in the clouds with the saintly friar. Strange things were happening inside his own body. Though he scarcely realised it, he had resigned himself to the fact that Marti's diagnosis was a virtual death sentence. Now, all of a sudden, he was feeling better – much better. He did not attempt to discover the cause of this welcome reprieve. It could have been Julia May's force-feeding or the Doc weaning him off most of his medication – especially the steroids. Then again it could have been the fresh air and mountain walks that had replaced the exhaust fumes and frenetic pace of the Eternal City. Or even Divine intervention. Whatever the reason, he now began to immerse himself more deeply in what he had originally regarded as a dull backwater. In some ways Brulagh's intrigues and personality clashes were just as violent as those in the Vatican.

One of the national papers quoted the Bishop as objecting to 'individuals claiming to have seen moving statues, heard revelations from Padre Pio and imposing their wishes on other people'. Now that the press were homing in, the Bishop phoned him daily for his advice. The poor man had been given the bishopric as a reward for long service in the mission fields. He was completely at sea where the press were concerned and made it clear that he was leaving the whole matter in the capable hands of the parish priest *in situ* – unfortunately not before his secretary had issued another statement that criticised 'those who, in seeking self-glorification or commercial gain, deliberately misled people and damaged their faith!'

The harsh words could only have hastened Maggie's departure from reality. The way she twisted her rosary beads between her white knuckles when her fingers stopped their tattoo on the bench during Mass bore this out. The defection of Julia May served only to strengthen Maggie's conviction. His housekeeper's surprise at this soon gave way to exasperation.

'I wouldn't mind, Father, but she was the one who thought I was seeing things at the time. Now she's twice as bad as I ever was. She spends half the night on her knees at the grotto. 'Twould be more in her line to look after her business. That last bag of flour she sent us was a pure disgrace. 'Twas crawling with weevils, so it was.'

Whatever about crawling weevils, the statue not alone wept and moved but did so nightly before a growing audience. Convinced that an important message would be delivered by Our Lady on her Feast day, Maggie had taken to announcing this at the grotto each night. All this and more she confided to Mick when he took her to task. She agreed with him that some might attribute her sudden zeal to the income from the car park and chip van operated by their children. Such begrudgery she dismissed by reminding him that the visionaries of Knock, Lourdes and Medjugorje had to endure even worse slurs. Warming to her theme, she said it was just one more cross she had to bear in a life already ruined by an errant husband and a failing business. Hastily abandoning that line of attack, Mick warned her instead that she was looking far from well. His suggestion that she was working too hard in the shop met with a better response. So much so that when he suggested it might be a good idea to have a check-up with the Doc, she agreed. He made the appointment for the following day in case she changed her mind.

When Father Jerry saw Maggie outside the surgery, he prayed hard that Mick had remembered to coach the Doc. If he had, then the grotto might yet revert to the original role it had played in the rich tapestry of life in Brulagh – a mere walk-on part in the great religious production of Mass, novenas, funerals and christenings. Had he been a fly on the wall, the opening exchanges in the surgery would have done little to raise his hopes.

'Good morning, Maggie. By God you're a great one for time. Was that Michael down by the pier with the priest?'

'Yes, he serves Mass every morning . . .'

There was a rasp of reproach in her voice. It implied that this was something he could not possibly be aware of since he was not a regular Mass-goer.

'. . . then if it's fine, they go fishing afterwards.'

'Do they catch anything from there?'

'Not much. Just the odd mackerel. Usually all they get is a few congers.'

'Not much eating in those. I hear the French think highly of them but that lot would eat anything. They go mad for dogfish, too. Could you credit it?'

If she could, she kept it to herself. He knew by her expression that this was going to be one of his more difficult consultations. It was eight years since she last set foot in the surgery. He hoped this visit would be more rewarding than the last. Then he had warned that another pregnancy might be fatal. She had not taken kindly to his suggestion that she use some form of birth control; in fact she stormed out. He understood from Mick that she had chosen the thorny path of abstinence – to the extent that they now slept in separate rooms. Perhaps she felt that after providing him with seven children she had contributed enough to the cause of Mick's immortality. Whatever the reason, she was looking well on it. Celibacy suited her. There was a glow to her cheeks and a spring to her step.

Mick appeared to bear his cross lightly. There were other fish in the sea and he spent much of his time trying to land them. He did most of his fishing in Dublin, where he stayed while the Dáil was in session.

'How's Mick?'

It was a foolish question and he quickly regretted asking it.

'No fear of him. You would know better than myself how he is, anyway. You certainly see more of him! That Golf Club will be the death of the two of you. Poor Bernie must have the legs run off herself drawing drink to the pair of you at all hours of the day and night.'

What should have been a tirade was instead delivered in a dull monotone – unemotional as a newscaster announcing hundreds dead in a distant earthquake. Only her eyes betrayed the inner agony. Maggie appeared to be in deep shock. He thought it better to defend his leisure activities while he had the chance.

'Go on out of that, Maggie! You're not going to tell me that you listen to that kind of silly talk, now are you? The old ones around the village have been gossiping like that for years but I'm surprised that a sensible woman like yourself would pay any heed to it.'

Having countered her accusations as best he could, he pressed on smartly before any more shafts could be launched in his direction.

'It's been quite a while since you last sat in that chair.'

She nodded. 'It has indeed. Mick insisted that I came to you for a check-up though I can't think why. It would be more in his line to have one himself. His coughing in the mornings would wake the dead. Anyway he said that I looked a bit off colour. He keeps pestering me that I'm doing too much in the shop.'

'I'll take a look at you all the same. A check-up never did anyone

156

any harm. Have you had one since I saw you last? A check-up, I mean?'

'Of course not, you're our doctor. Where else would I go?'

Where else indeed? An olive branch, perhaps? Even a tiny sprig such as this was to be grasped at firmly. Reflecting that if the rest of his patients only needed him at eight-year intervals his finances would be even worse than they already were, he rummaged through the card index to find her file.

'Here we are. A bit out of date though. Better take your blood pressure first. That was a problem the last time, I think.'

He lied. Then, as now, it was quite normal. The file held details of her Caesarean delivery, and that was all. The woman was as healthy as a trout. He read off her pressure from the dial.

'Yes, just as I thought. Definitely on the high side. Do you have any idea what might be driving it up so high? Could Mick be right about you working too hard in the shop? Lifting sacks and boxes, that sort of thing?'

'No, not really. Now and again I have to bring in a bag of potatoes or a gas cylinder from the shed if one of the children isn't around, but that's all.'

'Well something is causing it. Are you worried about anything in particular? Under stress, maybe?'

These were dangerous waters to fish. If she saw the bait, she might turn her nose up at it and swim away. He wished he had some legal training. Just enough to lead his client as he had seen lawyers do in the courtrooms.

'Well, to be perfectly honest, this grotto thing is upsetting me.'

'Why don't you tell me about it. Then we might find out if that's the cause of your trouble.

Good. The fish was nibbling the bait.

'Sure you know all about it already. You probably think I'm losing my mind. The new priest and the Bishop certainly do . . .'

She paused for a moment to collect her thoughts. Then she continued in a stronger, more defiant voice, 'Well I don't care what they think. That goes for Mick and yourself as well. I know what I saw!'

'Maggie, go easy. I know very little about it, I promise . . .'

He tried to sound as soothing as possible.

'Why don't you make yourself comfortable in the chair and tell me all about it?'

20

Soho was swarming with rush-hour traffic as the little man struggled with the heavy shutters. He carried them out, one at a time, from inside the shop and placed them in front of the window with considerable effort. A certain amount of pushing and heaving was necessary to slot each one into the niche that had been cut for it in the window frame. The sign overhead read

JOHANN FLEUGEL & SON, TRADING SINCE 1837

This was not strictly true as there had been a few unavoidable interruptions in trading since his great grandfather had fled the Russian pogroms. Several of these had been due to fire yet the Fleugel name rose, refreshed, like a phoenix from the ashes on each occasion. The longest and most recent hiatus had occurred when the present owner had a misunderstanding with the law over some goods alleged to have been stolen. Unable to resolve the impasse, he spent just over two years in Wandsworth prison before purging his debt to society. It was not time wasted, however. While inside he discovered a more lucrative trade than fencing – the hiring out of sawn-off shotguns to the less scrupulous denizens of Soho.

He was not surprised, therefore, when two rough-looking types brushed past him into the shop as he was about to lock up for the night. As he padlocked the shutters into place, he regretted the lawlessness that made such precautions necessary when one might have expected that his selfless service to the criminal community of Soho would have ensured his immunity from break-ins. Experience had proved yet again that there was little honour among thieves. Hence the shutters and the sophisticated alarm system.

'Sorry gentlemen, I'm just closing. Call again tomorrow . . .'

He would have explained that he had an important engagement were it not for a hand placed roughly across his mouth and a gun jammed into the side of his head. The taller of the two closed the door and flicked the sign to 'Closed'. The brute who was holding him in a vice-like grip smelt strongly of cheap aftershave.

'We would like to talk to you about shotguns you hire out. You have been telling people that they come from an IRA deserter, right?'

The hand over his mouth moved slightly, to let him answer. The pressure from the gun barrel continued to bruise his temple.

'I . . . aaah . . . I mean, yes. That's true. Who wants to know?'

'We'll ask the questions.'

The voice was faintly Irish, quite like Terry Wogan's in fact.

'What's the name of your supplier?'

The gun was pressed so hard against the skin that it burned.

'Eddie. That's all I knew him by. Never knew his surname. He wasn't Irish. Said he had a friend in the IRA who supplied him with shotguns.'

'If you didn't know his name, how did you contact him?'

'Phone numbers . . . he gave me the numbers of a few pubs in Liverpool where I could leave messages. No need for the gun. Put it away and I'll get you the numbers.'

The gorilla removed the gun from his head at a nod from his accomplice. As Johann rummaged in a drawer for the numbers and wrote them down on a piece of paper, he prattled on nervously. Whatever hole these vermin had crawled out from, the sooner he gave them what they wanted and saw the back of them forever, the happier he would be.

'Yes, he seemed to be able to lay hands on all the guns I could handle. All brand new with the numbers filed off. I paid him three hundred quid apiece. No, I rarely sell them on. Prefer to hire 'em out with the barrels sawn off. More money in it that way. Got to know your customers of course. That's one of his guns over in the corner.'

His interrogator examined it closely and put it back where it had been standing.

'OK Barney, let him go. Now, Mister Fleugel, listen carefully. This conversation never took place. I'm going to Liverpool this minute to check out your telephone numbers. If they are not genuine or you have been a feeding me a load of rubbish, I will come back and kill you, understand.'

The little man was too terrified to attempt to speak. Instead he nodded vigorously. His two tormentors left as silently as they had arrived, vanishing into the neon glare of a Soho evening. He rubbed his temple gingerly and examined the red weal that the gun barrel had left beside his ear. Well, that's another supplier closed down, I expect. Pity, he seemed a nice lad, that Eddie even if he looked a bit rough. Those two were trained killers or I'm a Dutchman. Their every movement was calculated and synchronised. Could have been the Mafia – or the IRA. Might as well be from the Salvation Army for all he cared.

He had told them the truth. After that it was up to them. He locked the door and made for the basement drinking club at the end of the road. He hoped Rita would be on duty. He had quite a story to tell her.

The one called Barney steered the black Nissan into the car park of the Adelphi hotel. His boss, McCain, made for the bank of telephones in the foyer and started calling the numbers. A barmaid in the third pub knew Eddie well. When they drove round to where she worked, she snatched the twenty-pound note from McCain's outstretched hand and stuffed it into her handbag before revealing that Eddie's surname was Simcox. She was pretty sure of the street he lived in but not the house number.

The man in the cigarette kiosk was glad to have someone to talk to. Everyone was in such a hurry nowadays they didn't have time for a proper chat about anything. Twenty Rothmans and bang . . . they were gone. Hardly waited to pick up their change, some of them, so great was their hurry to be off about their business. Not like the old days at all. Then everyone had the time for a chin-wag. It was all that telly they were watching nowadays – killed the art of conversation, it did and no mistake. To tell the truth, some of the people round here couldn't hold a decent conversation even if they wanted to. Couldn't speak English proper, you see. Just enough to get by but not half enough to have a real conversation, you understand. Spoke bloody Urdu or something all the time so how could you expect them to learn English, for Heaven's sakes? Still that was the price we had to pay for being an empire, he supposed. Pity though, really, didn't he think? Nobody talking to each other nowadays, he meant. McCain nodded patiently and repeated the question.

Oh yes, the Simcoxes. Of course, he was forgetting all about them, wasn't he? Well, well, one had to expect that from a man of nearly eighty, he supposed. Now then, the Simcoxes. They were in number 37, half-way down the street on the right. Yes, that was quite correct. There was a young man, an Irishman actually, living there as well. Living with the Simcox girl, as a matter of fact. Jenny was her name. Nice girl, that Jenny even if she did keep to herself a bit. The

Irishman, oh yes, a nice lad he was. Yes he did know his name, as a matter of fact. It was a funny sort of name, so it was. Irish, he supposed. Sean, sir, yes that was it, Sean Flannery. He remembered the name because the lad cashed his cheques here sometimes when the banks were closed. His cheques were always honoured too, not like some he could mention. People living in posh houses not a hundred miles away from here either. Oh you'd be surprised what went on around here sometimes, that was for sure.

Yes, they made a fine couple, Sean and Jenny. He was a quiet lad. Never loud or tough like those Simcox boys. Yes, Sean had been with Jenny a couple of years now. Expect they'll be getting married one of these days. They have the house divided in two. One half for Jenny and Sean, the other for the two brothers, Eddie and Denis. Oh that Jenny was a fine girl. Ran the house like a proper mother so she did after their aunt died. And she just a kid herself at the time. The neighbours helped out as best they could but mostly she managed away on her own. Glad for her sake she had a nice steady fella now, even if he was Irish. Her brothers were rough diamonds, though. One heard talk about them every so often and it wasn't nice, not by a long shot. Not that there are many saints around here. Quite the reverse, in fact. The law are regular callers to the Simcox home, oh yes they are. Nothing really evil, you know. No drugs or violence or anything like that. Oh my goodness, no! Hot merchandise, sir. Whisky with funny labels, cartons of cigarettes that fell off the back of a lorry, that kind of thing. They could fix you up with a nice car, if you wanted one. Oh yes, tough as nails those two but no real harm in them. Eddie, the older brother, was in the Scrubs a few times. Are you from Ireland yourself, sir? Nice people the Irish, I always say. Oh yes, I was forgetting about the cigarettes. Twenty Benson & Hedges coming up, sir. Your change sir. Oh, thank you very much, sir. Been very nice talking to you, sir. Goodbye.

McCain elected for the direct approach. They would snatch Flannery and wring the truth out of him. If he was being supplied with shotguns by a renegade, they would find out who it was. If Flannery was using the Provos as a cover for his own activities they might even kill him there and then. It depended on the circumstances. McCain had already made up his mind that this was precisely what Flannery was doing. Shotguns were never an important part of the Provo armoury. Bank raids and kidnaps were the only time they were used. A shotgun fired into the floor or ceiling put the frighteners on most people and made them do as they were told. They were never included in any arms shipments that he had heard of because, not being essential weaponry, they took up as much room in a crate as the more lethal Armalites and Kalashnikovs. Jenny answered the doorbell. In her mid-twenties she was petite, her blonde hair cropped close like a boy.

'No,' she told them firmly, 'No one of that name lives here. Never even heard of him. You must have got the wrong address.'

The door was slammed in his face before he could pursue the matter further. As they waited in the car, parked well back from the house and out of sight of its windows, he warned Barney not to take his eyes off the street while he was gone. Sure that the instruction had been understood, he got out of the car, stretched the ache out of his back and walked back to the kiosk.

'Hello sir. Didn't expect you back here quite so soon, if I may say so. Another packet of Benson & Hedges it is, sir? A fine cigarette too even if I do say so myself. Do you get them over in Ireland, sir, may I ask? Oh you do. Well, that's nice. Sean Flannery, you say? Oh I'd say about thirty, maybe less. Tall and thin, short black hair. Wears glasses with big frames. Is that the gentleman you're looking for? It's not. Oh dear. Not the same man at all, you say. Ah well, more's the pity. Enjoy your cigarettes, sir. Goodbye.'

Back in the car, he sent Barney to a café they had passed earlier. Just as they were finishing the last of the chips, their vigil was rewarded. A white Porsche driven by a strongly built youth came to a screeching halt in front of the Simcox house. The driver got out and let himself in the door with a latchkey. Shortly afterwards a maroon Volkswagen camper pulled up behind the white car. Two men got out. Both were tall. The younger-looking of the two had a moustache. He wore a fur-lined bomber jacket and heavy boots. The ends of his jeans had a two-inch turn-up. They went inside, emerging at intervals laden with suitcases and cardboard boxes which they stowed in the camper. Apparently they were leaving. McCain wondered why.

He would have liked to report back to the London cell that was running him but it would take too long. It involved phone calls to cut-out numbers at fixed times and waiting for a return call at prearranged public phones. The cell was a 'sleeper', not an active unit. It would be used occasionally as an information conduit in safe operations like this just to keep it on its toes. Otherwise sleepers had a tendency to live up to their name. Then it would go into action once and once only before disbanding and regrouping elsewhere. Its target for the one-off operation would be important. Another Brighton or Aldershot, perhaps.

He had no faith in Barney's ability to deal with an unexpected crisis while he was using the nearest phone-box which was out of sight, quite a distance behind the cigarette kiosk. There was a phone in the kiosk but the chatty old man would inevitably remember not only his face but every word he said. If Flannery had to be executed there and then, they might have to silence the old man as well. He hoped he had put him off by saying that Flannery's description did not fit the man he was seeking. Just have to see what happens, he decided. Didn't want to leave a trail of carnage after them if it could be avoided. If necessary he could make it look like an armed raid on the kiosk that went badly wrong. He was slumped in the car, examining his options, when the three men and Jenny came out. They drove off hurriedly in the Porsche and the camper.

McCain told Barney to follow them without being detected. The trail led to Fishguard, a ferry crossing to Rosslare and then a long drive to some godforsaken village called Brulagh. On the narrow roads, they had to let the two vehicles get well ahead so as not to arouse their suspicions. In doing so, they lost them just outside the village. It was reassuring to learn that it had happened on what was virtually a cul-de-sac in that it was the only road into the place. It was even more so to hear that it was Flannery's home town. This they learned from the pseudo-patriot who owned the hotel they booked into. It was just a question of driving round until they found the Porsche or the camper. Flannery had probably gone to visit some relation or other. Shouldn't be too difficult to find him in a dump like this. McCain moved away from the upstairs window and told Barney to fetch the car. They had paid to park it among many others in a field outside the village. As they walked the short distance to O'Shea's they passed through a large crowd saying the rosary around a grotto. This pleased McCain, not because of their devotion but because he was a firm believer in the precept of safety in numbers.

21

Looking through the fly-spattered windscreen, Eddie Simcox surveyed his tiny world. The small clearing was surrounded by bushes and trees heavy with leaves. A buzz of insects and the chirping of unseen birds were the only sounds to disturb his reverie. It was difficult to realise that twenty-four hours ago he had been breathing in the smog and exhaust fumes of Liverpool. Ireland really was a strange land. On the road over the mountains to the village he hadn't seen a single car or lorry. No traffic of any sort except for an elderly cleric reading a book as he strolled along and a lone cyclist. Labouring up the hilly road on the steepest part where they would place the first diversion sign, the cyclist looked at the end of her tether. Nice looking she was too, with her spray-on jeans and leather boots, even if she was not quite in the first flush of youth.

Not in the least like the colleens in the picture postcards for sale on the ferry. The bag on the carrier of her bike looked as if it might fall off at any moment. Maybe she was the last person left on this strange world of shimmering greens, purple mountains and crystal-clear water. Her cheery wave caused the bike to wobble as Eddie returned her greeting. Why not stop and invite her to disappear for ever with him into this earthly paradise. Perhaps she would not consider a wave sufficient grounds for restarting the human race, he decided, even if it did look as though they were the last two humans left on the face of the planet.

Still, Adam and Eve can't have had much of an introduction either. He tried to recreate the scene in his mind's eye. Great big guy with a beard wearing a sheet and sandals appears in the sky above them.

'Hallo you two! I'm God. Adam, say hello to Eve. Eve, this is Adam, a mate of mine. Say hi to Adam.'

The whole story was probably a load of rubbish. Even the silly sod with his collar back to front seemed less than convinced as he read it to them at the Sunday School their aunt made them attend. Like them, he probably secretly believed that the whole business started with gas flying round in space and creeply-crawlies slithering out of the slime. He knew a few types in the car business who just had to be direct descendants of that lot. That part of his life might have been a million miles away for all he cared as he watched a small bird sporting a golden waistcoat peck at a berry. All this waving fascinated him. Driving off the ferry some guy waved at them and Eddie thought he was signalling them to stop. Then he saw Sean wave back.

'Do you know him?'

'Of course not. Never saw him before in my life. Why do you ask?'

'Well he waved to you, didn't he?'

'For goodness' sake, everyone in Ireland waves to each other.'

'Why?'

'I don't know why. I expect it's just the way we are.'

'You don't wave to anyone back in Liverpool, unless you know them, do you?'

The waving continued to confuse him. Eddie wanted to get to the bottom of it but Sean wasn't being of much assistance.

'Well, it's different in Liverpool. I know . . .' – Sean held up a hand to forestall the inevitable – '. . . before you remind me that there are nearly as many Irish in Liverpool as there are here, but it's *still* different. One reason might be that this is our home here and we do as we like. Anywhere else we have to behave like the natives. "When in Rome" kind of thing. We do it all the time so you might as well get used to it.'

The explanation was so unhelpful that they broke up in childish giggles. Now Eddie was waving with the best of them. Ridiculous, he thought, bloody ridiculous. Still, Sean was right. They were all at it. Farmers with caps down over their noses, leaning on gates and gazing into space, described a languid arc with their hands as they drove by. Shopkeepers standing at their doors, chatting to neighbours, broke off their conversation to salute their passing. Even the road workers breast-feeding their shovels with a dedication equal to that of their British counterparts, managed a limp salutation. The roads were astonishing. Apart from their narrowness, the number and variety of animals that shared them was beyond belief. Stray horses, hairy monsters with black-and-white coats, roamed at will, nibbling at the grass by the roadside. They didn't in the least resemble the sleek flying machines that strutted round the parade rings under the gaze of tiny jockeys and fat men affecting fur-collared coats and big cigars.

Cats and dogs also played their part in the menagerie. They wandered across the tarmac surface as though they owned it. A sheepdog or a small terrier would launch an attack on the spinning wheels of the camper but it was obvious that their hearts weren't in it; he could see from their eyes that they did so only because it was expected of them. Cats were lost in a cocoon of concentration as they stalked unseen prey in the hedgerows, oblivious to the dogs and the almost non-existent traffic. Back home they would have been smeared to the motorway within seconds of venturing out in the path of hurtling rubber and steel. Here they enjoyed an immunity like that granted to sacred cows in India. Speaking of which, he never realised there were so many damn cows in the world.

Herds of black-and-white milkers peered glumly over the fences or ambled along the middle of the road at snail's pace, chewing the cud and lowing contentedly. Now he was on the straight stretch of road just outside the village. This was where Jenny would pass the Land Rovers and cut in sharply behind the security van. Sean was right. There shouldn't be any problem with a manoeuvre like that. Even with traffic coming against her, there would still be enough room to squeeze the Porsche past the convoy. Anyway, a pretty girl blaring the horn of a white Porsche would get right of way from soldiers any day of the week. Hope she wouldn't meet a herd of those stupid cows though. He supposed that they only travelled along the road at milking times – early in the morning and late in the evening. The rest of the time they would be tucking into a feed of grass, safely locked up in a field. With the raid due to take place around midday, the cows should not be a problem. A large metal sign with black lettering on a white background welcomed him to Brulagh. Some mumbo-jumbo underneath presumably repeated the greeting in Gaelic. The sign was where Jenny must accelerate hard to pass the Land Rovers. Given the car's turn of speed, she would have plenty of time to duck in between them and the van, brake hard and skid to a halt sideways on, blocking the road.

Sean was a clever lad and no mistake. Before meeting him, Eddie had always regarded the Irish as being straight out of the turf bog – a shovel clenched in one hand and a pint of Guinness in the other. Those he had met up till then had been a dangerous lot who kept to themselves except at weekends when they went on the rampage. His aunt had always warned him to keep out of their way. At school the Irish, with their funny accents and enormous families, had been the butt of everyone's jokes. Until Jenny and Sean got together, neither he nor his brother Denis would pass the time of day with a Paddy if they could help it. But Sean was different, very different.

Shame about the gun racket, though. Still it was great while it lasted. That was Sean's idea too. Dressed to the nines he would call on a gun dealer and explain that he was looking for a gun suitable for clay-pigeon shooting. He had an easy, self-confident manner that reassured even the most suspicious: within minutes he would have the run of the shop. He would check this gun for balance, that one for fit. He showed both familiarity and a respect for the weapons that led the dealer to anticipate an early sale. Having seen what he wanted, Sean would then make his excuses and leave, declaring that he would like to sleep on it before deciding which gun to buy.

Wearing balaclavas, the three of them would return a few mornings later just before opening time. The talking was left to Sean, who had developed a strong Belfast accent for such occasions. Choosing about a dozen guns, pump-action repeaters if possible, they would make their escape in a car stolen the previous night. Later Denis would burn it to destroy their fingerprints and clothing fibres. Like the headgear, that too was standard practice for the Provos.

It was so easy it was laughable. Violence was never needed. It was enough to hint that it would be used if everyone didn't behave sensibly and not make a fuss. Every gun shop had an alarm button, usually under the counter, near the cash register or the credit card machines. Often Sean would have located it on the earlier visit and one of the trio would position themselves beside it. If there was another one, the frightened dealer would sidle furtively towards it. He might as well have used a spotlight to show them where it was. When that last avenue was closed, the victims gave up in despair. One terrified man actually helped them load the shotguns into the car. They never hit the same area twice. Not once did they see a policeman in the course of a robbery.

Their's was a small but profitable niche that did not cause the smallest ripple in the overall crime scene. Each raid was recorded as yet another unsolved firearms theft, possibly by the IRA. The Simcox brothers had no record of stealing guns. As far as the law in Liverpool was concerned, they dealt in stolen cars and the odd case of whisky or cigarettes. Nevertheless it was a fact that long before those two strangers arrived on the doorstep asking questions about Sean, the gun racket was played out. They had run out of shops, unless they hit some of their original victims again. The other option was to try London. But the further they moved from base, the more insecure and exposed they became. Might as well quit now while they were ahead. It was only a matter of time before they were caught or some gunsmith cut up rough and they had to hit him over the head. It was a consolation to know that if this lark with the security van came off, they would be set up for the rest of their lives.

Sean had seen in the paper his mother sent him every week that a festival was being held in his home town. In describing all the exciting events that were planned, it mentioned that an extra cash collection would be made from the traders and the bank on the Monday of the Festival. Sean's plan was to separate the security van from its escort of armed soldiers and police. This would be done by using Jenny in the Porsche to delay the soldiers in the Land Rovers and police in squad car while the van was diverted down a side road and emptied of its contents. By the time the convoy reached the road where the van had turned off, the diversion sign would have been removed and they would speed along the main road in pursuit. They would not be unduly worried at losing sight of their charge. No attempt to rob an escorted security van had yet been made.

Jenny had been the most difficult to persuade. At first she refused point blank to have anything to do with it. Soldiers and police toting sub-machine guns sounded far too dangerous. When Sean went over the whole plan again, this time more slowly and in greater detail, she finally relented. That visit of the two strangers with Irish accents had frightened her. She hadn't been living among petty criminals all her life not to recognise mavericks when she saw them. Both those men had the dull, empty eyes of psychopathic killers.

Eddie believed, however, that what finally persuaded her to fall in with their plans was her hope that Sean might be reconciled with his family. From what he had said about them, they might not have been anything to get too excited about; none the less they were family. Family was very important to Jenny. When their parents abandoned the three Simcoxes, they were reared by a maiden aunt. Food and education were skimpy. The school attendance officer ensured they got the minimum education, enough to read and write but little more. Boredom and the ever-present shortage of money ensured that he and Denis stayed at school only as long as was legally necessary.

When the aunt died, they were on their own. They did their best to look after Jenny but the two brothers were no substitute for a proper family environment. They were away a lot – even when they were not in jail. Until Sean knocked on their door looking for lodgings Jenny had never had a relationship with anyone. That was two years ago, and now they were closer than ever. Why Sean should choose to cut himself off from his family was beyond all understanding.

Of course he had told them about the silly incident that caused

168

the break. For quite a while they were sure that there had to be something more sinister in his past – an accidental killing or a pregnant girlfriend at the very least. When it proved to be a mere trifle like getting drunk, stealing a bloody statue and drawing the probation act, they didn't know whether to laugh or cry. They could count on the fingers of one hand the number of people living on their street who were not on probation. More than half of them had done time for one crime or another and no one took a blind bit of notice. Imagine cutting yourself off from your family for such a piddling offence! The Simcoxes had heard that the Irish were different but this was too bloody ridiculous for words. Jenny told him of the times she had tried to reason with Sean but all to no avail. It was the one area of his life he refused to discuss with her. For the time being, he wanted nothing to do with his family and that was the end of the matter.

Now this caper would bring both families into the same arena. Sean had repeated over and over again that there was no way he would contact his parents while in Brulagh. Not only had he no wish to do so but it might ruin the whole operation. It was Sean who insisted that they camp in a wood half-way up a bloody mountain and well away from the village. Despite such an unpromising scenario, Jenny had blind faith in her destiny. All through the hard times, she promised herself that, when it happened, she would have a white wedding in a proper church like the royals did on the telly.

She revealed this to no one save Eddie. Her wedding, to be properly staged, would require the presence of Sean's family. After all someone would have to make a speech informing Denis and Eddie that they were not losing a sister but gaining a brother. Someone would have to stand up and applaud the uniting of two distinguished families. She longed for the snow-white wedding dress, the three-tiered cake, bridesmaids, champers, soaring organ music, the ivy-covered church, white linen tablecloths and milling guests wishing the happy couple well. Not for her the Registry Office with ham rolls and a booze-up in the pub afterwards. When Jenny tied the knot, she would do it in style.

Now there was a chance of her dream coming true. If they did succeed in ripping off the security van without getting blown away or caught by the law, they could afford ten white weddings with all the trimmings. She had already promised Eddie that he would be best man because of his way with words. Denis would have to content himself with the role of giving her away at the altar. At the far end of their street the pub on the corner was up for sale. Forty thousand would buy it. It had a big flat overhead – just right for a young couple starting out in life. Her aunt had always said that the Irish made good barmen. Of course she *had* told them other things about the Irish that they preferred to forget. Anyway, none of it applied to Sean. They had never seen Sean drunk or looking for a fight. Mind you, when he did get stuck in one, he could look after himself. He had told them that he once spent a year in a place called a seminary where some queers took a shine to him. That was when he began to study karate rather than theology. Just like the Scrubs, really.

Wonder why those two strangers were asking about Sean? It had to be that bastard we nicknamed 'London'. When I set up the deal, London wanted a guarantee that the guns would not come from the British army. That was when I fed him the story of an imaginary IRA defector. London did most of his drinking in a club where a bottle of Haig cost forty quid and the girls wore too much make-up and too few clothes. The hostess who brought the bottle to their table was an old friend of London's, or so he claimed. He introduced her as Rita, paid her for the drink and fondled her bottom absent-mindedly before sending her out of earshot. It was then that they agreed on three hundred quid a gun.

Yeah, Eddie decided, when this lark is all over, I'll call on London. There was no way those two snoopers, whoever they were, could have got on to them except through London. How they got hold of Sean's name was a mystery. Had they been looking for Denis or himself, that would have been nothing out of the ordinary. Whenever a car was stolen in Liverpool the law came knocking on their door to make 'inquiries'. Yes, he decided, as he drove up what appeared to be the main street, he would certainly have a quiet chat with London one of these days. However, all that was in the future. Right now he had to get petrol. He also needed nuts and bolts to put on the number plates he had stolen on the ferry and the materials to make a convincing diversion sign.

22

The Sergeant hated the telephone on his desk. Invariably it proved to be the harbinger of bad news. This phone call was no exception.

'Here it is, the address you were looking for, Super. Yeah, Sean Flannery's. Thirty-seven, yes, three seven. A for Andrew. Thirty-seven A, OK? Laburnum L-A-B-U-R-N-U-M, that's right. Avenue. Fishmarket Street. Addington A-D-D-I-N-G-T-O-N, Liverpool. Got that? Good! Maggie wasn't sure if he's still there but that's his last known address. Is that all you phoned me for? No ... it was just that the first time you asked me for it, I thought we agreed I'd post it on to you. Oh they were, were they? I see now what your hurry is. The Special Branch, no less. I hope the lad is not in any trouble, is he?'

His brow furrowed in concentration as he tried to catch every word that crackled across the line. The Superintendent rarely bothered to phone. Never before had he done so on a Saturday when the station was closed. It was just sheer coincidence that he had been there with the priest looking for the key of the practice room to give the band their instruments. He had met Father Jerry on the street and invited him to listen to the band's recital. Then he realised he had yet to find the key. Mary Mullarkey must have seen him open the station door because he never went near the place at weekends. For a moment he had considered not lifting the receiver. He had enough on his plate without adding further complications to what already looked like being a hectic weekend.

At first he was glad it was the Super. He might think he was working unpaid overtime. As the conversation progressed he became less happy. The Super told him of a startling new development. The telephone was not his favourite means of communication – he preferred to see whoever he was talking to rather than have to shout into the elderly instrument from which a worried voice was babbling frantically.

'Could you spell that again for me, Super? This is a really bad line. Ah yes, I see! There's an "i" in it. I thought you said McCann. Yes, yes, I have it now. *McCain*, John McCain.'

The pencil stub flew across the paper as he jotted down the description of McCain and his accomplice, known only as Barney. Spotted leaving the Rosslare ferry the previous evening, they had been tailed to Brulagh. Their car, a black Nissan, was rented from Hertz at the Victoria Station desk. McCain was well known both to the Special Branch here and to the Interpol counter-terrorist squad. He was thought to be a procurement officer in the Provisional IRA. Little was known about him except that he had trained in Libya. Posing as a carpentry instructor teaching backward communities, he received training in bomb-making and assassination techniques. That was three years ago.

Since then there had been occasional sightings as he criss-crossed European borders. His base was a tiny apartment just off Dam Square until an arms deal went wrong. Though a large deposit had been paid, the shipment failed to materialise. The Dutchman disappeared. Later he was found floating between moored barges in a muddy Amsterdam canal. There was a bullet in his head. McCain left Holland two days before the body was found. The Dutch police would have liked to interview him but there wasn't a shred of evidence to link him to the killing. He was next sighted disembarking at Rosslare and followed to O'Shea's. Nothing was known about the other man, except his first name.

'They stopped outside O'Shea's you say? I'll check it out but I can tell you this much, there was no black Nissan there five minutes ago. I walked past the place just now and there wasn't a car of any sort outside the place. Unless it's in the car park at the back, of course.'

The voice at the other end became even more agitated. Even the priest across the desk, busily feigning lack of interest while straining to catch every word, sensed the sudden urgency. It was imperative that the car be found and its two occupants kept under strict surveillance. God alone knew what dangerous bastards like those two were up to. McCain was known to be a thoroughly bad lot, the Super shouted down the line, and the one called Barney wasn't likely to be any better. Keep them under observation but make no attempt to apprehend them. Could they be cooking something up with the armchair rebel, Tom O'Shea? Gus waited for the torrent of words to subside.

When it did, Gus grinned at Father Jerry as he spoke into the mouthpiece.

'Super, you've already turned down my request for extra men to help out over the weekend. As you well know, my junior is out on sick leave with pneumonia. We have a Festival about to start with the usual late-night bar extensions. Then there's the mob around the grotto every night waiting for some miracle or other to happen. On Monday, we're opening the new stand and Maggie Flannery says the Blessed Virgin Mary is going to deliver a message to the world at the same time. To cap it all, Donnelly, the bloody bank manager, arranges an extra cash collection for the same day. The fool is forgetting that it is a Holy Day of Obligation. That means the street will be jammed solid with cars parked outside the church for last Mass. He couldn't bother his arse checking with me first. Instead he phones you. Then, as usual, I'm the last one to hear about it. No, I didn't get out of bloody bed the wrong side this morning! I'm at this game long enough to know you have to take the rough with the smooth but this is the last straw. On top of minding the village single-handed for what is going to be the busiest weekend in its history, you now want me to mount a close surveillance operation on a car and two complete strangers that I haven't even seen yet. Jesus Christ, Super, even you must realise that it's a bit much to ask one man to do!'

Soothing noises babbled from the phone but Gus would not be mollified, though he wished he hadn't sworn in front of the priest. It was all very well for the Super. He didn't give a damn. His retirement was coming up shortly and then he could devote himself full-time to his blasted bridge. In the meantime, Gus Moriarty was expected to play John Wayne for the weekend and not even get paid for it. It was too ridiculous for words. The Super re-entered the fray with a nervous laugh.

'Will you for God's sake stop complaining! I didn't invent the cutbacks. If the Minister for Justice says there is no overtime or reinforcements available for Mickey-Mouse festivals and the like, then that's that. If you don't like it, fair enough. Tell *him* about it, not me. I only work here, like yourself.'

The voice now became almost wheedling.

'Look Gus, do the best you can. You could never claim that Brulagh is a hotbed of crime! It's hardly going to turn into one over the weekend. Quite the reverse, probably. Everyone will be too busy praying their heads off at the grotto or trying to get on TV. Look, I'll see what I can do about getting you a few extra days off before Christmas to make up for the overtime. That's the best I can manage. In the meantime, try to keep an eye on McCain and his pal but be sure to give them a wide berth. That lot would shoot their mother before breakfast and not give it a second thought. Good luck.'

173

Without waiting for a reply, he hung up. Abandoning the search for the key, Gus looked quizzically at Father Jerry to see how he had reacted to the conversation. His expression gave nothing away. Nor did he pass any comment. In reality Gus was not as annoyed as he pretended to be. As Superintendents go, this one was all right. One of the best, in fact. No lightning swoops to catch him unawares. He knew that this happened at bigger stations and was the bane of every sergeant's life. As long as Gus kept Brulagh peaceful and did nothing to besmirch the Super's record as he cantered down the home straight to retirement, he was left to his own devices. The reference to the Festival as a Mickey-Mouse affair was not meant as an insult, but as a feeble attempt to be amusing. The Super was prone to attaching himself like a limpet to certain words like Mickey Mouse, close surveillance and intensive policing. Spoken by a man approaching seventy, Gus thought they sounded bloody ridiculous.

First things first, he reminded himself. You have to find the missing key. If it wasn't in the desk, then either the Doc or Pat must have it. No key meant no instruments. No instruments meant no band. No band meant no parade and what festival worth its salt had ever been opened without a parade? No that key must be found, he told himself, as he started to go through the drawers in his desk slowly and methodically. Then he would let the priest listen to what mayhem the band tried to inflict on the National Anthem while he went in search of McCain and his partner.

First he would have a chat with O'Shea. They had been on worse terms than ever since Easter, when Gus had been instructed to arrest anyone selling Easter lilies in a public place. The proceeds from the sales of these paper badges depicting a lily were rumoured to go to subversive elements, as his Super liked to call the Provisional IRA. Gus preferred to label them murdering bastards and leave it at that. O'Shea, as Brulagh's token Republican, was the lily seller. He stood outside the church gates after the Easter Masses with a collection box and his sheets of stick-on lilies. Gus could not fathom if his success was due to an undercurrent of nationalism in the village or because people were reluctant to upset the only publican for miles around.

Whatever the reason, it had been his job to tell the old fool to move away from the church gates or he would have to arrest him. O'Shea made the point that if poppies could be sold on Poppy Day why not lilies at Easter? Gus replied mildly that he didn't make laws, he just enforced them. Secretly he loathed O'Shea. Though many in

174

his beloved GAA shared O'Shea's sentiments, Gus regarded extreme Republicanism as both stupid and dangerous. To him it was unreasonable to declare Britain, who employed half the sons and daughters of Brulagh, a sworn enemy. He still couldn't find the blasted key anywhere.

He pulled the door of the station shut and walked with the priest to Pat Mullarkey's office. They paused on the kerb to let a camper with an English registration pull in at the petrol pumps.

'I'll tell you something, Father. If Pat doesn't have the key, music-lovers the world over will heave a sigh of relief.'

As they approached the glass door, there came from behind it the sound of a strange incantation. It was Pat trying out his speech.

'A Chairde Gael, tá áthas mór orm – A Card-yuh Gale, thaw awe-huss moor orrum – My dear friends, it gives me great pleasure . . .'

It would give him even more pleasure if he could think of something to add to his opening remarks. He was staring at a blank sheet stuck in the office typewriter. He had tried scribbling something down on a scrap of paper and that hadn't worked either. The muse, if such a thing existed for aspiring politicians and bilingual orators, had flown off he knew not where. Thank God the damned loudspeaker was mended at last. If that Flannery child had said 'Testing, testing, one two three' again, there would have been one less of the tribe to grossly overcharge the faithful for hamburgers and chips at the grotto. For a moment, Pat had seriously considered stringing him up from the instrument through which his young voice was squeaking, accompanied by a high-pitched whine and shrieking static. It would have been preferable to trying to resolve the argument raging within. Was he going to deliver a speech on the subject nearest his heart – the dying rivers? Or would he take the easy way out and tell them how wonderful they all were and that the future was safe in their hands?

For once, Mossy had been quite helpful. He pointed out that the Department of Agriculture would not welcome one of their staff publicly airing a matter of some embarrassment to them. It was, after all, they who had caused the problem even if it was the likes of Mossy and Pat who preached salvation through silage. Now that its effluent proved lethal to the environment, to complain of dying rivers would be tactless in the extreme. The Department, who were already wielding the axe because of drastic cutbacks in their budget, would not take kindly to his pointing the finger, however indirectly, at them.

If Pat wanted to put his head on the block, he was going the right way about it. Anyway, Mossy said resignedly, it was all the same to him. He retired in two years and if they kicked him out sooner, so much the better. His pension was secure. He had no qualms about bailing out, he declared sarcastically, when he knew that the future of farming was safe in the hands of the likes of Pat. However if he wanted to get fired for discussing confidential Department matters from a public platform, then that was his own decision. Though it was obvious that his chief concern was not to lose an assistant who covered for his frequent absences, it had to be admitted that he had a point.

'Better play it safe and leave the crusades to others. Give them the Olympic Spirit recital. You know it well enough by now. Every team you ever trained heard it over and over again. Participation is what counts. Sure it's always nice to win but winning must not be an end in itself. Tell them that and try to sound as if you believe every word of it. If you wanted to be petty you could get in a sly dig at the Legend. You could use the stand as an example of community effort rather than individual glory. Don't be tempted, though, to tell them that the fact that it is still without a name only goes to prove the point.'

It was then that Pat saw the two figures through the frosted glass. He got up from the desk and opened the door. Gus spoke first.

'We could hear you practising the speech. We were afraid we might give you a heart attack if we jerked you out of it too suddenly. How is it coming along, by the way?'

'Still working on it. Well, what can I do for you?'

'The band is waiting all dressed up to the nines but their instruments are locked into the practice room. I hoped you had the key. I've turned my place upside down but I can't find it anywhere.'

'No wonder. I had it yesterday. Hold on a second.'

Pat rummaged through his pockets, then looked in the desk drawers, all without success.

'Not here. It must be with the rest of the keys in the supermarket. I'll walk over there with you to get it. You'd never find it on your own. Let me just have a quick word with the loudspeaker expert.'

He said to the young Flannery who was near the top of the pole, 'Come down out of that before you kill yourself. The whistle seems to have gone out of it now. A while back it would have woken the dead.'

Josephine Donnelly was cycling out of the village. As she passed them, she waved, which sent the bike into a wobble. This elicited a comment from Gus.

'I wonder where she is off to? Never saw her on a bike before. What are you going to tell us? In the speech, I mean.'

'I was trying to decide that very thing just as you arrived. I think I'll give them the usual stuff about community spirit, the value of the GAA, a healthy mind in a healthy body. That sort of thing. Do you think that would be all right?'

'Fine Pat, that sounds fine. Just the thing for them,' Gus reassured him.

'And you, Father, what do you think?'

'Absolutely the right note, I'd say, Pat.'

Gus chimed in, 'Speaking of notes, will you try to find that key before the lads in the band disappear off in every direction. Trying to keep them together in the one place is like trying to mind sheep at a crossroads. As for the speech, to be honest I was afraid you were going to give them a sermon on dead fish.'

He laughed, unconvincingly, as though the idea was so outlandish as not to merit consideration.

'I was seriously considering doing just that. I expect Mossy told you as much. He thought I was crazy. Hinted I might even get fired if I went ahead with the idea. Mary didn't think much of it either so I decided to drop the idea, for the moment anyway. Anyway who gives a damn if every fish in the river goes belly up? As long as the Festival goes ahead and the stand is officially opened that's all that matters. The show must go on, eh?'

It was unusual for Pat to be so bitter. Gus and the priest wondered what had got into him. As they walked together into the supermarket, Bernie Murphy was deep in conversation with Pat's wife.

'Good morning Mary. Good morning Bernie. Are you ladies all set for the big day?'

Gus and the priest lingered at the door to talk to them as Pat, with a curt nod to the two women, hurried to the post office at the back. Mary whispered, 'Does he have his speech ready yet?'

Gus gave her a conspiratorial wink and answered softly, 'I think so. He's just told us it's about sport and the community spirit. Completely fish-free, thank God.'

'I'll say "Amen" to that.'

Mary sighed as though a huge weight had been lifted from her shoulders, as a triumphant cry from the back of the shop indicated the missing key had been found. Gus ushered Father Jerry across the road and into the practice hall. Within moments the sad wail of Saint Fintan's Brass and Reed Band warming up their instruments rent the air. It was interrupted by the roar of an engine. A black Nissan screeched to a stop at the intersection on the main street. Its two occupants peered right and left as though looking for something in particular. After a moment's hesitation they roared off up in the direction of the Golf Club. The two women at the door looked on in amazement.

'Just as well Gus didn't see those two or he would soon put a stop to their gallop,' Bernie commented.

Mary replied casually, 'You're right. That's about the fifth time that pair have passed here this morning, each time going like the hammers of hell. As for Gus, he probably didn't even hear them. With the racket that lot across the road are making trying to murder the National Anthem, he'll be lucky if he can ever hear anything again.'

23

A notice in the bedrooms listed many things the management declined to be held responsible for and ended by reminding patrons that breakfast was served between the hours of 7.30 and 9 a.m. The pressmen beat Charley to the table by the shortest of heads. Two crumb-scattered place settings proved the two strangers in their midst to be early risers. Last night, when he saw them in the bar, Colum thought that one of their faces was familiar. Perhaps he had seen it before in the pages of the Journal, or down in the basement that housed the Picture files for the paper. Colum used to browse through them when he wasn't out on an assignment. The basement was a safe haven from the News Editor who would have found something for him to do had he remained hanging around the Newsroom.

O'Shea eyed their arrival with distaste. Another five minutes and he would have been within his rights to refuse to cook for them. It would have pleased him no end to inform the press that his kitchen was closed, to exact revenge from those who kept him up half the night. He took the order for thirteen 'Traditional' Irish breakfasts – orange juice, cornflakes, bacon, egg and sausage plus tea or coffee. His hatred of cooking showed in the plates he slapped down before them. The orange juice and cornflakes were beyond his powers of destruction but he made up for lost ground in the main course. The strips of bacon, uneven and marbled with fat, concealed shards of razor-sharp bones crudely slashed from an elderly pig who had given itself up to whatever butcher O'Shea was still on speaking terms with.

'What's the schedule for today, Charley?'

Colum looked the picture of rude health. To judge from his appearance he might have retired to bed early with a cup of cocoa. In fact he had spent most of the night pouring drink into Charley and signing him on as a helper. Money had changed hands and Charley was now, to all intents and purposes, a stringer for the Journal. He was also feeling unwell. A severe throbbing behind his right eye gave way to a dull pain that started just below his nose and lanced outwards in several directions. He was absorbed in rescuing a tiny piece of lean bacon from the clutches of a hairy rind and a swamp of congealed fat. Abandoning the struggle, he took a deep draught of orange juice to clear a path for his voice through the swarm of frogs in his throat.

'Well, you said last night you wanted me to set up some interviews.'

What passed for a fried egg glared up at him from the plate. Its rheumy yellow eye twitched as though it were alive. Perhaps it was trying to escape from its prison of slippery, white plastic fringed with a collar of burnt lace. The Borgias could have taken lessons from O'Shea, he decided, as he lowered his voice so the others would not hear.

'We had better pretend to be covering the Festival. We'll ask a few questions about Mick Flannery, the four-in-a-row team, Saint Fintan's, the new stand – that sort of thing. Then you can switch to the grotto as an afterthought. If you jump straight in with direct questions about it, they'll shut up like clams.'

'Point taken. Will you set up something with the priest . . . ?'

He looked across the table at the photographer, 'so that Joe and I can go along with you to interview him?'

Colum's plate was empty except for a piece of bacon rind. Charley's respect for him grew. Not alone had he been up for most of the night but now he was champing at the bit, impatient for the 'off' having swallowed the worst that O'Shea could throw at him. Maybe he really did earn those press awards after all. Up to now, Charley believed they were distributed among the big dailies like snuff at a wake.

Perhaps that piece he had done last night might win him some well-deserved recognition. It was certainly one of the best things he had ever written. Charley Halpin – Reporter of the Year, had a certain ring to it. Yeah, he concluded cynically, the ring of fantasy. His reporting of Mick Flannery's election promises might qualify for a fiction award but that was about the size of it. No Pulitzer prizes for hacks reporting moving, weeping statues. He pushed away his breakfast in disgust and turned his attention to Colum.

'I've already fixed that. He'll see us as soon as you're ready to go. He could hardly refuse us an interview in his capacity as Chairman of Saint Fintan's GAA club. Then we work around slowly to the grotto. Everyone knows that he regards it as the ravings of a few daft old biddies. How to get him to say so will be your job. Maggie Flannery, who started it all, is as mad as a March hare . . .'

The photographer interrupted by asking the world at large in a very loud voice, 'What does the guy fry this muck in? Axle grease?

180

If the bastard can't cook, why doesn't he get someone in to do it for him?'

Believing the question to be directed at him, Charley made sure O'Shea was out of earshot before replying.

'Too bloody mean, that's why. He wouldn't give you the itch, don't mind a half-decent breakfast. Anyway, what woman in her right mind would work for him? Mick Flannery's daughter was supposed to have a summer job here but she ran out of the place inside an hour. He's still a randy old bastard, more luck to him. I only hope I'm that healthy when I reach his age.'

Colum ignored the aspiration and steered the conversation back on course.

'Fill me in on this priest. Father what's his name.'

Charley did so, without mentioning the line he was pursuing about the priest's unusual past. He had come to a dead end with Johnny, his poteen supplier. Something had happened to make him silent as a tomb on the subject though it was he who had mentioned it to Charley in the first instance. He fell silent as O'Shea cleared away the plates, passing no comment on the fact that most of his cooking had remained untouched.

'I see . . .'

Colum was thinking hard even as he spoke. *Maybe this little shit might yet be worth the money he had paid him after all. One thing was beyond dispute. The money would last him quite a while if his reluctance to buy a drink was anything to go by. He had met up with some cheapskates in his time – reporters who would rather die than pay good money over a bar counter – but when it came to keeping his hands in his pockets, Charley Halpin was up there with the best of them..*

'. . . He sounds worth a few minutes of our time. Did you say you'd already talked to him?'

Charley thought hard before replying.

'Yes, I did. Got nothing out of him, though. Just the usual line the clergy trot out every time there's a crisis of any sort. If God appeared in a fiery cloud, loudhailer in one hand and flaming sword in the other, warning the good people of Brulagh to run for their lives, the Bishop would set up a Commission of Inquiry to take depositions from eyewitnesses. Parish priests have to watch their ass in case they get a belt of a crozier. Anything of interest in the papers is sent to Rome by the Papal Nuncio. If the bigwigs in the Vatican don't approve, the Bishop gets it in the neck. Then he takes it out on the PP and so on down the line. I expect the altar boy eventually goes out and kicks the sacristy cat. What I'm trying to say is that even if Father Jerry thinks the grotto thing is a load of old cobblers, he can't come right out and say so. How can he accuse his congregation of being religious maniacs one minute and then complain about them being late for Mass or not putting enough in the collection box the next?'

Colum nodded in agreement but said nothing. Judging by his expression, Charley had something on his mind. It soon became clear what it was.

'What will the others be up to while we're at the Parochial House?'

So that was it. Charley was afraid the stage was becoming a bit too crowded. Colum's words were not designed to comfort him.

'Dunno really. They're not with me, Charley. Some of 'em are stringers for the English papers. The rest are freelances looking for a scoop. They get paid so much per word if it gets printed. They just tagged along when they heard there might be a story here. In August the tabloids will print anything to fill empty spaces. The dafter it is the better they like it. I call 'em "pilot fish" but not to their faces!'

'I see. That explains it,' Charley said. 'Joe Gallagher tells me he has another crowd coming in from London this morning. News travels fast. I wonder who they are?'

'We'll know soon enough. You can bet that the pilot fish are asking the same question. All the more reason for us to get our interview done quickly.'

As they walked up the street to the priest's house, a Nissan with an English registration screamed around the corner. Moments later a camper, also with English number plates pulled up at the petrol pumps. Maybe Joe's people had arrived already. It added urgency to their meeting with Father Jerry. It was agreed that Charley would introduce both of them to the priest, ask permission for the photographer to do his job and then hand over to Colum. If it looked as though he was getting anywhere, they were to shut up and stay quiet. Julia May greeted Charley coldly. Was this because the *Clarion* had ignored her retraction or did she still disapprove of the cookery section? Whatever the reason, she looked grave as a judge donning the black cap when she announced, 'Father O'Sullivan will be with you shortly.'

She left them standing in the hall, twiddling their thumbs and making small talk. After about ten minutes Father Jerry appeared. This time the interview was to be more formal; not in the untidy den but in the stark splendour of the parlour. Sucking on a large pipe, he ushered them into the austere room and nodded absently as Charley made the introductions. He seemed to be emitting as much smoke as possible into the hermetically sealed room. The high windows looked as if they had not been opened within living memory and the enormous sideboard glowered at them, looking more overpowering than ever. Even Saint Sebastian looked unhappier than the last time. Only the flowers in the heavy cut-glass vase had been changed. When the pipe was drawing to his satisfaction, the priest coughed to clear his throat before opening the proceedings.

'Well gentlemen, what can I do for you on this, the Feast of the Assumption of Our Blessed Lady into Heaven? Before you answer, I must tell you that I have a Mass to say in fifteen minutes' time. Then there is the home-made wine competition in the Festival marquee which may interest your readers. I am reliably informed that the rhubarb wine is excellent this year, though the white gooseberry has yet to peak. Immediately after that I go for a long walk during which I read my office. Then lunch, after which I attend the opening of the Festival. A rather tight schedule, you must admit. However, for the next ten minutes I am at your service.'

Charley opened the bowling with a nice slow ball.

'Perhaps you could tell us, Father, what your reactions are to the Festival and the opening of the new stand?'

Father Jerry sucked on his pipe for some time before replying, adding considerably to the smoke already drifting around the parlour. The photographer loosened his tie and ran a finger round the inside of his collar. There would be no indoor shots in this atmosphere, the smoke had seen to that. Charley wondered if this was a form of biological warfare designed to unsettle them. The tobacco was of an aromatic variety that gave of a sickly perfume not unlike the aftershave affected by that weirdo in O'Shea's last night. A strange-looking bird, he asked about the Flannerys, especially young Sean, while his companion remained silent. After listening to a long-winded bromide, delivered slowly and without much conviction, on the value of sport in general and the need for good leisure facilities for the youth of Brulagh, Colum jumped the gun when he realised that nearly half their time had been used up.

'What about the moving statue and the message that is promised for today?'

The priest applied another match to the pipe, which greatly increased its smoke output. He appeared in no hurry as he answered.

'In her wisdom, our Holy Mother the Church treats all such phenomena with suspicion. One might even go as far as to say that she views them with a jaundiced eye. While shrines such as Lourdes, Fatima and our very own Knock have now been accepted as places of special devotion to Our Blessed Lady, you will search long and hard before you find any senior cleric asserting it as doctrine that she actually appeared in any of these places. You are perfectly at liberty to believe that she did so, if you wish, but it is not a required Article of Faith. You may have noticed that claims relating to her appearance at these places are made by younger and more fervent people. It is no coincidence that many other places have claimed similar sightings in the past, with or without moving statues, dry-eyed or otherwise. They all appear to share certain similarities, however. The alleged sightings occur in relatively remote areas such as here. Those claiming to have witnessed the events are invariably both impressionable and devout . . .'

Colum was determined to break into the monologue which promised to swallow up their remaining time.

'Are you saying that Maggie Flannery is mad?'

'I most certainly am not. Nothing of the kind. Mrs Flannery is a devout church-goer, a daily communicant and a pillar of the Legion of Mary.'

'What about the statue moving and tears coming from its eyes? More than just Maggie are saying that they saw both these things happen.'

Colum had to be quick off the mark to catch the priest, as he paused for a moment to puff on his pipe.

'If you don't mind, I'll finish what I have to say first. Then you can ask your questions. If we have enough time to get around to all of them, that is.'

Ah sweet Jesus, that has to be the good old Diplomatic training. That creep Halpin did say there was a Vatican background somewhere in his past. Wonder why he got out. Booze? Women? Stress? Doesn't matter anyway. He's not going to give anything away. Better concentrate on the daft old bat who saw the statue move.

In a moment the priest will look at his watch and leave before he can be asked any awkward questions. The oldest trick in the book – set an unbreakable time limit, then talk right through it to avoid the tricky bits at the end. Sometimes you can hassle them into saying something. That wouldn't work with this beauty. He seems to have invented the adjective 'imperturbable'. No wonder the guy saw us right away. With Mass coming up, it gave him the perfect 'out'.

'Now you were asking about the statue,' Father Jerry continued. 'You wondered whether it moved or not. Also if it wept. My answer to that is simply that I cannot say. I have not been present at the grotto on any of the occasions when it is reputed to have done so. As you must have heard by now, my housekeeper has changed her mind about the whole affair. She now believes it was simply a trick of the light played on tired eyes. Why don't you print that? Or perhaps you would not regard it as sufficiently newsworthy?'

'You're right, Father, we wouldn't. Why didn't you attend the prayer meetings at the grotto? As leader of the flock, surely your place was with them at a time like this? I believe the Legion of Mary extended an official invitation to you to join them in prayer.'

That ruffled his feathers a bit. He flushed and an icy note crept into his voice.

'Gentleman, that is quite simply not true. I have never received an official, as you term it, invitation from the Legion of Mary to join them at the grotto. I act as chairman for their meetings so I should know. The only official invitation I have received from them is to head their pilgrimage to Lourdes.'

'Is there not some doubt about that trip going ahead?' Colum asked.

'Stay at home pilgrims!' Villagers say why fly to Lourdes when we have our own miracle on our doorstep? – Maybe something could be done with that angle. At least it would be a fresh approach. The priest was playing a straight bat again.

'I hadn't heard. Did you happen to hear the reason? You appear to know more about what is happening in my parish than I do myself.'

'Be that as it may, that's what I hear. The word is that the lady who invited you to the grotto is now saying that the trip to Lourdes should be cancelled. Says it would be better for the Legion of Mary to keep a proper vigil by the grotto. What do you have to say about that?'

'Nothing, absolutely nothing at all.'

By now the smoke made Father Jerry almost invisible. Perhaps this line of questioning might yet bear fruit in the dying seconds of the game.

'Why did you refuse Mrs Flannery's invitation to join her in prayer at the grotto?'

'No particular reason except, of course, that her's was a private, informal invitation. I refuse and accept invitations all the time. For instance, someone wanted me to go out to dinner last night. I refused because I had to hear confessions at the time. Again I refused an official invitation from the Festival committee to make the opening speech because I believed that people would have heard more than enough of me from the pulpit. I refused another invitation to go sea-angling recently because I get seasick. So you see, gentlemen, I refuse invitations, public and private, formal and informal, all the time. It is one of the few prerogatives left to an ageing cleric.'

The silky sarcasm was wasted on them. Father Jerry made to gather up his matches and tobacco pouch in readiness for his departure. His pipe made a sucking sound like a blocked drain.

'And when are you leaving?' Colum asked.

'I beg your pardon, but I don't quite understand the question.'

'I'm told that you were posted here on sick leave from the Vatican. When you recover from whatever it is that is wrong with you, you will be moved on to some other trouble spot. Maybe even back to the Holy See.'

That might do it as a headline – POPE'S TROUBLESHOOTER FAILS TO CRACK GROTTO MYSTERY!

The priest was getting to his feet as he replied wearily, 'Well now, Mister Jones, it seems that once more you have the advantage of me. It's certainly the first I heard of it. I'm hardly of an age to go scuttling round the world as a sort of clerical "fixer" but if you want to believe it, that is your privilege. We both know that a priest can be moved anywhere at any time as his superiors see fit but, as I say, I am not aware of any such move in the offing. However, you never can tell, can you?'

'No, you can't. Now about your housekeeper, Julia what's-her-name. You must have brought pressure to bear on her to . . .'

Whatever it was he had in mind would have to keep for another day. Father Jerry walked to the door, removed the pipe from his mouth and said drily, 'I regret to say that our time is up. I have to lead my congregation in the celebration of High Mass in honour of Our Blessed Lady. No one will be more surprised than myself should she appear in person during the ceremony. Nevertheless, who can tell what may happen in these turbulent times? Perhaps the three of you might care to join me in the church. The Mass shouldn't take much more than an hour.'

Without waiting for a reply, he gathered his cassock about him, stuck the pipe back in his mouth and was gone. The interview was at an end.

24

If this is your home town, Sean, I don't blame you for getting out as fast as you did, Eddie Simcox thought as he steered the camper down the grey street with its drab buildings on either side linked to each other by lines of small flags hanging limply downwards. They tried, without success, to convey an air of gaiety. To Eddie it looked as if they were mourning the passing of an important citizen, except for the giant banner stretched across the street, bearing the legend 'Welcome to Brulagh'. He had passed the petrol pumps before he saw them in the mirror. They stood close together like rusted sentries, their hoses wrapped around their shoulders, curved handles protruding from their sides. They were set back from the footpath in front of a corrugated-iron shed that served as both forecourt and garage.

Reversing to the nearest pump, he got out and looked around. The shed was deserted save for a small, angry terrier. From a distance three men stood watching him in a disinterested fashion. One was dressed like a vicar except that he wore black. Another in a blue uniform and matching peaked cap could have been an ambulance driver; it was only when he spotted the three stripes on his sleeve that Eddie realised he was an Irish copper. Except for his height and big feet, he didn't look in the least like the law back home. The third was younger and wore a check sports jacket over grey flannel slacks with a shirt and tie. He looked like a civil servant.

There was a large building across the street. A plastic sign proclaimed it to be The Allied Banks of Ireland. Gold lettering on its windows assured him it had assets of more noughts than he could count. Of more immediate interest were its trading hours. It was not open for business until 10 a.m.

At the end of the street stood a huge church, its steeple pointing the faithful in the direction of their Heavenly reward. At its front gate a gaily decorated platform had been erected. A small boy stood alone under its striped canopy, clutching a microphone and looking anxiously at a loudspeaker. Outside a shop with a sign that read 'Mullarkey's Supermarket' two women were deep in conversation. *Supermarket my foot! The whole village would fit comfortably into my local Co-op.* He was startled by a piping voice.

'Is it petrol you want, sir?'

A girl emerged from behind the shed. She had red hair and freckles. He guessed she was no more than eight years old.

'Yes please. Fill her up.'

She uncoiled the hose, turned the handle until it clicked loudly and put the nozzle into the tank. This was her job and she was obviously very proud of the fact. Her gaze was fixed on the bunks that she could see between the chinks in the curtains of the camper.

'Do you sleep in that yoke?'

'I beg your pardon, could you say that again?'

The child giggled with embarrassment. She repeated the question slowly and clearly as though to a backward playmate. To further clarify the matter, she added, 'I mean, do you live in it?'

'Not really. Not all the time, if that's what you mean. Only when I'm on holiday.'

He felt his explanation was less than adequate. He still had difficulty in understanding what she was saying. The accent was singsong, almost a lilting Welsh, but the delivery was much faster. One word ran into another making it even harder to grasp.

'Are you here for the Festival?'

'Yeah, I am. Will it be any good, do you think?'

Again she dissolved into giggles at the thought of a grown-up asking such a silly question.

'Of course it will.'

Indignation replaced shyness as she replied, 'It's going to be a great gas altogether. Donkey races, talent competitions in the pubs, fancy dress. When the Sergeant finds the key they're going to have a parade with the band. That's them waiting over there.'

She pointed helpfully across the street to a low building around which a group of young and not so young bandsmen were loitering in an embarrassed fashion. This could have been due to their dress. From top to toe they were attired like traditional Scottish pipers, complete with kilt and sporran. The younger elements whiled the time away flicking each other's kilts upwards and then rushing away, shrieking with laughter.

'How much do I owe you?'

'Fourteen pounds, sir. If you please.'

Eddie counted out the crisp notes he had exchanged on the ferry. The punt looked quite like the English pound except the lady on the Irish note looked even sadder than the Queen.

188

'Do you know where I could buy small nuts and bolts? Also some decorating gear, paint, brushes and that sort of thing?'

'Try Flannery's sir, they should have what you want.'

'Where's that?'

'Go to the end of the street. Opposite the church. You can't miss it.'

He made a U-turn and parked in front of the bank. Waving goodbye to the child, who was coiling the hose around the pump, he crossed the street and walked in the direction she had pointed. Passing Mullarkey's, he looked in through the window. In fact it was quite big. The shop stretched back a long way to some kind of office with a brass grille in front of it. Still, it took some bloody cheek to call it a supermarket. Beside it was a small office with big picture windows. It, too, was closed. Lettering on its windows showed it to be the Office of the Department of Agriculture. Next to it was a neat house of much earlier origin with a badge of ceramic tiles over the door. It read 'Garda Siochana'. Must be the cop shop, he reckoned. It, too, showed no signs of life.

As he drew level with the boy on the platform, who was still clutching the dead microphone, they eyed each other warily. Suddenly a group of men were striding towards him. As they parted to let him through, he noticed one of them was wearing a green anorak across which were slung several cameras. They were talking animatedly among themselves, totally oblivious to his existence, as they turned up the avenue to an imposing grey house beside the gaunt church that so completely dominated its surroundings. Flannery's seemed an unlikely place to get what he needed even if the GENERAL MERCHANTS bit tacked on at the end of FLANNERY'S, GROCERS held out some hope.

Inside, amid a welter of bric-à-brac he was relieved to see tins of paint and a good selection of brushes. His freckled guide had directed him to the right place after all. He would have gone there on some pretext or other in any case. Sean had told him his mother ran the shop; this was his opportunity to get a look at her. Though Sean rarely mentioned his family, he obviously had great affection for his mother. She must feel the same way about him if she continued to send him the local paper. If it weren't for her persistence in sending it without any acknowledgement of its arrival the four of them wouldn't be here right now. Anyway Jenny would never forgive him if he hadn't inspected what she hoped would be her future mother-in-law.

The place was spooky – it reminded him of a nightmare he once had of being trapped in a cave. Sean's mother appeared. The resemblance was there for all to see. A tall, attractive woman of middle years, she seemed less than pleased to see him.

'Mrs Flannery?'

He had not meant to address her by name but she looked so like Sean that it seemed only natural to do so.

'That's right. Who wants to know? If you're a reporter you can clear out of here this minute! I have nothing to say to any of you!'

Her voice was brittle with tension. Eddie was mystified by the unexpected onslaught.

'I don't understand. I'm not from any paper. I just want to buy a few things, that's all. The girl at the petrol pumps said you might have what I want.'

He felt aggrieved. This bloody village was already getting on his nerves. First he could barely make out what the kid at the petrol pumps was saying. Now Sean's mother was practically kicking him out of her shop. If a good beginning were half the battle, it didn't augur well for the job they had to do in a few hours' time.

'Oh I'm really sorry.'

She sounded genuinely contrite. If he closed his eyes, it might have been Sean speaking.

'I thought you were one of those reporters. There's a mob of them running around looking for something to write about me for their papers. With your accent, I thought you might be one of them.'

'Well, I'm not! What would they want to write about you, if you don't mind my asking? I thought they must be covering the Festival or something like that.'

From what he had seen of it so far, they could easily have written a full description of it on the back of a postage stamp.

'I'm not sure what they're after. Probably the grotto, I expect. Are you English?'

'Yeah, that's right. Liverpool . . .'

He could have bitten off his tongue at the slip. Luckily she didn't pick it up. Hurriedly he went on, 'I'm looking for eight nuts and bolts, small ones if you have them. About an inch long, please.'

'I'll show you what I have. Eight, you said?'

He nodded. She made her way to a section of the counter that lifted upwards on hinges to allow her through. As she passed a statue standing on a niche high up on the far wall, she crossed herself just like that Everton centre-forward did on the rare occasions that he scored. She made for a stack of small, brown boxes and selected one. Taking off the lid, she offered it to him.

'Are those the sort you're looking for?'

'They'll do fine. Could I also have a big tin of white hard gloss and a small tin of black enamel paint? Oh yes, and two brushes, one large and one small. What was that you were saying about a grotto?'

'Oh it was nothing. It's just that there's a grotto a few hundred yards down the road from here. You must have passed it on your way into the village. Well there's been a lot of excitement over it recently, that's all. Between it and the Festival, we'll all be driven out of our minds before this weekend is over. Will you be staying on for the Festival yourself?'

After the Liverpool slip, he was not going to make the same mistake twice.

'I'm not sure. The girl at the pumps said it would be starting soon. She said it would be great fun. What do you think?'

'Did she say that? A fine cheeky one she is for sure. All the same, it might be true for her. Time will tell. There's to be a parade first, led by the band. I haven't heard a squeak out of them yet so it could be a while before they're ready. Will there be anything else?'

He decided he had pushed his luck far enough. No point in over-staying his welcome. If he didn't leave now, she was sure to ask him questions he would prefer not to answer. When the police made enquiries afterwards, he wanted to appear as an ordinary visitor to the silly Festival. The only copper he had seen so far looked as if he couldn't catch a cold. Nevertheless, you couldn't be too careful when you were trying to pull off a stunt like this one.

'Yes, I'll take those two trays over there by the window as well . . .'

They looked about the right size for a diversion sign.

'Now what does all that come to, Mrs Flannery?'

'The two tins of paint and the brushes come to six pounds, eighteen pence. The trays are one pound fifty each. That's nine pounds eighteen pence in all. Make it an even nine pounds, if you like.'

She had not touched the cash register or used a scrap of paper to work out the sum. Eddie was impressed by her mental arithmetic; he could see where Sean had got his brains. She took his money and pressed a key on the till. This opened the cash drawer with a staccato ring of a bell from somewhere deep inside the machine. It reminded him of the panic buttons in the gunsmiths'. Obviously Mrs Flannery was into bells in a big way. Handing him a pound note from the cash drawer, she slammed it shut, causing another peal.

191

'I hope you have a nice weekend. Good day to you.'

Barely a minute later the bell over the door announced the arrival of another customer. This time it was the priest. To his considerable embarrassment, it was the first time he had been inside the shop. He had been putting it off for far too long and now he wondered what excuse he would make for his overdue visit. Or, indeed, whether he should make any at all. Probably the safest course would be to buy a tin of tobacco and find out for himself if the Doc's medication was having any effect. If he got the chance to dissuade her from becoming the bearer of God's message to the world, then so much the better.

From the outside, it looked like the Old Curiosity Shop. Two tall windows on either side of the door were empty save for a few dead flies and a partly decomposed wasp. White wicker screens acted as a backdrop to the empty stage. They also cut off a view of the interior. Reaching half-way to the ceiling, each bore a different message. One modestly declared, FLANNERY'S FINEST TEA – A BLEND OF THE BEST TEAS FROM ALL OVER THE WORLD. The screen in the other window read, FLANNERY'S – GROCERS AND GENERAL MERCHANTS SINCE 1913.

No merchandise nor 'special offer' poster was to be seen. The barren windows gave no indication whatsoever, apart from the writing on the fly-specked screens, of what lay behind them. To reassure the sceptical that this indeed was a shop and not the headquarters of some obscure religious sect, there was further information on a small frieze above the window frames. Etched in minute, flowery script was, LICENSED TO SELL WINES, BEERS AND TOBACCO.

As he entered the shop, a bell above the door gave out a sharp ping. It made him start. The noise caused a movement at the back of the shop whose only source of light was that which came through the windows and filtered through the screens. As he waited for Maggie to emerge from the dark recesses, he wondered at the cash register – big as a Wurlitzer organ. On the counter beside it lay a book that might have been a bible. It had LEDGER picked out in faded gilt on its leather spine, and looked older than many of the late Canon's beautifully bound volumes. Did it hold the financial skeletons of the village, he wondered?

These he would be spared in the confessional, where only spiritual and sexual matters were discussed. His flock believed that the Ten Commandments were suspended where money was involved. He wondered idly how the last entry for the parochial house would read. He would have liked to steal a quick look at his account in the huge tome to see if it had been credited with the defective bag of flour but

192

his nerve failed him. Relations were likely to be sufficiently strained without Maggie catching him prying into her ledger. Nevertheless it would have been interesting to discover who was ahead in the battle between the two women for the trade of Brulagh.

The shop was claustrophobic. It reminded him of the catacombs that housed the dead in caves beneath the Eternal City. Rows of hayforks, rakes, shovels, spades and replacement handles tied in neat bundles stood like sentinels against the wall. Above them were shelves stacked to the ceiling with tins of paint, bottles of turpentine, weedkiller and sheep dip. Next to them, for no logical reason, were multi-coloured cartons of seeds, fighting for space with small bags of compost and fertiliser. Overhead, hanging upside down like bats from hooks in the ceiling, were pots and pans, kettles and teapots, baking tins, watering cans, coal scuttles and buckets. Further on, they gave way to hot-water bottles, frying pans, cake tins, and coils of nylon and manila ropes of varying length and thickness. Further back in the dim recesses of the shop from where Maggie was just emerging, dangled endless pairs of wellington boots.

As he approached the counter, Maggie moved to the far side. Tall and slim, there was a faded elegance about her tired face. She wore a blue shop-coat with a floral pattern and held a bag of what appeared to be tea-leaves in one hand. A silver-coloured scoop was gripped firmly in the other. She was not pleased by the interruption.

'I suppose you've come about the weevils!'

Her voice was dull, resigned almost. Certainly not angry, he was relieved to note.

'Not really, Mrs Flannery, though if you want to talk about them, that's fine by me. All I wanted was a tin of tobacco, as a matter of fact.'

'Julia May says I was trying to poison you. Do you believe that?'

'Of course not, she was upset, that's all.'

'Those things sometimes come in the flour. I was on the phone to the millers. They're sending someone around next week to take away a sample for analysis. I hope you realise it's not my fault. I had no way of knowing what was inside the bag. There was no sign of them when I was filling the bags . . .'

She just stopped herself from saying when. It was nearly six weeks ago, a long time for flour to remain stacked in a drawer. Mullarkey's had a special offer on flour and she had hardly sold a bag of it over the past month.

'Look, why don't we forget the whole thing. It's not very important. How much for the tobacco?'

They were interrupted by another customer, who wanted a handle for a hayfork. Maggie pointed to the wall where they stood. Examining each one carefully, he asked if he might take a few outside to view them properly in the daylight. When she reluctantly agreed, he made for the door with his selection. He could be seen on the footpath with his four handles looking for the knot that would cause a premature break. Not finding one, he checked for less obvious flaws by pressing each in turn against the pavement to test its strength and resilience. After each test, he ran his eye along the handle, as though sighting a rifle, to check if his efforts had left a kink in the timber. He was a man who would not be rushed into a foolish purchase.

'Do you really blend your own teas?'

'No, we don't. Not any more. We have this tea merchant in Dublin and he does it for us. His father and mine were great friends. That's how it all started. His son carried on the blending business. He knows what we want and whenever he gets it, he sends us on a couple of chests. He says it's getting harder to find good leaf every year. Something to do with the English planters being kicked out of India and Ceylon. Do you like tea yourself?'

'Not especially. Then again I've only tried it out of teabags. I expect you have them in Ireland too.'

'Indeed we have. The young ones nowadays wouldn't know how to make a proper cup of tea if their lives depended on it. The stuff in the teabags is only dust. The very same rubbish that we throw out from the bottom of the chest. I suppose it's easier for them to drop a bag into a cup of hot water than to go to the bother of warming a teapot and letting the tea draw for a few minutes. No one wants to take time over anything nowadays. It's the same with nappies. When I started here, you bought your nappies before you had your baby. You washed them until you didn't need them any longer. Then you put them away in a cupboard, ready for the next arrival. Now you can hardly take a step on the beach without tripping over one of those filthy paper things.'

She was amazed at herself talking like this to a priest. It must be those pills. She had been feeling odd all morning. Not sick or anything, just different. Sort of detached was the best way to describe the feeling. Like she was walking on air. Though she realised she was talking nineteen to the dozen, she didn't care. Usually she

194

weighed her words as carefully as her tea. The priest didn't seem to mind, in fact he seemed quite interested.

'Don't you sell teabags at all, then?'

'Not on your life. Most of my customers wouldn't touch them. Those that want them can find them below in the supermarket. That's the sort of trade they cater for. And the disposable nappies. I don't stock them either.'

The woman had a dazed look. Unless he wished to prolong the discussion on the merits or otherwise of the disposable nappy versus those of the teabag, a quick exit was in order. She had made no reference to the grotto, the press statement, the funeral fracas or the soon to be revealed Divine message. He knew that for him to do so would be a waste of time. Maggie Flannery was lost in a happy, hazy zombie-like trance. A wistful smile as if she was remembering some long forgotten happiness played around her lips.

'What do I owe you, Mrs Flannery?'

She walked slowly along the far side of counter until she reached the cash register. Her movements seemed mechanical in some indefinable way. The Doc's prescription was certainly having an effect. Whether it was the desired one was another matter. The woman was stoned out of her mind.

'Now let me see. The tobacco is one pound twenty. The nappies are two pounds and ten pence and the tea is one pound fifty. That will be four pounds and eighty pence please.'

Father Jerry paid for the nappies and the tea without demur – just relieved that they had not been produced. He could imagine Julia May's reaction should he leave them on the kitchen table. Instead he put the tin of tobacco in his pocket and waited for his change. He could not bring himself to ask her anything about the grotto. He knew he should but something deep inside told him that this was neither the time nor the place. She handed him his change, saying, 'Good day to you, Father.'

With that she turned on her heel and headed for the back of the shop to resume whatever she had been doing. As he opened the door to leave, the bell above his head bade him a last farewell. Outside on the footpath, the farmer was still testing the handles, undecided as to whether any of them met his requirements. Across the street, a big green van jerked to a halt. Its occupants climbed out hurriedly and approached him. One of them carried a TV camera big as an anti-tank gun on his shoulder and aimed it at him without as much as a by your leave. Beside him an assistant held a shiny aluminium suitcase strapped to his wrist. Power cables led from it to the camera and to the microphone cupped in the hand of the third individual, who was dressed in a smart blue blazer and grey flannels. Into the microphone he whispered the incantation of interviewers the world over: 'Testing, testing, testing, ah one . . . ah two . . . ah three.' Satisfied that it was working properly, he thrust it towards Father Jerry. The farmer had broken off from testing the handles and was watching the proceedings with growing consternation.

'Father O'Sullivan? I'm Stephen Walshe from Ulster Television. We're doing an item on the grotto for the *News at Ten* programme.'

'What sort of an item?'

'Oh just the usual. Interviews with interested parties. Shots of the faithful at prayer. Reactions of the local worthies . . . all that sort of thing. Might even do a documentary on it later if anyone thinks it worth the bother. Will you give us an interview?'

'You mean right here on the street?'

'Yes, unless you would prefer to do it with the grotto as a backdrop. Come to think of it, that would be better, much better.'

The impertinence of it flabbergasted him. The cameraman was fiddling with the controls, obviously getting ready to film. Father Jerry brushed aside the microphone with an impatient sweep of his hand and faced his tormentor.

'I have no intention of giving you an interview. It would serve no useful purpose except to blow what is essentially a trivial local matter out of all proportion.'

'That's OK, Father. Don't get mad, we're just doing our job. When we saw you, we thought we would give you the chance to put your point of view across to the world at large. If you don't want to, that's fine by us. Actually we're on our way to interview Mrs Flannery. We hear she's not too pleased with your attitude to the whole business. Did you not suggest that she might be making money out of it?'

Before he could nail the lie, another question followed.

'She *is* Mick Flannery's wife, isn't she? The guy in the Dáil with the four All-Ireland medals in a row, I mean?'

Father Jerry nodded as they brushed past him into the shop. He quickened his step, realising that he had less than five minutes to change into his vestments and say Mass.

25

The home-made wine competition was held in the Festival marquee. After Mass a large crowd gathered round the long trellis table, which was creaking under a vast array of bottles. Josephine Donnelly judged the entries and Mick presented the prizes. Father Jerry said a few words as well, relieved at the absence of the media in any shape or form. It wouldn't have surprised him in the least had Colum Jones come up with something like 'WINE-CRAZED WOMEN AWAIT DOUBLE VISION', or 'DIVINE MESSAGE COMES FROM HOME-MADE VINO!'

He wished he could have told Mick of the incident at the shop before handing over to him but there were too many spectators pressing around them for anything of a private nature to be said. Instead he discussed the merits of a very young rhubarb wine with an intense young man in sandals who, according to the Sergeant, also grew his own cannabis somewhere on the mountainside.

Though he sampled the wines extensively, Mick was not foolhardy enough to judge them. That would have embroiled him in needless controversy that might lose him a few precious votes. At the prize-giving, he praised the dedication of the wine-makers, congratulated the winners and consoled the losers with the prospect of there being another day. Already he pined for the Bloody Mary that usually kick-started him to cope with days like this. Father Jerry looked in even greater need of one. He was unaccountably jittery, his speech hesitant and uncertain, as he plucked nervously at the lapels of his coat.

Josephine, on the other hand, looked radiant in a smart red suit. It was chiefly because of her that the wine thing happened at all. Mick welcomed its addition to the programme as he did most drink-related innovations. There had been much heart-searching prior to its inclusion in the Festival. A vocal minority of teetotallers, one of whom was his wife, objected strenuously. They called themselves Pioneers, though they bore scant resemblance to the hardy souls who braved the Rockies and marauding Red Indians in their quest for a better life.

The Brulagh variety were to find Paradise in the next world. It would be a reward for their relentless efforts to turn the likes of Mick away from alcohol. Founded in the last century by a reforming priest,

197

the Pioneers received only lukewarm support from the clergy. Like Maggie, they chose the thorny path of abstinence. Total abstinence. It was a difficult concept to promote in a community where social life centred around the pub. That many priests were dedicated drinkers did even less to further their cause. It was not surprising, therefore, that the heart-shaped Pioneer badge – known as 'the pin' – did not adorn many lapels. That the home-made wine competition attracted such a large crowd was due, in no small measure, to the free tasting that followed the adjudication. It was then that Josephine beat Father Jerry by a short head for the ear of Mick Flannery.

'Hi there, lover boy . . .'

She spoke like a ventriloquist, her deliciously glossed lips barely moving as the words made sweet music in his ear. '. . . That went off OK, didn't it?'

Before he could agree and perhaps ask her back to O'Shea's for a quiet chat about the logistics of how they might progress their relationship, she floored him with her next question.

'What are you doing for the next couple of hours?'

He shrugged as he pondered the implications. He knew he should be doing any of twenty different things. Chief among these were preparing his speech for the opening ceremony, having one last shot at talking Maggie out of acting as God's courier to mankind, and sinking at least three Bloody Marys to prepare him for what looked like a trying day.

She continued without waiting for his reply, 'Because unless you had anything terribly urgent going on, I thought it might be fun to take a look at Rose Cottage.'

He spluttered in a mixture of astonishment and growing excitement as the suggestion hung in the air.

'Best idea I've heard in ages. Give me time to get the place straightened out. I'll meet you there in, say, half an hour. Would that be OK?'

'Terrific! I'll hop on my bike and see you then. Bye for now.'

As she swept out of the marquee, several women stared sourly at her body-hugging suit and put their heads together to bemoan the passing of an era when bank managers' wives dressed in a more becoming fashion. Though he could see Father Jerry trying to reach him through the heaving throng, Mick beat a hasty retreat in the opposite direction and made for O'Shea's as fast as his legs would carry him.

'A large Bloody Mary and a bottle of brandy, Tom. Make it as quick as you can, like a decent man, I'm in one hell of a hurry!'

He downed the miracle that even O'Shea's destructive powers could not harm and watched the tomato juice slide down the inside of the glass to form a small, a very small, red blob at the bottom.

'No bird ever flew on one wing, Tom. Better give me another one of those and wrap up the bottle, will you?'

'Right, Mick. I wasn't sure if you were going to drink it here or take it away with you!'

Mick chose to ignore the jibe. O'Shea was in a class of his own when it came to oddity. He had yet to meet anyone with a good word to say about him.

'I hear Maggie has just chased a TV crew out of the shop with a pitchfork,' O'Shea commented.

Mick had never liked O'Shea, less so since he tried to harass his daughter, Gillian. Nevertheless he needed somewhere to hold his clinics and the bar was the only suitable venue. For that reason alone, he tried to be civil to the shamrock-crazy little bastard.

'Jaysus, Tom, I hope you're joking!'

'On my oath, I'm not! Some old guy outside the shop saw the whole thing from beginning to end. Said he joined in himself and gave them a few belts over the head with a handle or something. Said 'twas the best fun he'd had since listening to you promising the new pier.'

Mick seriously contemplated hitting O'Shea hard between the eyes but thought better of it. It might only delay him from his tryst.

'I don't see anything funny about it. As it is, she's nearly demented over the bloody grotto. Now this will put the tin hat on it. What's a TV crew doing round here anyway?'

The prospect of free publicity made him bridle like an old warhorse at the scent of battle.

'Dunno. Your guess is as good as mine. Could they be here to cover your speech, I wonder?'

Not trusting himself to reply, he left hurriedly. He drove quickly along the narrow road. In the short time before he addressed the populace he was determined to make every second count. A dutiful husband would have been at his wife's side in her time of need, he supposed. But life, he consoled himself, was nothing but a series of choices. If you came right down to it, what red-blooded man in his right senses would forgo a few hours of bliss with the likes of Josephine for the hassle of trying to talk a crazy woman, even if she were his wife, out of kneeling before a statue that moved and shed tears and waiting for it to deliver a message from God?

Anyway he needed time to tidy the cottage before Josephine arrived. God alone knew what condition it would be in after the last occupant. First he would make sure that the bedroom was all right, then he might light a fire to lend a touch of romance to the proceedings. He would open the windows, of course, to air the place. The brandy would have to be introduced with considerable delicacy. He did not wish to convey the impression of a randy old lecher plying an innocent young thing with strong drink so that he might have his wicked way with her. None the less he needed several drinks before he gave of his best. Already the buzz from the Bloody Marys was wearing off as he sped past the rock-strewn fields carved into tiny squares by drystone walls. The need for another drink and the anticipation of what lay ahead made his fingers beat an anxious drum roll on the steering wheel.

He was nervous as a teenager on his first date. *Ridiculous*, he told himself. *You've had more affairs than your constituents have had hot dinners.* They had, however, had been conducted further from home. This was the first time he risked defecating on his own doorstep. Rose Cottage, as if he needed reminding, was less than two miles from the doorstep whose purity he was so keen to preserve. He would hide his car in the garage in the backyard of the cottage, which was hidden from the road. Otherwise, he might as well put an advertisement in the *Clarion* to the effect that Michael Flannery, Esq., legendary sportsman and politician without equal, was having it off with one Josephine, the beautiful and compliant wife of the universally loathed Thomas Donnelly. Perhaps it would have taken something of that magnitude to distract Maggie from her mission. Fair play to her, though, for taking the pitchfork to those shaggers. If she found out about himself and Josephine, he could expect a similar fate. Not that it would happen, he reassured himself. Rose Cottage was well off the beaten track.

Safely ensconced, his car out of sight, all he had to do was to remain indoors – which shouldn't be too difficult. Josephine Donnelly was a good-looking woman and no mistake. Not a day over thirty, if he was any judge. Maybe he *was* old enough to be her father but what did that matter? Half the bloody Dáil would happily sacrifice their eye teeth to get into bed with her. Anyway, you were as old as you felt. To this original observation, he added another. A few hours with the voluptuous Josephine would compensate in some measure for the slings and arrows that had been raining down on him with even more than their usual ferocity.

Apart from the GAA not naming the stand after him, he had just discovered that Mullarkey was snapping at his heels yet again. This time it was over the temporary car park beside the grotto. The little bollix was going to bring it up at the next County Council meeting as an example of flagrant disregard for planning regulations. Add to that Maggie's moving statues with their messages for an unbelieving world, the bloody village crawling with reporters and the VAT man going through the books with a fine toothcomb and there was enough aggravation surrounding him to give Job a nervous breakdown.

Rose Cottage was the home of Maggie's uncle Tim. He died last year without making a will. He did, however, leave behind a large debt in the shop ledger. Tim had never paid for anything in his lifetime, preferring to charge everything on the vague promise of riches to come in his will. When these had failed to materialise, Mick decided that generous provisions for VAT and a lifetime's credit could be added to the bill before he submitted it to Tim's solicitor. How this would be received by the swarm of bloodsucking relatives hoping to benefit from the estate was anyone's guess. Mick calculated that his share would clear his debts and perhaps leave a something over and above for incidental expenses. The first of these would be a trip to Lourdes for Maggie – if she could be persuaded to go. It might just bring her back to her senses. She had always been more relaxed for a few weeks after her annual pilgrimage. Now, thanks to those shagging Mullarkeys, he would have to pay for her ticket because of her resignation as mother hen to the Legion of Mary. If she made the pilgrimage he could look forward to several encores in Rose Cottage during her absence.

As an executor to the will, he had been given a key to the cottage in the hope that he might let it to some of his wealthier Dublin cronies. In this he had been quite successful. The last tenant had left at the end of July so the place had been empty for the past fortnight. The fellow was an accountant with a wife and a child so he hoped to find the place in good order. In case it wasn't, he wanted to get there before Josephine. There was no greater passion-killer than dirty dishes in a sink or an unmade bed. If this encounter turned out less than idyllic, it would not be for lack of preparation. Despite the cottage's isolation, it was an attractive place with fuchsia-covered hedgerows and a panoramic view of the green hillside sweeping down to the sea. A tiny front garden was festooned with roses. It was reached by a narrow, twisting back road, which only hardy souls like the late Uncle Tim used as a short-cut to the main road over the mountain.

The memory of Tim made him smile. His coffin had been draped in the national flag. At the graveside a volley of shots was fired by his comrades from weapons even more ancient than themselves. Such tributes were reserved for those who had fought in the War of Independence. The myth of uncle Tim, freedom fighter *extraordinaire*, persisted right to the end. The true facts of the ambush that made his name a legend in his own lifetime were hard to come by.

Mick was told by one who had been there that there were no more than six of the local flying column – free-range guerrillas on bicycles – present when the Model T Ford chugged its way up the steep mountain road. It carried four members of the notorious Black and Tans – a rag-tag mercenary unit loosely attached to the British Army. Recruited from demobbed soldiers and petty criminals, they had a well-deserved reputation for ferocity. The ambush took less than a minute. A volley of rifle shots from behind a low stone wall left one dead Tan on the roadside. Two of the flying column received flesh wounds as they made their escape. When satisfied that their attackers had fled, the Tans brought the corpse back to the barracks. That evening they descended on Brulagh, where they roughed up a few villagers but failed to get information on the movements of the flying column. Maggie's father was dragged from behind his bar when he protested at their behaviour. He was put up against a wall and might have been shot out of hand but for the intervention of a senior officer. Con Murphy built a long and distinguished career in politics out of that incident.

As he told it later, despite torture and the threat of execution he refused to divulge the whereabouts of his gallant brother Tim, the hero of the ambush that sparked off the reprisal. Tim had to be rehearsed carefully in his contribution to the cause of Irish freedom because he had been fishing two miles offshore during the ambush. He learned his lines well enough to qualify for a good pension and a disability allowance for being wounded in action.

As he eased the car into the backyard of Rose Cottage, Mick recalled the TV interview that Tim had given on the fiftieth anniversary of what by then had become a benchmark in the Fight for Freedom. Historians had pinpointed it as the opening salvo in the conflict that finally resulted in an Irish Free State. While the passage of half a century had increased the Black and Tans from four to twenty, the precise numbers of the flying column remained shrouded in mystery. Tim insisted that it was impossible to give an exact figure as 'the lads were coming and going all morning' as they lay in wait. The forty-two still drawing pensions on the strength of the ambush had reason to be grateful for his less than total recall.

Firelighting was not one of Mick's skills. The contents of the grate looked as if all they needed was a lighted match to get a fire going. After three attempts he had used up all the paper and was still faced with a tangled web of blackened twigs and two lightly grilled milk cartons. He returned to the garage. While parking the car he had scraped against a lawnmower lurking in the gloom. Where there was a lawnmower, he reasoned, there had to be petrol. There was no sign of a petrol tin anywhere. Cans of paint, long since hardened into uselessness, two drums of a lethal weedkiller and a bottle of disinfectant were all he could unearth. A flash of inspiration sent him to look in the tank of the mower. It was half full. He emptied the contents into one of the discarded paint tins, splashing a good deal of the fuel over his trousers in the process.

Back inside he poured the petrol carefully into the scorched grate, fearful that an unseen spark would blow the whole thing up in his face. When it didn't, he stood well back and threw lighted matches at the grate. Nothing happened. The matches burnt out long before they reached their target. Moving closer, he allowed the flame to get a firm hold on the match before trying again. This time he succeeded beyond his wildest expectations. With an explosion that blinded him momentarily, the contents of the grate erupted into a blazing inferno. It settled down into a glowing core that promised to develop into a decent fire. Another trip to the garage produced a bale of turf briquettes, some of which he placed on the fire. As he made for the bedroom, he was pleased to note that the stench of petrol had lessened somewhat.

The duvet and pillows were arranged neatly at the end of the big double bed. He plugged in the electric blanket and switched it on. Arranging the duvet on the bed, he gave it an affectionate pat in anticipation. Drawing back the lace curtains, he opened the window and gazed down the valley to where his native village nestled by the sea. The whine from the loudspeaker could still be heard in the distance, an unwelcome reminder that he should be preparing his speech were he to let his head rule his heart – or points south. Just this once, he muttered, Mick Flannery is going to put himself first! He had to prove to himself that there was life in the old dog yet.

Don't be bloody ridiculous, he told himself. You're not even sixty. Some of those old goats in the European Parliament are over eighty and they're still at it morning, noon and night. A change is what you need, he assured himself, as he put the brandy beside the toaster. Lighting a cigarette, he considered the possibility that the Doc might have been serious when he ordered him to stop smoking. He had looked suitably grave as he donned the black cap and handed down the verdict. Well to hell with the Doc, this was no time to quit the habit.

Of course he wanted to live as long as the next man but there were sacrifices he was not prepared to make in the pursuit of longevity. Come to think of it, the Doc had never promised him a long life. What he *had* said was that he would be dead if he didn't stop drinking and smoking. Not the same thing at all, not by a long shot. A quick inspection proved the loo to be in good shape. One hundred pounds a week and the place left looking like a new pin! Why would anyone want to sell a money-spinner like this? Even if they could find a buyer, the price they would get for a cottage at the back of beyond would be a pittance. With any luck they could get a couple of thousand every year from letting it to good tenants like the accountant and still own the property at the end of the day. But try telling that to the flock of vultures he had for relations. It would be easier to convince them that the earth was flat.

If he had any money, he would buy it himself. It could double as an investment and a love-nest. Sadly, it was out of the question for the time being. The shop was losing money hand over fist and even without the VAT problem, his credit was already overstretched. Of late, Donnelly had taken to writing letters. While their tone was still respectful, as befitted correspondence addressed to a public figure, certain phrases were creeping in too often for comfort. Recurrent themes such as 'endeavouring to reduce your overall indebtedness' and requests for 'a meeting at your earliest convenience' made him uneasy. He wondered how the bloodsucker would react if he knew his wife was about to jump into bed with a delinquent borrower. Probably write him a letter about it.

As though on cue, he heard a noise from the yard. Opening the back door he saw Josephine guiding her bike through the narrow space between the garage and the whitewashed wall. A small bag was tied to the carrier. She was wearing jeans, leather boots and a wool sweater that displayed her charms to good effect. He was entranced. She really had a superb figure. Forget your troubles Mick

Flannery, he told himself, and count your blessings. There's a lot of men would give their right arm to be standing in your shoes this minute. Pausing only to move the brandy to a slightly less obvious position, he went outside to welcome her to Rose Cottage.

'Josephine, you're looking great!'

It may not have been on a par with Shakespeare in the matter of great opening lines but it was the best he could think of in the circumstances.

'Thanks Mick, you're not looking so bad yourself. When I saw the smoke pouring out of the chimney I thought you were electing a Pope. Am I late?'

'Not at all. Just perfect, as it happens. I was getting the place into some sort of shape,' he lied cheerfully, 'the last family that rented it left it in a mess.'

'Well lover boy, aren't you going to give me a welcoming kiss?'

Her lips were warm and soft. Being a head shorter she had to stand tip-toe and put her arms around his neck to reach his mouth. A surge of excitement ran through his body like an electric current. As her tongue forced his teeth apart and waggled provocatively against his, they embraced tenderly at first, then with greater urgency. He was about to explore what lay beneath the sweater when she broke away with a giggle.

'Mick Flannery, I'm surprised at you! Can't you control yourself at least until we get inside the house. What if someone saw me glued to the local TD in a backyard miles from anywhere? We'd never hear the end of it.'

Removing the bag from her bike she strode across the yard to the open door. He followed a few steps behind, mesmerised by the movement of her firm buttocks beneath the overstretched denim. With a woman like that on the premises, it was a miracle that Donnelly had the time to write those letters. To judge by the way she launched herself at him, maybe he had been writing too many of them.

26

For McCain and his partner, Barney, the whole business was becoming more chaotic by the minute. Having left the room above the bar for a breakfast of inedible fat and gristle, they drove around the area all day looking for the camper or the Porsche. The closest they got to either was when a young girl at the petrol pumps told them a camper had filled up the day before. They spent the rest of the time driving up and down the side of a mountain, vainly seeking their quarry. The Festival had completely taken over the village, making their quest even more difficult. Any methodical search was out of the question. Crowds milled around a donkey race or followed a fancy-dress parade in a swirling, ever-changing whirlpool of faces. Finding needles in haystacks would have been easier than trying to pick out a face or a car in the turgid stream of traffic that flowed through the thronged roads. Finding their quarry now would be purely a matter of chance.

By midday McCain feared that he had lost them. It would have been easy for them to slip away unseen amid the confusion. Then again they could be camped in some remote spot, lying low and waiting for the Festival to end. But to what purpose? They had no reason to suspect that they were being followed. By night, McCain had left their car not in O'Shea's car park but in a field beside the grotto where at least two hundred other vehicles were parked in random fashion at all times of the day and night. The unspoken thought in both their minds was that the birds had flown and they were wasting their time. Indeed McCain was on the point of calling the exercise off and returning to the motel to collect their belongings when a horn blared behind them. Moving over to the side, he was passed by a girl driving a white sports car very quickly. It was the Simcox girl in the Porsche.

They gave chase but from the start it was an unequal contest. The Nissan was no match for the Porsche. In a moment she had vanished from sight. They doggedly pursued her, falling further behind with every passing second. McCain had given up hope when they came to a straight stretch of road where the sign 'Welcome to Brulagh' peeped out from behind a clump of tall nettles. Just ahead was a convoy of three army Land Rovers with an unmarked police car bringing up the rear. They were scattered haphazardly across the road as though they had braked hard to a sudden halt. They must have stopped for the Porsche, which was stalled sideways across the road. Jenny, her miniskirt riding up almost to her waist, was leaning over its wing, peering under the raised bonnet. Three soldiers were around her, tinkering with the engine. Their colleagues remained in the Land Rovers, their eyes glued to her shapely rear, hoping that she would lean over even further. McCain reversed quietly back around the corner, stopped the car and got out. From behind a bush, he watched and waited.

He did not have long to wait. Jenny got back into the Porsche and took off hurriedly, wheels spinning on the dry tarmac. The soldiers returned to their vehicles, sniggering and throwing lewd remarks at each other. In a moment, the convoy moved off at a sedate pace. Even if McCain had wanted to, he did not have enough room to overtake them on the narrow road. It was better, he decided, to keep a discreet distance behind the procession of vehicles. For the second time in five minutes, Jenny disappeared from view.

'Jesus, what's going on? The whole place is crawling with fucking soldiers,' Barney complained.

McCain just shrugged his shoulders, not bothering to reply. Barney, apart from his aftershave, had the added vice of stating the obvious as though it were freshly minted wisdom. Neither did he tell him that the police car belonged to the Special Branch. There were only sixteen such cars altogether, most of them unmarked. He made it his business to know their registration numbers. The question nagging him like a sore tooth was what one of them was doing in a place like this. He knew that sometimes, in an emergency, they were pressed into duty for bank escorts. But if that was their present assignment, where was the vehicle they were supposed to be escorting? McCain disliked mysteries.

He took a right turn down the side road that would eventually bring him back into the village. The convoy drove straight on. He would get to hell out of here as quickly as possible. Everything had become too high profile for his liking. Blondes in flashy cars were fine for TV or the movies but not the sort of thing freedom fighters wanted around them at a time like this. The presence of the Special Branch was the last straw. He had to be high on their list of people they wished to 'interview'. They might have a few questions to ask him about that cheating bastard for starters. The Dutch police must have sent them on his file by now even if they had dropped the case like a hot brick. Not that he had committed any crime in Ireland except to be a member of an illegal organisation. That in itself, of course, would be enough to put him away for two years or more.

He had an uncomfortable feeling about O'Shea. For all the trappings of patriotism, the portraits of rebel leaders that covered his walls and his love of bile-green shamrocks, some sixth sense told McCain that the old man was watching them without pretending to, almost as though he had been alerted to their true identities. With so many splits within the IRA nowadays, McCain often felt that he had more to fear from his own than from the enemy. That had been one reason for parking the car in the field by the grotto. The other was that the design of O'Shea's car park created a bottleneck which might present a problem should they wish to make a quick getaway. It would have been nice to interrogate young Flannery but it wasn't worth two years in jail just for the sake of executing him. When he had collected all the available evidence, he would send it to his section head for evaluation. As for the girl and her brothers, they were just petty criminals and not worth bothering about. What really gnawed at his conscience, though he could not bring himself to admit to it, was that he was disobeying orders.

He should have checked with the London cell before dashing back to Ireland. Had this mission been a success, he could have shrugged off the oversight. Now that he was going to abort it, he would have trouble in justifying his wild chase from Liverpool to here. His masters had specifically warned him against using ports and airports unnecessarily since his cover had been blown in Holland. At least that crook had got what was coming to him, even if it earned McCain his unwelcome fifteen minutes of fame – his face scowling out from TV screens and the front pages for one long weekend.

Some might interpret his ferry crossing as acting against orders for no good reason, thereby endangering the security of the organisation. McCain had enemies in the Provos who would be happy to kill him on lesser pretexts than that. They would argue that he could have been recognised by immigration control, his identity checked and passed on to the Special Branch. That would explain the presence of one of their cars in the middle of nowhere, providing an escort for an invisible charge.

Lost in thought, he turned the car down the back road that would bring them in a long, winding loop back into the village. They passed a priest walking briskly. He was reading his office from a small leatherbound book and scarcely noticed their passing. Around the next corner they found their path blocked yet again – this time by the Porsche, the camper, a blue security van with its back doors open and a tractor and trailer which completely sealed off the road. Three men in balaclavas were unloading the last few bags out of the van into the camper, helped by two security men. Everyone froze as he braked the Nissan to a skidding halt.

Barney spotted the girl first. She was turning the Porsche towards them as though she was either going to ram them or make a run for it. He loosed off a few wild shots at her. She braked hard, jumped out of the car and dashed for the cover of a nearby cottage, screaming as she ran. The other three in balaclavas, one with a sawn-off shotgun, followed her. Rank amateurs, McCain realised. Real pros would have stood their ground. He had arrived in the nick of time. The van's contents were already loaded into the camper, its engine still running, as they raced past it towards the house.

McCain was thinking of the man with the shotgun as he kicked in the front door and threw himself out of the line of fire behind the jamb. Barney saw the shotgun pointing to the floorboards and barely resisted the urge to shoot its owner on the spot. Instead he screamed at him to drop it as McCain stepped across the threshold. Barney came into his own, McCain conceded, in situations like this. The idiot was dead if the balaclava had the balls to use his gun. They herded the four into the kitchen and took stock of their surroundings. A trail of clothes, obviously discarded in some haste, led to a locked door.

'Jesus Christ, what was that?'

Mick was roused into sudden wakefulness. The sound of revving engines and confused shouting came through the open window. It was a split second before he could get his bearings. They must have fallen asleep after their exertions. It slowly dawned on him that the commotion was coming from somewhere outside. From where he was lying, Josephine's nubile form splayed out beside him, he could see little through the open window except a cloudless sky. Slipping out of bed as quietly as possible, he pulled on his trousers. By craning his neck, he could see part of the road in front of Rose Cottage. It was empty; nothing to be seen but the trees swaying in the breeze. The engine noises had dropped to a low hum, replaced by excited voices shouting to each other. He drew his head back inside the window and padded stealthily to the front door. He would get a better view from there. He inched it open just enough to peer out without being noticed. It took a while to grasp what was happening.

A dark blue van was stopped a few yards down the road from the cottage. A tractor and trailer blocked its path. Behind the van was a maroon camper. Men in balaclavas were grouped around the cab. One of them, apparently the leader, was shouting instructions. He was pointing what appeared to be a sawn-off shotgun at the driver inside. Another balaclava had a can, the contents of which he was emptying over the cab of the van. A third balaclava stood some distance away, flicking a cigarette lighter in a meaningful fashion. After a moment, the driver's door was opened from the inside and two men in blue uniforms scrambled out. Immediately the gun was jammed into the driver's ribs. He and his helper were marched to the back of the van, where they opened the heavy loading door. In the distance, a shrill siren wailed further up the mountain.

Mick was riveted to the doorstop. That was a northern accent, Belfast probably. What he was witnessing was a heist. Probably Provos, ruthless usurpers of the proud tradition of Uncle Tim. Everything seemed to happen in slow, jerky movements like an old black-and-white movie. His mind was a kaleidoscope of jumbled thoughts, unable to take in the images freeze-framed before him. The place would soon be crawling with police and soldiers. The security van must have been diverted down this back road while its escort continued along the main road, blissfully unaware that anything was amiss. The siren might indicate that they now realised how they had been tricked. If so, they would here within minutes. There was no way he and Josephine could slip away unseen. Even if they could, by some miracle, reverse the car through the narrow gate on to the road without being spotted and probably shot, their escape was blocked in both directions by the various vehicles scattered across the narrow road.

They were trapped. Any movement, even the closing of the door, might attract attention. Perhaps if he remained still as a statue, the nightmare might pass. Then he remembered that in Brulagh statues were not necessarily immobile. Oh Christ, today's the day Maggie is to get the message! What message his wife would get if his bedding the fair Josephine became public knowledge did not bear thinking about. Desperately he hoped and prayed that events would so arrange themselves that he could get back into bed with Josephine and spend the rest of the morning lost in her arms. Oh sweet Jesus, he was supposed to deliver the opening speech. A quick look at his watch told him that he was already late. Mullarkey, the little bollix, would be only too delighted to take his place on the platform. Still, it had been worth it. Josephine was a lover of extraordinary skill and enthusiasm. Even in the midst of this crisis, he stirred at the memory of what had happened earlier.

As he treated himself to an instant playback, another part of his mind rebuked him for such lascivious thoughts. What was happening before his eyes was an armed robbery. More likely, he would spend the rest of the weekend making statements rather than energetic love. Quite a few people would be eager to hear his explanation of how he came to be in Rose Cottage, more so should they discover that Josephine was there too. Even more curious would be the media bloodhounds. *Four-in-a-row Flannery found in love-nest with banker's wife!* should provide a much-needed boost to flagging summertime sales. Then there was Maggie. The appearance of every angel in Heaven at the grotto was unlikely to divert her from vengeance on a scale hitherto undreamt of.

Not a sign of the bloody police, nor the army escort, needless to say. It was always the same. Park six inches across a yellow line and they were crawling all over you, notebooks and pencils at the ready. How many times had he listened to endless Dáil debates bemoaning the cost of protecting these security vans? Now here was one in the middle of nowhere being robbed before his very eyes and not a guard or a soldier to be seen. Just then a white car, an expensive-looking machine, screeched to a halt behind the camper. The driver's helper, also in blue, was lugging the last of the bags from the van to the camper. A blonde in a miniskirt climbed out of the car. She must have been part of the gang, as her arrival caused no excitement. She began to help with the loading. A siren sounded again, this time much closer. None of the group around the rear of the van appeared to take much notice of it. Perhaps they were too absorbed in their task.

He sensed Josephine behind him. She was rubbing the sleep out of her eyes, a diaphanous robe draped loosely about her shoulders.

'What's happening, lover boy? I heard noises and you were gone.'

Her voice was husky with sleep and spent passion.

'There's a robbery going on. Keep your voice down.'

'Shouldn't we be doing something?'

Mick had a crystal-clear picture of what they should be doing were it not for this unwelcome development on their doorstep.

'Such as? We're hardly going to rush out like this. We'd be shot,

211

for one thing. Or taken hostage. Then the whole world would know about us. I'm supposed to be opening the bloody Festival and you're going for a cycle in the mountains, don't forget. What are we doing half naked in Rose Cottage? How do we explain away that? I've had to tell a few lies in my time, believe me, but I can't think of one good enough to talk our way out of this.'

He refrained from adding that if she thought he was going to get himself shot full of holes to recover a few quid stolen from that bastard of a husband of hers, she was greatly mistaken.

'No. I suppose not. Will we go back to bed?'

'Maybe we should. Or hide in the cupboard till this thing blows over. That fellow with the gun looks like he means to use it. Not that there's anything we could do to help . . .', he added hastily, lest she might harbour ideas along the lines of the one he had just abandoned.

The girl was talking to the man with the shotgun. Whatever she was saying, he obviously agreed with her, as he nodded vigorously. He signalled to the two security men to hurry up as the girl started to turn the white car. The operation appeared to be drawing to a close. Another two minutes and the van was empty. The security men were bound hand and foot and locked into the van. The three in balaclavas were about to climb into the camper.

Mick breathed a sigh of relief. In a moment they would be gone. Then there would be room to reverse the car out of the backyard and on to the road. They would slip away at the very first opportunity, telling no one what they had witnessed. The bloody banks were insured for that sort of thing anyway. He might yet be in time to deliver that speech. He inched the door closed as the white car's engine burst into life. They returned to the bedroom and waited for the raiders to be gone. When he unfolded his plan, she protested at first.

'What about the poor wretches locked in the van? Won't they suffocate or something?'

'No fear of that. I saw two big ventilators on the roof. They'll be all right. If we were to do anything for them, we'd be involved up to our necks. Like I said, that would take some explaining! As soon as those IRA bastards clear off, we'll slip away quietly. You take the bike back to the village and I'll drive back by the other road. OK?'

'Sounds fine, lover boy. We might as well go back to bed while we're waiting. At least we'll be out of sight there.'

She unleashed a high-pitched giggle loaded with promise – a trait he found more endearing than ever now that the crisis had almost passed. They retreated back beneath the duvet and resumed where they had left off.

Suddenly another car screeched to a halt. There came the unmistakable crack of two shots. Somewhere a woman screamed. Footsteps pounded up the path to the cottage. In the same instant the front door burst open with a loud bang. A faintly familiar accent demanded to know if there was anyone at home. They pulled the duvet over their heads, scarcely daring to breathe. An excited babble of voices came from the hall. Then a loud crash as though the door had been kicked in. This was followed immediately by a new voice screeching, 'Drop it, you bastard!'

The same voice that enquired earlier if anyone was at home now pleaded 'OK, OK. Don't shoot us for Chrissake!'

Mick snuggled ever deeper beneath the covers and reached for Josephine. It looked like being a long day.

27

In his mind's eye, the headline shrieked at Mick from the front page.
He could imagine only too well what a meal those shaggers in the
media would make of *this:*

NAKED TD DRIVES PROVO RAIDERS FROM LOVE-NEST.

Michael Flannery, Brulagh's evergreen sporting and political
legend, single handedly put to flight an armed gang of dangerous
subversives. Surprised in their vicious attack on a security van,
they took Mr Flannery hostage in a cowardly attempt to save
their own skins. Because of his capture, Mr Flannery was unable
to perform the opening ceremony for the Brulagh Centenary
Festival. This was a cause of universal regret. His place was
taken at short notice by Councillor Patrick Mullarkey who,
despite his best efforts, was driven from the platform by a
fusillade of empty bottles and decaying vegetables. The opening
ceremony was then postponed indefinitely. It may be restaged
when Mr Michael Flannery is sufficiently recovered from his
ordeal to explain certain matters to his wife and bank manager.'

His journalistic efforts were shattered by the bedroom door being
kicked in. Evidently criminals never opened doors. It was then that
he remembered locking it after witnessing the heist. A harsh voice
penetrated the duvet.

'Stand against the wall over there, the lot of you. One move out
of any of you and you're dead. Barney, see what's under the bed-
clothes, will you. I thought it moved there a second ago.'

The unveiling of the two naked bodies evoked a mixed response.
The most memorable was that of the thinnest and tallest of the
balaclavas.

'Oh Christ, what are you doing here, Dad?'

As a question, it had to be rhetorical. Even to Barney, not the
brightest of men, it was plain as a pikestaff what the embarrassed
couple were doing before they were, literally, exposed.

'OK, everyone out to the hall again.'

If McCain was surprised, shocked, disgusted or amused, his voice did not betray it. As they were going through the door, he grabbed the balaclava Sean was wearing and wrenched it off his head.

'Are you Sean Flannery?'

Sean nodded reluctantly. Mick's reaction to the family reunion, as unwelcome as it was unexpected, surprised even himself. Still lying on the bed in a perfect foetal position, hiding his nakedness with cupped hands, he roared furiously at his unmasked son.

'Jesus Christ Almighty! What brought you back here? Didn't I tell you not to set foot in Brulagh until you got yourself sorted out? Sorted out, my arse! I might have known a blackguard like you would end up in something like this. Your mother will lose her life if she finds out!'

Then realising the delicacy of his own position and that of Josephine he did not pursue that line of argument any further. Even had he wished to do so, McCain would have cut him short as he turned on Sean.

'We've been looking for you. You led us a merry dance from Liverpool, so you did. We'd very nearly given up on him, hadn't we Barney?'

Confirmation came via a curt nod. Conversation was not one of Barney's stronger points.

'Tell me Sean, have you been pretending to be the Provisional IRA while stealing guns?'

'I haven't the faintest idea what you are talking about.'

Sean's accent hadn't altered much in the six years since Mick had last heard it.

'We'll see about that very soon, my lad . . .'

McCain's voice oozed menace as he turned to the pair on the bed and ordered, 'Get dressed you two! Don't try jumping out the window. I'll kill your son if you get up to anything silly. Out in the hall the rest of you.'

As they filed through the door, Mick rushed for his clothes. They were strewn across the floor in an untidy trail that charted the course of their energetic coupling.

'We're in a cruel fix now, that's for sure. What are we going to tell the police, not to mind your husband or Maggie? As for Sean, he's sure to get a stretch in prison for this caper.'

'If he's lucky. That animal said he was looking for him, remember? Something about passing himself off as a Provo . . .'

She was struggling into a bra that was more shadow than substance. Mick watched her efforts with a vague, erotic pleasure, much as one might glance at a saucy advertisement while labouring to complete the crossword. The fires of his passion had been well and truly dampened by the appearance of hordes of voyeurs. That bloody Sean had always been the bane of his life but never more so than at this moment. Trust the black sheep to turn up like a bad penny at the worst possible time. If only the last few minutes had been just a bad dream. Then he and Josephine could slink back into the village without the whole place knowing of their liaison. Josephine continued, '. . . I don't know much about that crowd, thank God, but I'll bet they don't take kindly to crooks passing themselves off as Provos.'

Mick nodded absently. His mind veered off in another direction. Where was the shagging army anyway? Probably half-way up the mountain right now, playing at being soldiers and dressing up as trees when they should be rescuing innocent taxpayers like himself from the clutches of a shower of murdering Provo swine. Would they use him as their trump card in any negotiations? As he pulled on his pants and carefully zipped up his flies, he was in two minds about how he would react to being a hostage. With the press already crawling all over the place, there might yet be valuable publicity to be milked from the situation. Then he remembered his immediate circumstances and had second thoughts.

Should their captors require a shield to make good their escape, his girth, if not his status, would make him the obvious choice. In that event, he hoped that his decades of devoted public service would deter the soldiery from opening fire. Of late much, far too much, had been written about the need to take a firm stand against terrorism. Editorials penned from the safety of a dozen lounge bar counters praised the Israelis for shooting first and asking questions afterwards. Every Jew was a frontline soldier in the struggle against terrorism, was the catch-phrase. Indeed he, himself, had echoed it approvingly on more than one occasion. Now he saw it for what it really was – a crude vote-catching slogan that merely endangered innocent lives.

Even if they did, by some miracle, manage to extricate themselves alive from this mess, how was he going to explain away his presence in Rose Cottage with the fair Josephine when he was supposed to be opening a bloody festival? It would require a lot more than Charley Halpin's creative writing to work that trick, he reminded himself as the waves of self-pity washed over him. Nothing less than a miracle would save him this time. Speaking of miracles, he wondered if the message had yet been conveyed to an expectant world through his wife. He prayed hard that the Mother of God would put in her promised appearance. A few thunderbolts unleashed from Heaven would not go amiss either. Anything that would distract the press, the public and Maggie from what was going on at Rose Cottage would be more than welcome.

'You're dead right, Josephine. Did you see Sean's face when your man said it to him? I'd say that's exactly what those clowns were doing – pretending to be shagging Provos! It's just the sort of stupid thing Sean would get up to! First stealing bloody statues ... now robbing guns, for Jaysus' sake. I wouldn't mind but he was away to be a priest. Can you imagine what sort of one he would have made if he had stuck it out? If he's lucky, he'll be walking with one leg six inches shorter than the other. That lot go in for knee-capping, you know. When they're not shooting people in the back of the bloody neck, that is.'

He was tying a knot in his tie while holding forth on his eldest son's shortcomings as priest and patriot. Still in her bra, Josephine was carefully applying eye-liner with a trembling hand. Whatever might be their fate, they were going to present a good appearance for the *grande finale*. A sharp knock on the window made them jump with fright. The pale face of Father Jeremiah O'Sullivan gazed at them both in amazement.

Father Jerry raised his eyes from the turgid prose to gaze at the deep purple mountain towering above him. Up there somewhere the Doc would be helping the Widow Slattery into the ambulance. He would have met it outside the village and guided it to the remote cabin where she lived. A bed had become available overnight and the Doc had to honour his promise to accompany her on what was her first, and probably last, visit to hospital. The Doc had told him this in the stifling marquee as they watched Mick and Mrs Donnelly present the prizes for the home wine-making competition. It meant that there would be one less of the committee on the platform for the opening ceremony.

Brulagh and its citizens never ceased to astonish him. When he had arrived from Rome, sick and mildly depressed, the place enveloped him like the whitewashed walls of a prison cell. Now that his health was improving and he got to know his flock, the beginnings of a strange inner peace had stirred inside him. He tried to hide his dislike of both Mullarkey and the bank manager: they were probably both good men but they did not make him feel at home. The Doc and eventually Gus had taken him into their confidence and shared their problems with him in a way that stitched him into the fabric of life in the village. As for Mick, why was it that the Devil always had the best tunes? He had taken to the burly reprobate from the first moment he set foot in his study.

He envied his zest for life and his obvious enjoyment of life's pleasures. Which reminded him to watch out for squalls where Mick and the bank manager's wife were concerned. Unless he was greatly mistaken, there was something going on between those two. Their relaxed, almost affectionate, attitude to each other during the wine competition, added to the haste with which they departed the moment it was over, would suggest something more than just camaraderie. His priestly disapproval of such a possibility was tempered by a more human satisfaction at the prospect of someone like Donnelly getting his come-uppance.

On reflection, he decided that was not precisely what he meant but it would have to do until something better entered his head. He wondered if the cuckold's sign, two fingers protruding from the forehead like goats' horns, so popular in Italy had acquired a foothold on this island.

He was striding along the ring road that meandered past Rose Cottage and back into the village. It was part of the exercise routine mapped out for him by the Doc. He felt much the better for it and the walk was just long enough for him to finish his office. Its daily reading was an obligation on every lay priest in Christendom. Monks in enclosed orders sang it in plain chant, which was marginally less boring. He seldom encountered anyone – but today was different. First a blonde girl in a white sports car rounded a corner so fast that he had to jump out of her way. Minutes later a black car, travelling at a more sedate pace, edged past him on the narrowest part of the road just before the cottage. He wondered idly if it were the car the Superintendent described to Gus. Dismissing the idea as too preposterous for words, he resumed his reading.

When the orchestra of excited voices, a woman's scream, fast-revving engines and two staccato backfires reached him, he was less sure that it was quite so preposterous. He thought of turning back and alerting Gus but that would take almost an hour. By then it might be too late. And, of course, there might be a perfectly innocent explanation for it all. Gus would not thank him if he were dragged away on a wild-goose chase to Rose Cottage while the village became grid-locked with traffic on this, the most important day in its history. Maggie would be kneeling before the grotto at this very moment, awaiting the message. He had sent Julia May there to report back to him on what, if anything, happened there. Despite her protests, he knew that she wouldn't have missed the occasion for anything. Since he couldn't go there himself and yet would be expected to file a detailed report on the matter to the Bishop, Julia May would have to act as his eyes and ears.

As he rounded the corner before Rose Cottage he stopped dead in his tracks. The usually desolate stretch of road was festooned with vehicles pointing in every direction. He reached the black car first. Yes, indeed it was a Nissan and its engine was still running. As was that of the blue security van, its driver's door ajar as though it had been abandoned in a hurry. A thudding sound came from the back. When he tried the rear door it was locked. He approached the cottage as stealthily as he could. Fresh gashes of splintered wood showed the front door to have been forced. Curiosity overcame his better judgement as he decided to investigate further. He crept as quietly as he could between the side of the cottage and the whitewashed wall of the backyard. He noticed Mick Flannery's car parked in an outhouse, a lady's bicycle leaning against it. There were voices raised in anger, coming from within. Just then he passed an open window.

By now he was feeling very uneasy. The presence of the Nissan and the security van indicated that something out of the ordinary was afoot. It looked like the same van that had been taking cash from the bank an hour earlier. He would have slipped away quietly to alert Gus were it not for an unfamiliar voice coming from the front door. His escape route was cut off, at least for the moment. The words did nothing to reassure him.

'I can hear a siren but there's no sign of the fucking Army, thank Christ!'

Nervously he approached the window and peered inside. When he saw Mick in the bedroom with the bank manager's wife he did not know what to do next. A police siren sounded again, this time more loudly. That was what decided him. He rapped sharply on the window. When Mick saw him, he jumped like a gaffed salmon, almost strangling himself with his tie. Mrs Donnelly hurriedly reached for her blouse and struggled furiously to get back into her jeans. She was pulling a wool sweater over her head as Mick approached the window.

'I was passing by on my walk when I saw all the cars. Is there something wrong?'

Mick put a finger to his lips. Mentally awarding the priest first prize for the understatement of the century, he was about to whisper to him what had happened when the bedroom door burst open. McCain saw the figure at the window. Aiming his gun at the priest he screamed at Barney, 'Go outside and bring in the fucking priest!'

Then, in a quieter tone, full of menace, he addressed Father Jerry. 'As much as a twitch out of you and it will be your last!'

Turning to the other two, he snarled, 'Didn't I tell you to hurry up and get dressed? What's taking you so fucking long? It's not a party you're going to, you know! Come on, get to hell out of here the two of you.'

With a last look round the bedroom for evidence of their brief but memorable visit, she picked up her bag and they made for the hall.

'Get over there against the wall with the others. Leave that bag on the ground. Put your hands behind your heads, all of you. Any sudden move and Barney here will put a bullet between your eyes. He enjoys that sort of thing, don't you Barney?'

His accomplice did not bother to reply. The shotgun lay on the floor. They were now using handguns. The casually expert way they handled them did nothing to lessen Father Jerry's anxiety. He had been hustled in with a gun in his ribs. Another siren wailed; it seemed to be nearer than the last one. He had run errands for Castelli in some of the most dangerous trouble spots imaginable but this was the first time anyone had pointed a gun at him. Brulagh, he decided, was full of surprises. He hoped he would live long enough to relish them.

'Why don't you put down the guns for a minute till we talk things over.'

Mick's appeal for reasonableness earned no response other than a blow from Barney. The blood from his nose dripped on to the tie he had so carefully knotted. Josephine shrieked her anger but was ignored. Father Jerry thought to intervene but decided against it.

'Another word out of you, you fat old bastard, and I'll shoot you where you'll feel it most!'

It was not clear to the priest whether the blow or the unflattering description hurt Mick most. There could be no doubt, however, which part of the Flannery anatomy Barney had in mind.

'Here you, watch your tongue! That's my father you're insulting.'

Sean's reproach earned him a pistol-whipping from McCain that left his face a raw, bleeding mess. The speed and efficiency of the beating was as horrifying as its result. Sean was grabbed by the shoulder and pushed towards the bedroom.

'Get inside there, you! I want to talk to you. Barney, remember – shoot the first one that moves!'

As they disappeared behind the door of the bedroom so recently vacated by the two lovers, the rest of the players in the drama were frozen into immobility. With Barney pointing an unwavering pistol at Mick's groin, the group looked like a tableau in a waxworks. Two sirens shrieked outside. Father Jerry decided that much as he would have wished it to be otherwise, they sounded further away than before.

28

With the Festival opening ceremony yet to start, the Mass-goers drifted down the road to the grotto. Their arrival on the perimeter of the crowd already there added considerably to the crush and exerted almost unbearable pressure on those kneeling at the railing. This made it difficult for Maggie to force her way through to her usual place in front of the statue. Wearing the full regalia of the Legion of Mary she made an impressive sight as the onlookers fought and struggled to make a path to let her through. Exhausted by the effort, she flopped to her knees, reached into her handbag for her rosary beads and looked up at the plaster face of the Mother of God. The neon tube of the halo had begun to flicker – probably because it had been on for months on end. In former times it was switched off at the end of May. Even with the winking halo, try as she might Maggie could not detect the slightest movement – not even the merest flutter of the Virgin's eyelids.

As she knelt and prayed silently she was struck by the medley of different sounds that assailed her ears. They were much sharper than usual. It reminded her of those childhood swims off the pier, when the sounds from the shore were magnified as they drifted across the water. The sawing and scraping of the rope as it rubbed against the hole in the floor of the belfry could be heard as clearly as though she were standing beside the sacristan. At midday and six o'clock he would tug it twelve times to remind the faithful to say the Angelus – a pot-pourri of prayers in Old English that made little sense to even the most erudite. Still, the peals told those without watches the time of day.

She was the only one of her family that could swim. The older generation thought it dangerous and immodest. Her mother warned her to wrap a towel round her the moment she left the water. The wet bathing costume clung to the body in a way that could arouse dangerous desires. She also feared that the salt water would wash the natural oils out of Maggie's body with unpredictable, perhaps fatal, results. Uncle Tim, who spent most of his life fishing out of a leaky boat miles from shore, insisted that it was folly to tease the sea by swimming in it. He often told her in a solemn voice that the sea always claimed its own. This was why he never learned to swim and regarded the practice as both dangerous and provocative. Such grim fatalism in no way interfered with his belief in an almighty and merciful God. When the sea eventually claimed him, it returned him to his mourning relatives after the traditional nine days.

Today the sounds were very different. From the car park came the frenzied roar of revving engines as drivers jostled with each other to find a parking space near the exit. This morning her children had opened yet another field to accommodate the cars. She told herself that it was as much to oblige Gus as to make money. The Sergeant had complained that the cars were causing an obstruction when they were left by the roadside. Assuring her that he would see to it that Pat Mullarkey would not make trouble for her in his role as planning supremo, Gus designated the field a 'temporary' car park to relieve traffic congestion for the duration of the Festival.

From another quarter blaring music mingled with the smell of frying chips and burgers. The Flannery Fast Food operation was in full swing. From behind the serving hatch crudely cut out of the side of the caravan, the perspiring Gillian and her younger brothers frantically exchanged food for an unending flow of pound notes. On the far side of the road, a gap in the ditch was manned by young Michael Flannery, who was using his schoolbag to collect the car park money. Large signs on either side of the entrance announced that parking was available within, admission one pound. They were painted in the same hand that had scrawled in red paint along the side of the caravan, GET YOUR FAST FOOD HERE.

In the beginning Maggie meant it to be a feeding station providing sustenance to hungry pilgrims free of charge. Her children balked at this and Mick pointed out that it would cost a fortune. The first night they charged reasonable prices that required vast amounts of change. They ran out of change in the first hour and after that the children took matters into their own hands – they charged a pound for everything. There were few complaints and business prospered. Even though it had become the core business of the family – far more profitable than the shop – Maggie refused to have anything to do with it.

Gillian had taken charge of the chip van after her short-lived job in O'Shea's. Maggie hoped that her daughter was still getting some study done. It would be nice if she changed the tape that was now blaring out – or, better still, switch it off. A bleating tenor informed the throng at regular intervals that 'The night has a thousand eyes'.

It had become the anthem of the grotto. Maggie thought that hymns to Mary would have been more appropriate but none were available on tape. Anyway she doubted if her children would have given them much airtime. Out of the corner of her eye she noticed that the camera crew, with whom she had had a row earlier in the day, were involved in a confrontation with a section of the crowd. Walking sticks and ash-plants were being raised in a threatening fashion.

To her right, Gus was doing his best to clear a path for a dark blue security van and its escort of police cars and the green Land Rovers carrying soldiers with their vicious-looking guns and flak-jackets. Unaware of the disturbance caused by the TV crew, he silently cursed the seed, breed and generation of Thomas Donnelly from whom the van and its escort would soon make a cash collection. That done, the convoy would turn around and have to retrace its path through the crowd to get out of the village. Gus wondered if the black Nissan would appear. When he had warned the Detective Inspector at the wheel of the police car, he seemed to know all about McCain, and dismissed him as a dirty piece of work before resuming his efforts to force a path through the crowd as Maggie stared hard at the statue to see if there was any indication that a message might be forthcoming.

Oh Holy Mother of God, give me some sign that will convince the unbelievers that your Son has a message for the world and that it will be revealed here on this, your very own Feast Day!

She was unsure whether the statue or Padre Pio would be the messenger. Unlike that turncoat Julia May, Maggie had not actually seen the friar in the sky but she increasingly sensed his presence. To those who asked when they could expect the message she made the same reply every time: 'All will be revealed on August Fifteenth! Be patient until then and pray with me to Our Lady of the Most Holy Rosary.'

Well, the fateful day had dawned. In fact it was now past midday and nothing had happened yet. Expectancy would soon change to uncertainty. Then impatience would give way to outright frustration. How those who had been coming every night for weeks past in anticipation of this day would react if nothing happened did not bear thinking about. Even now, amid all her other concerns, she was worried sick about why Gus was looking for Sean's address. Did he know that she had been sending Sean the *Clarion* all these years? There would be ructions if Mick ever found out. She had sworn to him that she would break off all contact with her son until he had, as Mick put it, 'sorted himself out'. In some ways, she had been as good as her word. The newspaper was sent direct from the *Clarion* office and no letter of any sort accompanied it. For all she knew, he might have moved on by now. All she could be sure of was that he was there last Christmas. The card bore the address and nothing else but 'Love to all from Sean'.

She started to say the rosary. 'Hail Mary, full of Grace, the Lord is with Thee . . . Holy Mary, Mother of God, pray for us sinners, now and at the hour of our death, Amen. Hail Mary, full of Grace the . . .'

Her mind slipped into neutral. From there on fingering the beads told her when to chime in with a 'Glory be to the Father and to the Son . . .', which marked the end of each decade. The break was marked by a small gap in the beads followed by ten in succession for the Hail Marys, after which the isolated bead triggered an 'Our Father who art in Heaven' that preceded the next mystery. Her nightly recital was taking its toll not just on her vocal chords. Her body felt exhausted and she found it difficult to concentrate on anything for long. Constant worry made sleep difficult. She had taken an extra four of the Doc's pills before she left the shop after the incident with the TV crew. That had upset her so much that she hoped the pills would calm her down. She would have to be alert and in top form to receive the Divine message when it came, as come it certainly would.

The responses washed over her like the waves in those childhood swims. How she wished she could return to those happy, carefree days. Things were so much simpler then. No moving statues, Divine messages, errant sons or straying husbands – just long, golden days of weighing tea with her father and those lazy, lonely swims off the pier. An unfamiliar sound penetrated her cocoon of yesteryear. It was definitely not Padre Pio for it had a piercing, electronic crackle that cut through the hum of murmured prayers. Nor was it the voice of her husband, though it issued from the loudspeaker high on the platform before the church gate. Where in the name of God was Mick? What could have possibly gone wrong that he would pass up such a glorious opportunity for self-congratulation? Why was the high-pitched squeak that offended her ears that of Pat Mullarkey declaring the Festival open?

The piercing whistle returned to the loudspeaker at intervals. As Pat was trying to make himself heard, it drowned out his words to the audience gathered in front of the platform. Mick Flannery had failed to show up though he had been in the marquee earlier that morning. Surely the old fool couldn't have taken offence at this late stage over the stand not being named after him? Still you never knew with Mick, especially if he had a few drinks in him. Father Jerry was missing too. Probably keeping a discreet eye on Maggie at the grotto. In fact the platform was empty save for Mossy and Bernie. Secretly, he was quite pleased that so few of the committee would hear the blatant lie he was about to tell.

'. . . because it is entirely due to the . . . EEEEEEEEEEEEEEK . . . and unflinching support of the people of Bru . . . AWAWWWWWWWWWWWWWWW . . . EEEEEEEEEEEEK . . . stand rises proudly as a testament to . . . SSSSSSSSS-SSSSSSSSSSSSSSSSS . . . Flannery who in no small way contrib . . . AWAWAAAAAAAAAAAAAA . . .'

In frustration, he moved the heavy microphone out of harm's way to the back of the platform where it continued to hiss like a bad-tempered snake. Beside it sat Mossy in his best suit. At a safe distance sat Bernie, looking smart in a summer frock. All three pricked up their ears at the sound of a siren drifting down from the mountain. The absence of the Doc, Father Jerry and, most of all, Mick Flannery presented Pat with the opportunity he had been waiting for all his life. He grasped it with both hands. With the rogue microphone safely out of the way, he sought to restore direct communication with his audience.

'What I was trying to say to you before this bloody thing . . .' – he cocked his thumb in the direction of the offending microphone – 'started acting up was that both the Festival and the new stand are the creation not of one man, nor even of the GAA Committee. They are nothing of the sort. They are, in fact, the direct result of the support and generosity of each and every one of you here today!'

As he waited for the applause to die down, he was relieved that the lie did not stick in his gullet. Even the sprinkling of reporters mingling with the crowd in the street knew by now that but for Gus and himself, the stand would still be an unsightly rubbish dump beside the pitch. As for the Festival, it would have been no more than a late-night drinking session dreamed up by Mick Flannery and his cronies in the Golf Club. Now the die was cast. After all, he had promised Mary and told Gus and the priest that he would follow the Flannery precept and tell the people that they wanted to hear. The truth would have to wait for another day.

From his elevated position on the platform he could see the bunting stirring in the midday breeze. At the back of the crowd were a dozen or so ladies dressed up to the nines. They were pushing large prams ahead of them. The 'Bonny Baby' competition was the first event after his speech. Like Mick, Pat had declined to judge this competition. What was the point in gaining the winner's vote if the other competitors were mortally offended? The judges were Julia May and Tom O'Shea. Neither of them had chick nor child and could, therefore, be deemed neutral. No doubt the presence or otherwise of shamrocks would colour Tom's judgement, whereas regular attendance at daily Mass could be a deciding factor in Julia May's final choice.

The street was empty beyond the prams at the outskirts of the crowd. The sound of cars revving drifted towards them from the unofficial car park in Flannery's front field. Even from this distance, the grotto was black with people. The smell of frying grease wafted from the chip van. Honours were about equally divided as to which event was drawing the greater numbers. Apart from Maggie, most of those at the grotto were strangers. The villagers were clustered round the platform, eagerly awaiting the next pearl of wisdom to fall from his lips.

'And I'll tell you something else! If we can only nurture the same spirit of co-operation that launched this Festival and built our stand, we can turn Brulagh into a thriving, vibrant community. A community of which each and every one of us will be proud to be a member!'

More deafening applause. Above the din he could hear Mossy shouting encouragement from behind:

'That's the stuff for the troops, Pat. That's what they want to hear!'

'And when I say thriving,' he continued, 'let me remind you that I do not just refer to the prosperity that will inevitably be our reward when we put our shoulders to the wheel and get this community moving forward once again. No indeed I do not! What I mean by thriving is not a collection of factories belching out poison into our clean air and blue sea. What I mean by thriving is a community with a common goal. And what, my friends, should that goal be?'

In a detached way he noticed that his voice was at least twice as loud as normal without any extra effort on his part. His hands, too, seemed to have taken on a life of their own. They sliced the air, lending emphasis to his every point. He had the rapt attention of every man, woman and child in the audience. He caught his wife's

227

eye. She winked her approval. This eloquence was new to him. When he had spoken at committee meetings, a glazed look descended on his listeners like an opaque film. Not this time. This was a public meeting with an open platform, not some stuffy room filled with self-important worthies. The crowd were hanging on his every word – waiting for him to reveal in the fullness of time what this goal might be. As he had long since departed from his prepared script and was flying on automatic pilot, he was just as curious as they were to find out.

'The goal of each and every man, woman and child here today must be this. To turn Brulagh into a community that our children will refuse to leave. A community where good jobs in a clean environment will hold more attraction than high wages across the water. A community where they can indulge their talents in sport, work and play. A community where we can raise the next generation in a Christian atmosphere where neither crime nor drugs hold sway and . . .'

He had to stop right there. Wave after wave of clapping and shouting drowned out his words. Charley Halpin and the other pressmen were scribbling furiously. A part of his mind hoped that they would describe the applause as thunderous. Another part was refereeing a struggle between two different schools of thought. One claimed that he was spouting the greatest load of rubbish to be delivered off a platform since Mick Flannery's last election campaign. The other viewpoint, now rapidly gaining ascendancy, was that while this might indeed be true, his listeners were lapping it up and baying for more. Were he to stop now, he would not only be leaving the admiring throng in an angry, cheated vacuum but he would also be missing the chance of a lifetime. For the first time he knew what it felt like to have a crowd in the palm of his hand. It sent a charge of adrenalin – almost orgasmic in its intensity – surging through his veins.

So this was the reward that Mick Flannery reaped in exchange for running errands and generally arse-licking the voters – the buzz that came from delivering a rousing speech to a delirious audience. *So what am I going to say next? I'm not sure it matters. What counts now is how I say it. At this moment if I tell them that the world is flat and that they will fall off the edge if they venture outside the earthly paradise that is Brulagh, they would believe me!* Not being foolhardy enough to put that proposition to the test, he chose a less outlandish one. He picked up the sentence that had been interrupted.

'. . . where pollution is something that we only read about in the newspapers. Where our rivers and sea teem with fish safe from the deadly poison of environmental terrorists. In an atmosphere where those who do break the law will be fined and imprisoned should they persist in their criminal actions . . .' – this was followed by the loudest and most prolonged applause yet. He was surprised to see that three farmers who were responsible for the last big fish kill were clapping and cheering as heartily as the rest – '. . . and I can assure everyone here today that I will work every hour that God sends to turn this dream into reality. Not by promising castles in the air, fictitious factories, imaginary processing plants and God knows what else . . .'

This time laughter accompanied the jeering and clapping. The barb directed at the absent Mick had struck home.

'Instead of that nonsense, our dream will become reality by harnessing the vigour and enthusiasm of everyone here today to build a better future. And . . .' – he paused for a moment, then pointed towards the crossroads – 'also those good people gathered round our grotto. Their fervour and devotion can also be made to work for the good of our community. No one knows better than our new parish priest . . .' Here he paused again, about to point towards where Father Jerry would have been sitting when he suddenly remembered he, too, was missing.

'. . . and myself the amount of goodwill towards improving our small community that fills the hearts and minds of each and every one of you. Our telephones haven't stopped ringing all week with offers of help and encouragement to make this the biggest and best event ever staged in the long and glorious history of Brulagh.'

Once more he had to stop until the cheering dropped to a level over which he could make himself heard.

'Some people have said it is a bad thing that we are opening the Festival at one end of the village and waiting for a miracle at the other end. Father O'Sullivan has had half the press of the free world camped on his doorstep and pestering him about the carry-on at the grotto. Sergeant Moriarty has had complaints about traffic jams, Doctor Buckley is treating half the village for high blood pressure and the phone in my office has hardly stopped ringing for people wanting to know what we are going to call our new stand. I say this to you. All this excitement and concern is good thing. It is a sure sign that our spirit is alive and well. We may not always see eye to eye with each other on every issue but we are all dedicated to the same goal – the improvement of our community. Today we see with our own eyes the huge numbers that have gathered here today to honour both God and Brulagh. There is no conflict between these two goals. Why should there be? Not when they both stem from the same desire in everyone's heart to better themselves and their surroundings. This is why we are holding this Festival today and opening our new stand. It gives me great pleasure, therefore to declare both the Festival and our new stand well and truly open!'

Above the din, a siren wailed. It was quickly followed by another. And another.

29

As the door closed behind McCain, Sean stumbled towards the unmade bed. What followed was clearly audible in the hall.

'I already know you steal guns and sell them to a crook in Soho . . .'

The voice had a vicious rasp that would brook no argument even if Sean could have managed one through his swollen lips.

'That doesn't bother me. What does is that you told the little shit that the guns came from the Provos. If that's true, you had better tell me who you got them from. Then I'll think about not shooting you here and now! Lie to me and you get no second chance. I know the name of every freedom fighter who has access to arms caches so don't waste my time. After that you can tell me what sort of stunt you were trying to pull just now with the security van. Were you playing at being Provos there too?'

A long pause followed. Then Sean realised the futility of any further pretence. Now he just wanted to get out of this alive. Jenny was right, as usual. It was a crazy idea right from the start. He barely recognised his own voice as it slurred through smashed lips and teeth.

'OK, OK . . . we had a nice little thing going for us. We would do a gun shop every week or so. We wore the same clothes we have on now. Never said we were IRA or anything. Why should we? The guys behind the counter were in too much of a hurry to hand the stuff over to worry about who we were. Then a few days ago, some bloke came looking for me in Liverpool. That was you, I suppose . . .'

Without waiting for a reply, the words tumbled out in a nervous outpouring. There was red mist forming before his eyes and he thought he was going to faint with the pain. He wanted to say it all before he got hit again.

'. . . It was then that we decided to pack it in and try our luck with the security van here. We figured that if we pulled it off, we'd never see a hungry day again. Then the two of you turned up. Who the hell are you anyway? I thought you were the law at first, now I know you're not. Are you IRA or what?'

'I'll ask the fucking questions. Now get back to the point. Someone told the dealer in Soho that the guns came from the Provos. I still don't believe your story and I'm running out of time and patience.'

'Look for Christ's sake I never even met the Soho guy. Eddie, he's out in the hall, handled that end of the business. He's into motors in a big way. He stole the Porsche and the camper just before we came over on the ferry. Before I met him, he was selling cars he nicked in Liverpool to this guy in London. He told Eddie he was looking for shotguns to rent out to blokes he knew. We never asked what they were used for. It was big business though. Took as many guns as we could get. Paid well too. But I swear to God I never even saw the guy, much less told him the stuff came from the Provos. As for Eddie, he wouldn't know a Provo from a hole in the ground!'

'We'll soon find out.'

McCain opened the bedroom door and shouted into the hall, 'Eddie, whichever one you are, get in here.'

A sullen but defiant Eddie joined Sean on the bed.

'Did you tell the dealer in Soho that the guns came from the Provisional IRA?'

'What's it to you? Might have told him they came from fucking Toyland for all it concerns you!'

The bullet struck the bedhead, less than an inch from his left ear.

'Haven't time for idle chit-chat. Next time you get it in the knee. After that, between the eyes. Understand? Now I'll ask you just once more. Did you give the IRA as the source of those guns? Why I want to know is my business.'

'Trying to find out if one of your babykillers is shopping you, is that it? I thought you was the law when you fucked things up for us. Now I reckon you're just an IRA hit-man. So what? Big fuckin' deal! Shoot me if it makes you feel any better. Shoot the whole fucking lot of us, in fact! The ponce out in the hall would love that. Just itching to plug someone, he is. Well, in case you don't know, there's a bleedin' army out there somewhere. And a load of coppers. They'll be along in a minute. Even that lot can't miss from twenty yards. You fire another shot and they'll be in here like a ton of fuckin' bricks. Then it won't matter a tuppenny damn whether I told that little London git that the guns came from your lot or the Pope of Rome because we'll all be stone dead. OK, so if they know what they're about, they'll probably not shoot the women. But they must have a description of me, my brother and Sean by now. They'll probably think we're the Provos, not you, so they'll shoot us first anyway. So what the fuck difference does it make whether you or some Mick squaddie takes us out?'

Every word of Eddie's outburst was heard in the hall. Its force and logic made quite an impression. Even Barney looked nonplussed. When Father Jerry heard the shot from the bedroom, he was staring at Barney. The creature didn't bat an eyelid. That finally convinced Father Jerry that they were in the clutches of two psychopaths to whom killing was as natural as voiding their bowels. His own loosened considerably as he strained to hear McCain's reaction. In doing so, he thought he heard a shuffling noise from a room no one had been in yet. He looked around to see if anyone else had heard it. Apparently not, to judge from the intent expressions on their faces as they waited for the confrontation in the bedroom to escalate further.

It didn't. Instead the eerie silence lengthened until it became almost unbearable. They were not to know that the trio in the bedroom were engaged in a battle of wills, each trying to stare the other down. Eddie had struck the only chord that could stop McCain dead in his tracks. The conviction with which he said that he didn't care who shot him rang true. It mirrored exactly McCain's own view of life – and death. In other circumstances, a reference to his fellow Provos as babykillers would have earned a bullet between the eyes. Now McCain seemed frozen into immobility, though his gun never wavered.

They continued to sit still as statues until the silence was shattered by the wail of sirens. With a screech of brakes, the Land Rovers skidded to a stop, an unmarked police car on their tail. The convoy had found the security van. McCain pushed Eddie and Sean back into the hall. The others, with the exception of Barney, were relieved that the shot they had heard from the bedroom did not appear to have hit either of them.

'What's that, Barney? Take a look out the door.'

Barney did as he was told.

'A fucking ambulance would you believe and a blue Ford. Oh Jesus, half the fucking Army are right behind them!' he reported.

'Get inside and close the door after you,' McCain ordered.

The voice might as well have been inviting him in for a cup of tea. It betrayed no emotion whatsoever. McCain had regained his composure. For all his ruthlessness, McCain was more embarrassed than anyone by the sight of the naked couple on the bed. He had never really come to terms with sex. What experience he had of it was bought off the shelf. Then there was Eddie's outburst. That had unsettled him even more. But the priest was the last straw. The Provos respected no one, not even each other. But they feared the clergy. And with good reason. The hierarchy might publicly condemn their outrages till they were blue in the face but they stopped short of the final sentence. Excommunication. Though most Provos never darkened the door of a church from one end of the year to another, their funerals were staged in accordance with the full rites of the Church.

In some parishes, the priest might not permit the tricolour to be draped over the coffin while it lay inside the church but that was as far as it went. At the burial, a firing party loosed off a volley of shots over the grave and then melted away into the crowd before they could be arrested. The Church's ambivalence towards the Provos was crucial to their continued existence. It was the very oxygen that allowed them to live. No one knew this better than McCain. Now he was stuck with a priest in this bloody cottage. If he got killed or injured, McCain's reputation would be mud for ever more.

'McCain, I'm talking to you! You have exactly one minute to come out with your hands up. Leave all weapons behind in the cottage. Starting from now . . . one, two, three . . .'

The voice jerked McCain back to reality. The barrel of his gun jammed into Mick's rib cage.

'OK Mister Flannery, now's your chance to prove how good a fucking politician you are. Both of us are going to walk out that door to the camper. Barney and your lady friend will be doing the same thing right behind us. At the slightest hint of something wrong, the two of you will be as dead as mutton. Like our friend Eddie here, we don't really care how we go. Unlike him, we have a cause to die for though you wouldn't understand that, being a fucking politician.'

'Don't talk rubbish, McCain . . .' Father Jerry was pleased that his voice did not betray the cold fear that gripped his heart. So this was what it felt like, the first step to the next life. He wondered if that poor wretch on the mountain felt the same when he stepped off the bale of straw into the dark void of eternity.

'. . . Take me, instead. They'll recognise my clothes and they won't risk shooting at a priest. Bringing the woman along will only confuse them. They may even think she's one of your crowd.'

'No way, we'll take Fatso. And his woman. We need a shield each, thanks all the same. Anyway, I don't like priests, they make me nervous. In fact I shouldn't be risking your neck out here in the hall. If you got shot, I'd never hear the end of it from my superiors. Go into a room and stay there. If you're thinking of climbing out a

234

window, just remember that the crowd outside will mistake you for one of us trying to escape, so I'd stay put if I were you!'

As Father Jerry made for the room from where he thought he had heard a noise earlier, McCain pointed the gun at Mick, who was asking himself if this was how his father-in-law had felt when the Tans dragged him out of his shop all those years ago. The cunning old bastard would never have built a political career on the incident had he been found stark naked in bed with someone else's wife, that was for sure. Of even greater certainty was the fact that his own future in politics was finished if he were found out. Just imagine what that little bollix Mullarkey would say! . . . *Couldn't turn up for his own Festival, if you don't mind. Instead he had to go screwing himself blind in Rose Cottage with the bank manager's wife. OK, so we all knew Mick was in trouble with the bank, but that's a novel way of getting an extension on your overdraft!*

And it wouldn't be any easier for Josephine. A banker's wife, like Caesar's, was expected to be above reproach. Being found in bed with a legend in his own lifetime would not fit in with the image Allied Banks of Ireland sought to project, despite their sponsorship of sport in general and hurling in particular. These dark broodings were interrupted by McCain's ice-cool voice.

'Right, off we go. First, open that front door and explain to the crowd outside what we are going to do. Tell them that any attempt to interfere with our escape – road-blocks, shooting out tyres, nails on the road sort of thing will result in both of you being shot. You can tell them anything you damn well like as long as you convince them that we mean business. That shouldn't be too difficult . . .' – McCain's voice was heavy with scorn – '. . . as it's all in a day's work for you. Persuading people, I mean.'

Mick treated the jibe with the contempt it deserved. The loudhailer was at forty-seven and counting . . .

'What about the others here?'

'They can stay here for the moment. Tell 'em there's explosives strapped to everyone left in the house and that we'll blow them to Kingdom Come if they try anything. A kind of insurance just in case your oratory fails to win them over. Understand?'

The door creaked open, grating against the broken hinges, and Mick experienced a sensation he hadn't felt for years. Butterflies in his stomach. Not quite fear but more the sudden surge of adrenalin. He hadn't felt it since he led his team out on to the pitch for his last match – the one that earned him the fourth medal in succession. He fought back the sensation of wanting very badly to pee. Facing the ring of soldiers, police, reporters and assorted onlookers, he cupped his hands around his mouth and began, 'I want you all to listen carefully to what I am going to say . . .'

The loudhailer cut him off before he could begin to explain.

'Come out with your hands above your heads. Leave what weapons you have in the house and come out through the front door in single file!'

McCain's reply was to grab the shotgun with his other hand and jam it against Mick's head. As he did so, he rasped into Mick's ear, 'You and I are out here to make those bastards listen to us. Try making a run for it and I'll blow you to bits before you've taken two steps. You, Mick Flannery, are going to be our passport out of here. Barney, keep an eye on the woman. Shoot her if you have to. By the way, who is she?'

'No one you'd know.'

Mick had things on his mind other than formal introductions. The scene had changed dramatically since he had looked outside twenty minutes earlier. The vehicles already abandoned there had been joined by many more. To the fore were the army Land Rovers, parked facing away from where he stood. From the back where the soldiers travelled on the hard bench seats, the snout of a sub-machine-gun on a steel tripod pointed from each vehicle. Barely visible in the dark recess, a soldier squinted along the barrel. A rough cordon had been thrown around the cottage. From behind the stone wall on the far side of the road, helmets and the occasional green flak-jacket could be glimpsed. Everywhere he looked he saw black Uzis with their rectangular magazines that spewed out death through their stubby barrels at God alone knew how many bullets per second.

'Not Sean's mother, I'll bet,' said McCain, glancing at Josephine. 'Now, let's talk to those bastards.'

He prodded Mick with the gun towards the gate that led up the short path to the cottage.

'Open it real slow, if you've got any sense. Remember what I said about making a run for it. Don't speak unless I tell you to.'

Mick nodded and the gate creaked loudly as it opened. McCain shouted from behind him, 'I have a hostage here so don't shoot. He's Mick Flannery.'

There was a moment's silence. The loudhailer came on with a distinct click.

'Mick who? Why don't you just give yourselves up and stop fucking about?'

'Listen, I'm not fooling around. Mick Flannery's the guy's name. He's a TD or something round here. We are taking him with us as soon as you clear the road. We'll be generous and give you half an hour to sort everything out. Move those fucking soldiers away from there, for starters. They're making me nervous. I'll be back out here in half an hour. Have the road cleared by then or we start killing the hostages. Got that?'

'Yeah, most of it. We'll need more time. We have to confirm your hostage's identity for one thing. Then we've got to set up communications network with our Commanding Officer. As it is, we've no authority to negotiate with you. That'll take three hours at the very least.'

'OK, you've got an hour. But that's all.'

McCain dragged his hostage back inside the cottage and pulled the door shut behind them.

In the spare room, the first thing Father Jerry saw was an array of cardboard cartons stacked neatly against the wall. By the window stood a bed. Out from under it crawled a weasel of a man wearing a shiny suit and a tweed cap that looked as if it could only be removed from his head under a deep anaesthetic. As he brushed the dust and fluff from his suit with the back of his hand, he arched his back to get the stiffness out of his bones. At the same time he extended a hand in greeting and muttered in a conspiratorial whisper, 'Bit of a shindig going on out there, by the sound of it. First of all a man and a woman were hardly inside the front door before they started at it hammer and tongs like it was going to be taken off the market tomorrow. A while later who arrives but some crowd of shagging lunatics fighting and arguing among themselves. At that stage I thought it better to hide under the bed till everyone cleared off. Then you came into the room just now. When I spotted the black shoes and the ends of the trousers I said to myself "Freddie, if those aren't the feet of a priest, I'm a Dutchman." You wouldn't be Father O'Sullivan, by any chance?'

'I am indeed and who . . .'

Before he could frame the question, the answer dawned on him with appalling clarity. The little man stuck out his hand in greeting and confirmed the worst in an accent not unlike McCain's.

'Then meet your only surviving relation this side of Heaven! Freddie Bartholomew O'Sullivan at your service. I was doing a bit of business in the neighbourhood when all this excitement started. I'd have slipped away quietly only that I wanted to keep an eye on my investment.'

Father Jerry cocked a thumb at the cartons lining the wall and asked, 'Did you buy that off Johnny?'

'Faith then I did, Father. Two thousand pounds in used notes I paid the divil for it and it's worth every penny of it, I can promise you. As fine a drop of the hard stuff as I've tasted in many a year. That Johnny is a genius and no mistake. Would yourself like to try a drop, while we're waiting?'

'Certainly not. You don't seem to realise the seriousness of our situation. There are two IRA killers holding hostages just outside the door. The Army and police have the cottage surrounded. At this very moment they are trying to persuade them to come out peacefully. They sent me in here so that I wouldn't get shot if the negotiations broke down and the Army has to storm the cottage. Unlike civilians, the IRA apparently have a close season on priests. Now, to crown it all, I meet my only surviving cousin. And where do I meet him? In a room full of poteen, that's where! Do you realise, Freddie, that all it needs is for just one stray bullet to hit your load of paint-stripper and we're all blown into smithereens?'

'Oh Holy Mother of Divine Jesus, you're right. I never thought of that. What are we going to do? With all the bottles stacked against the wall and the Army using high-velocity bullets, we're odds-on favourites to go out with a bang! What are we going to do at all? Do you think if we told those lunatics out in the hall about it that it might make them give themselves up?'

'No, I don't. They would be far more likely to shoot you before you could get a word in edgeways to explain who you were and what you were doing hiding here. Far better for me to go out in the hall and try to talk sense to them.'

He went to the door and turned the handle. The door was locked. He pounded on it for a minute or so but to no avail. As he turned back he noticed for the first time the uncanny resemblance Freddie's features bore to those of his father. What had disguised the similarity up to now was the fact that his face was so small, like a gilt-framed Victorian miniature or a shrunken skull from Borneo. In a flash, Father Jerry was back again beside the turf fire on a winter's night with the howling wind rattling the latch on the half-door. There was no electricity and the turf that flamed in the grate had been cut from the bog with their own hands. As a lad of seven or so, he was allowed to join in on the mouth-organ. His mother played a concertina that reminded him of a caterpillar when it was at full stretch. With his father sawing away on the fiddle and the uncle expertly clicking the spoons, there was no need for a crystal wireless set even if they'd had the money to buy one.

Sometimes the neighbours would arrive and an impromptu party, a ceilidh, would start. Then sparks would fly from the hobnailed boots as they clattered off the flat stone slabs of the floor in time to the music. They all drank out of chipped mugs but even a seven-year-old soon realised that such euphoria could hardly be generated by the tea-leaf alone. As the mugs were filled out of a nondescript bottle, references to the 'pure drop' were made in the hushed tones used by wine-tasters sampling a particularly fine vintage. When it ended, often as the first streaks of a new dawn sidled in through the tiny windows of the small thatched cabin, they ended with a rousing chorus of his favourite ditty.

'I'm a rambler, I'm a gambler. I'm a long way from home.
And if you don't like me, just leave me alone.
I eat when I'm hungry and I drink when I'm dry
And if moonshine don't kill me, I'll live till I die!'

Father Jerry sighed, 'Well, Freddie, that settles it. We are stuck with each other for the time being. One thing in your favour is that no one except me knows that you're here. If I were you, I'd climb back in under that bed and stay quiet as a mouse. The reason I chose this room was that I thought I heard something moving in here.'

'Oh that was me all right, Father. I was trying to stack the poteen so it wouldn't fall.'

'Yes, well I'd kiss goodbye to it, if I were you. Then I'd clear off out of here the first chance I got. Unless you want to be shot, of course. By the way, I saw the letter you wrote to Johnny and I didn't like it one little bit. I thought it sounded as if you were trying to blackmail me about our uncle being in the business or something like that. Or worse still, trying to embarrass me about my poor father, God rest him, dying dead drunk in a ditch.'

The alliteration pleased him as he watched Freddie's expression register alarm, anger, and finally contrition.

'Oh God between us and all harm, Father, what ever gave you a daft notion like that? Sure it was only a joke. I swear on my poor dead mother's grave that the thought of blackmail never even crossed my mind. Sure I wouldn't have a day's luck out of it and you a priest. I swear before Almighty God and his Blessed Mother that if I get out of here alive, you'll never see sign nor light of me ever again.'

'*Will* you swear on that, Freddie?'

When Freddie nodded emphatically, Father Jerry produced the leatherbound breviary from his pocket much as magician might have drawn a white rabbit out of a top hat. To the uninitiated, it looked just like a bible.

'Then swear to that effect on the most holy Bible.'

Freddie took the breviary in his left hand and raised the other in salute to his Maker. 'I do solemnly swear by Almighty God that if I get out of here alive, I will never come near Brulagh or my cousin, Father Jeremiah O'Sullivan, for as long as I live.'

'All right Freddie, that should suffice. Now if I were you I would get under the bed. I won't say a word to anyone about your being here.'

'Thank you, Father. One thing though, will I have to leave all the merchandise behind me?'

'Unless you want to declare yourself its legal owner, that would seem to be your only choice. I must tell you that the local Sergeant pursues bootleggers with relentless energy and enjoys nothing more than sending them to prison for long periods.'

'I know all about that Sergeant. Johnny told me he had the heart put crossways in him from hounding him morning, noon and night.'

'There you are then. Listen Freddie, why don't you give up the business altogether. Today will cost you a pretty penny if any one of us lives to count the cost. Anyway, poteen never brought a day's luck to any of our family.'

'Begor I don't know about that Father . . .'

From under the bed, Freddie had the last muffled words ever to pass between them.

'. . . didn't it make a parish priest out of you!'

Father Jerry had the grace to smile at this parting shot. Then as he paced the room, trying to work out what his next move should be, he suddenly remembered another line of the old song –

> 'Oh moonshine, oh moonshine, oh how I love thee!
> You killed my poor father but please don't kill me!'

In the circumstances, it seemed unpleasantly apt.

30

'The fourth glorious mystery, the Assumption of Our Blessed Lady into Heaven. Our Father who art in Heaven, hallowed be thy name. Thy Kingdom come. Thy will be done on . . .'

Maggie had to raise her voice yet again. The buzz of excitement from the crowd at her back was almost tangible. Sirens were now wailing with increasing frequency, fighting for airtime with the screaming gulls overhead. The convoy with its charge had long since gone, inching its way back on to the mountain road. To judge by the lack of microphone static from the platform, the Festival had been well and truly opened. A tiny part of her mind wondered where Mick might have got to. It was completely out of character for him to miss an opportunity like this. After all, it really was his Festival even if Mullarkey had persuaded them otherwise.

She could recall every last detail of the celebrations after Mick brought home his last medal. Bonfires lit the night sky as crowds gathered to welcome the lorry bearing the captain and his all-conquering team. Gus had stayed with her as she waited for Mick to arrive. Cheering supporters reeled drunkenly in the firelight, drinking from bottles of stout and bellowing snatches of song to celebrate a feat never to be equalled. Four All-Ireland medals in a row was a record that would surely stand for ever. Mick built a career out of it even greater than her father's – at least Mick's was based on fact rather than fiction.

So why had their marriage failed? She knew everyone in the village blamed her. Mick could philander to his heart's content all over Dublin and no one would be any the wiser. Let his wife move to a separate bedroom and she might as well have taken the entire Brulagh hurling team as lovers. Then there was Sean and the disappointment of his failed vocation. He would have made a grand priest who might have been a support to her now in her hour of need. The picture of him climbing down from the bus clutching his battered suitcase and wearing the dark suit of the clerical student was as clear now as though it had happened only yesterday. Much clearer, in fact. Of late she found that recalling incidents from the distant past was far easier than remembering what happened yesterday. As for the trouble with Sean and his debating team in Oxford, that was all Mick's fault for wanting to turn him into a politician.

Anyway, that was all water under the bridge. Today her life would change utterly: she would shed her cares and woes like an old skin and emerge like a butterfly, clean and new, free for ever from her ugly caterpillar past. Any moment now the Blessed Virgin would reveal the message from her Son that would prove to be the salvation of the world. The still invisible Padre Pio had whispered as much into her ear just as the helicopter, clattering noisily overhead, had scattered the terrified seagulls and completely drowned out the responses to the rosary. Her mind suddenly became a vast, grey wasteland of emptiness. Focusing on mundane matters like Gus tugging at her veil was like trying to drag her feet through the turf bog at the foot of the mountain.

The harder she struggled to concentrate, the deeper she seemed to sink into the morass of drowsy oblivion. Was this the trance-like state she had read about in the *Lives of the Saints*, where they assumed a slightly dazed expression as messages from God were revealed to them? Or was it merely the effect of the pills she had swallowed before leaving the shop? Who knows? Who cares? Overhead the mighty rotors continued to flap noisily like a huge, wounded bird frantically seeking a safe haven. Eventually the helicopter settled in an open space in the car park – to the amazement of most of the onlookers, who had never seen one before.

Suddenly she knew! She knew with a blinding flash of absolute certainty. In the midst of the incredible din it came to her as clearly as if the Virgin had climbed down from her pedestal and whispered the message into Maggie's ear. *Go forth and save China.* That was it. The message ricocheted around inside her head, repeating over and over like a looped tape. 'Maggie Flannery, you have been chosen to convert heathen China to the One True Faith . . . Go forth and save China, go forth and save China!' again and again until it was driving her out of her mind.

Gus was trying to tell her something. The rotor blades were still churning, though more slowly and with less noise. The voice of the Virgin kept repeating the message. Maggie desperately wanted to tell the people around her of the miracle that had just been wrought in her mind. There would be no apparition. No spectacular revelation to the crowd of the will of God. Instead, Maggie Flannery was to be the handmaiden of the Lord. It was her bounden duty to inform them of the immense task that had been set for her. The very first

242

one to know must be her husband. But where was he? Where had her fellow missionary disappeared to just when the Lord's work had to be done? She was further distracted by Gus squeezing her shoulder and shouting in her ear, 'They need you up at Rose Cottage. Come with me now. I'll explain on the way!'

He forced a path for her through the crowd to the helicopter. No sooner were they aboard than it swooped upwards. The draught from the rotors blew hats from carefully permed hair as the faithful who had gathered at the grotto to celebrate the Feast day of the Assumption of Our Blessed Lady into Heaven looked heavenwards at the helicopter. Many of them believed they were witnessing if not quite the real McCoy then at least an impressive re-enactment of the miracle they had come to see. The noisy metal bird came to roost a short distance from her late Uncle Tim's cottage.

'We need you to describe the layout of the cottage to Colonel Lee. Where the doors into the rooms are, that sort of thing . . .'

Gus introduced her to a fair-haired young man in combat fatigues who wanted to know everything from the size of the fire grate to whether the windows opened freely and in which direction. He also asked what the interior walls were made of and what sort of handles were on the doors. This and more he relayed to a small group dressed in different battledress to the rest of the soldiers.

When he had gone Gus explained to her that they were a special unit called Rangers, set up to deal with hostage situations. They had just flown in and were preparing to launch an assault on the cottage as soon as they had all the relevant information to hand. Mick and possibly several others were being held hostage inside by the Provisional IRA. Maggie was not in the least surprised by this. In fact it made perfect sense to her. The forces of darkness were already at work to prevent her accomplishing the will of God. Mick she would need to unravel the red tape involved in her imminent journey to China. He might even accompany her in her mission and thus atone for the many sins of his past. Now the Prince of Darkness was determined to thwart her by kidnapping her aide.

Perhaps the Devil had deceived Gus into helping him. And what of the fair-haired colonel walking back to them? He too could be in the grip of Satan. From now on Maggie could have no doubt about where her duty lay. It had been shown to her in the clearest manner possible by the Son of God through the persona of His Blessed Mother. Gus moved away to talk to Lee. They both came back towards her after a hurried conversation.

'Have you any idea how Mick came to be in the cottage? He was supposed to be opening the Festival, wasn't he? The officer in charge of the convoy tells me he passed a priest walking in this direction. From his description, it has to be Father Jerry. Now he's gone missing as well. We're worried that he may be inside the cottage too.'

She shook her head sadly. What was the point in telling them that what they were witnessing was not just an IRA kidnapping but yet another round in the eternal struggle between God and the Devil? If the priest were there too, then perhaps God had sent him in to fight on his behalf. Or – a darker thought – maybe the Devil had won him over too. Whatever the true reason, she would have to act fast if the battle were not to be lost. Gus was talking again. She could barely hear him through the roaring in her ears. It was the same sound that had preceded the revelation of the Message.

'They think there might be up to ten people inside. It is hard to get an exact number with infra-red equipment, especially as they are moving about from room to room. The Colonel says he can't send his men in unless they know which are the IRA and which are the hostages. Otherwise in the confusion, the hostages might get hurt and the IRA escape.'

He did not mention that just before they landed in the helicopter, the captors had said they would be coming out using human shields. At the first sign of trouble the IRA would kill the shields and blow up those inside the cottage by remote-control detonators.

The door of Rose Cottage crashed open. The soldiers around her tensed visibly. Colonel Lee gave a flat wave of his hand that instructed them to hold their fire. Five snipers, rifles resting on the bonnet of the nearest Land Rover, fiddled with their telescopic sights and snuggled the stocks of their weapons against their cheeks for a more comfortable firing position. Several of them were chewing gum and one was whistling a low, tuneless ditty through his teeth. The door was about twenty yards away. Suddenly the portly figure of Mick Flannery was framed in the doorway.

In the same instant everyone gaped in amazement as a figure, her blue-and-white robes flying in the wind, dashed headlong towards Mick. She seemed to cover the distance between them in a split second. Just before she reached him, she struck her foot against a loose flagstone in the crazy paving of the path. She stumbled forward and crashed into the man standing behind her husband, a revolver jammed against Mick's neck. The impact knocked him to one side and sent the gun spinning away. Another man, holding a woman in

244

front of him, rushed forward. A volley of shots rang out. The tall man behind Mick spun round in a half-circle clutching his left shoulder, from which blood was already beginning to spurt. The man by the door, who was hiding behind the woman, had one hand raised upwards as though trying to grip something in the air. He shrieked for mercy. His other hand clutched his thigh. Blood was seeping through his fingers as his mouth opened and shut wordlessly like a stranded fish. Then Maggie fainted.

She came to in a bouncing ambulance. The Doc was leaning over her, saying soothing words and promising her everything was going to be all right. She gave a nod of recognition to the Widow Flannery who was sitting on a padded bench seat across from her, her shawl wrapped tightly around her shoulders and a rosary clenched in her gnarled fingers. There were others there as well but her eyes couldn't focus well enough to see who they were. The Doc said they were going to the hospital, and gave her an injection. From then on she slept. She felt so very tired that she was quite sure the Son of God and his Blessed Mother would not mind terribly if she left China until tomorrow. Or the day after.

31

As the shots rang out and McCain fell to the ground holding his wounded shoulder, Mick displayed a presence of mind for which he would be grateful later on. Turning on his heel, he dashed back inside the cottage, pausing briefly to implant his shoe in Barney's face as a farewell gesture. Then as now, Mick never believed in leaving the field of play without settling a score. He pushed Josephine, who had not been seen properly by those outside, further back into the hall.

Gus and half the Army crowded in after them. As the local representative of the civil authority, Gus read the two wounded Provos their rights and then charged them under the Offences Against the State Act. As McCain and Barney were led away by the Army and police, Father Jerry joined Mick in the hall, locking the door behind him with great care as he cocked an ear to what Mick was saying.

'It's all over now, bar the shouting, Father. Maggie saved the day, fair play to her. Came flying at me and knocked McCain sideways. The two of them were wounded by the snipers. They've been taken into custody but not before I got in a good belt on that Barney one. God forgive me but that bastard had it coming to him.'

'Good man yourself, Mick. Those are my own thoughts entirely. Pity you didn't give him another one from me while you were about it. Don't you think you had better go outside . . .' Father Jerry laid great emphasis on the word *outside* as he whispered into Mick's ear, '. . . and talk to the press rather than have them swarming all over the cottage. They might uncover something both you and I would prefer remained a secret.'

Mick clapped a hand to his brow.

'Oh Jaysus, you're right as usual. What'll I say to them? I can't think straight at the minute.'

'Oh I think something along the lines of this not being the right moment to interview anyone and that you'll hold a press conference later. Promise them that they'll make their deadlines and they'll probably leave us alone.'

Mick went outside. A cordon was still in place. He beckoned Colum Jones to a private audience by the front gate.

'Listen', he said confidentially, 'there's no way anyone here is in a fit state to be interviewed at the moment . . .'

As Mick spoke he could hear the whirr of cameras, their zoom lens focused on him as spoke urgently to the reporter.

'Why don't you shag off for a few hours and we'll hold a press conference when we're a bit more organised.'

'Can you promise me that? I'll look a right fool if I go back and tell them that, only for the lot of you to go missing. You know yourself what our editors would say if we missed the story of the year and we sitting right on the spot where it happened!'

'That won't happen. You have my word on it . . .'

Mick tried desperately to sound convincing as he pressed on, 'A few of us will make ourselves available to you before six this evening. Then you can ask us all the questions you want. But you must leave us alone till then. Is that a deal?'

Colum Jones looked dubious but eventually shook hands on it.

'Do we have a choice? Let us know where it's on. We'll be in O'Shea's.'

'Have a round on me while you're at it,' Mick replied. 'Now I want you to do something for me. I'd appreciate it if you played down Maggie's part in the seige. You can see that the woman's not well in herself. She's gone to hospital, as a matter of fact!'

'I'm sorry to hear that, Mr Flannery. I'll see what I can do. See you later.'

Out of the corner of his eye, Mick saw him rounding up his fellow hacks and piling them into cars for the short trip back to their natural habitat – a public house. The police escort had already left with Barney and McCain. The last of the Land Rovers disappeared down the road as Mick went back inside. From another direction Gus was reversing the Doc's car up to the back door. As he got out, he warned the last few sightseers that there might still be explosives in the cottage. That was enough to send even the most curious scurrying back to the village. Gus opened the large boot of the car and moved the golf-bag from it into the back seat. Leaving the boot open, he went back inside.

He brought Jenny and her two brothers into the bedroom he had already used to charge McCain and Barney. As Gus did so, he told Sean to slip quietly out the side door and climb into the open boot, pulling it shut after him. He was to stay there if he knew what was good for him until someone let him out later on. Then Gus turned to the three Simcoxes.

'I need a statement from the three of you. Here are three sheets of paper. You will write what I tell you. Then Mister Flannery and I will witness them as being signed of your own free will and not under any duress. Understand?'

They nodded dumbly, barely grasping what he was saying.

'Right, this is the gist of what you are to write down, though be sure not to make all three statements exactly the same. You three are English tourists on holiday in Ireland. As you were passing through Brulagh, you thought it would be fun to stop off and see what a traditional Irish festival was like. While you were sightseeing – now be damn sure you get this bit right – in your hired Nissan you got caught up in an armed robbery. This was carried out by one John McCain and his accomplice known only to you as Barney. Got that?'

They nodded furiously. It was beginning to dawn on them that things were happening which they did not quite understand. None the less, the thrust of what the Law was saying sounded favourable, very favourable indeed. It was beginning to look as though, for some reason best known to himself, this Sergeant bloke was not going to throw them into jail after all. Probably covering up for Sean's old man caught between the sheets with someone else's wife, but who cared?

'As for your friend Sean Flannery, you never even heard of him, right?'

Again they nodded. They had most certainly got that.

'And as for the blonde lady called Josephine, she never happened either.'

'Never saw her in our life, Sarge.'

'Good, I'm glad to hear it. Now get on with writing out those statements and call me when they're ready to be witnessed. One more thing. Just in case any of you change your mind and decide to do something really silly like selling your story to the press, I'll arrange for the Liverpool police to throw so many charges at you you'll think you're a dartboard. OK?'

Again they nodded. This time with somewhat less enthusiasm.

'Right then, get on with it. The sooner those statements are finished, the sooner you can resume your touring holiday in Ireland. The Nissan is due back at the Avis desk in Victoria Station next Friday so you'll get to see a bit of our country before you go back to England. Keep well away from here though and remember, no interviews of any sort to the media.'

Gus closed the door without waiting for a reply. He found Mick and Father Jerry in the kitchen. They were drinking the brandy Mick had brought with him to smooth the path of love and were talking earnestly, their heads bowed and close together. Mick looked up and said, 'Gus, you seem to have everything under control. But where's Josephine?'

'When the crowd outside moved off, I put herself and her bike into the ambulance. Poor Maggie was under so much sedation she didn't know where she was. For sure she won't notice anything out of the ordinary. The Widow Slattery never laid eyes on her before this so she won't be any the wiser either. The Doc will drop her off at the crossroads and she can cycle back into town. That way no one but ourselves will know the true story. The Doc won't say anything to anyone and Mrs Donnelly can say that she was out for a ride on her bike.'

They both looked at him with ill-concealed awe. Father Jerry, well accustomed to machiavellian plotting, clapped his hands in delight. Mick sounded hoarse with gratitude and deep embarrassment.

'You're a bloody genius, Gus. That's for sure and certain. Now all I've got to worry about is that clown of a son of mine, young Sean. He could get ten years for this caper, you know, and there's not a damn thing I can do for him this time.'

Gus and Father Jerry looked at each other, each waiting for the other to speak first. Finally the priest looked at Mick.

'The Sergeant and I were discussing that problem a little earlier. Just as soon as we have finished the brandy, I will drive the Doctor Buckley's car back to the parochial house. There Sean will get out of the boot – where he should be hiding by now – and stay, unobserved, as my guest for as long as he pleases. From what you told me about his experiences in the Seminary I think the Church owes him that much at the very least. I look forward to meeting him under more relaxed circumstances. We seem to have quite a lot in common. I see him much as I myself might have turned out had I abandoned my vocation.'

His listeners let it pass. Both of them tacitly decided he was talking as much to himself as he was to them. He blinked several times, took a final sip of brandy and concentrated on matters of more immediate importance.

'Mick, I hope and pray that your wife will recover her senses. Though perhaps it would be better that she did so *after* Mrs Donnelly leaves the ambulance. Good day to you both. See you at the press conference.'

With that Father Jerry was gone. Several efforts to start the engine ended in a spluttering death rattle. Then a loud backfire was followed by a triumphant roar from the broken exhaust and the crashing of gears as Father Jerry tried to accustom himself to the eccentricities of the Doc's elderly Ford. A shout from the bedroom informed them that the statements were ready. These were duly signed and the Simcoxes sent on their way with renewed warnings about not talking to anyone ringing in their ears. At last Gus and Mick had the place to themselves.

'I owe you one, Gus. Several, in fact.'

'Not really, Mick. You did a lot for me in the old days. Getting me on the hurling team and, later on, seeing that I was transferred back here. I'd say we're about even at this stage.'

'I'm glad you feel that way about it, Gus, because there is just one more wee thing you might do for me. Actually, you would be doing it for that decent man, Father Jerry.'

'Go on, Mick. Spit it out. What do you want me to do now?'

'Well, it's a bit complicated really. Supposing you were to look in that room over there, you'd find it full of poteen.'

'Oh God no! You're not telling me Johnny was using the cottage as a store? And I with the legs walked off myself trying to find where he had hidden the stuff up the bloody mountain!'

'Well, no. Not quite. What I mean is, the stuff isn't Johnny's. Not now, anyway. He sold it to a cousin of the priest's, as a matter of fact. The cousin's a bit of a hard nail. It's my guess he was trying to get money out of the priest on some pretext or another.'

'By blackmail, do you mean?'

'Well I don't rightly know the details but it could have been something like that. Anyway the cousin has shagged off back to wherever he came from and Father Jerry tells me we won't be seeing sign nor light of him ever again around these parts. Which is all to the good except that it leaves you and I with a roomful of poteen. I'm supposed to be looking after Rose Cottage till the place is sold and it wouldn't look good if poteen were found in a place that an elected representative of the people like yours truly had charge of, now would it?'

'No. I suppose it wouldn't at that. But you must remember too, Mick, that it's my job to confiscate any bootleg liquor I find.'

'I know that, for God's sake. But my point is that if I hadn't told

250

you about it just now, you mightn't ever had found it. Or, worse still, someone else like Colum Jones might have heard about it. Then it would be plastered all over the papers that Sergeant Moriarty of Brulagh was looking for poteen all over the mountain while it was stored safe and sound, under his very nose, in Rose Cottage. That's just the sort of story those shaggers would make a meal out of, wouldn't you agree with me?'

The Sergeant's voice had become deep with suspicion as he enquired, 'So what should I – sorry, I mean we – do about it?'

'Well I was discussing that with Father Jerry and we decided . . .' – it was here that Mick's narrative departed from the truth – '. . . that the best thing would be for someone to tell Johnny that the stuff was here and that if he got it to hell out of the cottage before six o'clock this evening, no one would ask too many questions. He'd have to promise, of course, to send his mother to Lourdes and give the rest of the proceeds to the young widow to spend on the children's education.'

They looked at each other silently for a long time. Then Gus rose to his feet and said, 'I must get back to the village. God only knows what sort of a tangle the traffic has got itself into while I was gone. Will you give me a lift down the mountain?'

'My pleasure, Gus.'

Mick pulled the broken front door closed behind them and made for his car.

Indoors there was nowhere large enough to stage a press conference. Eventually they decided to use the Festival platform. A trellis table and three chairs were arranged facing outwards. One each for Father Jerry, Gus and the hero of the hour, Michael Flannery, TD. The media were gathered round the front, TV cameramen and press photographers elbowing each other aside as they jostled for the best positions. Sound-men and reporters thrust microphones towards the platform to catch the words of the speakers. Two television crews were screaming at curious onlookers to keep clear of their cables. Further back but no less attentive was a very relaxed group of villagers. Many of them had started off the day at the grotto. With nothing of interest happening there except for the whisking heavenwards of Maggie in the helicopter, they had adjourned to O'Shea's to review the events to date and to digest the rumours of strange events at Rose Cottage that had filtered down from the mountain.

O'Shea, who should have been pleased at the increased custom, was strangely silent and ill at ease.

Just as the proceedings were about to start, Colum Jones shouted up at Mick that he was wanted on the telephone. Mick roared back to tell the caller to wait until they were finished. When he heard it was the Prime Minister and leader of his party, he vaulted down from the stage with the agility of a man half his years. After a few minutes he resumed his place on the platform, beaming widely.

Colum Jones had the first question.

'Mr Flannery, what did the Taoiseach want you for?'

'Oh just to congratulate me on getting out alive, that sort of thing. He also offered me a seat in the European Parliament.'

'Which one?'

'The one left vacant by the death of my esteemed colleague, James O'Rourke.'

'Will you accept it?'

'I just did.'

His reply provoked a round of appreciative sniggers from the press and whoops of delight from his supporters at the rear of the crowd. From another quarter a voice asked, 'What were the names of the men involved in the siege?'

Gus cleared his throat and spoke in his best courtroom manner, slow and deliberate. Everyone pressed forward to catch what he was saying.

'John McCain and Barney. I am not yet aware of the surname of the second miscreant. When asked he refused to give it. Both of them have been charged under the Offences Against the State Act and will be brought before the Special Criminal Court at the earliest opportunity.'

'What are they charged with?' This time the accent was distinctly Oxbridge. The English TV crew had made it after all.

'Armed robbery, kidnapping and being members of an illegal organisation.'

'Anything else?'

Whether it was intended to or not, this provoked an outburst of laughter. The charges mentioned would be more than enough to put the pair away for several lifetimes. The owner of the Oxbridge accent was not so easily deterred.

'Who else was in the cottage?'

Gus again answered that one.

'Father Jerry here on my right was grabbed by them when he

happened on the raid during his morning walk. As were three other English tourists on a touring holiday. Then, of course, Mr Flannery.'

This was greeted from the back of the crowd by delighted cries of, 'Good man yourself, Mick!' and 'Aha, ya boy ya!' One voice even attempted to sing the National Anthem before he was silenced by his comrades.

Oxbridge had one last arrow in his quiver. 'What were the names of the three tourists and where can we interview them?'

Gus coughed to clear his throat before answering, 'I'm afraid that's privileged information. We cannot divulge their names or their whereabouts. For their own protection, you'll understand. Where subversive organisations are concerned, every precaution must be taken to protect witnesses.'

Colum Jones was next. 'Does that mean we can't talk to them?'

Gus again fielded the question. 'Yes, that is exactly what it means. We try to co-operate with the press as much as we possibly can – but not to the extent of endangering innocent lives.'

'Will those three be required to give evidence at the trial?'

Mick decided it was time he took a hand in proceedings.

'I wouldn't think so. Father O'Sullivan and myself saw the whole thing. Our evidence should be enough to put the two Provos away without anyone else risking their lives testifying against them.'

This was accompanied by more whoops from the back and the odd snatch of song from the more excited of his supporters.

'Was that why you couldn't make the speech for the opening of the Festival?'

Mick recognised the accent immediately.

'That's right Charley. I was walking out the road, trying to compose a speech in my mind when they grabbed me and forced me into the camper at gunpoint. Then when the raid went wrong, they took myself, Father O'Sullivan and the three tourists inside the cottage as hostages.'

'Were any of you injured during the siege?'

Father Jerry shook his head silently and Mick took up the reins once more.

'I got a belt on the forehead . . .' – he pointed to a patch of dried blood above his right eye – 'but it was nothing. I often got worse on the hurling pitch!'

This time the outburst of cheering and shouts of encouragement from the back of the crowd lasted over a minute. When it subsided enough for Jones to make himself heard, he asked, 'Was there a woman being used as a shield by the second gunman?'

'I think so . . .'

Mick had already formulated the answer to this long before it was asked. 'The one called Barney, the bastard who gave me this . . .' – again he proudly pointed to his battle scar – '. . . grabbed one of the tourists and tried to push her ahead of him out the door. Then when Maggie, God bless her, ran up to me, I gave my fellow a belt on the jaw and went for Barney . . .'

This slightly amended version of events drew sustained applause from every quarter, including the hard-bitten hacks who, by now, were caught up in the general euphoria. The rest of the questions were mere ritual.

'Is Mrs Flannery recovered from her ordeal?'

'I hope so, I saw her off in the ambulance. Doctor Buckley said that she got a knock on the head but would be all right in a few days.'

Charley Halpin was not to be outdone on his own patch. 'Who do you think will succeed you here when you go to Europe?'

'Haven't the foggiest, Charley. For the sake of Brulagh, I hope it will be someone from the locality.'

'Pat Mullarkey, for instance?' Charley persisted.

'They could do a whole lot worse!'

'Were you disappointed that they didn't name the stand after you?'

'To tell the truth, Charley, I was.'

Colum Jones decided to interrupt this cosy chat about local issues. 'Father O'Sullivan, I have a question for you.'

The priest smiled bleakly and cocked an ear.

'Was any message revealed at the grotto and did the statue move?'

Father Jerry examined his fingernails before replying. He availed of the breathing space to force something akin to a smile on his face.

'Not so far as I know. As you must be aware by now, I spent most of the time in the hands of the two gunmen. I therefore had no opportunity to observe what was happening at the grotto. It is my understanding, however, that nothing out of the ordinary occurred there. I believe that to be a good thing in that it will allow us all to get back to normal and recover from what, I think you will agree, has been an unusually hectic day in the long history of Brulagh.'

With no more questions forthcoming, the press conference was at an end.

32

The mob whistled their disapproval. From a thousand throats there came a high-pitched twittering. With Castelli sweating in terror as the tumbril rattled across the cobbled square, his own feelings were less obvious. Of course he was afraid, but the knot of fear had a strand of elation running through it. Why? Dying for the One True Faith, he supposed. Had he not learned at his mother's knee of the eternal reward for martyrdom? A ticket to Heaven and an entry in the *Book of Saints*. A lifetime at the very heart of Roman Catholicism had failed to unearth one shred of evidence to prove the existence of either. But his mother's word was good enough for Jeremiah O'Sullivan, Defender of the Faith. Would not that be his title after the guillotine had done its work? He mounted the rough timber steps ahead of the whimpering Italian. Wordlessly he tossed his head in contempt at the still twittering masses. Placing his neck on the block, he waited for the hiss of the bloodied blade that would signal his entry into Paradise.

A tap on the shoulder startled him into wakefulness. Julia May placed the breakfast tray on the bedside table. He lay still for a moment, trapped somewhere between the Place de la Concorde and Brulagh. His body sat up in bed while his mind clawed in desperation at the vanishing wisps of his dream. He tried to cope with the disappointment of not dying for the One True Faith before a blood-thirsty mob. Knuckling the sleep from his eyes he struggled to escape from the crater in the middle of the old Canon's bed. A new bed had been ordered for some time but the supplier seemed in no hurry to deliver it.

Julia May handing him a steaming teacup finally dispersed the last shreds of his noble martyrdom. What a pity! It would have been so much easier to save his soul in a single blaze of glory than by the daily grind of pastoral work. Sipping his tea, he wondered if Castelli ever had the same fantasy in his Vatican apartment. Probably not, he decided. Castelli would never have allowed himself to be beheaded or to travel in a tumbril. He would have come to an arrangement with his jailers whereby Jerry would be thrown to the mob while he, a true Prince of the Church, would escape in a gilded coach drawn by four prancing, white stallions.

Now only the twittering remained. If anything it had grown louder. 'What's that noise?'

July May threw him a look of condescension as she replied, 'Swallows, Father. The dirty divils have my windows ruined with their droppings.'

She parted the curtains to reveal another sunlit morning. Small, black projectiles with crescent wings hurtled themselves towards the window like kamikaze pilots, swooping upwards at the last millisecond to settle in the eaves of the roof, from which their nests clung precariously. As Julia May said, they made a mess. Their droppings scarred her windows and formed dirty mounds on the sills. Yet even she was not brave enough to destroy their summer homes of mud and feathers. To do so would bring bad luck on the house and all those who dwelt within.

As a small child, he was caught throwing stones at the ball-shaped nests. Retribution had been swift and severe. His mother, too, believed that to disturb the swallows was to invite disaster. This superstition did not conflict in any way with her more formal religious beliefs. If anything, it strengthened them, especially when the head of household died tragically so soon afterwards. Father Jerry sometimes wondered if she had not held him responsible, in part at least, for his father's drowning.

Of course she also believed that if she received communion on the first Friday of the month for nine consecutive months her soul would be spared the everlasting flames of Hell. Just to make certain, she did the exercise several times in case the magic faded with the passage of time. Even today, serious sinners availed themselves of this attractive offer. Then, as now, he harboured the greatest reservations about the whole matter. It seemed odd that receiving the Body and Blood of Our Lord at, admittedly inconvenient, fixed times would provide *carte blanche* to even the most hardened reprobate. Without disclosing whether he himself had managed this First Friday feat, Mick had remarked that most of the bad debts in Maggie's ledger were run up by 'those Nine Fridays shaggers'. Nonetheless it was intriguing to observe how fire insurance in one form or another played such an important part in the lives of his flock.

Outside the window, the swallows rose and fell. They looked like waiters in a restaurant hovering attentively around an important diner in their perfectly cut tailcoats and starched white shirts. Sometimes a different cry, harsh with protest, rose above the din. Squatters were being evicted from the nests where they had sought refuge. Was there no sanctuary to be found for them, not even under a priest's roof? Apparently not, he reflected, as he bit into the hard toast, except of course for Sean. Much to everyone's relief, Julia May instantly adopted him as the son she'd never had. Sworn to secrecy, she fed him like a gamecock and delighted in recounting his feats at the table.

'It wouldn't surprise me in the least if that poor lad hasn't had a decent meal inside him since he left the village. Nothing but chips and burgers, he was telling me, for the bones of six years. No wonder the craythur is as thin as a whippet. I won't be long in putting a bit of meat on him, I can promise you.'

He didn't doubt her boast, having already put on nearly two stones himself. He hadn't been as well in a long, long time. He was walking several miles every day, playing golf three or four times a week and during the recent spell of warm weather he swam off the pier. He found the sea colder but far cleaner than the dying Mediterranean. He no longer missed Rome, its food or its people. Indeed for long periods he never thought of the place at all. He was becoming part of the landscape in Brulagh. Now people merely saluted him as they passed. No longer was he the topic of conversation in the chattering groups that formed like eddies in his wake as he sailed past on his daily walk. How many of them knew that Sean was hiding out in the parochial house? Julia May's discretion was not to be relied on, if the grotto business was anything to go by. Anyway it was time to engineer Sean's official homecoming, now that the excitement of the Festival weekend had evaporated.

The siege had drawn lots of media attention but all of it was the approved version of events. Colum Jones had been as good as his word. No reference was made to the part Maggie played at either the grotto or the siege. In a tightly written account of events at Rose Cottage he praised Mick for his sang-froid. It had taken Father Jerry five minutes of gentle persuasion to convince Mick that Jones was paying him a compliment rather than suggesting that he had contracted an anti-social disease. Recalling Mick's prowess on the hurling field, Jones expressed the opinion that the four-in-a-row legend had saved his finest performance till last. Mick emerged as the hero of the hour – a role he did nothing to play down in the interviews that followed his appointment to the European Parliament. His new remit had almost four years to run before he again faced the electorate. To no one's surprise, Pat Mullarkey was contesting the by-election for Mick's vacant seat. What was more, he was expected to win comfortably now that he had obtained the unexpected blessing of his predecessor.

Rumour had it that the two sworn enemies had done a deal, the nature of which was anybody's guess. Father Jerry suspected that in some way it involved directing Sean Flannery into the mainstream of political life. The lad had admitted as much after a long session with his father in the priest's den. When it was dark, Father Jerry and his house guest walked along the shore in the moonlight. They spoke of many things. Despite the difference in age and background, they shared similar views. Sean claimed that his experience in the Seminary had not blighted his life. Rather it had, he claimed, been an ideal preparation for the hostile world outside Brulagh. The hell's kitchen of Liverpool's back streets had merely strengthened his resolve to change the world. He had great affection for his father but regarded him as a political dinosaur.

As they walked along the beach, Sean kicked at the sand in frustration as he recalled for the priest how his father once asked him what he should do to get a bigger slice of the youth vote. He could still see the horror in Mick's face at his reply.

'They need something of their own here. A community hall to meet in to get them out from under the feet of their families, for instance. Sure they have a hurling club but nothing happens there at night except a game of cards. Anyway it smells of sweat and old socks. What they want is a place of their own with bright lights, a juke-box and a bar. Only minerals, of course. No alcohol. But it must be their own place. They'd even build it themselves if you could get them one of those EC grants everyone is talking about. They might even call the place after you if you did that for them!'

He hoped that might have made a tempting bait. To his surprise the fish just sniffed at it and swam away.

'It would never work. For starters, the young crowd around here wouldn't get up off their arses to build a sand-castle, never mind a bloody community hall. Anyway, where would we put it? Build it on the street and half the people will be up in arms, complaining about the racket, saying they can't get a decent night's sleep. Put it outside the village and the shopkeepers, your mother included, will be moaning that we're trying to take the bread out of their mouths. Then we'd have that lot up in Saint Fintan's saying we were seducing the youth of the village away from their national heritage with strobe lights and loud music. Add in the Canon thinking half the girls in the parish would be put in the family way and you'd have the makings of a fine old mess, I can tell you. And all because of a bloody building named after me! No, son, believe me a community hall spells nothing but trouble.'

Soon afterwards, Sean had to leave in a hurry. He presumed that Mick made no further efforts to woo the young voters. As luck would have it, they must have stayed at home and not bothered to vote, believing one politician to be as bad as another. If they ever realised the power they wielded, Mick and many more like him would be thrown on the political slag heap. The fact was that Sean's vision of the future was much closer to Mullarkey's. They had already met several times in the den but Father Jerry had not enquired, nor had he been told, what emerged from these meetings. It may have been sheer coincidence that Mick gave his backing to Mullarkey after the last of these sessions.

The ritual of his morning cup of tea, a drink he had until recently despised, had taken on for Julia May the significance of a tea cere-mony to a geisha girl. She would wait until he tasted it and emitted a long 'Aaaaaah!' Then she would beam with satisfaction and return to the kitchen. She had visited Maggie in hospital and reported that it would be some time before she would be out and about again.

'I declare to God, the poor woman is half demented, so she is. One minute she is clear as the air, talking about the shop and the trip to Lourdes. Then the next minute she is off to China with Mick to convert the little yellow shaggers. Do you know what I'm going to tell you, Father?'

He knew from experience that the question would be rhetorical. He continued to sip his tea in silence and tried not to let the swallows distract him from whatever Julia May was about to add to the sum of human knowledge.

'A visit from Sean would do her all the good in the world, so it would.'

She was quite right, of course, but his attention had been snared by the swallows. Some of them could have flown across Italy on their migration from North Africa. Until recently such a thought would have made him ache for sunlit piazzas in which man and machine vied noisely for supremacy. Not any more. Now when his thoughts drifted to his adopted country, they were more likely to focus on Boggola. He remembered how Agostini seemed unaware of his idyllic surroundings among the wooded hillsides of Tuscany. His tranquillity seemed to come from within. With the passing of each day, he too came closer to this state of inner happiness.

He no longer thought of the parochial house as a giant mausoleum reeking of polish and disinfectant. Rather he had begun to regard it as more of a community centre where his flock would come and visit him, telling of their good and ill fortune and using its rooms for their meetings. Now, of course, it also served as a sanctuary for Sean. He wondered if Mick was aware that Jenny was coming back to Brulagh tonight. For the sake of decorum she would be staying in O'Shea's until the wedding details were finalised. There were rumours, too, of O'Shea's imminent departure for Boston. Not even Julia May could fathom the reason behind his decision to leave. It certainly was not lack of custom. Being the only hotel and bar for miles around, it had to be a licence to print money for its new owner – whoever that might be. For one dreadful moment he considered the possibility that it might be Freddie. Then reason prevailed as he remembered with relief that his sole surviving relative's only venture to date in the village had been a financial disaster. As he climbed out of bed, he tried vainly to recall the cure he had discovered yesterday for hitting the golf ball too far to the left. He might need it this afternoon.

The ball was about five feet from the hole. The green between it and the flagstick was far from level. It was a difficult putt.

'I'll give you that one!'

The concession was as welcome as it was unexpected. The Doc stooped to pick up his ball before Mick could change his mind.

'I suppose I owe you that much. Would you agree with me, Gus?'

'That's for sure,' Gus replied. 'If the Doc hadn't smuggled Mrs Donnelly away from the cottage, there would have been some explaining to do. Not to mention Father O'Sullivan doing the same for young Sean. Is he all right again, Father?'

'Oh he's fine, Gus, just fine. Julia May's feeding him like gamecock. As soon as things quieten down, he can start leading a normal life again. I felt the Church owed him something in return for what happened at the Seminary. It's called "sanctuary" in some parts of the world. Julia May informs me that round here it's known as "looking after our own." '

It was a bright, sunny morning. A few wispy cotton-wool clouds hovered above the shimmering sea. Otherwise the sky was clear save for the swooping gulls. Joe Gallagher's boat was ploughing a creamy furrow across the bay, followed by his usual escort of screaming seabirds. His visitors had left and Joe could concentrate on his twin duties as fisherman and sacristan. The village below them had reverted to normality, the excitement of the Festival weekend fast evaporating if not quite forgotten. The gaily decorated platform, the chip van and the bunting were gone. Only the flattened grass in the car-park fields bore testimony to recent events. The four players were the sole human presence on the golf course. They had their usual quota of spectators, small flocks of curious black-faced sheep tempted by the lush grass on the fairways.

'I suppose we won't have another fourball like this for a long while, with you going off to Europe and all that?'

As usual it was hard to know when Gus was being serious. His long, lined face was expressionless. Father Jerry reflected that both he and Mick owed Gus a few favours after what he did in the cottage; not least his turning a blind eye to a roomful of poteen. Knowing Gus, he would refuse to accept anything in return, except the job of administrator in charge of the Flannery Leisure Centre. A hasty meeting of the GAA Committee had voted the name change proposed by Pat Mullarkey, no less. Afterwards Mick expressed the view to his son Sean and the priest that if he couldn't squeeze a few francs out of those shaggers in Brussels for such a worthy undertaking, then he was a Dutchman.

The only outsiders aware of Sean's presence in Rose Cottage were the two Provos. Under Section 31 of the Broadcasting Act the media were not allowed to interview members of an illegal organisation. The terms of the Act were familiar to Mick because he had been up half the night waiting to vote each of its clauses into law. The proceedings of the Special Criminal Court where the Provos would be tried were held in camera. His good friend, the Taoiseach, described such measures as 'cutting off the life-giving oxygen of publicity to those murderous bastards'.

As for Josephine, she would be silent as the tomb. She and her husband were being wined and dined by the bank directors in celebration of the bloodsuckers getting their money back. Now with the generous salary of a Member of the European Parliament, Mick might even start to pay them back too. After the VAT man, of course. As for the Simcoxes, they were so relieved to get out of the country without being arrested, they could hardly wait to shake the dust of Brulagh from their feet. Except for the girl, that is.

'Of course we will,' Mick replied. 'I expect to fly home most weekends. I'll have to keep a closer eye on the business now that

Maggie is in hospital. Have you any fresh report on her since yesterday, Doc?'

'No I haven't. She has had a mild nervous breakdown, that's all. She needs lots of quiet. Time will do the rest. When she's a bit stronger, Sean can visit her. That will do her a power of good. You can say that he came home unexpectedly and the two of you made it up after all those years. That would be better for her than all the medicines under the sun. Everything's all right again now between the two of you, isn't it?'

'Oh yes indeed, thanks be to God. Never better. Just like the old times. Sean's going to look after the shop while Maggie's getting better. After that, who knows? He seems keen on the Simcox girl. What was her name again?'

This seemed a golden opportunity for Father Jerry to put his spoke in.

'Jenny. Yes he does indeed. He had a phone call from her as a matter of fact. She's arriving off the eight o'clock bus tonight. Julia May booked her into O'Shea's. Sean says he wants to marry her. Jenny, that is!'

Seeing the surprise of Mick's face, he thought he had better explain further.

'He was telling me that they have been together for two years so an engagement is hardly necessary at this stage. Anyway I told him I would marry them whenever they wished.'

Mick's reaction was even more favourable than Sean could have anticipated.

'That's great news altogether. I was wondering what he'd do with himself after this . . . Gus, you were telling me that O'Shea is thinking of going back to Boston, weren't you? Something about him not finding the climate in Brulagh to his liking. Didn't those two Provos stay with him? That wouldn't have anything to do with his change of heart, now would it?'

Gus shrugged his shoulders. As he prepared to tee up his ball to play the next hole he said, 'I just passed on something I heard McCain mutter about informers as they were taking him away, that's all. If O'Shea wants to believe McCain was talking about him, then that's his own business. I just felt it was my duty to tell him what was said, in case he found himself walking with one leg six inches shorter than the other. Knee-capping is a nasty business and O'Shea is short enough as it is.'

Just managing to keep a straight face, Mick coughed as though to clear his throat, 'The reason I asked is that Sean was thinking of renting the pub from him while he's away. If he's going to get married, that makes it an even better proposition. It's as good a place as any for a young couple to start out on their life together. Donnelly might even give him a loan to buy it now that I'm back in his good books again . . . Credit wise, that is!' he added hastily. The others studied the sky. One of the sheep bleated its forlorn approval.